Praise for Mary Ellen Taylor

"[A] complex tale . . . grounded in fascinating history and emotional turmoil that is intense yet subtle. An intelligent, heartwarming exploration of the powers of forgiveness, compassion, and new beginnings."
—*Kirkus Reviews*

"Absorbing characters, a hint of mystery, and touching self-discovery elevate this novel above many others in the genre."
—*RT Book Reviews*

"Taylor serves up a great mix of vivid setting, history, drama, and everyday life."
—Durham *Herald-Sun*

"[A] charming and very engaging story about the nature of family and the meaning of love."
—seattlepi.com

Winter
Cottage

OTHER TITLES BY MARY ELLEN TAYLOR

Union Street Bakery Novels

The Union Street Bakery
Sweet Expectations

Alexandria Series

At the Corner of King Street
The View from Prince Street

Winter Cottage

MARY ELLEN TAYLOR

 Montlake
Romance

Published by Montlake Romance, Seattle

www.apub.com

Amazon, the Amazon logo, and Montlake Romance are trademarks of Amazon.com, Inc., or its affiliates.

ISBN-13: 9781503903883
ISBN-10: 1503903885

Cover design by Laura Klynstra

Printed in the United States of America

Winter Cottage

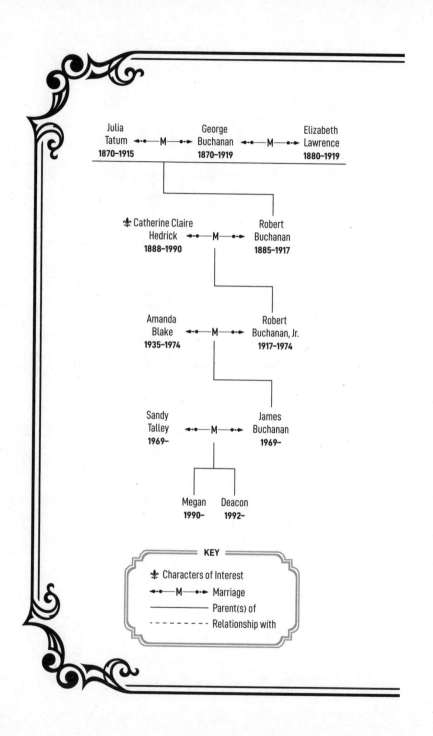

Julia Tatum 1870–1915 ◄●─M─●► George Buchanan 1870–1919 ◄●─M─●► Elizabeth Lawrence 1880–1919

⚜ Catherine Claire Hedrick 1888–1990 ◄●─M─●► Robert Buchanan 1885–1917

Amanda Blake 1935–1974 ◄●─M─●► Robert Buchanan, Jr. 1917–1974

Sandy Talley 1969– ◄●─M─●► James Buchanan 1969–

Megan 1990–   Deacon 1992–

═══════ KEY ═══════

⚜ Characters of Interest

◄●─M─●► Marriage

─────── Parent(s) of

- - - - - - - Relationship with

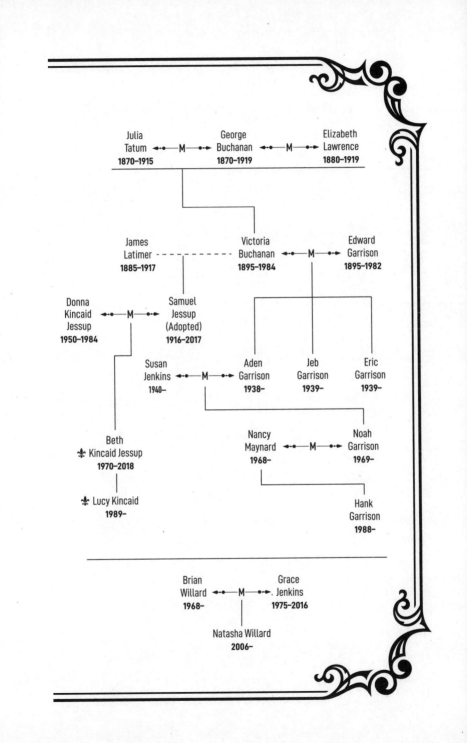

In the depths of winter, I finally learned that within me there lay an invincible summer.

—*Albert Camus*

CHAPTER ONE

Mrs. Catherine Buchanan

May 2, 1988
Cape Hudson, Virginia

In coastal Virginia on a warm spring day, Mrs. Catherine Buchanan settles tired bones into her cane rocker. She carefully adjusts her green knit dress with gnarled but precise fingers. She is dressed for this occasion, but no amount of fussing or preening can approach the reckless beauty of the girl sitting across from her.

The girl has straight blonde hair and sharp blue eyes that remind the old woman that once her thin white hair was an unruly red mass of thick curls that tumbled down over tanned shoulders and full, high breasts. She was filled with hopes and dreams, and she too knew a man's sensual touch. She was never as stunning as this girl, but she turned her fair share of heads.

The girl's name is Elizabeth Kincaid Jessup—Beth to her friends. She has asked Mrs. Buchanan if she can record her stories with a camera borrowed from the high school library. It's a living-history project, she says, and then adds quickly with refreshing honesty that she needs an A, so don't hold back on the good stuff.

Youthful hands carefully unfurl the microphone wire attached to the camera. She has a devilish smile that reminds the old woman of another girl who lived here so long ago. And like the other girl, there are whispers about Beth. She runs with a fast crowd, drinks, and has been seen with several boys in town, some not so nice.

Girls like Beth think they have invented rebellion. They believe they're the first to ignore the rules, but they are simply reinventing a wheel that has been rolling for hundreds of generations.

"Can I clip this to your collar?" Beth asks. "It'll pick up the sound better when you talk."

"Of course."

Beth's gaze is drawn to the chandelier and then to a portrait of a young woman dressed for her wedding day. The painting hangs over the pearl marble fireplace embellished by a French mason with flowers, scrolls, and greenery.

Mrs. Buchanan doesn't need to glance to see the portrait. She is the woman in the painting wearing a white satin dress fitted with a beaded bodice and an apron tunic of lace. Woven through red curls are strands of pearls and a waterfall of tulle that graces the floor behind her. The portrait was painted in this very room.

"Do you remember when it was painted?" Beth asks.

The old woman's coy smile is for the man she loved. "Yes, I remember it all."

The girl adjusts the focus button as she peers into a lens and then settles onto the floor, easily folding and crossing her legs. "You've lived by the bay for nearly a hundred years."

"I have, for the most part."

Beth grins. "I heard you know where all the bodies are buried."

"Bodies?"

Beth shrugs. "A figure of speech. I don't mean real bodies. Just the juicy stories about the area."

Mrs. Buchanan straightens but keeps her expression in check. "Yes, I have stories. And buried in those stories is perhaps a body or two."

"Really?"

Secrets bubble up as time loosens the bindings. There is no one left alive to protect now. "Shall we begin?"

The girl clears her throat and presses the record button. *"I'm Beth Jessup, and I'm a senior at Cape Hudson High School. This is my final exam project for Mrs. Reynolds's history class. I live on Chesapeake Bay's Eastern Shore in Virginia, and today I'm interviewing Mrs. Catherine Buchanan, who was born in Cape Hudson in 1888. Mrs. Buchanan, can you tell me about your family?"*

The rocker squeaks as Mrs. Buchanan leans forward a fraction. *"My mother was Addie Smith, and my father was Isaac Hedrick. When my father wasn't doing carpentry work, he was sailing with the merchant marines. I am the oldest of seven, and my mother died giving birth to her last child when I was twelve."*

The girl looks up, and her blue eyes reveal the pain of the loss of her own mother. At first glance, they might seem to be an odd pair, but strip away money and age and they are simply two motherless girls hungry for love.

"What happened after your mother died?"

"My father could not go to sea and also care for seven children, so he farmed us out. The boys went to the Jessups, a childless couple in town. My sisters were sent to live with families on the mainland, and I went to work for the Buchanans."

"That must have been terrifying."

Mrs. Buchanan locked this pain away a long time ago and is not anxious to handle it again. But when she agreed to this interview, she promised herself the truth would not die with her. *"The Buchanans took me with them back to New York City. I was so homesick. The city was noisy. Bright. I didn't really sleep for months. But I eventually learned to adapt and move forward."*

"Did you ever see your sisters or brothers again?"

"Eventually. But it would be a long time." The words hung between them for several seconds before Beth cleared her throat.

"What did you do for the Buchanan family?"

"I assisted the ladies' maids, and then later I became Miss Victoria's personal maid."

"Who was Victoria?"

A breeze sneaks past the silk taffeta curtains, and she feels the pull of the spirits that have been circling closer these last few months. Old pains bob like distant buoys.

"Mr. Buchanan's daughter. She would later become my sister-in-law. In fact, you remind me of Victoria. She was restless like you."

Beth's grin is sly, as if she's been busted. *"What happened to her?"*

The old woman smiled, pleased by the girl's genuine curiosity. *"Maybe if you come back another day I'll tell you."*

"You've barely told me anything today."

"If you want to know more, then you'll have to come back. I'm old. I get tired easily." A half truth at best. She wants to see the girl again. She enjoys talking to her.

"I work in the afternoons at the restaurant. I can't afford to come back."

"Then I'll pay you. Consider it a new job."

The wariness in the girl's eyes reminds her of a wild fox her father once captured in a trap baited with fish. *"I'm a pretty good waitress, Mrs. B. I make good tips."* Beth names her price but seems to expect some haggling.

"Agreed."

Blue eyes widened. *"Seriously? All I have to do is tape while you talk?"*

"Correct. And be punctual."

Beth seems to wait for the catch. When none comes, she says, *"I'll do it. But you have to pay me as we go."*

"Of course. Can you return this Friday?"

4

"*Sure.*" The girl's gaze catches the portrait again, and she asks, "*Was it love at first sight?*"

Mrs. Buchanan is silent for a long moment. The drumbeat of secrets grows louder. "*Yes. But that love wasn't for my husband, Robert.*"

Beth's blue eyes are calculating, just like the fox's were when he sniffed fresh fish in the trap. "*Who?*"

"*See you on Friday.*"

CHAPTER TWO

Lucy

January 15, 2018
Cape Hudson, Virginia

Lucy Kincaid arrived with a nor'easter pressing against her back, its sharp, cold winds heavy with the scents of Tennessee whiskey, smoky honky-tonks, fried and glazed doughnuts stuffed with chocolate custard, burgers cooked on a greasy griddle, and the sickly sweetness of death.

The icy fingers of the storm's remnants brushed her cheeks, startling her awake from a restless night's sleep. Hand to her face, she glanced into the mist rising over the tall reeds by the swirling waters of Chesapeake Bay. She was in her Jeep, parked in the spot she'd chosen in the early-morning hours. Beside her was Dolly Parton, her mother's two-year-old German shepherd, nestled under the blanket, sleeping peacefully. The back seats were packed with everything she owned: a duffel bag full of clothes, sketch pads, her mother's guitar, a sleeping bag, and a grocery sack filled with sodas, peanut butter, and bagels. In between the seats lay the scuffed wooden baseball bat, dubbed the Peacemaker, and beside it, the metal urn that held her mother's ashes.

When she'd crossed the seventeen-mile Bay Bridge–Tunnel, driving toward the Eastern Shore shortly after two in the morning, the waves were choppy, and the gusts had forced her to slow and turn on her hazards. In the middle of the bridge, over an expanse of water and under a blanket of stars, she'd felt as if the universe were daring her to turn back. But if anything, Lucy was stubborn, and she never shied away from a challenge.

Once on shore, it'd been too late to find the man she'd come to see, and she'd been too broke for a motel room. A barren stretch of road beside a barn near the bay had had to do. When she shut off the engine to save the last of her gas, she'd discovered that without the heater running, the air in the Jeep quickly chilled.

Under the light of a full moon skimming choppy waters, she'd covered Dolly and herself with her mother's large, worn quilt and tried to sleep as the rain beat against the car.

Lucy shuddered, wrapped the blanket closer, and stared at the orange-gold sunrise as it nudged above the waters stretching to the horizon. The rains were gone, and fresh light danced over the tips of frosted seagrass bending to wind that teased the rippling waters of the bay.

"What do you think, Dolly?"

Dolly raised her head and snorted before returning to the warmth of her blanket.

"We're going to have to love it. It's all we've got for now." Her mother's medical bills had drained Lucy's savings, leaving her with a hundred bucks in her pocket, a quarter tank of gas, and the best possibility of a job a thousand miles away in Nashville. To uproot her life and just start over, even for a little while, was insane and the kind of thing her mother had often done.

She glanced toward the tarnished secondhand urn the funeral director had sold to her for thirty bucks. There was a large dent in the top, which had something to do with a dispute between two wives and one dead husband. The urn's dramatic history would have appealed to her mother, and the price had been right.

Her mother had died two weeks ago of brain cancer. She had never been sick a day in her life, so she'd chalked up her first migraine to the half a bottle of rye whiskey she'd drunk the night before. Not enough sleep had explained the next one away. The third had crippled her for days and driven her to call Lucy, who'd been managing a bar on Lower Broadway in Nashville. The emergency-room visit had led to an MRI neither could afford and a doctor's devastating news. The tumor had been malignant and inoperable.

Lucy had given up her place and moved into her mother's small apartment in November. She'd administered painkillers, comforted her mother, and waited for the end. On their last day together, Beth had stirred. Her eyes had opened and focused on Lucy as they hadn't done in days.

"You take good care of Dolly for me."

"You know I will." Lucy reached for an extra blanket and covered her mother as Dolly nestled closer to her thin frame. As death circled closer, her mother was growing more anxious about the dog's fate. Other than Lucy, Dolly was her best friend.

"She hates being alone."

Her mother winced and struggled to catch her next breath. Lucy reached for the bottle of prescribed morphine. A few drops on her tongue relieved the panic that came as her body shut down.

A sigh shuddered through her mother. "I need you and Dolly to take my ashes to Virginia."

Lucy and her mother had had their share of troubles, but they didn't keep secrets, so she figured this first-time mention of Virginia was just the morphine talking. "Mom, you've never been to Virginia."

Her mother struggled with her next breath. "A letter came about a month ago."

"What letter?"

"Under my mattress. Look."

Lucy lifted the mattress and found the large manila envelope lying beside a crumpled cigarette pack and a taco wrapper. Lectures about eating well and not smoking had long passed, so she simply scooped up the envelope. The letter was from Henry Garrison, Cape Hudson, Virginia.

"What's going on, Mom?"

Her mother moistened her pale lips. "I've come into some property, but it'll be yours now. It could be a real home. Just like you always wanted when you were little."

A real home. At twenty-nine, she didn't know what the hell that meant.

Now rolling her stiff neck from side to side, Lucy pulled a rubber band from around her wrist and wrapped her hair into a ponytail. Why hadn't her mother told her about Virginia? Why the secrets? Her mother had always prided herself on brutal honesty. Told it like it was. Shot from the hip.

"Why the lie?" Lucy tightened her hands on the steering wheel, wishing for just a few more minutes with her mother.

Cold, hungry, and needing to pee, she searched the woods and the thick, tall grass that skimmed the hundred yards between them and the water. She opened her door and grimaced as the morning wind bit at her skin.

She coaxed the dog out. "Come on, girl. I know you have to go." Dolly flattened her ears. "None of that. You've got it easier than me."

The dog rose slowly and crossed over the gearshift. Yawning, she hopped down. Dolly, part human as far as Beth was concerned, didn't need a leash.

"Don't chase anything. You'll freeze your ass off if you get lost, and I'll freeze mine off looking for you."

Together they trotted toward the reeds. Lucy's brown cowboy boots, inlaid with turquoise leather, squished in the soft soil as she tried to keep up with the dog, who bounded, snorting, into the cold air, finding a burst of energy she'd not had in weeks.

Dolly squatted and raised her nose into the wind. She sniffed and ran along the reeds.

"Remember what I said about wandering off." Lucy reached for her zipper and tugged down her pants. The wind blew over her naked backside, and she peed as quickly as possible. By the time she tugged up her jeans, she'd lost sight of Dolly.

"Hey, we're not supposed to leave each other alone. That was the deal. Come on, girl! It's freezing!"

Dolly dashed toward the water. Weeks of being cooped up in Beth's apartment with only short walks hadn't been enough for the seventy-pound dog. She was now free, on a scent, and loving it.

Lucy wrapped her arms around her chest and stamped her feet. "Dolly, don't do this to me now. We need to get back in the car and get warm. I promise, you'll get a chance to run later."

The dog barked, and a bird flew from the reeds that jostled as the dog moved through them. "Treat!" Lucy shouted. "Dolly, want a treat?"

The reeds stilled, and the dog's head popped up, a clear indication that she could be bribed. She ran up, tail wagging, as Lucy opened the car door. The dog gave her a quick glance, hopped over her seat, and settled into the blanket on the front passenger seat to wait for her treat.

"I'm a little lean on treats," Lucy said, closing the door and scrounging for a fast-food bag. She fished out a few stale fries, which Dolly promptly gobbled.

She rubbed the dog between the ears and dug out a container of hand wipes, one of the last things that she'd taken from Beth's apartment. She plucked out one and slowly rubbed the damp cloth around her hands, savoring the scent and imagining the way Beth used to clean her hands when she was a child. Beth had always had a thing for wipes. They might have lived in a one-room apartment in East Nashville, but her hands were always clean.

She crushed the wipe in her hand, reached for the key in the ignition, and twisted. The engine turned, groaned, and stopped. On the second attempt it sputtered and coughed. She glanced at Dolly, who stared at Lucy as if she expected her to make something happen.

She leaned into the wheel, willing life into the engine. "Jeep, don't screw with me now." She turned the key. It didn't fire. The universe had sent her enough bad breaks lately, and by Lucy's way of thinking, it was time for some good, at least for a little while. A safe harbor waited for her, and she wasn't changing course.

The third time, the engine caught and rumbled and rattled. For a moment she didn't breathe or move, fearing it would sputter off. When it held steady, she turned the heat up, and both she and Dolly leaned forward to take in the warm air.

She shifted into reverse. "Onward and upward."

The dog perked up her ears. Her tail wagged.

Lucy pressed the accelerator and turned north on Route 13, the main road on the peninsula. At first she saw only a few marks of civilization, and then a motel appeared with ten cabin-style rooms and a red VACANCY sign blinking in one of the cottage windows. Beyond the motel were several broken-down tractors with FOR SALE signs hanging on them. Her first sight of a human was an old man in camouflage pants and a jacket, picking up a newspaper. And then she passed a tiny strip mall with several boarded-up stores.

She slowed when she saw the sign CAPE HUDSON, 8 MILES and thought about the blog posts she'd read about the town. It had been settled in the late nineteenth century as a railroad depot serving Norfolk and the northeast; however, there were land grants dating back to the time of King George I and records of indentured servants brought to the Virginia colony in the mid-1600s. Ruins of old plantations and hunt clubs stood watch over the waters of the Chesapeake.

The summers here were fairly busy, but there weren't enough hotels and cottages to make it a big vacation destination. The town's population of ten thousand tripled at the end of each November with the annual five-day oyster festival. In January, nothing happened in town.

The streets, one blogger wrote, were "just about rolled up." Another called it "a land of untapped potential."

She slowed and followed the directional signs that took her down an even smaller road toward town.

According to the map on her phone, two streets ran east and west, while another two ran north and south. The buildings were brick, one or two stories tall, and hearkened back to a time when the town had been a moderately successful hunting destination and railroad town.

There were businesses that catered to tourists, and many bore signs reading CLOSED UNTIL MARCH.

At the end of the main drag she spotted a diner in a brick building. It already had several cars out front, and it was the first sign of real life. She parked alongside them. The sign out front read ARLENE'S.

A few early risers passed by her bright-yellow Jeep, glancing at her and then at her plates before disappearing into the diner. She shut off the engine. "Wait here, girl. I'll get a to-go box."

She ran to the front door, then pushed it open to the sound of bells jingling over her head. Warmth, heavy with the smells of bacon and pancakes, greeted her. God, it felt good.

Standing behind the counter was a woman in her late forties. Her hair was a bright red, and she wore an oversize black T-shirt that read OYSTER ROAST VOLUNTEER. Her name tag read ARLENE.

Lucy caught her attention instantly. "Morning. Could I get something to go? My dog's in the Jeep, and I don't have enough gas to keep the heat running."

The woman stared at her for a second or two, blinked, and then grinned. "Baby doll, just bring that puppy right inside. It's the off-season, so it's just the regulars and you today."

"Are you sure? She's pretty big."

"Folks, you mind if this little girl brings in her pup?"

Almost in unison, the regulars raised their coffee mugs in approval. Arlene picked up a coffeepot and a stone mug. "I'll pour while you get your dog."

"Thanks."

Lucy dashed outside to find Dolly staring at her through the driver's window. Her ears were down, and her eyes looked as if she thought she'd been put in a time-out.

Lucy opened the door. "They're letting us both in. We can sit at a real table and enjoy a real meal." She hooked a leash on Dolly's collar, and the dog climbed out.

"How about a bacon biscuit?" she said to Dolly.

Dolly wagged her tail.

They pushed through the diner door. The bells jingled as Lucy again savored the rush of warmth that swept over them. She didn't realize how much she'd been craving food other than powdered doughnuts, fast-food hamburgers, or overcooked eggs on English muffins. And God, she needed coffee.

She kept Dolly close and beelined for the table in the corner outfitted with hot coffee and a bowl of water on the floor. She sat, wrapped her fingers around the hot mug, and took a sip of the rich coffee, feeling herself coming back to life. Dolly lapped up the water.

The diner was long and narrow. A chrome breakfast bar lined the wall to the right, and across from it eight booths nestled against a wall filled with dozens of framed black-and-white pictures depicting the area through the decades.

Arlene came around and refilled her cup. "Tennessee is a long way from here."

"Fourteen hours."

She leaned down and rubbed Dolly's head. "What brings you two out this way? If you're here for the oysters, you're a little late or a lot early. And you don't look like duck hunters."

"We're here to see Henry Garrison."

Nodding, Arlene glanced out the diner's front window toward a brick building across the street. "Well, his lights aren't on yet, so there's no rush. And by the way, everybody calls him Hank."

"I knew we were early, but we're hungry."

"Menus are in the holder on the wall. Let me know what you'd like."

Lucy looked up and, for the first time in months, beamed. "Thanks."

The woman hesitated, head cocked with a question. "Do I know you?"

"I've never been here before."

She stared as if recalling an old memory boxed away for decades. "But I know you."

"I'm Lucy Kincaid. This is Dolly. My mother tells me she was from this town. Beth Kincaid." She hoped Beth's name would ring some kind of bell that validated this trip.

Arlene shook her head, puzzling over information that wouldn't reconcile. "Haven't heard of the Kincaids. You got any other names I might recognize?"

"What about Jessup?"

Arlene laughed and rolled her eyes at the obvious staring her right in the face. "Your mother was Beth Jessup, wasn't she?"

Lucy set her cup down, tapping a nervous finger on the side. "She was."

Arlene studied Lucy like she was looking at an old friend. "I thought of Beth Jessup the second you stepped in here. We went to high school together. Tore this town up from time to time." A rediscovered youthfulness sparked in her brown eyes. "Good Lord, I've missed that gal. What the heck is your mama up to these days?"

The coffee cup stilled inches from Lucy's lips. "She died two weeks ago."

The smile, triggered by memories of Beth, crumpled. "I'm so sorry to hear that, honey."

Lucy sat a little straighter, still not comfortable with the words herself. "She had brain cancer. She asked Dolly and me to visit her home. Bring her ashes."

Arlene cleared her throat. "Bless your heart. Good Lord, in my mind Beth's still a wild teenager. And now she's gone. I really am sorry."

Sadness she'd done her best to ignore crept up beside her. "Thanks."

The creases between Arlene's brow deepened. "I suppose you're here about Winter Cottage?"

News traveled fast. "Mr. Garrison mentioned something about a cottage. Where is it?"

"It's just outside of town near the lighthouse."

"I have no idea what I'm getting into."

Arlene swatted her concern away with a wave of her hand. "Don't worry. Hank will take good care of you. By the time you eat breakfast, he'll be at his desk. He's an early riser. So what can I get for you two?"

"I'll take the pancakes," Lucy said. "And extra bacon for Dolly."

"Sure thing. I'll get your order started right away."

"Thanks."

The woman's grin was warm, genuine. "My word, it sure is nice to have Beth's daughter in town."

Beth had only been in her teens when she'd had Lucy. She'd never once mentioned Cape Hudson, but the locals might shed some light on her mother's life before she moved to Nashville.

As she waited for her order, more people arrived for breakfast. Several older men now sat at the bar, eating and talking in hushed tones. An older couple took a booth adjoining hers. She caught more than a few inquisitive glances in her direction.

The pancakes and bacon arrived, and she fed several strips to Dolly before she took her first bite. The pancakes were soft and buttery, and she couldn't remember the last time she'd sat at a table and eaten. Most meals were grabbed in the kitchen behind the bar, and at Beth's there'd been no tables. Beth hadn't been a fan, opting always to sit on the floor and eat out of a bowl.

The door to the diner opened again several more times, bringing with it gusts of cold air. The diner was almost full.

Arlene approached her and set down a white to-go container. "Extra bacon. Good to see you girls have real appetites. By the way, your check's been paid."

"Who?" Lucy asked.

"Consider it a welcome gift."

Arlene had a warm smile and she'd known Beth, prompting Lucy to ask, "My mom never talked about this place. Do you know why she left?"

"No one knew the answer to that. One day she was here, but then the day before graduation, she was gone. I was sure she'd be back. We used to share a beer on the beach each Friday after the football games all through high school. I must have kept those Fridays open for a year before I finally figured out she wasn't coming back." A customer called Arlene, and she shook her head. "I missed that girl something fierce."

Arlene turned to her other customer, who spoke in quiet tones, occasionally glancing at Lucy.

"We're the talk of the town," Lucy whispered to Dolly.

The two ate in silence for nearly twenty minutes, aware of more glances. For every bite Lucy took, she fed two to Dolly, and soon her plate was empty. She dug a few dollars out of her pocket for Arlene and tucked them under the salt and pepper shakers.

Again, she could feel folks watching as she and Dolly left. The lights in Mr. Garrison's office were still off, so turning up the collar of her coat, she led Dolly down Main Street, and they crossed the dunes to the beach. A stroll on the sand, in theory, was a nice idea, but the cold wind cut across the water, through her jacket, and into her bones.

Back up Main Street, she realized the lights in Mr. Garrison's office were on. "Ready or not."

CHAPTER THREE

Lucy

January 15, 2018

Lucy and Dolly climbed the three stone steps leading to the entrance of the two-story blue building on Main Street across from the diner. She glanced briefly at the sign **GARRISON & ASSOCIATES, LLC** and found the door unlocked.

The entry office was furnished with a rich oriental rug, walls painted a deep hunter green, and four large paintings that depicted the bay in the different seasons. There was a receptionist's desk, but it looked like it hadn't been used in a while. She reached down and dusted the sand off Dolly's paws as she wiped her own feet on the mat.

"Hello?" she said, closing the door behind her. When she didn't get a response, she moved toward the stairs and shouted, "Mr. Garrison?"

Footsteps sounded on the second floor and then upon the stairs. The man who appeared was lean, easily over six feet, and in his early thirties. Short dark hair, still damp from a shower, was brushed off stark, angled features. He was dressed in khakis with sharp creases as hard as his eyes and a crisp white shirt rolled up to his elbows. If Beth were here now, she'd have said he had the aura of an old soul.

He stared at her, as if searching for meaning that explained the songbird tattoo on her inner wrist, the streak of blue in her blonde hair, and the band of red-and-blue beads that wrapped around her other wrist. "You're Lucy Kincaid."

"Arlene called ahead from the diner, didn't she?"

"Yes. Welcome, I'm Hank Garrison. When did you get in from Nashville?"

"Last night."

"Where'd you stay?" Dolly walked up to him, and he extended his hand and allowed her to sniff his fingers.

"In my Jeep."

He shook his head, frowning. "It was cold last night." Dolly licked his fingers and settled onto the expensive rug.

"Yes, it was. Do you mind if the dog stays? It's cold."

"Sure, she's fine." He drew in a breath, still studying her, and then said with genuine sadness, "I'm sorry for your loss."

For some reason, the simple statement added to her loss. "Thanks."

"How are you two holding up?"

"I ditched the grief at the Bay Bridge–Tunnel last night." Beth wouldn't have wanted her to hold on to sorrow, and Dolly didn't need the bad energy. Now all she had to do was find a way to really wrestle free of it.

Garrison cleared his throat. "Did you bring the papers I requested?"

He'd been up front on the phone that she'd have to produce proof of identification before he could speak to her. She hadn't been able to find her birth certificate, so she'd gotten a copy when she went to the department of vital statistics for Beth's death certificate. It listed *Elizabeth Kincaid Jessup* as her mother. *Unknown* for her father.

Lucy dug into her satchel and pulled out a stack of papers. "Here are the certificates as well as the letters you sent."

"Good. I thought after all the times your mother ignored me, you'd do the same." He studied the papers, but especially her birth certificate.

"My mother never said a word to me about this place or you. But maybe you could fill me in. I could also use help with that *Unknown* father on my birth certificate."

"Come on into my office." They crossed the small lobby to the adjoining office, and he opened the door and flipped on lights. Dolly and Lucy entered, and he motioned for her to sit while he settled behind the desk. Dolly drifted off to sleep by Lucy's chair.

The furnishings were tasteful. The solid-mahogany desk looked old, as did the tall leather chair behind it and two smaller chairs for visitors. There was an undergraduate degree in political science from the University of Richmond and another picture of Garrison and three men about his age, all dressed in marine uniforms.

"You were in the marines?" she asked.

"I was."

"Can't be a bartender in a Nashville honky-tonk and not know the branches of the service. Tips rise when you can belt out the right armed-services fight song. I can sing the marine hymn right now, if it would break the ice?"

A small smile twitched. "Thanks, not necessary."

"Too bad. I'm pretty good at it. Semper fi."

The last time she had been in an office like this, she'd been dealing with Beth's landlord, who'd sued her for six months' back rent. As a cosigner on Beth's lease, she'd been liable and forced to pony up the last of her savings to avoid a lawsuit.

"So about your father's identity. Your mother never told you about the will set up by Mrs. Catherine Buchanan?"

"The first time my mom mentioned Cape Hudson was a few days before she died. I'd have pressed her for details, but she slipped into a coma."

"I want to go home, Lucy. To Virginia."

"Why Virginia? Nashville is your home."

"No. Virginia."

The weight of those words had tipped the first domino.

"Beth always told me she'd been born in Nashville. Tennessean through and through, she used to say. Honestly, I'm still not convinced you found the right Beth Kincaid."

"Jessup," he added without hesitation.

"A name she never used. She was always Beth Kincaid."

"Except on your birth certificate, Lucy."

"You know more about me than I do. Got to say, Mr. Garrison, it's unsettling."

Again, studious eyes searched for depth and meaning as a muscle pulsed in his jaw. "Elizabeth Kincaid Jessup grew up in Cape Hudson. Her father lived by Winter Cottage the last years of his life."

"Her father?"

"Samuel Jessup. He married Donna Kincaid, your grandmother, in 1968."

She sat back, tapping a ringed finger on the mahogany arm of the chair while calmly trying to take it all in.

"Your grandfather passed away last year, which is what prompted me to reach out to your mother."

Hearing about Samuel and Donna, blood kin and total strangers, poked a hole in her heart. She threaded her fingers through her hair, not sure if she was grateful to finally fill in these pieces of her life or if she was pissed that Beth had lied to her. She opted for pissed because it hurt less to be mad than sad. "Did my mother have any brothers or sisters?"

"Your grandparents had an infant son born before your mother, but he passed when he was a couple of months old. Donna Kincaid Jessup died in 1984 when your mother was about fourteen."

"Did my grandparents have siblings? Are there at least extended cousins?"

"Your grandfather came from a family of five children. So you have quite a few second cousins."

"Where are they?"

"A few are in town, but most have moved away."

In third grade, Lucy's teacher had told her students to draw a family tree with their parents. Beth insisted it was just the two of them, so Lucy had drawn a single trunk with one branch. She'd been content until she'd realized her classmates' drawings were filled with endless branches. "I understand there is an inheritance called Winter Cottage."

"The inheritance is from Mrs. Catherine Hedrick Buchanan." Sharp green eyes locked onto her, waiting for her to acknowledge a name that he assumed was familiar.

"If you're waiting to see if the name means something, sorry. I got nothing. You'll have to start with the basics."

"Mrs. Buchanan owned Winter Cottage, and she wanted your grandfather, your mother, and now you to have it."

"What was Mrs. Buchanan's relationship to my grandfather?"

"I don't really know. Your grandfather was a merchant marine, and he didn't retire until he was eighty. That was 1996. According to family lore, Mrs. Buchanan offered to send your grandfather to college, but he refused. She made a similar offer to your mother, but she also refused."

"So why was this woman guardian angel to the Jessups?"

How many times had her mother told her college, especially art college, was a waste of money? She'd always figured the attitude had more to do with financial feasibility. Apparently not.

Lucy's teachers had always said she had potential, but in the end her grades had been too average for a scholarship. The first few years out of high school, she'd tried to save up for college, but whenever her bank account grew, something went wrong. The transmission in her car failed. Uninsured appendicitis. Beth was short on rent money again. It all chipped away at savings. By her early twenties, she'd earned a solid reputation on the Nashville strip as a bartender. Life rolled on, she sketched when she could, and college got left behind.

"When did Mrs. Buchanan die?" she asked.

"March 1990 at the age of one hundred and one."

"About a year after I was born."

"Yes."

"When did you first reach out to my mother?" she asked.

"Last year, right after your grandfather died. After she ignored all my letters, I finally got her on the phone four months ago. She said maybe you'd want whatever Mrs. Buchanan was offering and asked me to resend the documents."

"I had no idea." More hurt than surprised, she rubbed Dolly's head. "This is a lot to take in, Mr. Garrison."

"I know."

She thought about all the glances in the diner. "Beth must have made an impression. I got a lot of stares at breakfast."

"Your mother was hard to forget. My parents went to high school with her, and they remember her well."

"Have you asked them about her?"

"My dad said everyone has a Beth story."

She felt like she'd stumbled into a movie fifteen minutes late and was scrambling to identify the cast of characters. "What was his story?"

"She convinced a handful of students to skip school their sophomore year. They drove down to Norfolk and spent an entire afternoon eating ice cream and hanging out on the beach. The town sheriff, wanting to make a point, was waiting at the bridge when they drove home. With lights and sirens, he pulled them over, and everyone was scared but Beth. She laughed when the sheriff started lecturing them, and it got her a ride in the back of his squad car to jail, where she sat for a while. She emerged from jail a few hours later, and all the kids thought she was cool."

"That sums up my childhood. She was never one for the rules. Arlene said she left the day before graduation. Even I can do that math. She was pregnant with me."

"Yes."

"Do you know who my father is?" Now it was her turn to bore a hole in him and wait for an answer.

He didn't blink. "I don't know."

Her gaze steady, she tried to peer into his brain. "Can you tell me more about Winter Cottage?"

"It was built in 1901 and served as a hunting lodge. Mr. George Buchanan, Mrs. B's father-in-law, built the home for Elizabeth Lawrence because they both loved to duck hunt. She was his mistress for years, but they married in 1916."

"A hunting lodge. I'm imagining bear rugs, antlers, and lots of dark wood."

"Not exactly. You'll have to see it to believe it. The house also comes with three hundred acres of bayfront land that has several water access points. My family has leased one hundred acres from the estate for forty years. We run Beacon Vineyard."

"Land and a house. Beats a Jeep and the last hundred bucks I have in my pocket."

Mr. Garrison flexed his fingers as if he were about to handle something unpleasant. "There are conditions to the inheritance."

"Of course there are. What conditions?"

"All monies in the inheritance must be used to renovate and keep up the house. You can begin accessing those funds after you've lived on the property thirty days."

"Did my grandfather stay in the house?"

"He lived there thirty days and then moved to the guest cottage on the property. He was good about upkeep, but he never tackled any renovations beyond putting a new roof on the house."

"What's wrong with Winter Cottage? Why didn't my mother and grandfather want it?"

"It's old. Drafty. And taking care of a house like that is a commitment."

"And if I decide I don't want the house, then I get nothing."

"Correct. The property's renovation monies would then go to the heir descended from George Buchanan's daughter, Victoria. That's also odd, because back in the day, inheritance usually followed the sons, not the daughters."

"What about Mrs. Buchanan? She didn't have children of her own?"

"She had a son, who passed away in 1974. Her heirs were not listed in the will."

"Why not?"

"No idea."

Beth used to say possessions only weighed you down, and Lucy was starting to see some of the logic. "None of this makes sense."

"No, it does not."

"Who's the relative who gets this Winter Cottage if I say no?"

"Me."

"You?"

"Victoria was my great-grandmother."

She huffed out a frustrated breath. "So if I stay for thirty days in a hundred-year-old house, I then have the privilege of renovating it?"

"Yes."

"Could I sell it?"

"No."

"How much money is there for renovation?"

"There's fifteen million, but remember, the money will always stay with the house."

She blinked and sat back in her chair. "One five?"

"Correct."

"Damn." Lucy didn't know whether to faint or throw up.

He leaned forward, tapping the tip of a pen on the paper blotter. "I'm prepared to make you a cash offer if you'll surrender the inheritance."

"You want this cottage?"

"And the land around it."

"But you'd have to use the money for the house."

"Yes. The fifteen million will always be attached to the house."

"How much are you willing to offer?"

"Fifty thousand dollars."

She'd never seen that much money all at once. But as tempted as she was to take the money and run, she'd overheard enough wheeling and dealing in Music City to know the first offer was rarely the best. "Can I see this Winter Cottage?"

"I can take you out there now. We'll drive over in my car."

"I'll follow you in mine. Dolly tends to shed."

"Okay. I'm parked out front."

"I'm in a yellow Jeep."

"I know. Arlene already told me," he said.

She'd been here only a few hours and had more real clues to her past than Beth had supplied in a lifetime. The idea of unearthing this buried treasure of information made her suddenly restless and anxious to breathe fresh air.

She and Dolly waited as he shut off his office lights and grabbed his keys and coat. The cold, brisk wind felt good against her flushed cheeks as she and Dolly hurried to the Jeep. Dolly could tell something exciting was happening. She didn't miss much.

Garrison locked the office door behind him and slid behind the wheel of an old pickup parked in front. He made a forward motion with his hand and pulled onto Main Street. She put the Jeep in gear and turned the key. The engine groaned and spit.

"Don't do this to me now!" She leaned over the steering wheel, again hoping metal and rubber parts could be persuaded by pleading and wishing. "Please, be nice. I just need a few more miles."

The engine did not start.

Dolly barked, and she lifted her gaze to see Mr. Garrison striding toward the car. She rolled down the window. "It's a miracle it made it this far," she said. "The old girl just gave up."

"You two can ride in my car," he said. "It's fine if Dolly sheds."

"Thanks." She grabbed the keys, her mother's urn, and Dolly's leash, and the two slid into the front seat of the truck. "You don't mind if I bring Beth along, do you?"

"Not at all."

His truck was neat, which was fitting. He was a buttoned-up-tight kind of guy. "How long have you been back in town?"

"Six months."

"Just the facts, Joe Friday?" She settled the urn between her feet on the floor.

A smile tugged the edges of his lips. "Yes."

"Fair enough."

He drove through town and back toward the main road. He took a left and headed north. She made another stab at conversation, but he wasn't interested.

As they passed the flat landscape covered in farmland, she wondered what the hell was so terrible about this place. Beth had easily handled her share of shady characters while she'd tried to navigate the music industry. So why had a place like this chased her away?

As the scenery grew even more barren, she realized that she really didn't know this guy. No stickers on the back bumper of his truck, and no papers lying around his office that told her anything about him. It would be a real bummer to drive all this way and then get murdered by a serial killer. He certainly would have motive.

Okay, so worst-case scenarios were her thing. She'd spent most of her childhood devising and solving them. It paid to be prepared with the very spontaneous Beth Kincaid, a.k.a. Beth Jessup, as your mother.

She rubbed Dolly's head. The dog looked at her and thumped her tail. At least the dog wasn't giving off any bad vibes about Garrison.

The truck slowed in what seemed like the middle of nowhere and turned west onto a partially paved, graveled road. There was old Mace somewhere in the bottom of her purse, but she'd be dead before she found it. So if he tried to kill her, she'd scream and order Dolly to run.

Dolly yawned.

Garrison downshifted and slowed over the uneven road. "There was a hurricane that hit the peninsula about fifty years ago," he said. "It tore up the road, and it took nearly a year to fix it. Winter Cottage also became known as the House on Broken Road."

His sentences were getting longer. Damn near chatty now. He downshifted again as he approached what looked like a dirt driveway that cut through tall trees. He turned deeper into the woods. Here went nothing.

The line of trees gave way to a wide-open patch of land that stretched nearly a mile to the bay. It was covered in rows of neatly trimmed gray-brown vines twisting around trellises.

"I wouldn't think you could grow grapes out here."

"Vines like tough conditions."

Dust kicked up around the vehicle as he drove toward the white two-story house surrounded by windswept trees. The grass around the house was trimmed, but there was nothing that could have passed for landscaping.

The house had a wide front porch along with floor-to-ceiling windows streaked with salt. The red tin roof was tired and weathered. A lone rocker, grayed by weather and time, swayed gently in the breeze.

Garrison kept driving.

"Isn't that the house?"

"No, that's the old custodian's house where Mr. Jessup lived. There was a fire in the house last year, so it's not really livable. Winter Cottage is a little farther down the road."

"Mr. Garrison, this is starting to creep me out."

He frowned. "Why?"

"I don't know. Middle of nowhere. With a stranger. Serial killers. I have about seven or eight more reasons if you have time."

"I'm not a serial killer."

"That's what they all say."

Her worry and stress seemed to surprise him. He parked in the middle of the driveway, shut off the engine, and faced her. "Winter Cottage is one hundred yards ahead, around the bend. It sits right on the bay."

"We can't drive up to it? Oh yeah, Broken Road."

Ignoring the quip, he said, "A winter storm soaked the driveway last month. We've been waiting for it to dry out so it can be repaired in the next few days. For now, we have to walk in."

"Of course." Not sure how the dog would react in a new setting, she grabbed Dolly's leash and her mother's urn and got out. The wind again slashed through her, chasing away all the warmth from the truck's heater.

"The house is a responsibility," Garrison said.

"And I don't look like I can handle it?"

"I didn't say that."

"You were thinking it."

He removed a set of thick keys from his pocket. He set off down the road, taking her past deep ruts carved by heavy rains.

"How did the vineyard fare in the storm?" she asked.

"It did okay. In fact, we hope to plant more, but we haven't been able to negotiate a new long-term lease on the land."

"What have you been waiting on?"

"You."

The gusts seemed to be pushing her toward the waters. In the bending grass she imagined whispers and thought of Beth. She listened and hugged the urn a little closer, hoping for answers. But there was nothing. Typical Beth. Her mother was going to make her work for this one.

Dolly stopped several times to sniff all the new scents. She then snorted as if something in the breeze awakened her senses.

The road finally evened out. The tree branches, bent by years of bay winds, reached over the road as if they were lovers trying to clasp hands. Ahead she heard the lap of water against the shore.

When they rounded the final curve, she stood face-to-face with a huge French provincial–style house. Painted a faint yellow, it was elegant and simple all at once. Three stories tall, it was made of brick and sported twenty tall windows along the front. In the center was a massive wooden front door. No Trespassing signs were posted.

"Where's the cottage?"

"You're looking at it."

"It has to be at least ten thousand square feet," she said.

"Fifteen."

She dug deeper into her jacket. "Who decided to call this a cottage?"

"To the Buchanans, it was a cottage. Their other homes in New York City and Newport, Rhode Island, were twice the size."

She tried to picture Beth here but couldn't. The mother she remembered had stood on the stage of a smoke-filled honky-tonk, singing an old Dolly Parton song, or had sat at her card table on Lower Broadway, reading tarot cards for tourists. When she thought of Beth, she saw neon lights far from this cold, barren place that looked so *permanent.*

He walked up to the wide front door and shoved one of the large keys into the old lock. He wiggled it back and forth as if coaxing it until a bolt clicked open.

He pushed open the heavy door, stepped inside, and flipped on a bulb that spit out a faint ring of light by the door.

The front entry hallway cut through the house to a large bank of windows looking out over the bay. Thick rain clouds, remnants of last night's storm, lumbered toward the northwest, dragging with them choppy, white-capped waters. Still, the view was stunning. Lucy imagined that on a clear day, it could easily take her breath away.

Her footsteps echoed as she moved through the dark house toward the bank of windows. She set Beth's urn on a small table as goose bumps crept along her shoulders and Dolly's ears flattened.

She ran her fingers over Beth's red-and-blue prayer beads, which were wrapped around her wrist. If her mother had been reading her cards now, she'd have pulled the Tower. Destruction. Turmoil. Upheaval. Yep, that ticked all the boxes for today.

The air in the house was musty, and the light caught the dust dancing in its beams. On her right was a massive staircase, and on her left, a formal dining room. The furniture in the dining room was covered in white sheets, and only faint outlines remained of whatever paintings had hung on the walls.

This place was from a different time. There were no trendy restaurants nearby. You couldn't walk to get coffee or drift into a honky-tonk and listen to the newest country-music talent hone their craft. Time had flat-out stopped. It was surreal.

"Ready to talk about my offer?" Garrison asked.

CHAPTER FOUR

Beth

May 6, 1988

Beth sits quietly as Mrs. B sips her tea. She's quit her restaurant job and is ignoring Arlene's warnings about giving up a good job. Arlene is covering Beth's last shift in case she changes her mind, but she knows she won't.

Beth fixes her own tea with plenty of milk and sugar but finds the bone-china teacup covered with hummingbirds too delicate. The cup barely holds more than a couple of mouthfuls, which tastes like watered-down coffee. But the old lady is the boss now, so she drinks tea from the blue cup.

Again Mrs. B is dressed to the nines. Today it's a red Chanel suit with a white ruffled silk shirt. Her jewelry is the same simple-but-pretty scrimshaw ivory broach. It's old, but the kind of bauble tourists snap up at the shore because it's made by locals and isn't expensive.

"I told my teacher that we're going to keep talking. She's stoked."

Mrs. B sets down her cup onto the saucer. "Stoked?"

"Excited. She's curious about you and this place. All the kids know about you, but no one really *knows* you, if that makes sense."

Mrs. B studies Beth like she's either searching or trying to dissect. "Could you ever see yourself living in a house like this, Beth?"

The teacup rattles in the saucer. "God no! If I lived here, I'd never get out of this town."

"And that's a bad thing?"

"Well, yeah. If you're my age and haven't seen the world. You've traveled. The best I've done is a school field trip to the Washington, DC, zoo last year."

"Maybe after you've traveled a bit, to Nashville or wherever, you'll end up returning to Cape Hudson."

Beth reaches for a sugar cookie, which is kind of bland but grows on her after a mouthful. "How do you know about Nashville?"

"It was one of the cities you mentioned the last time you visited. I may be old, but I remember." She sips her tea. "I hear things about you, Beth."

Instead of being put off, she is intrigued. The old lady isn't the hermit she appears to be. "I bet you got an earful. I'll bite. So what did you hear?"

"That you were a cheerleader but got kicked off the team after an incident involving chickens set loose on the football field at homecoming."

Beth grins. "Don't ever dare me."

"You're dating one of the football players, but you also have an eye for my great-nephew."

"Well, I was dating Eddie, but now I'm on to Brian. Noah's your great-nephew, right? He is pretty good looking, and I wouldn't say no to a date."

"When you chase a boy, you give your power away." She raises her teacup to her lips.

"Power?"

"Sex, dear. Just because a boy smiles doesn't mean you should have sex with him."

For whatever reason, Beth laughs. "Believe me, just because I like to have a good time doesn't mean I'm letting any boy stop me from going to Nashville, or wherever."

Mrs. B studies Beth over the rim of that delicate porcelain cup, her eyes searching. "I've met girls like you before. They're drawn to the excitement. Moths to a flame. Be careful, Beth."

"Of what?"

She slowly sets the cup down. "Shall we get started?"

"Yep. Where do we begin?"

"We're going to start with Claire."

"Who's Claire?"

"Listen and learn."

Beth switches on the camera.

———— ⚬⚬⚬ ————

Claire

Cape Hudson, Virginia
October 3, 1904

The first time Jimmy Latimer saved Claire Hedrick's life, she was sixteen.

She was thrilled to finally return home to the Eastern Shore. Her charge, Victoria, was in school in Switzerland, and she had been invited to Winter Cottage as a lady's maid to Mrs. Lawrence, who spent most of the hunting season in breeches.

It was her free afternoon, and the air was warm and heavy with humidity on this Indian summer day. She wanted to be out on the water like she had been as a child. Nearly four plus years of caring for the spoiled Victoria, sewing for endless hours, and enduring homesickness had taken its toll. The water promised freedom, and it was so tantalizing she didn't worry about the dark clouds clinging to the distant horizon and the faintest rumble of thunder. She wanted to feel alive.

Claire pulled the small skiff toward the water, savoring the sunshine and the salt air teasing the copper curls framing her face.

"You're being stupid, girl," a man shouted.

The sharp warning came from Jimmy, the housekeeper's son. He was home on leave for several weeks from the merchant marines, and his mother, Mrs. Latimer, spoke with pride about her son's service. On track to be captain one day. Too handsome for his own good. Any girl would be lucky to have him. Mr. Buchanan claimed he was the best hunting guide in the county.

Jimmy was the favorite son. She was the forgotten daughter.

So when Claire's gaze met Jimmy's ice-blue stare and desire and longing rushed through her, she was more determined to dislike him. She tugged the vessel closer to the water, and his deepening frown only fueled her determination to prove him wrong. At sixteen, she could pretend she was sure of herself so that she didn't look cowardly before the handsome man watching her.

Unmindful of the water soaking her boots and the hem of her skirt, she pushed the bow over the smooth sand. She jumped into the small boat and gripped the oars, feeling a little smug as she pulled away from the shore. A rumble of thunder followed as she watched Jimmy walk to the shore, hands on hips, scowl deepening. But to stop was to admit failure, and so she kept rowing. Even the current fought to keep her on the shore.

The oars were heavier than she remembered, and she was quickly growing breathless. Sweat trickled down her back. But as Jimmy watched, she kept cutting the water with the oars. Soon she was a hundred yards from shore, and Jimmy's features had melted away. She sensed then that she'd made a mistake.

When the weather turned on a dime, the wind swept in dark clouds with falling temperatures. The sky was ripe with lightning and thick droplets of rain.

The boat rocked, and the wind splashed the waters against her face and chilled her body to the bone. Getting back to shore was urgent. She wrestled the boat around and rowed, ignoring her tired muscles and burning lungs. The choppy current, so fickle in storms, shifted and now pulled her farther away from shore. Even with every pull of the oar against the churning water, the little boat drifted farther from land.

She never saw the wave that struck and capsized the boat. Her first reaction was shock. Then panic.

Another wave hit her, and her arms flailed as she struggled to keep her head above water and reach the upended boat. Her clothes and boots, now saturated, pulled her under. Treading water became impossible. She fought, gulping water while scrambling to the surface. Her adrenaline was beginning to yield to the cold and exhaustion. The dark sky grew angrier as her lungs screamed for air. She'd been a fool, and it would cost her dearly.

A strong hand grabbed her by her collar, hauled her like a rag doll into the air, and dumped her onto the soaked wooden hull of a fishing boat. She coughed up water and sucked in a breath.

Claire looked up to see Jimmy and his most beautiful scowl. His weathered hands gripped the oars, and his muscles pulsed as he rowed with all his might. He was silent until they reached the pier.

"That was stupid," he said through clenched teeth.

Pushing hair from her eyes, she coughed, wiped the briny water from her lips, and sat straighter, hoping to salvage some dignity. The cold was almost unbearable.

He nodded toward a blue woolen jacket draped over the bench seat. "Did you not hear my warnings?"

"I did." She lifted her arms and shoved them into the warm folds of the jacket. His scent surrounded her.

"I've heard you're hardheaded. You're lucky I was watching you."

Her lips trembled. "Why were you watching me?"

He grumbled something, and with a flick of his head pushed back a thick lock of sun-streaked blond hair. Such a beautiful face. Such a muscular body.

Mrs. Latimer came down the pier, a blanket in her hands. She fussed over Claire, helping her out of the boat and wrapping the blanket around her. "What were you thinking, girl?"

Jimmy answered for her as if she were simple. "She's fearless like you said, Ma. But not as smart."

They'd been talking about her, Claire realized as Mrs. Latimer fussed over her. "Why did you do such a foolish thing?"

Claire couldn't answer as Mrs. Latimer led her to the house. She twisted around and found Jimmy still watching. Damp hair, blue eyes, and full lips turned into a puzzled frown.

He'd saved her, and pride or not, she was so grateful. Without thinking, she broke from Mrs. Latimer, rushed toward him, and wrapped her arms around his neck. Seconds passed before he gently patted her on the back and then pulled her hands away.

"Thank you, Mr. Latimer."

"I'm just Jimmy." This time he grinned, and just like that, she was in love.

Claire

January 10, 1916

Claire hadn't seen Jimmy for almost twelve years. To say she thought of him all the time would be a lie, but she did think about him often. She began a regular correspondence with Mrs. Latimer, and when she wrote, she always asked about Jimmy, though she was careful to sound polite, as if this were a kindness. *And how fares your son? What countries has he traveled to this year?* Claire collected all the tidbits Mrs. Latimer supplied.

The years had been good to Claire. She'd developed a reputation as a very talented seamstress and had received offers from couture shops and other society ladies who wanted to employ her. But in the end, she'd remained with the Buchanans, who were her surrogate family in so many respects.

Now she was back in Cape Hudson. The first Mrs. Buchanan had died in her Paris apartment, and Mr. Buchanan was finally marrying his mistress, Mrs. Lawrence. Claire had been readying Mrs. Lawrence's trousseau for months and had designed her wedding dress.

Thoughts of a grumbling Victoria, who had accompanied her from New York on the long train ride, and even the pressing alterations to the wedding dress were forgotten when she saw Jimmy. He was leaning against a polished Model T car parked in front of the train station in Cape Hudson.

His arms crossed, his lips flat in a deep, beautiful frown, he wore a dark coat and knit cap suited for a sailor and not a driver. He was taller than she remembered, and though still fit, the years had filled out his body and accented his tanned face with feathered crow's-feet at the corners of his eyes.

He'd been in the merchant marines nearly fifteen years and was rising through the ranks. His mother said he'd soon be captain of his own ship, but he was again on leave and would be doing odd jobs for the Buchanans as he always did.

His presence was a good omen. The way she saw it, it added to the euphoria of being back home where the salty breeze was fresh and the land open as far as she could see. No more skyscrapers, rattle of streetcars, and rush of city people.

It felt right.

Feminine laughter bubbled behind Claire, and she turned to find Victoria Buchanan giggling as she spoke to the train porter. The poor young man was already smitten by the stunning twenty-one-year-old woman, who possessed a youthful beauty that turned men's heads and tortured them with jealousy.

Curled blonde hair as fair as summer sand framed Victoria's oval face and accentuated her high cheekbones, bow mouth, and bright, expressive blue eyes. The wool fabric of her navy-blue velvet traveling coat nipped into a tiny waist and draped over perfectly rounded curves. The girl was a dream to dressmakers, though Victoria often complained about her large bosom and wished for sleeker curves like Broadway's Irene Castle, who was making lithe and boyish figures fashionable.

Claire was trim, but her build would never be as delicate as Irene Castle's. Though her own mother had dubbed her frame sturdy and dependable, she was not unattractive and knew how to alter her dresses to make her waist appear slimmer. She still had her share of men taking a second admiring look her way.

Today she'd chosen her own coming-home dress carefully, selecting a burgundy wool with a draped bustle and fitted jacket that fastened with pearl buttons and dipped below her waist to a point. It had been one of Victoria's castoffs, but the fabric was too fine to pass up, so she'd customized it with a fur collar from another rejected ensemble.

As Miss Victoria moved away from the porter, she raised a gloved hand to her mouth and stifled a yawn. The girl initially had planned to travel with her father and soon-to-be stepmother two weeks ago to Cape Hudson. But she'd begged, pouted, and pleaded with Mrs. Lawrence during one of their last fittings. *"Let me stay! Papa will listen to you!"* Mrs. Lawrence hadn't been convinced until Victoria offered Claire up, insisting she chaperone.

Claire had not wanted to linger in the city. She'd wanted to be in Cape Hudson before her father's ship set sail. But Mrs. Lawrence had seen the advantage to having her fiancé to herself for a couple of weeks, and in short order the arrangements were made. Claire's father had set sail by the time they'd arrived.

"Claire, this place is as dull as I remembered," Victoria said.

"I think it's beautiful."

Victoria wrinkled her pretty nose. "After all the places you've seen, you can say that?"

Claire brushed a curl from her face and imagined Jimmy behind her, staring. Would he remember her? "Because it's the truth."

Victoria's smile was aimed toward Claire, but she was truly focused on the young porter lingering by the train. "Your people were seamen."

"And fishermen."

She winked at the boy and then faced Claire, already growing bored with the game. "I wonder if Daddy would mind terribly if I just slipped back on the train. I'm sure he'll not miss me when he marries Mrs. Lawrence."

"He'll notice." When a man spent a small fortune on dresses, as Mr. Buchanan had with the frocks for this wedding, he expected to see his ladies on display.

Victoria raised a lace handkerchief to her lips. "Ugh. I know. He wants Brother Robert and me here with bright, shining smiles when he welcomes his new bride into our family." She continued to hold the handkerchief to her lips. "Is there some kind of facility where I can relieve myself?"

"Are you still feeling ill?"

"Mixing brandy and whiskey is now off my spirits list. But seeing Anna Pavlowa and *The Big Show* at the Hippodrome last night made me forget reason."

The evening before, Victoria and her third cousin Edward Garrison had arrived home at 2:00 a.m. Claire had been waiting in the kitchen over a warm cup of tea when she'd heard the front door bang open. She now hoped the twit retched for the rest of the week.

"There are facilities around here, but if you have a queasy stomach, they'll make it more so. I suggest you wait until you arrive at Winter Cottage." There was a special kind of relationship between a lady's maid and her mistress. Certainly there was a line that could not be crossed, but there was also familiarity. She was always abreast of the girl's exploits, which came close to crossing a line.

"How long will that take?" Victoria asked.

"Less than an hour."

Victoria slowly tucked the handkerchief inside her left cuff. "Ugh, again. At least Papa assures me there's indoor plumbing at the cottage now. *Thank God.* I can't imagine roughing it much more than I am. How do we get to the house?"

Claire nodded toward Jimmy. "I'm guessing he's been sent for us. No one else on the shore has money for a driver other than your father."

Victoria regarded Jimmy, and a slow grin dispatched her pout. "He's very attractive. Rugged. Strong."

"That's Jimmy Latimer."

"You know him?"

"I doubt he remembers me. But yes, I know the family. His mother is housekeeper at Winter Cottage."

Victoria pushed the edges of her right sleeve up, exposing a portion of her delicate white wrist. "I'm going to freshen up somewhere. And when I return momentarily, can you introduce us?"

"Of course." As Victoria ducked into the train station, Claire walked up to Jimmy, feeling a giddy tightness she'd not felt since that day he'd watched her pushing the skiff into the water.

Tipping her chin, she stood in front of him, waiting for him to say her name. He studied her, but she saw no hint of recognition. "I'm Claire Hedrick."

"Hedrick?" He sounded as if he were searching his memory. "I know an Isaac Hedrick. His ship sailed a few days ago."

"My father. So I've really missed him?"

"Aye." A genuine kindness wove around the word, making her sorry she didn't really mind missing her father. In the years she'd been gone, he'd never written her once. "So which of the four Hedrick sisters are you? Oldest, youngest?"

"The oldest." His question vexed her. "It's been over a decade since I was in Cape Hudson. I've been living in New York, Newport, and Europe."

"Fancy places I'd say, judging by the looks of you. I've not seen any of your sisters, but I see your brothers running about town from time to time. The Jessups are doing a fine job with them."

She'd written to Sally Jessup weekly through the years and received news back on the "little boys" often. Though they were hardly little boys now at fifteen, sixteen, and seventeen years old. "I'm looking forward to seeing them."

"Stanley plans to go to sea like his father."

"Does our father see the boys?"

"Whenever he can."

So her father kept up with his sons. She was glad for the boys but irritated for herself. Annoyance crept into her tone. "Are you my driver?"

He raised a brow. "I'm here to pick up Miss Victoria Buchanan."

"That is me," Victoria said brightly from behind Claire.

He looked past Claire to Victoria. Immediately he grinned that odd, silly smile men got when they first looked at her. He had the good sense to temper his reaction, but it was there. He tugged off his cap. "Pleased to meet you, Miss Buchanan. I'm Jimmy Latimer."

Victoria looked amused but didn't really smile—that was something she would make him work for. "And it's a pleasure to meet you, James."

"Not James," he said quickly. "That's too formal. Just Jimmy." His gaze skittered to her bosom, and he cleared his throat, dropped his eyes, and mumbled something about taking their bags.

He was a male and therefore powerless against Victoria's charms. Claire had witnessed similar effects on men as young as ten and as old as eighty, but this time she felt a jealousy she had little right to claim. He'd saved her life, but he'd saved countless lives, according to his mother's letters.

"Let me get your luggage loaded," Jimmy said. "Where are your bags?"

Claire cleared the thickness from her throat. "We have several trunks that I assume will have to come later. But the carpetbags on the platform should travel with us now."

"No worries, miss."

Her name wasn't *miss*. It was *Claire*. And she wanted to hear him say it with the richness of *Miss Buchanan*.

Jimmy packed the two small carpetbags in the car's rear trunk, opened the back-seat door for Victoria, and took her gloved hand, steadying her as she climbed in. Victoria held on to his hand a moment longer than necessary while situating herself.

Claire walked around to the front passenger seat and waited for Jimmy. He was smiling at Victoria, forcing Claire to clear her throat until he came around and opened her door.

"Sorry about that, miss."

He offered a gloved hand to Claire, but as much as she would've liked to show him she was quite capable, she wanted to touch him. She laid a gloved hand in his, and he wrapped his fingers around hers. His hand was stronger than she remembered, and the energy still radiated through him. Her annoyance flitted away as she climbed up into the seat and tucked her skirts around her feet. If she were the kind to giggle like Miss Victoria, she might have been tempted to do so now. But Claire did not giggle, flirt, or smile. She was far too practical and proud.

He closed the door with a loud thump; moved around the car with quick, purposeful strides; and unbuttoned his jacket as if he couldn't stand the constraint any longer. The wind teased the flaps of the jacket, showing off a hard, lean waist.

"There are goggles on the seats for both of you," he said.

"Jimmy," Victoria said as she scooped up a pair of goggles and inspected them, "I can tell you're going to be my one bright spot during this long, cold winter. Tell me there are things for the young people to do here."

"There are, miss, but I'm not sure you'd be interested."

She slid on her goggles, managing not to ruin her hair. "I might be, for the right reasons. Where I'm going is for old ladies who gossip and their husbands, who only smoke cigars and discuss politics."

Claire's vanity loathed the idea of goggles, but she knew in this case he was right. She fitted them carefully over her face.

"You must work on Jimmy for me, Claire. A strapping fellow like that must know of any gatherings for the younger folk."

"I don't know."

"But you can find out. Servants talk amongst themselves. You hear things I never would."

"I suppose," Claire said.

Jimmy got a boy to stand at the crank mounted to the engine before he slid behind the wheel. He gave the thumbs-up, and as the boy cranked, he pushed in the clutch and pressed the starter button. The engine turned and rumbled and then shut off.

Claire, simply to be annoying and pay him back for not remembering her, said, "The boy won't forget that we have twelve trunks? They're all very important."

Jimmy's jaw tightened and released as he motioned for the boy to crank again. "He won't forget, miss."

Miss. It's Claire. Remember me.

Jimmy pressed the starter button again, and this time the engine rumbled to life.

"Twelve cases."

"Got it."

"Don't worry, Claire," Victoria said. "I can tell after just a few seconds that Jimmy won't disappoint."

Victoria had never worried. Later, life's worries would find her, but for now she was the pampered daughter of a wealthy man who had protected her from worry. Claire had learned to worry as soon as she'd left the cradle. Each time her mother's belly had grown with her next sibling, it had brought a full dosage of fear. She dreaded the sound of her mother's screams during her long labors, the cries of a new squalling baby, and the increasing demands of the growing household.

The car lurched forward, forcing the boy standing in front to jump to the side. The engine abruptly cut off.

Victoria giggled. Jimmy mumbled an apology as he motioned for the boy to return. This time the engine sparked to life, and the boy handed him the crank. Jimmy put the car in gear and drove slowly away from the train station.

Victoria clapped. "Well done, Jimmy!"

He sat a little straighter. Men loved their compliments. As he drove, Claire's annoyance faded as her attention was pulled to the town of Cape Hudson, which had changed little since she'd left.

The town had been built by the railroad some thirty years ago, and its center was populated with several stores that seemed smaller than she remembered. Beyond the tiny retail center were compact, efficient houses that lined the few other streets in town.

The drive took them up a dirt road that cut along the shore north of Cape Hudson. Jimmy drove fast, nearly twenty miles an hour, and despite the rumble of the car engine and its oily smoke, she forgot about her fatigue, her hair, which surely must be a mess by now, and Victoria's spell on Jimmy.

Claire was enchanted by the land, the bright-blue sky, the white-caps that rolled over the bay's surface, and the flock of geese flying southward with the wind.

"Father must be in his glory," Victoria said, wrapping a silk scarf once again around her neck as she leaned forward. "Nothing gives him greater pleasure than to hunt fowl that love this cold, miserable weather as much as he. That's why he tolerates Mrs. Lawrence, you know, because she's happy to trot through the cold wind and rain like a bird dog. I swear, you'll never find me up before the sunrise in a hunting blind." She tugged at the edges of her white kid glove. "I'd have told my father so, but I know him. He'd have deliberately held the wedding in a blind before dawn just to teach me a lesson. Father and his lessons. I have learned not to argue, and let's hope for the sake of peace that my brother, Robert, has too."

The fortysomething Mrs. Lawrence was a widow with no children of her own. She'd met Mr. Buchanan at a society party in Philadelphia when his wife was ailing fifteen years ago. The attraction had been immediate between the two, and when Mr. Buchanan learned of her love of hunting, they became inseparable. The pair began to travel down to the Eastern Shore, where Mr. Buchanan maintained memberships in several hunt clubs. Of course, Mrs. Lawrence, as any woman, was not welcome at these clubs. So he built his own north of Cape Hudson. The next summer, construction had begun on what Mrs. Lawrence would call Winter Cottage. Only three months after the first Mrs. Buchanan passed in her Paris apartment, Mrs. Lawrence and Mr. Buchanan had announced their engagement.

As the car took them farther away from town, the land grew more and more desolate. It was very flat and covered in harvested cornfields. To the east were the waters of the Chesapeake Bay, and to the west, miles beyond the dense trees, the Atlantic Ocean. Her view now of the bay offered a reckless beauty she could never resist.

A sigh escaped Victoria's lips as she relaxed back against her seat and closed her eyes. "I could sleep for a week."

Jimmy's head cocked slightly, a sign he was paying attention.

"When will the trunks be delivered to the house?" Claire asked.

"As soon as possible."

"I have to dress the ladies for dinner. Will they arrive several hours before the dinner hour?"

"I suppose."

"That's not really an answer, is it?" She'd perfected the haughty tone of the women far above her station.

His hands tightened on the wheel. "It takes an hour. It depends on the road and the rain."

"And what would you guess based on today's conditions?"

A sigh slid across his lips. "An hour."

"See, Jimmy, that wasn't so hard, was it?" she teased.

Again his jaw pulsed. "You're mighty full of yourself, miss."

He would never have spoken to Victoria in such a way, but she fell into the world of the servants, so he was free to speak his mind.

"I could say the same of you."

"I've earned the right to some arrogance. What have you done but dress pampered ladies?"

Claire's retort vanished when she saw the flash of light from the lighthouse's Fresnel lens atop the tall redbrick spire nestled in a stand of trees near the bay. Despite herself, excitement swelled in her chest. Everyone who lived on these shores owed a debt to the men in the coast guard charged with sea rescue.

The lighthouse signaled that Winter Cottage was close. The cottage had been built in its shadow and rested just beyond the trees.

He slowed the car and turned onto a dirt road, and Claire found herself sitting a little straighter, curious about the cottage she hadn't seen in over a decade.

When the house came into view, Jimmy slowed, giving her a good look at the cottage.

If there ever were an inadequate word for this property, it was the word *cottage*. There was nothing small or quaint about the bright-yellow French provincial home that rivaled the fine estates outside Philadelphia or Paris. The high-pitched roof was made of slate and glinted in the bright sunshine. Twenty windows stretched along the front of the cottage, overlooking a meticulously manicured lawn.

She reached back and jostled Miss Victoria. It would not make a good impression if daddy's girl were sleeping when they arrived.

"We're here."

Victoria didn't open her eyes at first, but she released a sigh and rubbed the crook of her neck. "I was dreaming of Paris. Don't you long to be back in Paris, Claire?"

"Not often."

"Why not? It's such a stunning city."

For the rich, it was a city of lights and beauty. For others, not so much. She had dressed Victoria and Mrs. Lawrence in some of the most beautiful gowns draped in silks, ribbons, and pearls. But her contact with that glittering city rarely reached beyond the end of her sewing needle. Her Paris memories were of the small attic room where she lived and the cramped dressing room where she fussed over last-minute changes to gowns.

When she allowed herself to dream, it was of Jimmy sometimes, but always of this house. Her response was lost as Jimmy pressed the accelerator and the engine rumbled louder, and they drove down the long, graveled road that arched in front of the massive front door.

Victoria yawned. "It's not Paris."

Jimmy glanced toward Claire, searching her face. "What do you like about the house?"

All the letters from friends in Cape Hudson had mentioned the cottage, which to them had become a lifeline of employment and pride. "It's beautiful," Claire breathed.

"According to Daddy, the house is more of a marvel than the last time we were here," Victoria said, leaning forward again. "He says it's quite tolerable."

"Tolerable?" Claire shook her head, now annoyed at the spoiled young girl.

Victoria shrugged. "He's added luxuries to offset for all the talk I'll hear of waterfowl and politics."

Jimmy put the car in neutral, set the brake, and dismounted. He immediately shrugged off his driving goggles, which were darkened with soot, and opened Victoria's door.

She took his hand and smiled brightly. "Again, you're a delight, Jimmy. I hope you're one of our guides when we go hunting."

His grin flashed. "Yes, ma'am. I hope so."

Claire knew the girl would never rise so early in the cold to go hunting, not even for Jimmy. For Victoria, the rewards were expected with no hardships.

Mrs. Lawrence, dressed in hunting breeches, which were her preference here, greeted Victoria with a hearty hug. "Welcome, my dear. Your father is still in the marshes fussing over a duck blind but will see you at dinner."

Victoria yawned. "I need a nap."

"Of course you do," Mrs. Lawrence said. "Did you keep Claire up terribly late?"

"Claire is made of tougher stock than I."

Mrs. Lawrence looked past the girl to Claire. "Thank you for delivering the child."

Claire nodded. "Of course."

"We could not survive without you, my dear," Mrs. Lawrence said.

When the two vanished into the house, Claire removed her goggles and fluffed the soft curls around her face as she waited for Jimmy to stop gawking after Miss Victoria. He still needed to drive her around to the servants' entrance, but for a few minutes she'd have him all to herself.

He slid back behind the wheel and drove around the building to the side. He nosed the car toward the bay and shut off the rattling engine. As he strode around to her side of the car, he rolled his shoulders, releasing the stiff formality he'd maintained while Victoria was close. The swagger returned in the final steps before he opened her door.

"Welcome home, Miss Hedrick," he said. The deep tan of his face added richness to angled features that turned female heads in both small towns and big cities.

"So have you now managed to remember me?" she asked.

"A soaking-wet girl with red hair and too much daring for her own good? That girl? Certainly. But the woman before me in all her fine clothes and city ways is a stranger."

Gaiety and flirtations came so naturally to Victoria, and she'd spoken to Jimmy as if they'd been lifelong friends. Claire had managed only to sound like a harpy. "That girl learned caution."

His gaze slid up and down her. "She learned more than that."

"She also learned that impressions matter."

He leaned toward her until his face was inches from hers. "That foolhardy girl in the boat who dared the storm made a better impression than any dress."

His breath brushed her lips, and she wanted the man she had dreamed about for so long to kiss her.

"I'd have thought you'd like my dress."

"It's fine enough. But any monkey can dress up."

Her muscles stiffened with disappointment, frustration, and annoyance.

He winked and held out his hand. She lifted her skirts and, straightening her shoulders, laid her hand in his. Heat ran through her body and warmed her face. Climbing down quickly, she released his hand and entered the house. Immediately, the scent of bread drew her down the grand hallway.

"Ma!" he shouted. "You'll never guess what fine songbird has flown in from the mainland."

"I'm not a bird," she muttered.

"You flitter about like one, Songbird," he said so only she could hear.

She found Martha Latimer at the kitchen's butcher-block island, kneading bread. She was as short and stout as she remembered, but her hair was grayer, the lines around her mouth and eyes deeper.

Mrs. Latimer came around the corner, dusting the flour from her hands on her apron. A stern face that might once have been attractive split into a wide grin, deepening those well-used creases. "Jimmy, you devilish boy, where have you been? I was about to send out a scouting party. Is this our little Claire you've brought me?"

He kissed his mother on the cheek. "It is, and as you can see, she's all grown up into a fine, fancy lady. No hint of the wild child who dared storms."

Mrs. Latimer turned from her son and laid her hands on Claire's shoulders. "My word, that day still gives me nightmares. No more boating adventures for you, miss."

Claire hugged Mrs. Latimer, who smelled of cinnamon and nutmeg. "One per lifetime is enough."

Jimmy set Claire's bag down, and she could feel him lingering and watching. "I hope you saved something sweet for me, Ma."

Arched brows and a frown didn't soften the twinkle in Mrs. Latimer's eyes. "And why would I do that?"

"Because you love me." Jimmy plucked a freshly baked muffin from a basket by a cast-iron stove.

Mrs. Latimer swatted him away, but he only grinned and winked as he bit into the muffin. That wink chased away any of Mrs. Latimer's false bluster and made Claire feel giddy and foolish all at once.

"Fresh out of the oven," he said, sniffing the treat.

"The mistress told me Miss Victoria likes her sweets, and I thought I'd offer her a perfect welcome. Tell me Miss Victoria is safely here, Claire. Mr. Buchanan has asked me at least a dozen times since breakfast."

"Delivered safe and sound." Claire tugged off her gloves.

"She's a pretty one," Jimmy said. "She could be your sister, Ma."

"Now I know, boy, you're feeding me a line," Mrs. Latimer said.

"She's gone upstairs to rest," Claire said. "She didn't sleep well last night."

"Ah, I hope the girl wasn't too wild while she was left on her own in New York."

Claire didn't respond. The less said, the better.

Martha Latimer's blue eyes moved over Claire, taking in the cut of her dress as she rubbed her hands up over the soft sleeve fabric. "You look so much like your mother I could almost cry. She'd be proud to see you return home all fine and fancy. I still miss her dearly."

"I do too," Claire said quietly.

The old woman blinked and sniffed, shooing away the sadness. "You'll be pleased to know Jimmy got your brother a job on his next voyage."

"I didn't realize Stanley was old enough to sail."

Jimmy shrugged. "Seventeen is a very good age to get started, but for now they'll have him cleaning the equipment mostly. He's a good worker when he's not getting into mischief."

Mention of Stanley banished any lingering annoyance, and she asked Jimmy, "But he's doing well?"

Jimmy met her gaze square, no hint of teasing now. "He's going to be a fine seaman. He's a serious young man, and I'll wager he's a captain one day."

"You'll look after him?" Claire asked.

Jimmy's nod was so slight she almost missed it. "Aye, I will."

Her smile was genuine now. "Thank you. That means more than I can say."

He studied her as if he were really seeing her for the first time. Clearing his throat, he slid his free hand into his pocket. "Well, I'll leave you two be. As long as you don't get in Ma's way in the kitchen, you'll have a fighting chance in this house."

"Listen to you," Mrs. Latimer said. "I run a tight ship, and I make no bones about it. Which reminds me, I'll be serving the staff their meal promptly at 5:00 p.m. So if you're hungry, Jimmy, that's the time to come by."

He kissed his mother on the cheek. "Maybe another day. Catching up with some of the boys in town."

"Claire? You must be hungry."

Slowly Claire unbuttoned her overcoat and shrugged it off. "Thank you. I'll be very ready to eat by then. Where's my room?"

Mrs. Latimer fetched a fresh muffin from a tin, wrapped it in a napkin, and pressed it into Claire's hand. "You're on the third floor, last door on the right."

Jimmy grabbed another muffin for himself. "But while I'm here, I won't say no to another one of these."

His mother squeezed his hand tight. "I swear to heavens, boy, you could eat your weight in food."

"When it's your cooking, I surely can." He winked at Claire. "See you soon, Songbird."

CHAPTER FIVE

Claire

January 10, 1916

Suitcase in hand, Claire moved past a grand staircase on her right and around a corner to a smaller, narrower set of stairs. She climbed to the second floor and glimpsed several doorways leading into large rooms. This was the family's floor. A narrower set of stairs took her to the third floor, where she made her way to the last door on the right.

She pushed it open to find a beige room furnished with a twin bed, a compact dresser, a washbasin with a pitcher, and a cane chair. The last time she had stayed at the cottage, she'd shared a room with another servant, who she remembered hated the wind, snored, and was desperately missing New York and her large Italian family. But this time Claire had a room to herself. If she extended both her arms, she could almost touch both walls, but the private room was a sign of her improved position in the household.

She set her bag by the bed and carefully placed the muffin on the dresser. Closing her door, she hung her coat on the door hook and then removed her hat and placed it beside the muffin. From her bag, she removed a muslin-wrapped package, carefully unwound the fabric, and found the silver frame containing a picture of Claire, her mother, and her three sisters. The girls were gathered around their mother, whose belly was heavy with her fifth child, the first Hedrick boy, Stanley, who would become the apple of their father's eye, along with Joseph, born in 1899, and finally Michael, in 1900.

The photograph had been a luxury. Their father had done well sailing the seven seas, and the extra income had allowed his wife to splurge. Claire had been ten, Jemma had been nine, Sarah, eight, and Diane, seven. She remembered the photographer had smelled of engine smoke and spicy aftershave, and he'd kept ordering Diane to be still as he positioned her beside the settee where their mother sat. He'd instructed Claire to place her hand on her mother's shoulder, and when she did, her mother had instinctively covered it with her own. The photographer had taken this picture at that exact moment.

Claire kissed her fingertips and pressed them to the black-and-white image of her mother's face. "Love you, Mama."

She positioned the frame on the dresser and then unpacked a brush, comb, and other necessities, which she always arranged in the exact same order, no matter where she was staying. She carefully stripped off her jacket and then her blouse.

The sound of a barking dog drew her to the freshly washed windows overlooking the back property stretching toward the bay. Her gaze settled immediately on a man's broad shoulders. He was swaggering across the sand toward the lighthouse, and there was no mistaking it was Jimmy.

She raised her fingers to the glass and gently traced the outline of him. She'd hoped to see him again on this trip, and to discover he was the driver had thrilled her more than she should have dared to allow herself to feel.

As if sensing her, he stopped, turned back, and looked up, searching. Their gazes locked for a moment, and he touched his index finger to his temple in salute. Realizing she was in her shift, she stumbled back into the shadows, her heartbeat jumping a few beats as a blush warmed over her cheeks. Perhaps she should have been embarrassed, but she wasn't. She smiled, happy he had remembered her.

The wind pressed against the window, rattling the thick glass. She wanted to look again and search for him. She hesitated until she could summon the courage to approach the window a second time. As she did, the excitement rushing through her body quickly fizzled when she realized he was gone.

Disappointed, she wondered why she couldn't tease and tempt like Victoria. Even her sister Diane had had the courage to speak to people or joke with the boys in town when she was only nine. *"You're Mama's solid, dependable one,"* Diane had once teased.

Claire had been the daughter who kept the oven fires burning, watched after her siblings, cared for her mother after a difficult birth, and guided her sisters over the two-mile walk to the school. She'd wanted to be careless and to laugh more like Diane. She'd wanted to read more like Jemma or daydream like Sarah. *"You're the little mother while I'm gone,"* her father had always said before he left for one of his distant voyages. Being the oldest, it had been expected, just as it had been expected that she look after Victoria. She'd never once shirked her responsibilities.

She turned from the window and changed into a serviceable black skirt that skimmed her calves, a white blouse, and her very practical black boots. Sliding her hands over the skirt, she glanced into a small mirror and adjusted a curl before she headed downstairs for supper.

The utter silence of the third floor was comforting. In the city, there were always servants rambling about the large Buchanan house, the rattle and roar of the city streets, or the thump, thump of the sewing machine. Always noise.

On the second floor, the room on the right was painted a light blue and furnished with a simple four-poster double bed made up with a robin's-egg blue eyelet cotton coverlet. A polished pair of men's dress shoes were by the bed, and on a coatrack hung a black evening coat. She moved into the room and reached out to gently rub the garment's fabric between her fingers. The cut was the latest in fashion, suggesting this was the young Mr. Buchanan's room. Like his father, he enjoyed finely made clothes. On the dresser was a bottle of cologne, and beside it, a silver comb and brush. Entwined in the bristles were strands of thick, dark hair. Jimmy, she imagined, would laugh at such finery.

Floorboards creaked behind her. "Claire, you have found your way back to us."

She turned quickly, finding a smiling Robert Buchanan standing on the threshold. His suit was fitted to his tall, lean frame, and thick, dark hair swept away from pale, delicate features reminiscent of Victoria's.

She hurried toward the door, knowing she'd been caught snooping. "It's good to see you, Mr. Buchanan."

He blocked her exit, looking more amused than vexed. "Please, I've told you, it's Robert. If you're here, that means my sister has arrived." He cocked an ear. "Though I don't hear the phonograph or the endless peals of laughter. Are you sure you didn't forget Victoria?"

"She's here. Napping, I believe."

"Ah, she had a devil's night, I would imagine. Out with our cousin Edward again. That boy adores her, and she treats him like a piece of furniture. Tell me, what was she up to these last two weeks?"

"Nothing out of the usual." Although Robert could be charming, she never forgot her place.

He wagged an amused finger at her. "You're a wise woman to never speak ill of your mistress."

"Yes, sir."

"Oh God," he said, laughing. "Don't call me *sir*. I can't be much older than you, and frankly, you're too pretty to make me feel like an old man."

The compliment caught her off guard and teased hints of a smile. "Yes, Mr. Robert."

"No *Mister* either. Just Robert will do."

"Yes, sir. Robert."

He sighed like a man accepting that a dawning modern age couldn't banish the lines between social classes. "I suppose that's progress. Where're you headed now?"

"To check on the trunks. They hold the gowns for the next two weeks of festivities."

"Always the little worker bee. You're the most sensible woman I know, Claire. It's refreshing to see a woman who keeps her wits about her while herding all the women in my father's life."

"I enjoy what I do."

"Of course you do. You aren't a spoiled little twit like Victoria or Mrs. Lawrence. You appreciate what's given to you." He studied her face and then, dropping his gaze quickly to her chest and back up, cleared his voice and tugged the edges of his suit jacket down. "Mrs. Lawrence should return from the fields soon. She's tromping through the reeds as we speak, inspecting duck blinds with my father."

"She loves it here."

"She says she enjoys the sporting life, but I've never been convinced. Personally, I think the rumors are true that she's an accomplished stage actress and the mysterious Mr. Daniel Lawrence, a man of business, is a fabrication."

"I wouldn't know." It was common knowledge among the servants that Robert and his father clashed. When he'd been away at school, Robert's grades had been poor. Now that he worked at his father's finance company, he was often late to the office, and his choice of female escorts was a far cry from marriage material. Robert wanted the rewards and none of the responsibility.

"And if you did, you wouldn't say." His eyes crinkled with a smile. "Well, I suppose you better get on with your work."

"Yes. Thank you."

She stepped toward the door, and he shifted only a little, forcing her shoulder to brush him as she passed. The faint hint of sandalwood mingled with tobacco and brandy.

"It's good seeing you, Claire."

CHAPTER SIX

Lucy

January 15, 2018

Lucy's footsteps echoed in Winter Cottage as she moved away from the bank of windows and the thickening storm clouds lurking in the sky.

Mr. Garrison stood beside her, his impatience radiating around them. "Your mother really told you nothing about her childhood?"

"Once she told me she was born into a traveling circus. Another time her parents were rock stars, and another time they were Russian spies. I stopped believing the stories about her past about the time I gave up on Santa Claus. I didn't ask much about my extended family until I was about eight or nine. Beth had finally put me in school, and I noticed other kids had dads, grandparents, aunts, and uncles. I remember asking about my father, and whatever story she produced made sense to me at the time. It wasn't until I was about thirteen that I started to press for more details. That time, she said my father was a roadie named Charlie who died in a car accident. That was close to plausible, and I believed her at the time. I assume now Charlie was also a lie."

"Didn't it seem odd that your mother avoided basic questions about your family?"

"If you'd known Beth, you'd understand. She had a heart of gold, but details weren't her thing. I guess you could say she was a free spirit."

"Your grandparents, the Jessups, were anything but free spirits. Their families have been in this area since the Civil War."

"What did my grandparents do?"

"Donna, your grandmother, died nearly forty years ago. She was in her midthirties and had cancer. Your grandfather, Samuel Jessup, died last September. He was a day shy of his hundred and first birthday."

"Good to know there's some longevity in my gene pool." She sighed, trying to process all the information. "But what is my connection to the Buchanans?"

"I have no idea. And I've asked around. No one knows."

"I can just move into the house now?"

"Yes."

"It's quite the house," she said. The wind blew outside, bending the tall grass by the water and pushing cool air in through the cracks.

"It was a showpiece in its day. Built to withstand the worst storms."

"My luck, it's haunted."

That prompted a smile. "There have been rumors the last couple of years."

She arched a brow. "Since Mrs. Buchanan died?"

"Even before that. She always said she had enough company in the house, though she lived here alone."

Lucy laughed. "Did you start the rumor so you could buy the house from me?"

"I'm not that creative. But it's a good idea." His smile faded. "If this place bothers you, there's a nice inn in town. This time of year, it's off-season rates and there's plenty of room."

Even off-season rates were out of her budget right now. "Believe me, I've stayed in worse places. If there are locks on the doors, Dolly and I can handle a few ghosts." She slid her hands into her pockets.

"Beth asked me to bury her ashes in the Jessup family graveyard. Do you know where that is?"

"Not the Buchanan graveyard on this property?"

She shook her head. "She wanted to be next to her parents, so I assumed the Jessups."

"It's on the other side of the lighthouse, about a mile up the road. The Jessups were merchant marines for several generations, and some still serve. I've got appointments in town this afternoon, but I can take you there tomorrow."

"I've never buried anyone's ashes before. Is there some kind of protocol?"

"I'll be happy to check."

"I'd appreciate it." She shook her head. "This is the last spot I would ever picture as Beth's final resting place."

"Did your mother say why she wanted to be buried here? She's been estranged from her family for a long time."

"A simple explanation would have been way too easy for Beth, but it would have answered a lot of questions. Do I have to sign anything to take possession of the house?"

He frowned. "I thought you'd take one look at the place and run."

"Nowhere to run to, Mr. Garrison."

"Please call me Hank." Hank returned to the briefcase he'd set by the front door and removed a stack of papers and a fancy ink pen. "If you sign the papers, you can move in now."

She glanced at the two-paragraph statement. It was simple and straightforward. She had to live in the house at least thirty days before monies for renovation and maintenance could be released. With each new month she could draw more from the trust, and at the end of a year, she could take control of the trust, but all monies were entailed to the house.

"And if I leave before the year?"

"I'll take possession of the house, and you don't receive a dime from me."

"Sounds like Mrs. Buchanan wants a Jessup in this house." The old woman had not ensnared her mother or grandfather, but Lucy and Dolly had no qualms about staying for a little while. She signed her name. "So I'm the official occupant for the next thirty days."

He replaced the papers in his folder. "Unless you decide to leave earlier."

"Not much faith in me, Hank?"

"It's not an easy place to live. If you're used to nightlife, you'll find Cape Hudson somewhat restrictive."

"That experience talking?"

"It is. I spent summers here as a kid, but I'm still adjusting to the recent move."

"And how long did you say you've been back?"

"Six months."

"So you might leave?"

"No. I'm never leaving."

The finality in his tone silenced her next quip. The last thing she wanted to do was press a man who sounded like he had shit to work out. "Fair enough."

"The electricity and water will be paid out of the trust. There's also an account at the grocery store for you. There are a couple of cars in the garage that are in good working order."

"Sounds like you've thought of everything."

"Not me; it was Mrs. Buchanan who set up all the requirements. She wanted to give your grandfather, mother, and now you every reason to stay. She loved this place and hoped one of you would fall in love with it."

"So far my team's batting average isn't too good."

"No. It's not."

"How did you get roped into all this?"

"Your grandfather gave my dad and me power of attorney."

"If Mrs. Buchanan was so keen on us coming here, why didn't she reach out to us?"

"She was in contact with your mother when you were an infant, but she died shortly after you were born."

More secrets. And here she'd thought Beth had always been quirky but had her back.

"When Mrs. Buchanan became ill, she asked my father to speak to your mother about returning, but she refused."

"Your father talked to Beth? When?"

"You'd have been about fourteen months old."

"Beth confirmed this?"

"Yes. I spoke to your mother last September when Mr. Jessup died. She said I sounded like my father and mentioned her last conversation with him."

"Why did you call her?"

"I wanted to strike a deal with her, but she refused to discuss it or return for Mr. Jessup's funeral."

"I don't understand why she never said a word to me."

"She must have been thinking about our conversation, because she called me back several weeks later. She wanted to know if the deal was still available. I said it was. Your mother ended the call because she felt poorly."

"Sick in September? She didn't tell me she was ill until early November." Had Lucy's relationship with her mother always skimmed the surface? "Did Mr. Jessup ever say why he and Beth were estranged?"

"No." Hank stared out over the choppy waters as if the answer might be out there. "He was a merchant marine and didn't retire until he was eighty. According to my father, he wasn't around much, even when your mother was little. I suppose they weren't that close."

A hint of judgment hummed under the words, and she found herself rising to Beth's defense. "Don't think badly of Beth. She was a good mother. She loved me. And if she didn't tell me about this place, she had a reason."

"Of course."

She shifted her focus away from her mother's motives to the house. The light fixtures were made of a lovely Tiffany glass, illustrating collections of songbirds. Though the home didn't feel overly formal, the cork floors, board-and-batten walls, and hand-painted stencils were all the highest quality. "It clearly cost a fortune to build."

"For its time, it was state of the art."

To her left was a large dining room. The long table, high-backed chairs, and sideboard were covered with white dustcloths. A marble fireplace looked as if it hadn't held a fire in decades, and the pale-yellow walls looked faded and drab.

To her right was a wide staircase with a square mahogany newel and long handrails with diamond-carved balusters that stretched to the second floor and turned out of sight. Beyond the stairs was a long hallway leading past dark wainscoting to a sitting room filled with more draped furniture and another cold, large marble hearth. Like the other rooms, the paintings had been stripped from the walls.

"The bedrooms are upstairs," Hank said. "I ordered a service to clean out the bathroom attached to the pink room and to put clean sheets on the bed. It's the largest room and belonged to the Buchanan wives."

"You had confidence I'd stay?"

"No. But I'm always prepared."

"That's honestly refreshing."

"The bathroom fixtures are old, but they're in good working order. The kitchen is this way."

She followed him down another hallway to a kitchen that looked as if it had been pulled from the 1910s. The countertops were marble and led to a porcelain farmhouse sink. From here, the view took in the expansive back property with reeds farther off skimming the edge of the bay. The white enamel stove had four burners and two separate oven compartments.

"Does the stove work?" she asked.

"It does. I recently had the gas lines checked."

The only nod to more recent times was an olive-green refrigerator dating back to the eighties. In the center of the room was a large butcher-block island, and above it hung an iron rack sporting a collection of copper pots and pans.

"Mrs. Buchanan wasn't a fan of renovations, was she?" she asked.

"According to my father, Mrs. Buchanan felt the kitchen was modern enough for her. She liked remembering the way things were."

"Sad to think her best times were so far behind her."

Lucy twisted the hot water faucet in the kitchen. The pipes rattled and shook but shot out clean, cold water, which finally turned hot.

"The heating system is fairly modern. It was installed in the mid-1990s and should keep you warm. If you have any problems, let me know."

She ran her fingers over the fine grain of the wooden countertop, scratched with countless knife marks that could've dated back to the time the house was built. "Why did you call Beth with an offer for the house?"

"It's not the house I want but the land. The water access is valuable, and this is a prime area for a new development that would complement the vineyard. We'd also like to expand Beacon Vineyard to the eastern side of the property where the soil is richer and more fertile. This house would be renovated eventually, but it's not the priority."

"I thought winemaking was a hobby for rich people."

"I'm more interested in the jobs I'll create for the town and my men."

"Your men?"

"Men I served with in the marines. This land needs tending, the town needs to either grow or die, and my men are going to need projects when they separate from the service."

"And all that would be easier if I'd not shown up to claim the land and simply accepted your offer."

"Yes."

"The town looked deserted when I pulled in, but I thought it was the off-season."

"Even during the season, we're barely getting by."

"If you have so much to gain by me leaving, why are you being so helpful? You could make my stay here far more of a challenge."

"I refuse to be deceptive. Honor still matters. And I'm betting you and your dog will cut and run in a week or two."

A bright smile camouflaged her irritation over his quick judgment of her. "You underestimate how stubborn I can be."

"I can outmatch you on that front anywhere and anytime."

She could bluff with the best of them. "We shall see, won't we? You said there are cars in the garage. My Jeep is going to be out of commission until I can pay for repairs. I'll need one of them to go into town to talk to the garage people and buy groceries."

"Right." He crossed the kitchen to a pegboard sporting several sets of keys. "The two sets on the end are for the cars. One is to Mrs. Buchanan's 1972 Dodge Charger, and the other is to an '81 Chevy. Both are in good working order and are parked in the garage on the other side of the washed-out driveway."

"What are the other three sets of keys for?"

"Good question. I found them in the boathouse when I went to collect the cars. I still haven't figured that out."

"Does your father know about the keys?"

"He and my mother are on vacation and won't be back until tomorrow. I didn't see the rush, so I didn't disturb them."

"Makes sense. Thank you for all your help, Hank. If you don't mind, I'd like to explore the house. If the ghosts, rusty pipes, and isolation don't send me running back to Nashville, I'm sure I'll see you in town."

"I'll drop by the house in the morning with the road crews. It's going to be early. We've got to get the driveway repaired before the weather gets worse."

"Are we talking 'crack of dawn' early?"

"Eight a.m."

In her bartending days, 11:00 a.m. had been the crack of dawn, but since Beth's illness, she'd learned to be an early riser. "I'll be ready. I'd like to see what you're doing."

"You don't need to be on-site."

"Sure I do. This is my place, at least for now."

He frowned. "Sure."

As she walked him to the door, she asked, "Do I have any neighbors?"

"Brian Willard and his daughter, Natasha, live about two miles north of here. Don't expect him to be neighborly. He's back in jail after a drunk and disorderly."

She'd dealt with her share of drunks. "Good to know."

He gave her his card. "Call me if you need anything. My cell is on the back."

She flicked the edge of the white linen card with the tip of her finger. "I will."

She watched as he strode toward his truck. He moved with the straight-backed posture of a man who knew what he wanted. Lucky him. She didn't have a damn clue. Her breath released on a heavy sigh, and she closed the door.

As she walked to the windows, Dolly followed beside her. She rubbed the dog's head and stared at the churning waters of the bay. "There's got to be something to really love about this place."

The dog barked.

"Yeah, I know. You get to run around and play in the reeds and chase ducks. I get to live in a big creepy box that is possibly haunted." She ran her hands through her hair. "But on the bright side, it's *my* big creepy box, and there's something to be said for that."

The wind rustled outside, and somewhere deep in the house, she imagined the creak of footsteps. But this house promised her an address that no one could take away, and the town was the key to answering all the questions she'd had about her family. She'd never known any kind of permanence, and it both excited and terrified her.

The house groaned softly. Dolly's ears perked. "Please, house, no ghosts today. Or serial killers."

CHAPTER SEVEN

Lucy

January 15, 2018

Lucy, with her mother's urn in hand, climbed the stairs as Dolly bounded ahead, her tail wagging and ears perked as she sniffed a corner. At the top of the stairs Lucy flipped the small black switch, and an overhead bulb splashed out a ring of faint light big enough to reveal six doors that fed into the second-floor hallway. There were three doors on the left and three on the right. The first room was a bedroom furnished with two twin beds and a dresser. All the furniture was covered in sheets, and the walls were painted a robin's-egg blue.

"Door number one is not the one we want."

The next room came with a double bed, though by today's standards it looked small and cramped. The walls were painted yellow. Hank had said the pink room.

Lucy moved down the hallway to the next set of rooms. Both were painted in blues, and the furniture was missing. The radiators were cold and the floors dusty. The last room on the right was painted pink. The clean scent of fresh linens wafted through the room, and the dresser and floors were freshly polished.

"Home sweet home, Dolly." The dog all but galloped, her toenails clicking on the wooden floors as she sniffed around a queen-size bed.

Since Lucy had moved in with her mother, she and the dog had grown accustomed to sleeping together on the pull-out sofa. Quality of sleep had been spotty at best, and she was looking forward to sleeping on a real bed without paws digging into her spine.

Lucy set the urn on the dresser, took off her backpack, and sat on the edge of the bed. The springs creaked a little, but the mattress felt soft, and the sheets smelled fresh. "Dolly, the plan today is to stock up on groceries and check out the town."

Dolly jumped up on the bed and immediately began kneading at the pink coverlet. She kept going until the covers were just right and then, satisfied with her work, sat down.

Lucy moved to the closet and opened the door. She found the extra sheets, towels, and blankets Hank had mentioned.

She stepped into the adjoining bathroom, which was covered in pink square tiles on the walls and white geometric ones on the floor. In the center of it all was a large white porcelain claw-foot tub with crystal hot and cold water knobs. To her right was a pedestal sink, and across from it, a toilet with a suspended tank mounted to the wall above the white bowl.

On the sink rested a zip-top bag filled with soaps and shampoos. She opened one of the shampoo bottles and smelled it. Jasmine. "Hank's always prepared."

She turned on the water. The pipes rattled to an awkward beat that reminded her of a one-room apartment she and Beth had shared in East Nashville for six months. There was no flushing the toilet in that place when anyone was showering, or you risked being scalded. The water trickled and then flowed out cold. It took another minute before the water warmed. As a test, she flushed the toilet. The water didn't scald. Progress.

She glanced into the mirror above the sink. The silvering was fading around the edges, but there was enough left to reflect limp blonde hair streaked blue, hollow cheeks, and mascara under her eyes like a raccoon. "Hank must think I'm a real piece of work."

Dolly barked, and Lucy turned to see the dog rubbing her back against the bed with paws in the air and tongue hanging out. At least one of them felt at home.

When she'd left Nashville two days ago, this journey had been no more than a promise to Beth and an itch to know more about her family. Once both were addressed, she knew herself well enough to realize that she'd grow restless. Permanent home be damned, she should simply take Hank's money and move on.

Hank

Hank pushed through the front door of Arlene's and sat at the counter on the second seat from the right, the one he always chose. He didn't have to wait long before Arlene appeared and set an unsweetened iced tea before him.

"I saw you coming and put your burger on the griddle," she said. "Medium well, no onions, and extra mustard. Just like always."

"Thanks, Arlene."

It was noon, and the place was half-full, better than most days in the off-season. He drank the tea and opened his file. He wanted to dig into the loan documents.

Instead of leaving him to his tea and thoughts, Arlene wiped the already spotless counter in front of him. When he didn't speak, she shifted to polishing the napkin holder, salt and pepper shakers, and the artificial sweetener and sugar container. At the rate she was going, the stainless veneer would wear out, and her gaze would burn a hole in his head.

"Out with it, Arlene." Hank met her gaze and waited.

Arlene had the stones to look a bit surprised, as if she didn't know what he was referring to.

She shrugged and leaned in a fraction, though Hank didn't know why because everyone in town knew his business. "So what did she say? Half the town came in for breakfast this morning and asked about her. I should thank her for drumming up the off-season business."

"I'm not following."

She tossed her rag on the counter. "Don't play stupid with me, Hank Garrison. Is Lucy Kincaid staying at Winter Cottage?"

He traced his finger through the condensation on the side of the glass. "She is for now."

"What does that mean?"

"I don't know."

Arlene cocked a finely plucked brow. "If you had to bet?"

"I don't bet."

She grunted. "You're about to take the biggest bet of your life. How much do you have riding on that project of yours? And like it or not, your fortunes are tied up with that girl."

"Judging by the blue hair and cowboy boots, I'd say she's gone inside a week."

Arlene shook her head as she laid out a napkin for him with a fork and spoon on it. "What did she think of the house?"

"Overwhelmed. Just like everyone else who sees it for the first time."

"Did you offer her the go-away money?"

He closed the file and folded his hands over it. "Arlene, what are you talking about?"

"I overheard you and Rick talking. That's what he called it when you two were talking last week. 'Go-away money.'"

Rick Markham and Hank had served together in the marines, and Rick had taken the job as town sheriff six months ago. He'd said he was here to back up Hank, but Hank didn't believe that bullshit. Rick had his own agenda that just so happened to work well with Hank's.

"The property should be yours. Why she left all that land to Beth Jessup's kid is beyond me."

"Arlene, weren't you and Beth good friends?"

"We were. Good Lord, did we get into trouble. We cheered together until she turned those chickens loose at the homecoming football field." A smile tugged at the edges of her lips even as her eyes watered. "And if I'd known she was sick, I'd have driven to Nashville."

Dishes crashed in the kitchen, sending ripples of tension through Hank as he looked ready to come off the seat and fight.

"Damn. I can't afford too many more dishes," Arlene said as she wiped away a tear. "Natasha! What's going on back there?"

Seconds later a girl peeked out from the saloon doors leading to the kitchen. Natasha Willard was twelve years old. Her curly dark hair was pulled into a tight ponytail that didn't quite contain the soft wisps that framed wary brown eyes, a button nose, and mocha skin.

The girl tipped her chin up. She was grinning, but that was what the kid did when she was scared. Lately, she'd been smiling too damn much. "Some dishes fell."

"Yeah, baby, I got that," Arlene said. "How many?"

The girl looked back between the swinging doors. "Six, or maybe ten."

"All right." Arlene's calm voice sounded strained at the edges. "Don't clean it up. I don't need you cutting your hands. I'll get to it in a second."

"What should I do?"

"Just wash those potatoes for me."

"You want me to cut them up after they're clean?"

"No, baby, don't mess with the knife. I'll be right there."

The girl waved to Hank. "How's it going, Hank?"

"Good. Why aren't you in school?"

"It's a holiday. Teacher workshop or something."

"So you don't mind if I call to check?"

"Nope." The girl vanished back into the kitchen.

Hank sipped his coffee. "Isn't it against child labor laws to employ twelve-year-olds?"

"She came by after the early dismissal, asking if I had work. I fed her a big lunch, which she gobbled up like she was half-starved. She insisted on working to help me out, so I put her to washing dishes. I think maybe we'll stick to the potatoes."

"She's supposed to go to Brenda's when Brian's in jail."

"She swears she is staying at her neighbor Brenda's house like you told her to, but you know how busy Brenda is with her own six kids."

"This can't keep up."

"Brian swore to the judge he'd take better care of her, but already he's screwing things up."

"You see any bruises on the girl?" Hank asked quietly.

"No. And I was looking."

When Brian had regained custody of Natasha, Hank had been clear that if he saw one mark on the kid, *one mark*, he'd deal directly with Brian. So far, the not-so-veiled threat had kept the girl safe, but he wasn't naive enough to believe it was the permanent fix the girl desperately needed. Brian had already done two stints in jail for fighting and assault. This was number three.

"When Grace was alive, she always had an excuse for the bruises on her arms and legs," Arlene said.

A bell dinged behind Arlene, and she retrieved his burger and fries and set the plate in front of him. He reached for a fry. "I'll take care of it."

"And did I mention that Lucy looks just like her mama? I tried to play it cool when she came through the front door, but my word, you could have knocked me over with a feather. I thought it was Beth. I don't want to like her, but I do."

Lucy projected an air of calm, like a duck gliding on water, but he suspected that under the surface she was paddling as fast as she could.

Hank still didn't know what to make of Lucy. Maybe if Lucy had been dramatic or difficult, he'd have found a reason not to like her and summoned the resolve to see her gone. What Hank hadn't expected was the one-two punch to the gut when he'd seen her standing by the tall windows of the cottage as she'd looked out over the bay. Her directness and matter-of-fact mannerisms had fired up a sense of guilt he'd not expected. Cape Hudson was her only source of any potential family, but his success depended on her turning her back on it all.

"She seems *real* sweet."

He could almost hear Arlene dropping a fishing line with baited hook into the water. He bit into his hamburger, taking extra time to chew, hoping she'd get back to those dishes most likely scattered on the kitchen floor.

"She's pretty, and Lord, she has a cute little figure." Arlene put her hand to her heart. "And she's real good to her dog. Shit, I knew this would happen."

"What?" He ate another fry quickly, knowing he had only fifteen minutes for lunch.

"I kind of like her. I like having a part of Beth back. Be nice if she stayed around."

He slowly set down the burger and carefully wiped his hands on the paper napkin. "You don't know her. None of us knows who she really is."

"Maybe if she sticks around for a time, we'll all get better acquainted."

He bit into a fry, knowing damn good and well time didn't fix all problems.

She leaned forward, lowering her voice. "Don't kid me or yourself. You liked her too. You were always one to take in the stragglers."

"She's not a straggler, and it's to all our advantage she not stay." Once he had control of the land that went with the house, he could leverage the value of the land for the loan he needed.

Arlene looked befuddled. "I don't want to like her. But damn it all, I just can't hate her. Not yet, anyway. Of course, she is Beth's daughter, so that means it won't take long before she pisses me off. I swear, Beth Jessup was as confounding as she was fun."

"It's a fluid situation."

"Winter Cottage should have gone to you, not Lucy. You have plans and dreams for that property. Samuel Jessup never wanted it and could barely keep up the place."

"He maintained and inspected enough. He did what he could so his daughter or granddaughter could inherit."

"Miss Arlene." Natasha, her grin wide and full, poked her head out the swinging doors. "I think you better come here."

She mumbled a prayer. "Be right there, baby." She hurried into the kitchen, leaving him to his meal.

The house was the key to the land. Though the trust was attached to the house, whoever controlled the house had control of the land, which was not entailed.

Like he'd told Lucy, he'd never get rich, but expanding the vineyard, and ultimately building the bayfront development, would provide jobs and keep the area growing.

He had lots of big plans for the land. But until Lucy gave up her claim, he was in a holding pattern.

———— ⚬⌇~⌇⚬ ————

Lucy

With the keys to the Dodge Charger in hand, Lucy led Dolly through the front door. The old house keys felt cumbersome and heavy as she secured the lock. She crossed the tall grass covering the front lawn to the garage, also built of similar material and painted yellow.

The second key on her ring opened the lock, and inside, a flip of the switch revealed two cars that appeared to have been freshly washed and polished. The Dodge Charger was painted a bright pink, had a long, heavy body, and was trimmed in bright silver chrome. Paint it orange and slap an "01" on the side, and she'd be in a *Dukes of Hazzard* episode. She was glad the front door opened and she didn't have to slide through an open window like Bo and Luke.

She ran her hand over the smooth, polished finish as Dolly jumped in and took her place in the passenger side.

She pressed the automatic-door remote attached to the visor, and the garage doors rattled and shook as they slowly rose up on pulleys. Before her was a stand of trees, and beyond it, the top of the lighthouse, which was dark.

A turn of the key and the engine rattled to life, and she slowly pulled out. She turned onto the deeply rutted road, shifted to the lowest gear, and, holding her breath, drove forward. Her tires caught and spun, and she muttered a curse. She kept her pressure on the accelerator slow and steady. The tires felt underinflated, but they kept turning as she inched through the sand to more solid ground. A small but satisfying victory.

She retraced the route back into the town of Cape Hudson. With only a few streets crisscrossing through town, it was easy enough to find the grocer located on the block behind Arlene's diner. She parked in front with the engine running so Dolly could stay warm. "I'll be back in just a few minutes."

The dog barked, tossing her a sad expression that worked on Lucy every time. "I know. You're pitiful. I'll be right back."

The store was small, and though it didn't have a lot of variety, it did stock all the basic staples. Hank had said there was an account here, but she grabbed a cart and went straight toward the cashier. The tall woman smiled, her tanned face etched by lines from too much sun. Her name tag read PAULA.

"What can I do for you, hon?" Paula asked.

"I'm Lucy Kincaid. I'm supposed to have a store account."

"You sound like you're not sure about that, Lucy Kincaid."

"I'm not. Hank Garrison told me I did, but I thought I'd save us both the embarrassment and time before I loaded my cart with food. It's the Buchanan account."

Paula grinned. "Of course you're Lucy Kincaid. I'm just teasing. I know it's you. I went to school with your mama. Sorry to hear about her passing."

News traveled fast. "Thanks."

"My boss is a stickler for details. You got an ID?"

Lucy fished her wallet from her purse and produced her Tennessee driver's license.

Paula studied it and then looked at Lucy again. "Nashville is a long way from here. How long did it take you to make the drive?"

"About fifteen hours."

"I suppose you had to stop a few times for Dolly."

What didn't everyone know about her? "That's right."

Paula studied the driver's license picture again. "Your hair was bluer when you had this picture made."

"It's almost all grown out." Beth had asked Lucy to dye her hair a happy blue, but as they began, Beth's hair fell out in clumps. The chemo treatment was the culprit, but there was nothing they could do. Beth had started to cry, so Lucy offered to dye her own hair as a distraction.

Beth laughed and bet Lucy she didn't have the nerve. An hour later, Lucy was sporting blue streaks in her hair.

Paula handed back the license. "Arlene said you looked like Beth Jessup."

Lucy would have to get used to people referring to Beth as a Jessup. "I got that a lot growing up." She tucked the license back in her wallet. "How well did you know Beth?"

"We went to high school together. It was me, her, and Arlene. We were trouble waiting to happen, though I got to say, your mama was the instigator. We were all on the cheering squad until she got kicked off."

"What happened?"

Paula laughed at an old memory, then grew more wistful. "Chickens. She set loose a handful of chickens as a senior prank. Never was good at following the rules."

If Paula had been friends with Beth, then she'd have known who she was dating. "Did Beth date anyone in high school?"

"She dated a lot of boys. Very popular girl, your mama." The woman leaned in, studying Lucy. "Can't say you look like any of the boys I knew back in the day. It's as if your mama made you all by herself and just spit you out."

"That would be a neat trick. Who would be on the short list if a girl had to guess?"

"There was Noah, Brian, David, and Bill. And she did get into Norfolk on Saturday nights when her daddy was out to sea, which was all the time."

"She like any of them enough to leave town with them?"

"I didn't know she was pregnant until the day she left. I caught her throwing up in the bathroom at the diner. She tried to laugh it off as a hangover, but I have eight younger brothers and sisters. I know what pregnant looks like."

"How did she react?"

"Asked me not to tell, and I didn't. I figured we'd all find out soon enough, but then she just took off. I never saw her again. I was heartbroken."

"Any boys go missing from town about that time?"

"Nope. So I suppose if she did leave with a fella, it was one of the boys from Norfolk." She shook her head, as if seeing her old friend through an older lens. "Beth could be fun, but it couldn't have been easy having her as a mama."

"Beth was a good person. Not organized, but kind." And for Beth to turn her back on Cape Hudson meant something unspeakable had happened, literally. Lucy would be wise not to forget that. "Is there a limit on the account?"

"Nope. You could buy out the contents of the store, but I don't think you want everything."

"No."

"Well, then, it's whatever you want to eat."

"Thanks." She spent the next ten minutes loading up on vegetables, rice, lentils, two flashlights with batteries, wine, and a dozen cans of dog food. As tempting as the doughnuts and pastries were, she'd eaten her share in the last few months, and it was time to clean up her act.

When she returned to the register, Paula unloaded her groceries and bagged them.

"You're driving Mrs. B's Dodge Charger. Explains now why Hank took it to the auto shop last week to have it looked over." She rang up all the items. The tab came to ninety-one dollars.

"Do I need to sign anything?"

"Nope. I'll just make a note and bill the account at the end of the month."

"I appreciate that," Lucy said. "If I wanted to read up on the house, where would I go?"

"That would be the library on Main. It's a block from the water. You can't miss it. The librarian, Mrs. Faye Reynolds, can answer just about any history question about the town, and if she can't, she'll find the answer. Mrs. Reynolds was also our history teacher in high school and would have known your mama."

"And it's open tomorrow?"

"It is."

"Good to know."

"You're staying at the Buchanan house?"

"For now."

"That place is solid as a rock. It's not going anywhere in any storm. What do you think of the place so far?"

"Creepy."

"Beth always said the same thing."

"Why did she go to the house?"

"About a month before she left town, she got a job helping Mrs. B make her videotapes."

"What kind of videotapes?"

"Beth didn't talk much about the project but said Mrs. B wanted to tell her story and wanted it recorded. She paid good money to have Beth make the tapes."

"Do you know where the tapes are?"

"I don't have any idea. I suppose they're somewhere at the cottage. I'd start with the attic."

"Did you ever see the tapes?"

"No. Beth wouldn't say much, but it was mostly Mrs. B talking about a woman named Claire."

"Thanks, Paula."

Lucy tossed her groceries in the Charger's back seat, and Dolly rose up with her tail thumping. Lucy tugged a package of rawhide chews from one of the bags, tore it open, and gave one to Dolly. The dog immediately jumped to the back seat with the chew and got to work on it.

Back at the cottage, she parked at the end of the driveway and, hoisting her bags of groceries, walked along the path toward the house as Dolly set off with the remains of her chew stick. By the time she'd unloaded the supplies, her arms ached, and she looked forward to the day the driveway was repaired. She opened a can of dog food, and Dolly barked at the kitchen door. Lucy let her in and set down a plate for Dolly. The dog looked at the food, then at Lucy, and back at the food. She walked away from it and lay down on the kitchen floor.

"I know, we've been eating junk food for the last couple of weeks, and it all tasted good. But this food is actually good for you. It's time we both ate better. I'm swearing off powdered doughnuts, so you've got to get with the program too."

Dolly looked up at Lucy but wasn't impressed.

"Don't give me that look. I'm not feeling sorry for you."

She searched the pot rack for a small pan. "I'm going to cook up a bunch of vegetables and maybe some scrambled eggs. I'll share if you stop giving me that look."

She dug out a cutting board and a knife and sliced up the onions, carrots, celery, and mushrooms. She switched on the burner and set the pan on it. "We have heat. Progress."

Within ten minutes the veggies were cooking down in the pan and she'd scrambled three eggs in the bowl. Lucy opened the bottle of wine from the grocery store and poured herself a glass. She held it up. "Here's to you, Mrs. B. I don't know why I'm here or how long we'll stay, but thank you."

She sipped. The wine was passable. She served up the veggies and eggs on a plate and took a seat at the kitchen table. Dolly shamelessly inched closer.

She took a bite of her veggies, which were good enough but nothing like the burgers she'd lived on when she tended bar at Ray's House of Blues back in Nashville. Absently, she scooped up eggs with a spoon and fed them to Dolly. The dog gobbled them up. "You're not getting any more people food." She knew that wouldn't last. Dolly was her best friend now, and they both had been through a lot.

Dolly dropped her head and looked up.

"Don't go all pitiful on me."

She finished up her eggs and dumped what remained of the veggies in the trash before washing the plate and setting it in the drying rack.

She dug the flashlight and batteries from her shopping bag. "We should have a look at the attic. We've come all this way, so it's time to get to know our new home."

CHAPTER EIGHT

Lucy

With Dolly behind her, Lucy stood on the bottom step of a very narrow staircase that led to the fourth-floor attic. She flipped a switch, and a light bulb popped on.

Dolly edged past her and sniffed the air. Her hackles rose, and her ears dropped.

Lucy climbed into the attic and spotted an overhead bulb with a pull string dangling from it. It too clicked on, and she now had enough light to see what she was dealing with.

The attic was long and dusty but almost empty except for a collection of four black trunks and broken furniture on the west side. At each end of the attic were twin brick chimneys, and between them sat a massive engine with wheels and fan belts. She guessed this old generator was the original power source for the house.

With a house this old, she'd expected it to be chock-full of dusty relics. Yet everything was neat and organized. It would appear Mrs. B had no trouble dispatching what didn't serve a purpose for her. Ducking her head, Lucy crossed to the wardrobe boxes.

Each was a couple of feet wide and perhaps four feet tall. Cracked leather straps with brass buckles secured the top, middle, and bottom. A brass plate mounted on the front was etched with the letters *CHB*.

"*CHB*. Catherine Hedrick Buchanan?" She traced her fingers over the letters, wondering what had been so important to Mrs. Buchanan.

She rattled the lock and tugged, but it didn't give way. "I suppose if I'm going to find out, I'll have to find the key."

Dolly nosed Lucy in the arm and whimpered. "You don't like it here? Attics aren't your thing?" She rubbed the dog on her head. "I don't see any videotapes up here."

The dog barked.

She reached for the light switch and glanced back at the trunks. She'd come to Cape Hudson looking for answers but so far had found even more questions.

An odd sensation, akin to a breeze on the back of her neck, shuddered through her body like icy fingers. A little creeped out, she shut off the light, and the two of them trotted down the attic stairs, then past the third and second floors to the first. She grabbed a jacket and shrugged it on before bracing for the blast of cold air she'd come to expect. Dolly raced outside, loving the cool wind that ruffled her fur. The dog barked and ran toward a thick stand of seagrass.

Lucy followed the trail through the bowed trees that created a natural archway. Hank had said the family graveyard was this way, and she was curious about Mrs. B and her family.

She didn't have to walk long before she spotted the wrought-iron fence that ringed around three headstones surrounded by tall grass. The gate, rusted and worn, was stubborn and required that she pull hard before it squeaked and groaned open enough for her to slip through the opening.

She approached the three headstones. Centered was ROBERT BUCHANAN, 1885–1917. To the left was CATHERINE H. BUCHANAN,

1888–1990. To the far right was ROBERT BUCHANAN, JUNIOR, 1917–1974.

She smoothed her hand over the rough stone of Mrs. B's headstone, wondering how she must have suffered when she buried her husband and then her son. "It sucks to lose people. You must have felt so alone."

Lucy grabbed a fistful of scrub growing around the gravestone and pulled it up. She kept on pulling weeds until the space around Mrs. B's stone was clear. "I'll be back and get this area cleaned up."

Dusting her hands, she rose and called Dolly. Barks echoed from the reeds as she walked back toward the cottage. When she arrived, a red pickup was parked at the end of the driveway, and a woman was getting out.

The woman, in her late twenties, walked over the graveled driveway with quick, purposeful steps. Her black hair was pinned up in a topknot, and she wore jeans, an oversize sweater, and a padded vest. A red scarf wrapped around her neck, adding a pop of color that brought depth to her pale skin. She was holding a pie.

"Hello there," she said. "My name is Megan Buchanan. Welcome to Cape Hudson."

"Thank you. I'm Lucy Kincaid."

Her eyes twinkled. "Oh, I know. I've heard all about you. One thing you'll learn about Arlene if you stay for more than five minutes is she does like to talk."

Lucy couldn't begrudge the woman a little gossip. "Am I the talk of the town?"

"Are you kidding? You're ground zero for gossip now."

The woman's energy was light and positive and teased a smile. "Would you like to come inside?"

"I was certain I'd have to bribe you with pie to get inside."

"Not necessary. I'm happy to show you around. Though I still don't know much about the place myself. If Buchanan is your name, you must know something about Winter Cottage."

"Mrs. B passed before I was born, but my father, James Buchanan, spent a good bit of his summers here as a boy. Mrs. B was my great-grandmother."

"Hank said there were two lines in the family. One from Robert and the other Victoria, right?"

"Dad and I are descended from Robert Buchanan. Hank is descended from his sister, Victoria."

"Which leaves me descended from nowhere."

"The million-dollar question that has vexed the families and town since the late 1980s. Maybe you can solve the mystery."

As Lucy opened the door, Dolly dashed past, her wet paws leaving prints on the clean floor. "Mrs. B must be rolling over in her grave."

"I don't think so. From what Dad said, she never minded when he tracked through her house. She always loved having him."

Megan paused to wipe her feet and then looked around the foyer, marveling. "Mr. Jessup always guarded the place well."

"But he didn't live here?"

"Only for the first thirty days. Then he left. He said the place was too fancy for him."

"You've got to be a little hurt she didn't leave this to you," Lucy said.

Megan sidestepped the question. "It's a grand old place and deserves love and attention."

"And Mrs. B assumed some random woman from Nashville was going to take this place on?"

"Apparently so." Her brows wrinkled as if she had more to say. Instead, she held up her dish. "But I do have pie."

Lucy laughed. "It's your job to bring intel back to the folks in town."

"Reconnaissance."

"And your weapon is the pie?"

Her eyes narrowed, and she dropped her voice as if sharing a trade secret. "My apple will make the most hardened person talk."

A bit of the tension eased in Lucy's shoulders. "How old is your dad?"

"He's almost fifty."

About Beth's age. He could be her daddy, which would explain her inheritance, but not Samuel Jessup's.

In the kitchen, Lucy grabbed a wad of paper towels and dried the dog off before she let her move about the house. "I've got a feeling I'll be going through a lot of paper towels."

Megan set the pie plate on the butcher-block island. "She's a sweet dog."

"She was my mom's. We're still getting to know each other."

"She looks right at home." Megan shrugged off her jacket, and Lucy saw Megan's baby bump hidden under the folds of the sweater.

Lucy tried not to stare. "I just arrived this morning, and I haven't scrounged a coffeepot yet, but I'm hoping there's one here."

Megan walked to the stove, skimming her fingers over the vintage appliance. "I've seen these in pictures before but never in person. Have you tried it out yet?"

"Yes. It works well."

"Hank doesn't miss a detail."

Lucy opened a pantry and clicked on a light. The closet, like the rest of the house, was clean of clutter. There was a mixer, a blender, a toaster oven, and a drip coffeemaker. Beside it was a box of coffee filters and an unopened tin of coffee.

"Mrs. B wasn't much for clutter," Lucy said.

"According to my mother, she hired a crew every spring to clean the place from top to bottom. In the last few years of her life, she'd started giving away bits of this and that. She gave quite a bit of furniture to my dad. She only kept what was original to the house."

Lucy plugged in the coffeemaker and dug out the filters and coffee. "Who stocked the pantry with new appliances?"

"Your grandfather shortly before he died."

"Almost as if he expected his daughter to come home."

"I guess he hoped the house would lure her back, but she never came."

Lucy smoothed her hand over the brand-new pot. "Beth never spoke of her family. She was an easygoing person, but whatever happened between her and her father was too deep a wound to heal. She only told me about this place right before she died."

"But she told you. So she had some hope."

Megan searched the cabinets until she found a stack of white plates covered in roses, and then she fished a knife and a couple of forks out of a drawer.

"Megan, what do you know about the Jessups?"

"A proud history of serving in the merchant marines, and many are still in the US Navy." Megan sliced into the pie. "I know Rick Markham was the one who found old man Jessup. Rick paid regular visits to check up on him, and he found him passed away in his chair."

"That was September?"

"It was. He'd only been on the job a month." She was silent for a moment. "I hear you're going to bury your mother's ashes here."

The machine gurgled and spit out coffee. "I am."

"Let me know when. I'll come." She dished out two healthy pieces of pie.

Lucy cleared an unexpected tightness from her throat as she poured two cups of coffee. She fished a bag of sugar from a cabinet. "No milk, but I do have sugar."

"Excellent. That's my favorite food group."

Lucy grinned. "How many scoops?"

"Two. No, make that three. Eating for two and all."

Lucy ladled in the sugar. "When is your baby due?"

"Late spring."

"You and your husband must be excited."

"No husband. Just me. Funny, your mother flees Cape Hudson to have her baby, and I've fled back home to have mine."

"I'm sure you'll have a lot of help here."

"And some meddling. But that's small-town life, as I'm sure you're learning."

Lucy sipped her coffee, still trying to figure out what had been so terrible about this place. Why had Beth never come back? "I don't really mind."

Megan grinned over her cup. "Give it a week."

"So, your parents would have known Beth in high school."

"Mom did. Dad went to boarding school in Alexandria. He didn't come home that often," she said.

"Where are your parents now? Maybe I could talk to them?"

"I'm sure they'd be glad to visit with you. They live in Richmond most of the year. They're expected back here in the spring. My brother, Deacon, is also moving back to town, but I doubt he knows anything."

Lucy's relationship with Beth had been complicated. To say they'd grown up together wasn't exactly true. She'd grown up, but Beth hadn't. Her mother's carefree lifestyle could be fun and intoxicating, but it could also be frustrating when Lucy needed help with a homework assignment or assurance that rent had been paid, or when she wanted information about her family. Still, some of Lucy's best memories were because Beth hadn't been afraid to dress up as Martha Washington for a surprise visit to her classroom, to donate money to a homeless man who'd not eaten in days, or to pull her out of school for a day to pick blueberries or apples during the harvest season. "Beth wasn't perfect, but she did all right by me. I'm going to miss her."

Megan was quiet for a moment. This was more personal than a slice of pie warranted. Lucy liked Megan but reminded herself she didn't know her.

"You didn't mind growing up without a father?"

"I minded. That's part of the reason I'm here."

Frowning, Megan dropped her gaze to the dish. "Have you been to the lighthouse yet?"

Lucy grabbed a couple of paper towels. "I've seen it but haven't made my way there."

"When we were in high school, I went with a group of friends, and we broke the lock and climbed to the top. Two hundred and seven steps. We drank beer at the top and watched the sun come up. It was a sight to behold. Mr. Jessup realized what had happened when he saw the broken lock and double padlocked it after that. I don't think anyone's been up since."

"What kind of shape was it in?"

"It needs work, like the cottage. I think both are reaching a tipping point, just like the town. It all either gets saved or is lost." She pushed around the pie crust with the tip of her fork. "I have a confession to make."

"Okay."

"I have a master's degree in historical restoration. I wrote my thesis on this house, and if you decide to stay and fix it up, I'd like to help. Hank had said if the house came to him, I could have the job. It's a big part of the reason I'm back."

"I don't even know what restoration entails."

"A lot. Several years' worth of work for me and the crews." Absently, Megan rubbed her belly. "Working on this house, especially with the baby coming, would be a dream come true."

Lucy took a bite of the pie.

"I just figured putting the truth out there was best. And since I seem to be on an awkward conversation roll, if you ever want to see my restoration plans, I have them." Megan seemed to realize she was getting ahead of herself. "I often talk before I think. I kind of barrel ahead. The plan was to soften you up with pie. I wasn't even going to bring up the cottage, but I did. Right out of the gate."

"It's okay. I appreciate your love of this place. I think Mrs. Buchanan would have welcomed it." Lucy then shifted the conversation, just like she did when a bar customer started to talk about things she knew they'd later regret. "So you grew up in Cape Hudson, like your parents?"

"Oh yes." Megan looked relieved at the change in topic. "But I couldn't wait to get out of town. Wanted to see the big, wide world. But it truly is a great place to raise a family."

"Makes me wonder why my mother didn't see it that way."

Megan tapped the tip of her fork on the plate. "We've all made decisions we'd like to take back. Maybe Beth did want to return but didn't know how."

"She had every opportunity to return with me and never took any of them."

"But you're here now. Maybe that was her plan all along."

An alarm on Megan's phone buzzed. She fished it out of her pocket and turned it off. "I'm sorry, I've got to get going. Promised Arlene I'd have her pies to the restaurant by four."

"You sell your pies?"

"It's a way to earn a little money. I have a pretty good list of clients in Norfolk. If you're going to major in history, you've got to have a backup plan."

Lucy picked up Megan's coat and walked her through the door and along the driveway to her car. "Thank you for coming."

"And thank you for letting me prattle on."

"No problem." Dolly ran out the front door as the wind blew in from the south.

Lucy watched as Megan slid behind the wheel of the red pickup and, after a final wave, drove off. Lucy retrieved her coat and stepped outside. The wind had picked up, and the clouds on the horizon were turning a dark gray.

Dolly barked and wagged her tail as she nosed her snout into a thicket of bushes at the entrance to the lighthouse path. Lucy followed along the sandy, overgrown path. In the distance, thunder rumbled. The path opened up to the tall redbrick lighthouse. It was far more impressive as she stood at the base and stared up.

She climbed the front steps that led to a large wooden door, double padlocked with heavy iron locks. She tugged on it, wondering if any of the keys on her ring opened it. As tempted as she was to retrieve the keys, she questioned the logic of exploring a hundred-year-old lighthouse with an impending storm on the horizon.

Beth would have thrown caution to the wind and explored. Lucy could almost hear her mother's laughter ringing in her ears. *"Don't be such a fuddy-duddy, Lucy!"*

Dolly scampered up the stairs and nudged Lucy's hand. The breeze suddenly cooled, and she felt energy radiate up her arm as she held the locks. In the distance, thunder rumbled again as if to remind her a storm was coming.

"Let's get back, girl. We have a cottage the size of the Grand Canyon to explore."

When they returned, the phone was ringing. She ran toward the kitchen, where it was mounted to the wall with a rotary dial on its face. "Hello."

"This is Hank. I'm checking in to see how you're doing."

"Alive and well and admiring the phone that I'm talking to you with."

"You may have noticed that cell-phone service isn't good at the cottage."

She dug her phone from her back pocket. No bars. "Hadn't even noticed yet. This wall phone is beginning to grow on me."

"There's a storm coming. The worst of it won't be here for an hour or so. You'll likely lose electricity. Don't panic. There are candles and matches in the pantry. The electricity will be out for maybe a day, but that's considered fast around here. A backup generator will keep your refrigerator going."

"You've thought of everything."

A chair squeaked in the background, and she imagined him leaning forward. "So you've stocked up?"

"About a week's worth. Megan came by. I guess she's your cousin?"

"Second cousin. She mentioned she might make a visit when I saw her in town. Tell me she's on her way home."

"Stopping by Arlene's to drop off pies and then home. She's nice. And looking forward to renovating the house."

"If the cottage comes to me, I'm going to hire her."

Hank had the good sense to use *if*. Lucy sidestepped the remark. "Dolly and I checked out the lighthouse."

"What did you think of it?"

"We didn't go inside. I pictured us trapped inside during the storm, and Dolly is not Lassie. We would be totally screwed."

"If you run into trouble, you have my number."

"Why are you being so nice? You should be trying to run me off. Megan and you both have a lot to gain by me leaving."

"Mrs. B wanted you to have the house. I'm honoring her wishes."

"My staying is costing you a potential fortune."

"I'm still not convinced you're staying, Lucy. The longer you remain in the house, the more you'll realize it's one hell of a commitment."

She wasn't sure if he was testing her or helping her. He was impossible to read. "I'm stubborn."

Silence crackled through the line. "I'll call in after the storm."

Lucy decided that while she had electricity, she'd explore the house. She started in the main room that she supposed would have been the parlor. With Dolly on her heels, Lucy ran her fingers over the white cloth covering a settee. To her left was a covered table with several chairs around it, and on her right twin chairs nosed toward each other in front of the wide window.

She glanced again toward the space above the hearth and studied the faint outline of where a portrait had hung. Beside the hearth was another door that fitted almost seamlessly into the wall.

She pressed on the door, and it depressed slightly before opening with a small click. She felt around for a light switch, and finding one, clicked it on. It was a closet, maybe five by five feet, but what caught her attention were two large draped frames. She removed the first sheet and discovered a gilded mirror that tossed back a reflection of her blue-streaked hair, faded sweater, jeans, and cowboy boots.

She tugged off the second sheet and found herself staring at the portrait of a young woman. She was dressed in a white silk dress that nipped at a narrow waist and skimmed her legs down to her ankles. A beaded headdress and veil covered red hair that framed a heart-shaped face. The artist had captured the beadwork on the bodice with exquisite detail. The woman's smile was demure, but there was something in her blue eyes that whispered of mischief, as if she were sharing a private joke.

Lucy glanced from her reflection to the portrait. The woman in the portrait looked as if she belonged here, whereas Lucy didn't.

"Mrs. B, is this you?" She studied the woman's face, seeing nothing of herself or Beth. "Mind telling me what the heck I'm doing here? Everyone in town, including me, thinks you've made one heck of a mistake."

Smiling blue eyes stared back at her, silent.

She shifted her focus to the dozens of boxes meticulously stacked on the shelves and marked with black marker. *"Christmas," "Games," "Slipcovers," "Videos."*

Videos. The store clerk had mentioned that Beth had made videos for Mrs. B. She reached for the box and pulled it off the top shelf.

Dust floated in the air, and she coughed as she wrestled with the unwieldy box.

She carried it back into the parlor. Dolly sniffed and nosed Lucy's arm.

Lucy peeled the tape off the top and opened the lid. Inside were a dozen tapes, each marked in a youthful handwriting that reminded her of Beth. The first tape read *"Interview with Mrs. B. May 2, 1988."*

She ran her hand over the tape and then returned to the closet and found a television/VCR in one of the boxes. She hefted the box and carried it back to the parlor, where she set it on the table and plugged it in. She thumbed through the tapes, arranged them in order of the dates on the labels. Only then did Lucy push the first tape into the machine and turn it on.

Static appeared on the screen as she studied the buttons at the bottom of the TV. She didn't own a TV and watched whatever news she needed from her phone. Finally, she found the "Play" button, pressed it, and lowered to her knees in front of the screen.

White snow swirled over the monitor long enough for her to worry that the tape was compromised. And then the image of an older woman sitting in a chair by a window in this very room appeared.

White hair swirled into a chignon, accentuating small diamond teardrop earrings that dangled and caught the light. The woman wore a green knit dress, and a bright splash of lipstick added the pop that brought just the right amount of color to her face. If Lucy looked past the wrinkles and pale skin, she saw hints of the woman in the portrait.

A young girl's voice said in the background, *"I'm Beth Jessup, and I'm a senior at Cape Hudson High School."*

Emotions washed over Lucy like a tidal wave, and she immediately hit "Pause." Tears choked her throat and sprang to her eyes. It was her mother's voice. Months had passed since she'd heard her mother speak without battling pain. This was the voice she remembered from her childhood. Light, easygoing with traces of a devilish humor. This was the voice that had given her comfort and joy when she was a little girl.

"Mommy," she whispered as she touched the screen.

Dolly came to sit beside her and licked the tears streaming down her face. She rubbed the dog on the head. "Remember this, Dolly? We have a piece of her back."

Clearing her throat, she hit "Play." *"This is my final exam project for Mrs. Reynolds's history class. I live on Chesapeake Bay's Eastern Shore in Virginia, and today I'm interviewing Mrs. Catherine Buchanan, who was born in Cape Hudson in 1888. Mrs. Buchanan, can you tell me about your family?"*

The woman looked at the microphone clipped to her collar and began to answer. Lucy sat back, losing track of time as she listened to Mrs. B and Beth talk.

When Lucy reached the end of the first tape, she was eager to play the next tape and find out more about the woman who'd given her this home.

Outside, the wind kicked up. The storm announced its arrival with a loud crack of thunder, and the windowpanes rattled. Seconds later, lightning streaked across the sky.

The electricity blinked, and with that, the television and lights went dark.

"Shit!"

CHAPTER NINE

Lucy

January 15, 2018

Lucy scrounged for her flashlight and clicked it on. She stared at the television and VCR, willing them to turn on, but the electricity wouldn't cooperate.

As the minutes ticked by, the storm only worsened, and Lucy was forced to give up on the next videotape for now. In the kitchen, she gathered candles and matches, lit several, and then made herself a cheese sandwich with extra mustard. She dished out dog food to Dolly, who was still holding out for something better.

"It's a long time until breakfast, Dolly," Lucy said.

Dolly lay beside the bowl and whimpered softly.

"You're good. Very good. But I'll not be emotionally manipulated."

Dolly whimpered louder and touched Lucy's foot with her paw.

"Damn it." She tore off a piece of her sandwich and gave it to the dog. "That really is all you get. We're in a real home now, and we have no excuse not to eat right."

The sandwich gone, she rinsed the plate and returned to the VCR, hoping that the electricity would come back on.

The rain was coming down in sheets, and there was no sign of the storm letting up. The sun was setting, and soon they'd be in total darkness. "I'm going old-school, Dolly. Might just read a book."

Twenty minutes later, Lucy decided that reading by candlelight and flashlight sounded romantic, but it strained her eyes. She laid her head back on the pillow of her bed as Dolly curled at the end. The electricity had been out for three hours.

Lucy slid under the covers and draped a blanket over the dog. They'd been living in the Jeep the last couple of days, and it felt so good to stretch out on a real bed.

The wind outside continued to rattle the windows. The cottage creaked and moaned, but she'd bet this house had seen worse over the years.

The floorboards in the attic shifted and moved. If she believed in ghosts, she'd have sworn whatever entity still lurked in this house was fully awake and moving around. But she didn't believe in ghosts.

The dog peered out from under the blanket.

More boards creaked, and then a loud crack reverberated from the attic. She sat up in bed, blankets clutched to her chest as she listened. The wind and rain were relentless.

She didn't believe in ghosts. She *didn't*. And yet she was scared shitless. "How the hell did we get here, Dolly?"

She forced herself to settle back against the pillows. She closed her eyes, pretending she was in a yoga class and the instructor was playing one of her nature tapes with soothing sounds of a waterfall.

"Om," she breathed. "Om."

Slowly, the stress and strain of the last month pushed her over the edge, and she fell into a restless sleep. Lucy dreamed of a redheaded girl piloting a sailboat. Her gaze was toward the horizon. And she was searching.

When Lucy awoke, the room was dark, but the lights she'd left on downstairs had turned back on. She had electricity! Rising, she swung her legs over the side of the bed, her stocking feet curling when they touched the cold floor. She checked the time on her phone—1:02 a.m.

Dolly lifted her head and, seeing Lucy rise, followed.

She grabbed her flashlight from the nightstand just in case, clicked on the hall light, and padded down the front stairs. The wind still gusted outside, but the rain had slowed.

As she reached the bottom step, she heard the creak of floorboards in the kitchen. Stopping, she grabbed Dolly's collar and stood perfectly still. She'd locked the front door, but she still had no idea how many doors there were in this damn cottage.

She gripped the flashlight and listened. The floorboards groaned again, and the refrigerator opened and closed. Dolly's ears flattened, and the hair on the back of her neck rose.

If she had a ghost, it had the midnight munchies.

Drawing in a breath, she moved down the hallway with Dolly. A glass rattled. Dolly barked and lunged forward, pulling out of Lucy's grasp and racing toward the kitchen.

Metal clanged on the floor. A girl screamed.

Lucy raised her flashlight like a club, not sure what she'd find. Dolly barked. And then, silence.

She rounded the corner in time to see a young girl picking up a utility knife and feeding Dolly a slice of the cheese Lucy had bought earlier today. The girl had a trim, lean frame, and she couldn't have been more than twelve or thirteen. She wore jeans, a worn Carolina sweatshirt, and scuffed tennis shoes. A red headband held back a wild spray of damp black curls that framed the girl's light-mocha skin.

"Who are you?" Lucy said.

The girl fed more cheese to Dolly. "I'm Natasha. You must be Lucy."

Dolly nudged the girl's hand, giving her a forlorn look that only more cheese might fix. So much for being a guard dog.

"Don't feed her any more cheese, or you're going to clean up after her when she has an accident."

"Ew," Natasha said.

"Yeah, 'ew' is right. I made that mistake *once*." She set her flashlight down on the counter. "Natasha, how did you get into my home?"

"It's not your cottage. It belongs to Mr. Jessup."

"Mr. Jessup passed last summer. I'm next in line for it."

The girl looked up with doe eyes full of a sorrow that had Lucy's breath hitching in her throat. "I miss Mr. Jessup. He was my friend, and he always said I was welcome here."

"Natasha, do your parents know you're here?"

"My dad's sleeping in a drunk tank, and my mother is dead." Dolly nudged her hand, but Natasha kept the cheese for herself. "You know, everyone is talking about you in town."

"Is there not any other news in this town other than me?"

"Ah, no. You're the news of the century."

Lucy took the knife from Natasha and opened the refrigerator. She pulled out bread, mustard, and luncheon meat. "Do you want a sandwich?"

"Yes. I'm starving."

The kid looked scrawny, and she had a scrappiness that kids living alone developed. "Can you get me a couple of plates?"

The kid went to the right cabinet as Lucy rinsed off the knife.

"You know this kitchen pretty well. Do you come here often?" Lucy asked.

"When I need to get away from home."

She unwrapped the bread and set two slices on each plate. "Are you sure your father isn't worried about you?"

"I wish. He won't come looking for me for a couple of days."

"Who's your dad?" She'd just met this kid, it was the middle of the night in a raging storm, and she was asking the questions like their meeting was all routine.

"Brian Willard."

"That makes you Natasha Willard. The family that lives a couple of miles from here."

The girl settled on a stool by the counter. "Yes."

"Lucy Kincaid." She shook the girl's hand.

"I know."

"I know you know, but I thought a formal introduction might be nice before we eat." She doled out two slices of luncheon meat, slathered mustard on the slices, and set the second slice of bread on top of each. She cut both sandwiches, and then, grabbing a fresh bag of chips, sprinkled a liberal amount on both plates.

"You want a soda out of the refrigerator?" Natasha asked.

"That would be nice. Thank you."

The girl scooted off the seat and moved toward the refrigerator like she owned the place.

When the kid settled on her seat, Lucy pushed a plate toward her. She opened her own soda and took a long pull, wishing right now it was a cold beer. "So how long have you been staying at the house?"

"On and off for a couple of years."

"How old are you, Natasha?"

"You ask that like I'm some kind of kid. I'm eighteen."

"Don't con me, kid."

"Okay, maybe twelve and a half."

"I'm not judging. Just curious. It's not often I drive over a thousand miles to move into a haunted house and find a kid in my kitchen in the middle of the night, eating cheese."

Natasha popped open her soda can. "My mom used to clean for Mr. Jessup, and she was also his caregiver as he got older. He was nice, and a couple of times a year, he sent Mom up here to the cottage to check on it and clean it. I always liked it here because it was quiet and peaceful." She ate a couple of chips. "So was Mr. Jessup your grandfather?"

"That's what they tell me. I only learned about him yesterday."

"I heard your mom never told you about this place. You must be pretty angry at her." Natasha picked up the remaining half of her sandwich and took a big bite.

Lucy studied the chip in her hand. "Mad would be the easiest thing to feel right now, but I keep feeling sad for her. I miss her."

Natasha chewed quickly and swallowed. "I miss my mom too."

"I'm sorry about your mom."

"It sucks." She shrugged in the way teens did when they shielded their pain with indifference.

"Yes, it does." The two ate in silence until their sandwiches were finished. "Do you want more? I have plenty in the refrigerator."

"I might make a sandwich for lunch."

"You go to school, right?"

"Yeah. I'm in the fifth grade. It should be sixth, but I missed time after Mom died."

As independent as the kid appeared, a twelve-year-old had no business living on her own in an abandoned house. "What are your favorite subjects?"

"Math."

"Really? Good for you. I'm terrible at math, though I can do percentages very well."

"Why?"

"I'm a bartender. I can calculate tips off the top of my head. I suppose you do much higher math than that."

"Trigonometry and geometry are pretty fun."

Lucy sipped her soda. "Fun? I'm impressed. So do you want to be a scientist or professor one day?"

"Dad said if I stay out of jail, don't get pregnant, and get a waitress job, it's a win."

She didn't know Brian Willard, but she already didn't like him. "You can shoot higher than that, can't you?"

Natasha shrugged and sipped her soda. "Why's there an old-time television in the other room?"

"It's a television that plays videotapes. Kinda like a DVD."

"Those boxy things are the tapes?"

"Exactly. I was getting ready to watch a second videotape, and then the electricity went out. Do you want to watch some of the tapes?"

"What kind of tapes?"

"It's my mom when she was a little older than you, talking to Mrs. B."

"Mr. Jessup liked Mrs. B. He said he started working for her when he was twelve. He said she once paid him to move a pile of rocks from one side of the house to the other. And then the next day she paid him to move them back."

That would have been around the Depression. This farming community would have been suffering like most in the country.

"So Mrs. B just gave you this place?" Natasha asked.

"Basically." How had she fallen so easily into this conversation with a kid who should be home with her family or at least with someone who cared about her?

Natasha grimaced. "If I were you, I'd take the money Hank is offering and run as far away from here as I could."

"You know about the money?" Stupid question. There were no secrets in this town.

"Yeah. I heard him talking to Arlene earlier."

"So why should I leave?"

"There's nothing to do here. The kids at school, if you can call it that, are morons. If you're gonna do anything big in this world, it isn't going to happen here. My advice, take the money and run."

"Seems like a pretty nice place."

"You haven't been here that long, have you?"

"Barely a day."

"Give it five or six more hours. You'll go stir-crazy."

She pressed her index finger against the crumbs on her plate, trying to pretend this was all normal. "How did you get into this cottage?"

Natasha didn't have a rapid-fire answer this time. "Why do you want to know?"

"Maybe, if there are serial killers out there, it would be nice to lock up all the entrances."

"A serial killer couldn't get in the way I did."

"Why do you say that?"

"Because it's a little space."

"Out with it, Natasha."

She huffed out a breath. "There's access into the basement through a window. After Mom died a couple of years ago, and then Mr. Jessup passed, I had to find another place to disappear."

"Disappear?"

"A place where I can read or think or just not worry."

"Does your father hurt you?"

"Look, I don't want to get anyone in trouble. The last thing I need is social services breathing down my neck again. I've got enough on my plate."

"Plate?"

"That's right."

"You shouldn't have anything on your plate other than a hot meal with a loving guardian."

She scrunched her face into a prune shape. "I thought you'd be cool when I heard you had blue hair, but you sound like Hank."

"What's he say?"

"'Stay in school.' Duh. 'Look both ways when you cross the street.' Double duh. 'You can be whatever you want to be' or some crap like that."

"I know he can be bossy. But he's looking out for you."

"I can look out for myself."

But you shouldn't have to. As flaky as Beth had been, Lucy had known deep down her mother had her back. "What if I don't last here? What're you going to do?"

"Keep sneaking in."

"How about I just give you a key?"

The girl cocked her head. "Aren't you worried I'll rip you off?"

"Have you stolen anything from the house?"

"Just the food from your refrigerator tonight." She cocked a brow. "I heard you ran up a tab at the grocery store."

"What else did you hear?"

"I heard Hank talking to Arlene about you. Sometimes I help Arlene out in the kitchen. I wash dishes now, but she's going to teach me how to cook."

"And what did Hank say about me?"

She shrugged. "Mostly talked about this place and wondered what you were going to do."

"That's it?"

"What do you want me to say?" She dropped her voice as if doing an imitation of Hank. "'Lucy is hot and I want to date her'?"

Heat warmed Lucy's cheeks. "He didn't say that."

Natasha grinned, shaking her head. "No, but you blushed when I told you."

"I did not."

"Did too."

Lucy grinned. "Where do you sleep when you're here?"

"I have blankets in the basement."

"There are ten beds in this house. Pick one. Though I have dibs on the pink room."

"You can have that room. I never liked that one. It's the haunted room. If anything spooky is going to happen in this house, that room is ground zero."

A chill passed up her spine, but she managed a smile. "Who's the ghost?"

"I don't know. I guess it's Mrs. B. Or maybe it's some guy who got murdered."

CHAPTER TEN

Lucy

January 16, 2018

"Some guy who got murdered."

The phrase churned in Lucy's head for the remainder of the night. Every creak in the house, every snort Dolly made, every turn Natasha made in her bed in the adjoining room startled Lucy awake. As first nights in a free house went, this one sucked.

When the sun peeked up over the waters and cut through the lead glass, Lucy was startled awake by Dolly's barking and the sound of heavy machines rumbling nearby. Bolting up in bed, she blinked and searched her surroundings, which she didn't recognize immediately.

"Don't let the sun burn a hole in you," Natasha said from the door.

"What?"

The kid entered and handed Lucy a cup of coffee. "Hank's crew is outside fixing the road. It'll be nice to park by the house rather than a quarter mile away." Natasha studied Lucy, who must have looked as disoriented as she felt. "No, this is not a dream, Lucy Kincaid. This is your life."

Lucy sipped her coffee, hoping for some sense of normal. "I know that."

"You're looking a little dazed to me."

She took another gulp and swung her legs over the side of the bed. "How long have you been up?"

"A couple of hours."

"What time is it?"

"Seven forty-five."

"Why're you up so early?" She padded across the room toward the bathroom.

"I'm not such a good sleeper usually, but I made it to almost five today. Must have been the legit bed."

Lucy pushed her hair out of her eyes. She would talk to Hank today about the girl. Whatever was going on in her life was not even close to normal. "I never wake before nine."

"You sure were snoring last night."

"I was not."

Natasha laughed. "Oh yes, you were. Hey, what is that metal thing on the dresser?"

"My mother's ashes."

"Can I see them?"

"How about you let Dolly out? I'll be right downstairs."

"Sure. Come on, Dolly."

The dog jumped off the bed and followed the girl as if she'd been doing it all her life. Lucy moved into the pink bathroom and prayed for hot water as she twisted the crystal handles of the claw-foot tub. The pipes rattled and knocked behind the wall, and for a moment nothing came out, and then the water trickled and started to rush into the tub. The water was ice cold the first few seconds, but then it slowly warmed until it steamed. More grateful than she could say, she turned the cold water tap until the heat was just right, and then she plugged up the drain.

Lucy brushed her teeth and then sank into the tub. If this cottage were trying to win her over, the tub was a good start. It had been a long time since she'd soaked in a tub, and as the warmth seduced her body into relaxing, Dolly barked outside. Natasha called out the dog's name. And judging by the tone of the kid's voice, Dolly was not listening.

So much for the long soak. She grabbed a towel and dried off. Ten minutes later, she was in a clean pair of jeans, a thick black sweater, and her cowboy boots. She pulled her blonde hair into a ponytail, finishing off the last of her coffee before she hurried down the stairs. She found Dolly and Natasha waiting by the front door.

"Aren't you supposed to be in school?" Lucy asked.

"School starts at nine. We still have time."

She pulled on her jacket and grabbed her purse. "Do you have all your stuff?"

"You mean like homework? Yes. I did it last week."

"You work ahead? Hats off to you. Do you have a coat?"

"Sure."

"Where is it?"

"At home."

She grabbed her jacket draped over a chair. "Put it on."

"I don't need your coat."

"Wear the coat."

Natasha slipped it on. "Whatever."

Pulling the front door closed, Lucy locked it and hunkered farther down in her sweater. The rains had left as quickly as they'd come, and the sky was a crystal blue.

They walked through the damp, sandy soil down the dirt driveway until they saw the Dodge Charger parked on the other side of the section that had been washed out. Two bulldozers were pushing earth back toward the deep crevices while a dump truck full of crushed rock and gravel stood at the ready.

Lucy waved to the men in the trucks.

"Where did you get that tattoo?" Natasha asked.

Lucy glanced at her wrist. "It was a long time ago."

"It looks like a songbird."

"It is."

"Why'd you pick that?"

"My mom had one just like it."

"I'm not a fan of needles," Natasha said.

"Then you wouldn't like getting a tattoo. Besides, you have to be eighteen."

"I bet I could find someone who would do it for me. Money talks, right?"

"Not today, *okay*? You're way too young." Again, how did she find herself one thousand miles away from home in an old house with her mother's ashes, a dog, *and* a twelve-year-old angling for a tattoo? And when did she start sounding so disapproving?

"Whatever." Natasha jabbed her thumb over her shoulder. "Hey, how long do you think it will take them to fix the road?"

"Hank said a few hours."

Natasha scratched Dolly's head. "Did you see any ghosts last night?"

"No." She fished the Dodge Charger keys out of her purse.

"I didn't either."

"Good. So what's the name of the guy who died?"

"No idea. Ask Mrs. Reynolds at the library."

Lucy opened the car's back door and waited as Natasha and Dolly scrambled inside. As she reached for the driver's-side door, she had the immediate sense that someone was watching her. She looked up toward the cottage, expecting to see one of the crewmen. But there was no one on the path.

"So am I now being stalked by a ghost?" she muttered. A breeze blew over her skin, raising goose bumps. "Great."

Drawing in a breath, she hustled behind the wheel and shoved the key in the ignition. Once she dropped Natasha off at school, she'd swing by Hank's office.

As she turned the car around, she spotted his black truck rumbling toward her.

She stopped, her driver's-side window facing his. Natasha slid over the pink vinyl seat covers as she sank a little deeper in her seat.

Lucy glanced at the kid, sensing that if she was accountable to anyone, it was Hank. "What are you looking so worried about?"

"No one knows I'm here."

"No one? You mean Hank?"

"Maybe."

"I kind of figured that." Lucy rolled down her window.

Hank had showered, shaved, and changed into a dark-blue button-down shirt, hunter's jacket, and jeans. The faint scent of aftershave, which she could admit smelled nice, wafted out toward her.

His gaze shifted from her to the back seat. "Looks like I found who I was looking for."

"Hey, Hank," Natasha said. "You located me pretty quick this time."

"I'm getting wiser."

Lucy leaned back. "So you two have met?"

"Everyone knows everyone in this town," Natasha said. "Hank here gets the call from the school now if I don't show up."

Lucy fished her cell out of her back pocket and glanced at the time. It was 8:02 a.m. "She told me school started at 9:00 a.m."

"Nope, 7:45 a.m.," Hank said.

"The first class is PE, and it's lame," Natasha said. "And I really hate those stupid shorts we have to wear."

Lucy tapped her finger on the steering wheel, irritated she'd been played.

"I could have woken up Lucy, but she was sleeping pretty hard, Hank," Natasha said. "I figured she could use the rest. Seemed the right thing to do."

"How did you get into the house this time, Natasha?" Hank asked. "I nailed up the access door to the basement."

She grinned. "There's a window."

"I saw that window," he said. "It's pretty small."

"For you, not me."

The backhoes rumbled and beeped. "You've got to go to school," Hank said.

"I hate school," she said.

"It's not about what you like or don't like. It's about what you need. And you need an education."

"Why do I need an education? Brenda and Dad say I'm going to end up working at Arlene's anyway."

Hank tightened his hands on the steering wheel, and she imagined him counting to ten while his frustration diluted. "And I've told you that's not correct."

"Whatever."

Lucy could tick off at least ten reasons why a return to Nashville made sense. Her old job. Friends. Her favorite honky-tonk. Good bourbon. Zero complications. "She can stay here. I'm here for now."

Natasha grinned. "Perfect solution!"

Hank shook his head. "Natasha, I'm taking you to school."

"Lucy is taking me," she said.

His gaze zeroed in on her with all the force of a marine drill sergeant. "No, I am."

The girl locked eyes with him for a beat and then shrugged. "Sure. Whatever. Don't go all 'hoo-rah' on me."

His sights still on the girl, he said, "Lucy, why don't you and Dolly join us? If Natasha is going to stay with you, we'll need to let the school know. I'll run you back, and then we can check on the road repair."

Common sense was hard to argue with. "Why not? Kid, hop in the truck." She pulled to the side of the driveway and got out. Natasha piled in first, sliding over to make room for Lucy and Dolly.

Hank put the car in drive and headed back into town. He pulled in front of the school and shut off the engine.

Lucy and Dolly followed them as far as the door.

"Hey, what about lunch?" Hank said, reaching for his wallet.

"I made extra sandwiches," Natasha said. "Lucy bought some pretty nice bread and ham."

"Good."

"Don't break any federal laws today," Lucy said.

Natasha laughed. "Will do. But you said I could get a tattoo, right?"

"I did not!" Lucy said.

Hank didn't rise to the bait as he walked a grinning Natasha into the office. Through the window she saw him talking to an admissions secretary and then sending Natasha off to class. The administrator glanced toward Lucy a few times and nodded.

He joined her outside, and neither spoke until they were back in the truck with Dolly between them.

"All set?" she asked.

"It's one thing to be ambivalent about a house or staying in this town. But don't pull Natasha into this. The kid is drowning, and she can't afford to have you flake on her like everyone else has in her life."

"I offered her a place to stay for a few days. I didn't make any promises."

"She's not going to see it that way." He tapped a finger on the steering wheel. "Unless you can commit to staying in this house forever, don't make any kind of promises to that kid."

"Look, I was just trying to help."

"Trying doesn't cut it." He shook his head as if she hadn't spoken. "Can you make a promise that you're going to stay for good?"

"No."

"Then this conversation is somewhat pointless."

"What about this Brenda woman?"

"Not as reliable as I had hoped. And if she's telling the kid she'll never get out of this town, then I'm going to have to figure out something else. Natasha is smart as a whip, and she can do better."

"What's the deal with her father?"

"Brian Willard. Good-natured guy when he's sober but mean as a snake when he's not. More often than not, he's drunk."

"Natasha said she stayed with my grandfather when he was alive."

"Her mother was his caregiver, and Samuel did try to help. But he was in his late nineties when Natasha's mother died. He was in no shape to raise a child."

"How'd you end up in charge of her?"

"She landed on my radar when I came back to town six months ago. I've been trying to figure out a viable solution ever since."

Bourbon. Friends. Great music. No responsibility. The list ticked in her head. "I'm here regardless for the next few days. A few days will at least buy you some time to rethink your options with Brenda."

"Have you ever been around a kid before?"

"I had Beth." It didn't sound funny when she said it out loud. "There were plenty of times I felt like I was raising a teenager."

"It's not the same."

"I understand, but I respect the concept of sticking it out even when it's not what you want."

"What do you really want, Lucy?"

"Good question, Hank." When his frown deepened, she asked, "How much time do you need to get Natasha situated in a real home?"

"Two weeks."

"I can give you that. It'll give me time to send Beth off right and maybe find out more about my birth father. But I can't promise beyond that."

"You'll do right by the kid?"

"I may not look quite the part, but I can damn sure be responsible when I have to."

"But for how long?"

"For at least two weeks."

He didn't speak for several seconds. "I'll have to take you at your word."

The drive back to the cottage was tense and quiet. When he turned the corner onto Winter Cottage Road, they both realized the crews had stopped work.

"Damn it," he muttered.

They got out of the car, and she followed as Hank strode toward the dozer operator. "Matt, what's going on?"

Matt, a gangly guy in his midtwenties, took off his ball cap and scratched his head. "We found something."

"What?" Hank asked.

"It looks like an old well."

"A what?"

"Well."

"What's that mean?" Lucy asked.

"When the original property was built, the builders sunk several wells before they found one that would give them sufficient fresh water. The old ones were filled in. Mrs. B brought county water onto the property in the 1960s."

"You'll never guess what we found in this well," Matt said as he led them over the grated dirt toward a parcel ten feet from the driveway. "The wheel of one of the dozers got stuck, and we had to tow it out with the other one." He handed Hank a flashlight.

Lucy followed, figuring for now it was her place and she'd learn all she could about it. Hank approached the five-by-five section that had collapsed in on itself.

He gripped the light and held Lucy back until he tested the sturdiness of the area around the old well. He shone the light down the hole and studied it for several long seconds before he waved her over.

She edged close to him, and he handed her the light.

"Have a look," he offered with no emotion.

She followed the spotlight to the bottom of the well. Clustered at the bottom was a collection of bones.

CHAPTER ELEVEN

Beth

May 15, 1988

"I have a crush, Mrs. B."

The older woman is dressed in a burgundy wool jacket, black slacks, and a white ruffled shirt. "Is it the same crush since the last time we talked?"

"No, better." Beth rummages through her backpack, fishes out the microphone, and sets it on the small table beside Mrs. B. "This guy is going places."

"Going places is always a good thing." She fingers the ivory broach on her lapel. It's the same one she always wears. Ivory etched with black ink. It's the songbird.

"He wants to take over his daddy's land one day," Beth says.

"Do I know this boy?"

"You should." She clipped the microphone to her collar. "It's your great-nephew, Noah."

"He's a good boy. And dating a lovely young woman, from what I remember."

Beth snorts. "Nancy."

"They've been together a couple of years."

"She's getting fat. And he's getting tired of her. I can tell."

"Can you?"

"Sure." She sits cross-legged on the floor. "Men don't stick around, Mrs. B. They flutter around like butterflies. Pretty soon, Noah's gonna be flitting in my direction."

"And if he doesn't?" Mrs. B asks.

"He will."

Beth knew Noah would see her. And he would save her.

Claire

January 18, 1916

The Buchanans sponsored a party for the Cape Hudson community. It was their wedding gift to all those who'd worked hard on the upcoming nuptials and those who had served the family for years. Mrs. Lawrence had been clear she wanted everyone invited. No expense was to be spared, and she even hired a four-piece band from Norfolk and seen to it that there was a large pig to roast, breads, beers, and cake.

Claire and Victoria had only been in town a week, but as soon as Victoria had heard about the party, she had insisted on attending. Robert had been the one to remind his sister that the fete was for the servants, and she had obligations at Winter Cottage. But Victoria would not be swayed and saw to it that she and Robert would attend.

The air was warm, the wind calm, and the stars bright and brilliant when Claire, Victoria, and Robert joined Jimmy at the car parked in front of Winter Cottage. He was standing by the polished vehicle, the motor already running, wearing navy-blue seaman's pants, a cable sweater, and a peacoat. His blond hair was damp and brushed off his face.

Claire had plucked a white rose from one of the arrangements at the cottage and pinned it to her burgundy jacket. She'd only brought the one traveling dress, the one she'd worn from New York, but she hoped the rose updated the look just a little.

Victoria wore a baby-blue dress that skimmed her calves and a matching coat with a white fur collar, and she'd had Claire arrange her hair in a loose bun that allowed strategic curls to frame her face. Robert, as always, wore a black suit, a fresh collar, and a tie.

Jimmy helped a giggling Victoria into the back seat with her brother and then assisted Claire into the front. She was pleased to sit by Jimmy while Victoria and Robert were relegated to the back seat.

Jimmy tugged on his seaman's knit cap and shifted into first. The car glided gently forward, a sign he'd been practicing his driving. The slightly arrogant tilt of his chin told her he was proud of the new skill.

She'd only glimpsed Jimmy the last few days as he came to Winter Cottage to greet Mr. Buchanan and his male guests for their dawn hunts. The rattle of Jimmy's wagon had awakened her each morning, and then rushing to her window, unmindful of the cold floor, she would catch a glimpse of him. Jimmy was always smiling and at ease with the much older and far wealthier men. And it appeared that they held him in high regard, listening closely when he spoke. She couldn't hear what he was saying but imagined he was sharing details about the best hunting spots.

Conversation now was impossible with the rumble of the engine, but she hoped this ride to the party would be theirs alone. She'd planned to ask him for a dance.

When he pulled up the motorcar, a rarity in these parts, he drew the attention of everyone. Already the crowd had grown to fifty, and judging by the collection of boats rowing toward the shore, that would soon double. Parties like this were rare, and no one would want to miss it.

Jimmy, with a huge grin, rushed to open the door for Victoria. "Miss."

Victoria smiled as she looked up at him with doe eyes that rendered men immobile. "I must insist on a dance with you tonight," she whispered.

"Miss?" Jimmy said.

"Leave the poor man alone," Robert said. "Let him enjoy his people without your interference."

"I'm not an interference." Victoria made the most beautiful pouts. "And all I'm asking for is one itty-bitty dance."

Claire then stepped out and carefully removed her goggles. She dusted the bits of soot from her hands and lifted her burgundy velveteen skirts as she came around the car.

"Claire, please tell Jimmy I'm a very good dancer," Victoria said.

"She's quite good," Claire said.

Jimmy laughed. "Well, then, there's the problem. I'm not a dancer at all. Never tried it once."

"I shall teach you," Victoria said while the band was tuning up behind her.

"Perhaps in a bit, miss." Jimmy nodded toward a man in the crowd. "I see my old friend Eric Jessup."

Claire shifted from Victoria to the crowd. "I wonder if the boys are here as well."

"What boys?" Robert asked.

"My brothers. The Jessups have raised them."

"Ah, I remember hearing something about that." Robert regarded her as if he'd just glimpsed her as a real person. "I forget you come from this area and have a large family. Why haven't you snuck away to see the boys?"

"We've all been busy," she said. The truth was, she'd been a little afraid. The last time she'd seen them, the baby had been crying, and the other two were begging her not to go as her father dragged her from the Jessups' house. Her father had told her that her future was with the

Buchanans, but she'd wanted to stay with her brothers and sisters and the life she had here on the shore. "I shall see them soon enough."

"I haven't seen much of you either, Jimmy," Victoria said. "You're always out hunting with my father and his friends. You actually look as if you enjoy their company."

"I do," he said.

"I can't imagine a worse thing than rising early and traipsing through the wet and cold," Victoria said.

"What about you, Miss Claire?" Robert said. "You don't mind rising early, do you?"

Had he seen her peering out her window in the mornings? "I'm an early riser because there's so much to be done for the wedding. Just a few more days and so many last-minute adjustments to the gowns."

"Well, if your apparel is any indication," Robert said, his gaze skimming her body, "then the ladies will be stunning."

"Tell me you brought your flask," Victoria said to Robert. "You always have it."

"My job is to keep you sober," Robert said. "Be a good girl for once."

"I don't want punch." Pouting, she moved toward Jimmy and slipped her arm in his. "I'm looking for a bit of whiskey or maybe something stronger."

Jimmy glanced back toward Claire as if he wasn't sure what to say. Victoria was his employer's daughter, and he knew he was on thin ice. "I don't know about that, miss."

"Oh, of course you know, Jimmy," Victoria said. "No need to treat me like china. I've had my share of nips before, isn't that right, Claire?"

"Mr. Latimer, would you do me a favor?" Robert asked.

"Yes, sir."

"Escort my sister around the dance floor a few times. Perhaps a dance will burn some of this restless energy of hers."

Jimmy looked taken aback, but nodded, and was not that disappointed.

Victoria grinned and hugged Jimmy's arm tighter. "I won't tell Daddy if you three don't. I've been locked up in that house for over a week, and if I hear one more story about who shot which duck, I might go mad. A dance is exactly what I need." She tugged him into the crowd, looking just a little pleased with herself.

"You must dance with me," Robert said to Claire. "I'm feeling like an old third wheel."

"I could introduce you to a number of young ladies if you'd like to make their acquaintance."

"I'd much rather spend the time with you. I need an infusion of feminine common sense after sharing dinner with Victoria."

Claire wanted to tell him she was tired of being sensible tonight. She'd had a lifetime of sensible. "I don't think that would be wise."

The band began to play "Pack Up Your Troubles," a patriotic war song that had begun to make the rounds in New York and rouse many an audience. She was surprised the local band knew it.

She studied the crowd of people, trying to recognize anyone from her childhood. This place had been her home for her first twelve years, but she was more of a stranger here than Victoria, who was already laughing and talking to the others as if they'd known each other all their lives.

"Perhaps we should not be so wise right now," Robert said. "We appear to be the true outcasts here tonight. I know no one, and even though you grew up here, I suspect you haven't found a familiar face."

His insight was unsettling. "Everyone's changed so much."

"Whereas I'm who I've always been," he said, pleased with himself. "You know my good and bad traits. Dance with me. It will do both our spirits good."

Victoria and Jimmy were now lost in the crowd. "It would be my pleasure."

He offered her his hand. She took it, and he guided her out to the sandy dance floor where the other dancers were swaying in time to the tune. She placed her hand on his shoulder, and he settled his softly on her waist.

"You're stiff," he said.

"When have you ever known me to be carefree?"

"Never," he said, grinning. "But maybe tonight we can fix that."

"You're more optimistic than I," she said.

He quickened his pace, forcing her to glance at her feet so that she could match his steps. "Just enjoy the dance."

He was an excellent dancer and guided her around with such confidence, her own worries quickly faded. Claire relaxed, and her smile lost the nervous edges and widened. When the song ended, they stepped apart, clapping.

She readied to dance another song with him when another fellow approached. She didn't recall the man's name but decided his rawboned looks and coloring placed him in the Franklin family. Like the men in that family, he had a scruff of beard, and his dark, hollow eyes were sharp and wanting.

Robert's mild expression hardened, and he pulled away from her. "Claire, I have some household business to take care of with this gentleman. Save another dance for me."

She knew Robert pressed the edges of the law occasionally and that his father had intervened on his behalf a time or two. She didn't know what he'd gotten himself into this time. "Of course."

As the strings and the guitars plucked out the next song, Claire stood on the sidelines searching for Victoria and Jimmy. The girl had vanished and taken Jimmy with her.

"Claire, is that you?"

Claire turned to see a woman in her midthirties with curly chestnut-brown hair tucked under a straw hat. A brown checkered dress draped over a rounded pregnant belly and skimmed thick ankles. The woman looked familiar, but Claire couldn't place her.

"I'm Sally Jessup," she said, laughing. "We've corresponded for years, but I haven't seen you since you were twelve."

Claire shrugged off her shock and hugged Sally warmly. "My goodness, you're a sight to see. How have you been?"

Sally pressed her hand to her belly. "Pregnant."

"You never told me."

Sally's smile softened. "I wanted to make sure this pregnancy took. I couldn't bear to write about another lost baby."

Over the years, there'd been four miscarriages that Claire knew of. "Well, you look wonderful. How are Eric and the boys?" She couldn't bring herself to say *my brothers*, nor could she call them the Jessup boys as everyone in town did now.

"My men are constantly messing up my house, eating every scrap of food in sight, and wrestling at the slightest provocation, but I wouldn't have it any other way."

"Are the boys here tonight?"

"Eric is here, but Stanley has watch at the lighthouse tonight. He took Joseph and Michael with him. They all three marched out like fully grown men."

Sixteen years ago, they'd been babies and toddlers, and now they were men. She was disappointed they'd all not come. Surely they'd have known she'd be at the dance. "As soon as the wedding is over, I'd like to see them if I could."

"You're always welcome in our home, Claire. If not for the gift of your brothers, I'd have lived the last years childless, and I doubt I could have survived the miscarriages."

Claire looked at her rounded belly. "You must be close to delivery now."

"Less than a month."

"May I?"

"Of course."

Claire pressed her hand to the tight mound and waited and hoped for the baby to kick. "He's sleeping, I think. Do you have a name picked out?"

"Aaron if it's a boy. Anna if it's a girl."

"Lovely." She wanted the child to kick, but it remained mutinously still as if it were avoiding her like her brothers.

"He waits until I'm asleep in bed. Then he decides to dance his jigs." The swirl of the dancers caught her gaze. "We were thrilled to hear about this party. It's our last chance to get out before the baby. We both remember how confining it can be with small children." She pressed her hand to her belly. "That sounds like complaining, but it truly is not."

"I understand. I recall how hard it was when Mama had a new one. No one got much sleep in the first few weeks." She especially remembered the weeks after her youngest brother, Michael, was born. He was a pink and red-faced little fellow, and she alone had cared for him and her other siblings. It had been overwhelming and too much for her, but when her father had come home and announced the boys were moving to the Jessups', she'd been devastated.

Eric Jessup cut through the crowd, his broad shoulders and tall frame prompting people to step aside without a word from him. In his late thirties, he had a full, ruddy face and an easy grin.

He wrapped an arm around Sally. "Ma'am."

"Eric," Sally said, laughing. "It's Claire."

"Claire Hedrick?" He shook his head, scratching his black beard. "I didn't recognize you."

"Eric, you look well," Claire said.

He hugged Claire and then stepped back. "We're doing well. And your brothers are fine men. Come and see them anytime."

"I'd like that."

"Now, if you won't mind, Miss Claire, I'll be taking my wife for the dance I promised and then home where she's to rest."

Sally kissed him on the lips. "He worries."

As he should, Claire thought. Sally had skimmed over the loss of her four other pregnancies in her letters, but each time Claire had read the accounts she'd feared her brothers would lose another mother. "Enjoy your dance."

A laugh rose above the music, and it drew Claire's gaze away from Sally toward the smiling Victoria, who stood a hair's breadth away from Jimmy and scandal.

She did look stunning in the baby-blue dress. The soft silk draped her bosom, adding a seductive allure, and it nipped in at her very narrow waist. Blonde hair and her small pearl earrings caught the light from the torches ringing the dance floor. Every man at the party was aware of Victoria. The men of the peninsula were helpless to resist her siren's call.

Claire's fingers absently went to the rose she'd pinned on her lapel. Suddenly, it felt bland and a silly attempt to win the attention of a man who was smitten with Victoria.

The band on the stage tuned up again, striking a few lively chords to announce the next song.

It took another few notes to break Victoria's spell and for Jimmy to look up. When his eyes locked on Claire's, he turned and said something to Victoria that immediately produced a pout that looked both charming and vexing. He then marched toward Claire with the same steady determination he'd had the day he'd pulled her from the bay.

Before Jimmy could speak, Victoria rushed up and said, "Claire, you have bested me with this lovely man. He insists you get the next dance."

Claire wasn't his first choice, but she wanted to be his best. "I would like that."

Victoria's smile froze as if she'd expected Claire to stand down and give this victory to her. But Claire was going to be selfish.

"And you'll have the next," Jimmy said to Victoria. "Everyone wins."

He held out his hand to Claire, and she accepted it. "I'll warn you, I don't dance as well as Robert."

"You saw us dancing?"

"He's accomplished."

The initial blend of fiddles and guitars was smooth until one of the string players hit a shrill note that had a few folks cringing. But eventually the quartet found the right melody.

"I really don't know what I'm doing," Jimmy confessed. "I stepped all over Miss Victoria's feet."

Claire pulled Jimmy's hand to her waist and placed his other hand on her shoulder. "As I remember, you can tie any manner of rope knots when rigging a ship. This isn't different," she said, smiling.

Talk of the boats eased some of the tension from his shoulders. "We'll see shortly if you're right, miss," he said with a grin.

She placed one hand on his arm, feeling the ripple of muscle under her hand. "We're going to move in a simple square pattern. Pretend you're sailing your sailboat across the bay. We're the vessels, and you're the captain."

He flicked his head, tossing back a thick sweep of blond hair. "That makes sense."

"You're going to lead us back a step. Just lean toward me a little and nose us in the direction we need to go. Set your sights, just like you would on your sailboat. Then, when we take that step back, steer us one degree to the left and then retreat a step and then back to the harbor where we started."

"Sounds easy when you put it that way."

"It's easy. It seems so complicated the first time, but I promise you that sailing one of your boats in a storm is harder. Ready to set sail?"

He rolled his shoulders back like a sailor bracing for a storm. "Hold on to your oar."

Laughter bubbled, and he guided her back a big step that forced her to take two to his one. She nearly lost her balance and gripped his arm tight. "Steady there, Captain. You're putting too much wind in this sail."

His brow knotted as he dropped his gaze to their feet and directed her to the left. His body was stiff, and he looked more pained than amused, but he took them back several steps and then over to the right. They did this several more times, neither paying much attention to the music. He was analyzing the challenge of dancing while she was savoring a feeling she'd not had since he'd pulled her out of the bay and hauled her nearly lifeless body into his boat. She felt safe, steady, and that allowed all the joys she'd never dared to dwell on to peek out from the shadows.

The music picked up, and Jimmy quickly fell into a rhythm that smoothed out with each completed square. His hand on her waist eased up on its grip. He wasn't doing anything fancy in terms of dance steps, but he'd mastered the sway of their bodies in their small inlet on the dance floor.

"You're very good at this," Claire said. "I bet you could learn a few more dance steps."

"I'm not sure I'll have a need for any more moves." Talking threw off his next step. He frowned but righted their course almost immediately.

"It's supposed to be fun. Not a task to be endured," she teased.

"For the ladies, yes. We menfolk worry over stumbling in front of everyone and making a fool of ourselves."

"A good woman would not worry about a misstep. She would be happy to have you in her arms. I'm happy to be dancing with you."

His head cocked as if he sensed her deepest feelings for him. "Ah, but you were always a practical soul, Claire. Even when you were young, I remember how you'd help your mother in town with the supplies. She either had a little one on the way or one on her hip."

"You saw me with Mama?"

"I did. I remember her by the dock. You were seven or eight, and she asked you about the supplies for supper. You knew better than she what was in the larder."

"It was the way in our house. As soon as I could stand on a chair and stir a pot, I was helping."

"And when your father sent you to live with the Buchanans, he lost the last anchor for his family, and it drifted away."

"He cut the rope binding us."

"Sometimes in a storm, a sailor must make hard decisions. He took no joy in sending you away."

She'd been so angry when he'd first sent her away, but as the months became a year, she'd begun to miss him. She'd started to write, believing he'd respond. "He never wrote me back."

"But he had me read your blasted letters to him over and over."

Comfort mingled with sadness. "That was kind of you."

He muttered something gruff and unintelligible. "Will you be staying on the peninsula?"

"There isn't a place for me here anymore. Once the wedding is complete, I shall return to New York. I have a good job there and good friends." She'd been gone from the Eastern Shore longer than she'd lived here. Now she felt more like an outsider than a local.

But in this moment, in Jimmy's arms, she felt more at home than she had in years. She leaned into him a fraction, wanting to press closer but also fearing such a move would shock him. If she could wish for anything at this moment, it would have been Victoria's daring.

The music stopped, but Jimmy kept on a few more steps before he realized this sailing trip had ended. When the clapping of the other couples finally reached them, they looked at each other for an awkward moment and then each dropped their hands to their sides. A sense of loss rushed over her.

"Thank you for the dance lesson, Claire," Jimmy said. "I couldn't have done it without you."

"You're a natural, Jimmy. You don't need me."

The band rumbled through a new set of odd notes as they again set out on a search for the next tune. "Would you like to try it again?" she ventured.

"I promised this dance to Miss Victoria. I'm hoping to redeem myself after you kindly showed me the ropes."

Claire pushed aside the disappointment. "Yes, of course. I'm glad I could set you on the right course."

He saluted her. "I'm in your debt."

Victoria moved through the crowd of dancers who'd already recoupled and searched for a rhythm in the band's tune. Her smile was bright, and pinned to her lapel was a rose similar to Claire's.

"What do you think of my flower?" Victoria said to Jimmy. "I admit I stole the idea from Claire."

Jimmy's gaze dropped to the flower pinned above her bosom, and as he stared at the bloom, his cheeks reddened. He cleared his throat. "It's mighty nice."

Victoria boldly placed her hand on his arm and put his hand on her waist.

Claire was left to walk to the side of the dance floor as Victoria laughed at one of his missteps. If he was worried about the dance steps or making a fool of himself, he quickly forgot about it when she seemed to trip and brushed her body against his.

"My sister has spun her spell," Robert said.

His voice had her turning to find him holding two glasses of punch. "She's lovely."

He handed Claire a glass. "Lovely is her stock-in-trade. I fear the day when she walks into a room and not all the male heads turn and admire her. She'll be lost."

Seeing her now, Claire couldn't imagine such a day. "I'm sure she'll always turn heads."

He sipped his punch, and she noticed the raw skin on his knuckles. "Maybe."

"Did you hurt yourself?"

He glanced at his bloodied knuckles. "Naw. Just took care of a bit of business and in the process messed up my hand. Foolish."

"I'm glad to hear it's not serious."

"Not serious at all." He watched as Victoria laughed. "Claire, you have a style that none of the ladies here share. Even Victoria in all her finery wouldn't be able to make an ordinary dress look so amazing."

It was her turn to blush now. "Thank you."

"Would you like to dance again?"

She looked toward Victoria and Jimmy. The next dance was starting, and they were already moving to a rhythm all their own. Jimmy had forgotten about their dance and had moved on.

Claire looked up at Robert. There was no spark and no rush of excitement when she peered into his brown eyes. But sparks and flickers were treasures reserved for the less practical.

And if Claire Hedrick was anything, it was practical. "Why, yes."

Hours after Claire had left the dance, she stood at the kitchen stove in Winter Cottage, waiting for a kettle of water to heat. The cavernous room was quiet, but it would stir to life in two hours as Mrs. Latimer and her staff prepared for another busy pre-wedding day. It wouldn't be long before the household realized that Victoria hadn't returned.

The kettle whistled. She lifted it from the stove and poured the hot water into the waiting cup. How could Victoria be so foolish? This wasn't Paris or New York. It was Cape Hudson, and no one did anything without someone noticing.

"That was stupid, girl," she muttered.

The back door creaked open, and she turned to see Victoria peek into the kitchen. When she saw Claire's trepidation turn to relief, she said, "Oh, thank my lucky stars. I'm safe."

She closed the door behind her. Mushed hair, crushed petals of a tired rose still pinned on her bosom, and muddied shoes said so much.

"Where have you been?" The question sounded foolish to Claire the instant she asked it. She knew where Victoria had been and with whom. A surge of hurt and loss washed over Claire.

Victoria raised a finger to full rouged lips smudged by a kiss. "Not a peep, Claire."

"You could get him fired," she said.

Victoria arched a brow. "Who do you think we're talking about?"

"Don't play me for the fool. Jimmy."

"How do you know it was him?"

This was a game to Victoria. "You danced with him all night at the party. You've shown a sudden interest in the morning hunt."

Victoria handed her shoes to Claire and picked up the brewing cup of tea. "Are you jealous?"

She was. Terribly. But that didn't mean she wasn't right. "The rules of the game don't apply to you, but they certainly do to him."

"Of course the rules apply to me. Why do you think I'm sneaking about? Father would have a fit if he knew."

"You're playing with fire."

She would be forgiven eventually if found out. But Jimmy would find himself out of a job at best and shot at worst.

"But you won't tell, will you? And you'll clean my clothes before anyone is the wiser?"

As much as she wanted to see this foolish girl get her comeuppance, doing so would only risk exposing Jimmy. "Hurry to your room and pray your luck holds out."

CHAPTER TWELVE

Lucy

January 16, 2018

"Bones," Lucy said.

"Yep." Hank did not sound happy about this development.

She shone the light into the hole, which wasn't more than ten feet deep. "Who do you think it is?"

"There's no guarantee they're human. Either way, I'm going to have to call the sheriff, which means a delay." He dialed and seconds later said, "Rick. Need you out at Winter Cottage. We've found something."

She listened as he explained and wondered who or what lay at the bottom of the well.

"Naw, whatever it is has been there a long time. There's no rush." Hank shoved his phone back in his pocket. "He'll be right out."

Hank dug a roll of yellow tape from the back of his truck and strung it around the area. He ordered his men to finish up so the other crews that needed to come through here would have a solid road.

"It's been a week of surprises," she said.

Hank shook his head. "That's an understatement."

It wasn't more than a few minutes before the sheriff's truck appeared at the end of the driveway. No lights, no sirens, but a lot of questions.

Rick Markham climbed out wearing a ball cap that read SHERIFF. His hair was dark and cropped close. He wasn't as tall as Hank, but he had a muscular frame and a bearing that suggested he wasn't to be crossed.

Hank shook hands with him and then introduced Lucy.

"Some welcome, isn't it?" the sheriff asked.

"Everyone keeps telling me this is a sleepy little town, but my first twenty-four hours have been hectic."

"I hear Natasha spent the night here," the sheriff said.

Lucy didn't bother to ask how he knew. "She did. I've told her she's welcome for the next couple of weeks."

"She'll love the idea of bones in the yard. That kid likes puzzles," Rick said. "Let's have a look."

He strode to the edge of the well and looked in, shining his light. "You're right, Hank. Whatever the hell it is, it's been there awhile."

"Can't you tell if it's human or not?" Lucy asked.

Rick shook his head. "When it's been this long, it can be hard to say. Amazing how a bear claw can look like a human hand."

"So what's to be done?" Lucy asked.

"I'll place a call to the state and see what they suggest. You never know. They might want to send one of their own. I'd say for now, let's board it up so that no one falls in. Weather's supposed to be clear the next few days."

"Sounds good," Hank said.

"You're going to leave it?" Lucy asked.

Rick dusted the dirt from his fingers. "Just until I hear back from the state. My only concern now is folks coming to have a look and disturbing the site. If it's a human down there, they deserve to be identified properly."

Lucy checked her watch. She still had six hours before she needed to pick up Natasha.

"Rick, while I have you, Lucy would like to bury her mother's ashes in the Jessup graveyard. Any restrictions?"

"They in a proper container?"

Lucy nodded. "They are."

"Then I don't see a problem."

"Great," Hank said. "I'll set it up."

"When do you think you might be having the service?" Rick asked.

"I wasn't really thinking about a funeral," Lucy said. "Anything that formal wasn't exactly my mother's style."

"Wouldn't it help with closure?" Hank asked. "Maybe she wanted to do this for you."

"Perhaps. Then I guess anytime would be fine." She nodded to the hole. "When will you know about the bones?"

"When I'm dealing with the state, I never can tell," Rick said.

"I'm going to run Dolly back to the house and then head into town. I want to check on my Jeep."

"No need for either of you to hang around," Rick said. "I have this covered."

"I'll drive you," Hank said.

She called Dolly, who came prancing out of the woods, and the two ran up to the cottage. In the kitchen, she put a bowl of water down for the dog, along with food and a folded spare blanket for her to rest upon. Dolly lapped up her water and started nibbling her food. It wasn't a ringing endorsement but a step in the right direction. When the dog settled on the blanket, she went right to sleep. Too many months of not running and playing outside, and now Dolly had all the extra fun she could handle.

"I'll be right back," Lucy said.

To her relief, the dog didn't argue.

She hurried back to the construction site and found Rick in his truck on the phone and Hank standing nearby. When she slid into

Hank's passenger seat, he got behind the wheel and drove them toward town.

"I have the Charger. You don't have to drive me around," Lucy said.

"I don't mind. Glad to help."

Hank drove them past town to a small garage located off Route 13. It looked like a throwback to another time. The gas pumps still had the dials that spun as the dollars and gallons clicked off. It had a single bay and a small office with a soda machine in the corner. Two green vinyl chairs held together with duct tape sat on each side of a 1950s-style cash register. On the walls were vintage calendars featuring bikini-clad women and dozens of license plates from across the country.

A young man in his early thirties came out from the back, wiping grease from his hands. He moved with a slight limp but appeared fit and trim. "Hank."

"Rex." He extended his hand, unmindful of the grease.

Rex wiped his hands one last time before accepting it. "Hey, buddy."

"I'd like you to meet Lucy Kincaid. She's the owner of the yellow Jeep."

Rex arched a brow. "Oil change. That's all I got to say to you, miss."

"I know I've been behind on a few details," Lucy said.

"You nearly burned up your engine. I flushed out the systems, put in fresh synthetic oil, which will buy you more time, but it's not a free pass. The car's gonna need a major engine overhaul in the next year or so. I've bought you some time, but not much."

She nodded. "Yes, sir. I'll stay on top of it."

"I'm no sir," he said, grinning. "I was enlisted. The officer's bars belonged to Hank."

"Check. I'll keep that in mind. How much do I owe you?"

"On the house. Welcome to Cape Hudson."

Being beholden to anyone was always awkward for Lucy. She'd received enough charity when she was little and Beth couldn't make the rent, find money for a school lunch, or scrape together cash for back-to-school clothes. She'd had to take it all, but it always left her feeling like less. "Thanks."

"Lucy's stuff still in the Jeep?"

"Right where you left it," Rex said.

"Great. Lucy and I have to get going. There's going to be a funeral for her mother tomorrow," Hank said.

"Tomorrow?" Lucy shrugged. "Is that enough time?"

"It won't take much time to get the spot ready," Hank said. "Spreading the word in town takes all of five minutes."

"Why would anyone from town come?" she asked.

"Respect," Hank said without hesitation. "A lot of folks knew Beth Jessup. Let's say 4:00 p.m.? Natasha would be irritated if she couldn't come along. That kid hates to be left out of anything, even a funeral."

Rex wiped his hands. "Nice of you to look out for the kid."

"It's not a huge deal," Lucy said.

"It's a very huge deal," Rex countered.

She accepted the keys and made her way to the Jeep. Hank kept pace with her.

Lucy slid behind the wheel. It felt good to be around something familiar. "Thanks again, Hank. Beth would have appreciated the weirdness of this moment. She hated being ignored more than anything, and she loathed ordinary. Now she's front and center of what promises to be a unique tribute."

"Sure."

"I don't even know where the Jessup plot is."

"I'll pick you up at 3:30 p.m. tomorrow, and then we can get Natasha from school."

A breeze blew in from the bay, carrying with it the thick scent of salt, but also a growing sense of obligation. "Sounds like a plan."

She drove to the end of town and spotted the library on Main Street across from the beach. The Cape Hudson Library wasn't large, and it had a funky art deco facade dating back to the 1920s.

She hurried up the front steps, pushed through the doors, and strode straight to the information desk. The older woman behind it had short graying hair and glasses that reminded Lucy of a 1960s Hitchcock movie.

"Welcome, Miss Kincaid."

"You know my name?"

"I do. I also knew your mother. I'm Faye Reynolds."

"Do you recall assigning a history project to my mother?" Lucy asked.

"I do." Her frown softened a fraction. "She was supposed to interview one of the older folks in town. She picked Mrs. Buchanan. Did you find the tape?"

"I think I found that project at Winter Cottage, as well as half a dozen other tapes."

"Your mother was one of my best students. Smart girl. She loved to write. Very creative, but she wasn't the most disciplined student."

"That about sums up my mother."

"I will say, your mother went out of her way to appear inarticulate, but she was smart. The problem was, she became bored too easily."

"Mom always could figure out just about anything if she chose to put her mind to it." Give her the task of writing a song, and she would work tirelessly for days. But if you needed her to cook a meal or push a vacuum, forget it.

"I watched the first tape before the house lost power last night."

"I'd be curious to see it sometime if you don't mind sharing. I understand Beth and Mrs. B made over fifteen hours of recordings."

"You never saw the tapes?"

"Beth left town without ever presenting it."

"Do you know why she left?"

"I asked around. I'd heard she'd had a terrible fight with her father, but he never said a word about it when I confronted him. I thought she'd come back eventually or at least get in contact with Arlene, but she never did."

"Does this library have any information on the cottage or the Buchanans? I'd like to read all I can about it and them."

"Sure. The local newspapers were full of articles about them. I'll search through the microfilm and see what I can find.

"Let me do some digging today. The house dates back to 1901 and the paper started five years later, but I should be able to come up with several tidbits."

"Thanks. Trying to fill in this part of Beth's life."

"I understand."

"Do you remember her dating anyone about the time she left?"

The woman was silent for a few moments. "She dated a few boys."

"Any names?"

"I'm not sure I remember. I've taught so many kids over the years. Time jumbles things up sometimes. Let me think on it."

"Thanks. Hey, I'm having a funeral service for her tomorrow at the Jessup family plot at 4:00 p.m. You're welcome to come if you like."

"I'd like that. Can I bring anything?"

"No. That's not necessary. It's just going to be really informal."

Mrs. Reynolds picked up a pencil and made a note. "See you at four tomorrow, Lucy, and I'll bring what articles I can find."

"Thanks."

Lucy drove around town, trying to get the lay of the land. She'd thought maybe she had missed part of the town when she'd arrived, but as she drove, it quickly became apparent that her first impression had been correct.

Back on the main road, she headed north until she spotted the vineyard and then the cottage, driving over a small temporary bridge the road crew had just built. She thought the news of the discovery would have made it to town already, but there was no sign of anyone nosing around.

She parked by the side of the house and hurried through the kitchen entrance, greeted by Dolly's barking. "I told you I'd come right back. Don't run off. I don't have time to chase you down."

Dolly, nose to the ground and tail wagging, headed toward the reeds. Lucy unloaded the Jeep, carried all her belongings up to her room, and unpacked. With her clothes in the drawers, her makeup in the bathroom, and her sketches on the walls, she felt a little more at home.

With Dolly on her heels, she went into the main parlor, inserted the second tape, and then hit "Play." The static cleared, and the image of an eighteen-year-old Beth appeared.

The phone rang in the kitchen, and she hurried to answer it.

"This is Brian Willard."

"Natasha's father?"

"That's right." His deep southern drawl was laced with fatigue and she guessed a hangover. "I understand you took my daughter."

"Excuse me?"

"She was at your place last night. I don't appreciate you taking my girl like that."

"Well then, Mr. Willard, I suggest you call the cops. Oh, wait. Are you calling from jail? If you are, then it should be easy to report me. And then we'll see who ends up on the right side of this argument."

"I'm out of jail, and I don't know who the hell you are, but you ain't getting away with stealing my kid. I'm calling the police."

"Thank you for taking my suggestion." Her white-knuckle grip on the phone radiated up her arm.

"Smartass . . ." was all she heard as she hung up on him.

What a loser. She'd not had a father, and there were plenty of times she'd yearned for one. But at least she didn't have to deal with an ass like Mr. Willard.

CHAPTER THIRTEEN

Lucy

January 16, 2018

Lucy locked the front door seconds after she hung up with Brian Willard. She considered calling Hank, but she'd known him all of one day and didn't want him thinking she couldn't handle what appeared to be a drunken bully. She'd managed her share of drunks working in the Nashville bar scene.

She returned to the parlor, turned on the VCR again, and restarted the second video. She pulled one of the wingback chairs closer.

The image flickered back up on the screen. It was still amazingly good quality, given its age and the technology at the time. The older woman in the chair was positioned next to a bank of windows. The chair in the video was the same one Lucy sat in now, and it was placed almost in the exact spot it had been in thirty years ago.

She hit "Pause," studied the room, and realized it hadn't changed at all. Time marched on outside, but in Winter Cottage, it spun in place.

She watched Beth clip the microphone to the woman's collar. Again, she hit "Pause," wanting to really look at the woman who'd reached out of nowhere and brought her to this house. Hank and everyone in the town apparently had no idea why she had inherited the property, and she certainly was no closer to an answer herself. Maybe Mrs. Buchanan and Beth would drop her a clue if she watched.

She pressed "Play" again and watched as her mother fiddled with the microphone. She studied Mrs. Buchanan's expression as she watched the young girl at work. The older woman wore an ivory broach and pearl earrings that luminesced from each ear. Absently, Mrs. B fussed with the broach. Lucy hit "Pause" and studied the songbird painted on the broach. She had copied Beth's tattoo, which she could see now mirrored Mrs. B's songbird.

Pressing "Play" again, she watched as the video continued. Beth's jeans nipped in at her narrow waist, and a blousy pink T-shirt cut just above the high-waist jeans. The outfit could have made her an extra in *The Breakfast Club* or *Pretty in Pink*.

Lucy leaned forward in her chair, staring at her mother. Tears choked her throat, and she wanted so much to reach out to the young girl on the screen. She wondered what had happened that was so terrible that she would run a thousand miles away at such a young age.

"Damn, Beth, how did you find the courage?"

Leaning forward, she traced the outline of Beth's face. Her mother had always been an upbeat woman, and the girl in this video had the same enthusiasm. The interviews had been done in May of 1988, right about the time Beth had gotten pregnant with Lucy.

Lucy settled back and watched Beth ask a question or two before Mrs. Buchanan began to talk about a young woman named Claire who had returned to the area in 1916. Mrs. B explained that Claire's natural talent as a seamstress had won her the plum job of working in the Buchanan house for their young daughter, Victoria.

The old woman's face was stoic and distant until she mentioned James "Jimmy" Latimer. His name softened her pert lips, and her dark eyes brightened with the luminescence of a young woman. *Jimmy.* The young merchant marine and hunting guide had lived near this cottage. Several times when Mrs. Buchanan spoke about Jimmy and Claire, she raised a wrinkled hand bent with arthritis to her cheek, gently touching it as if imagining Jimmy's touch.

"Mrs. B was talking about herself. She was Claire," Lucy murmured out loud.

She found herself rooting for young Claire, who'd returned home only to discover she didn't really belong there anymore nor in the wealthy world of her employers. She was a woman moving between two separate worlds.

After nearly an hour of talking, Lucy watched Mrs. Buchanan draw in a deep breath and release it slowly. It was clear she had tired after only an hour but also that she had relished every moment of the retelling.

"This is enough for today," Mrs. Buchanan said.

Beth was silent for a moment. *"I'm kinda hooked, Mrs. B. I want to know what happened with Claire and Jimmy and Victoria."*

A sly smile tipped the edges of the woman's lips, still pink with lipstick. *"Then I suppose you'll want to return,"* she said. *"I have more to share, but I don't have the energy to give it the due it deserves. That will take some time and your help, Beth."*

"I can come back." Beth moved into the screen again as she unclipped the microphone. This time she knelt by the chair. *"I got to give you credit, Mrs. B. You have a great memory."*

"My husband said the same. Many times he wished I would forget, but I never did."

"What did he want you to forget?"

She patted Beth's hand. Her hand was wrinkled and pale, but the nails were neatly polished in a color that matched her lipstick. *"Come and see me a week from Sunday."*

"I might have a date on Sunday evening."

"Then we will meet in the afternoon. And when you dress for the evening, child, choose a darker color. The pink washes you out."

Beth laughed. *"I'll see what I have in my closet. So it's a date for Sunday afternoon. Say around two?"*

"Make it one. I will have tea prepared for us."

"I drink Tab, not tea."

The old woman appeared to shudder. *"We will have tea like proper ladies, Miss Jessup."*

Beth's laugh rang clear as a church bell. *"There's nothing proper about me, Mrs. B."*

"I said the same about myself at your age, and look where I am now."

The tape ended, returning to the black-and-white static. Lost in time, Lucy looked at the clock on the wall. It was after two and time to take a shower and clean up before she picked up Natasha. Remembering Mrs. B's advice to Beth, she thought about the dark V-neck sweater in her bag.

Hank

Hank stopped by the funeral home and confirmed there wasn't anything else required for Beth Kincaid's funeral. She'd been lawfully cremated, and the cemetery was private property, so as long as Hank had a good shovel, he could take care of it himself.

Next, he stopped by the sheriff's office and found Rick pacing, his jaw tight as he spoke on the phone. When he ended the call, he shoved out a breath. "We're on our own with the possible crime scene. County asked us to collect the bones and whatever forensic evidence we can find and then to send it to the state lab."

"Do you have what you need to excavate the site?"

"It's just me, but I'm going to need an extra set of hands."

"When do you want to do this?"

"First thing in the morning, and can you bring a ladder and rope?"

"For you, Rick, I'll even bring coffee."

Rick came around the desk. "What do you think of Lucy?"

"I have no idea. Right now, I think this is one big novelty to her."

"Have you asked her about extending the lease agreement?"

"Not yet. I'm hoping to ask her tomorrow. Figured I'd give her the chance to see her mother buried properly."

"And if she says no like her mother?"

"I spoke to Beth Kincaid only once. I realize now she was much sicker than she let on and likely not really herself."

"You said she lost her temper and hung up on you."

Hank could still hear the woman's tone shifting from hesitant to outright angry. "To her credit, she was calmer when she called back."

"But she never told Lucy about the lease."

"She didn't tell Lucy anything. Lucy doesn't even know who her father is."

"But you do."

Hank flexed his fingers. "Like I said, Beth was sick. She might have known what she was talking about when she told me, or she might not. She wasn't making a lot of sense, and I'm not going to pass on information that could very well be wrong."

"Either way, Lucy should know," Rick said.

"I'll tell her after the funeral."

"Don't wait too long."

"I could give you the same advice."

"What's that mean?"

Hank shook his head. "Megan?"

Rick's jaw tightened. "Let's call this a stalemate."

"Sure." The two parted, and Hank made his way to the Jessup family plot.

Samuel Jessup had been good about seeing to the family plot. He'd had the fence painted five years ago, and until he died, he'd kept the grass cut. However, since his death last year, the weeds had grown up. If Hank had had more time, he'd have called one of the boys from the high school to clean things up, but because the funeral was tomorrow, he'd decided to take care of it himself. Plus, he wanted it done right.

He pulled the Weed Eater from the back of his truck and spent the next hour trimming the tall grass and edging around the fifteen headstones laid in even rows. As he was wrapping up and putting the equipment in the back of his truck, his cell rang. It was one in the afternoon, and it was the high school.

"Hank Garrison."

"Hank, this is Principal Daniels."

"Everything all right with Natasha?"

"She's fine. Haven't heard a peep out of her. But her father came by looking for her. The vice principal chased him off, but he looks loaded for bear. I could call the police, but he's not really broken a law, plus he's my cousin's boy. I don't want to stir up family trouble unless I have to. Thought I'd give you a heads-up."

"Thanks, Mrs. Daniels. I'll pay him a visit."

It took Hank less than twenty minutes to track down Brian Willard, who was staying at his buddy Zeke's trailer. Hank parked in the graveled driveway littered with weeds and debris. A dog barked over the stench of garbage.

He banged on the trailer door. Inside, he heard the blare of a TV game show. He opened the door and found Brian napping in a worn recliner.

Brian Willard was a big man. He'd played high school football and in his day had been one of the stars on the team. He'd even managed a scholarship to Virginia Tech, and it had looked like he was on his way. Then a car accident his freshman year had sidelined him for half a season. Left to his own devices and self-pity, he'd started drinking. A DUI had gotten him kicked off the team and shipped back to Cape Hudson. It would be the first stop on his long road to totally screwed up.

It was still early in the afternoon, and judging by the beer cans littering the floor, Brian was at least ten beers into his latest drunk.

"What the hell do you want?" Brian didn't bother to get out of the threadbare recliner or to turn off the television.

"I'm here about Natasha," Hank said. "I got a call from the school. You came onto the property looking for her."

"She's my kid, and fathers keep up with their children."

"Stay away from Natasha. She doesn't need you meddling in her life."

"Meddling? I'm her father."

"An accident of biology."

"Doesn't matter how it happened, I am, and that's all that counts."

"If you go near that kid, the sheriff will see to it that your bail is revoked."

"You can't do that, you arrogant prick. She's my kid."

"I can." Hank's low voice was laced with controlled fury. "And I will. Stay away from the school and Natasha."

"That kid belongs at home. There are chores for her to be doing at the house. It's a damned pigsty. Clear she didn't do a damn thing at the house while I was gone."

"You were in jail."

"She's been hanging out at that Winter Cottage again. I told her before I left to stay the hell away. That house ain't for her kind or mine."

"Natasha is going to be staying at Winter Cottage for the next two weeks. The new occupant has agreed to keep her until you have your arraignment."

Brian shook his head as he jabbed a finger at Hank and rose up out of the chair. "The hell she is. I already told that woman to stay the hell away from my kid."

"You spoke to Miss Kincaid?"

"That her name? It don't really matter, because she's not going to want to have anything to do with Natasha after I get through with her."

"What did you say to her?"

He sneered. "Told her to mind her own business."

Hank took a step forward, putting him within a swing's distance from Brian. "One call, and your bail is revoked. And it won't be local but regional jail."

Brian tried using his size to intimidate. He was still sober enough to throw a cheap shot, which at that point Hank almost welcomed.

Hank stood his ground, flexing his fingers.

Brian set his beer can on the end table. He lowered, apparently ready to sit back down, when in one swift move, he whirled around, fist cocked, and fired.

Hank saw the punch coming and pivoted out of the way, so all he felt was the whoosh of air instead of bare knuckle.

He would never have thrown the first punch, no matter how tempting it was. Brian regained his footing, getting ready for a second strike. Hank thought about Natasha chatting and smiling, hoping it hid all the grief she had endured because of this guy.

Hank put his body weight behind the punch, connecting with the big man's jaw. The bare-knuckle strike was on the money. Brian stumbled back and fell into his chair. His arms flailed, knocking his beer over, spilling nearly a full can.

Brian looked shocked. He was just stupid enough to attempt another strike.

"Don't get up," Hank said. "I'll hurt you bad, and that won't be my fault."

"To hell with you." He rubbed his jaw but stayed put.

"Drink your beer, do whatever it is you do, but stay clear of Natasha."

"I could file assault charges against you."

"Really? You'll want to explain to the cops how you attacked first."

"There's no proof of that."

"Who do you think the sheriff is likely to believe?"

"Fine, the kid ain't worth the trouble," Brian said. "But once I beat this latest charge and I get home for good, she's not going to be staying at that damn house."

"We'll see." The arraignment was two weeks off, and in that time he would figure out a more permanent custody arrangement.

As Hank left the trailer, he was still plagued with worries over gaining control of Winter Cottage's lands, and his hand ached, but his mood felt a little lighter.

Lucy

When the school bell rang, Lucy and Dolly were in the yellow Jeep, parked by the main entrance. The buses had lined up behind her, and she was fairly certain she was illegally parked—a "no cars on the bus ramp" kind of thing. But because this was all new to her, she stayed put, ready to argue her position if anyone challenged her.

Her engine was running, the heater humming, and she'd found one country-western station out of Norfolk. The reception wasn't great, but anytime a Keith Urban song played, the world just felt right. She closed her eyes and imagined herself walking down Nashville's Lower Broadway with her friends past the neon lights of the honky-tonks as the music trailed behind her. She'd been so wrapped up with Beth the last few months she'd not seen her friends, and she suddenly missed them. There was a lot she'd loved about her life in Nashville.

She reached for her cell and, realizing she had bars by the school, dialed her friend Raven's number. They'd dated a few times, and she'd slipped him free drinks when he'd played guitar in the last bar where she'd worked. Raven, as his name implied, had thick shoulder-length hair and deep, dark eyes that implied an emotional openness that really didn't exist. He was about no strings. No ties.

Raven picked up on the third ring. "Luceeee. Where are you, babe?"

"Eastern Shore of Virginia."

He cleared his throat. "What the hell are you doing there?"

"You heard Beth died, right?"

"I did. Man, that was hard. I'm sorry I didn't get by to see you." He'd called once from Memphis right before Beth had slipped into a coma. He'd been a little drunk, but he'd tried to find the right words to make her feel better.

"What are you doing?" she asked.

"Just waking up. Played until 3:00 a.m. I'm in Tampa." In the background, sheets rustled, a sliding glass door opened, and she imagined him stepping out onto a balcony that overlooked calm, tranquil waters.

"Is it warm there?"

"It's eighty degrees and sunny. I might stay a few more weeks. You should join me."

The offer was tempting and reminded her she'd not done anything for herself in a long time. "Can't right now. Beth's funeral is tomorrow." Besides, I have a kid to pick up from school, a dog, and a creepy old house.

"Wow. That's rough. I'd come up, but there's no way I could be there in time."

"It's doable, if you start driving in the next couple of hours."

"Babe, I can't. I have a gig tonight."

He was the backup guitarist in a country-western band that covered the major artists. He could have missed a night or two. "Right. I get it."

"Don't sound all pouty on me. You know I'd do anything for you."

The front door of the school opened, and the kids began to stream out. "I know. Look, I've got to go."

"Hey, Lucy, before you go, I heard about a job. You remember Ray?"

"Sure." Ray-Ray, a.k.a. Raymond Tucker, owned several bars on the Lower Broadway strip.

"He's looking for a new manager. Paying good money. Your name came up."

"It did?"

"Yeah. I told him you were probably looking. He's going to give you a call. Could be a great opportunity."

"Thanks, Raven."

"I do look out for my girl."

"Yes. You do. Look, I've got to go. Talk to you soon."

"Take Ray-Ray's call. He's a heavy hitter. The job could mean some serious jack."

"Will do." She hung up as the Jeep's back door opened with a whoosh and Natasha tossed in her backpack and jumped into the car. "You made it!"

"I said I would."

She clicked her seat belt. "People say all kinds of things. Doesn't always mean much." She hugged Dolly. "She's like a big cuddly teddy bear."

Lucy shifted into first gear. "She's the best."

Natasha's eyes met hers in the rearview mirror. "You're going to have a reception back at Winter Cottage, right?"

"Why would I do that?"

"That's what people do after a funeral. They have folks over for food. Daddy didn't do it for Mama, but I know that's the proper way. It wouldn't have to be much. Maybe cake or something."

Lucy pulled onto the main road. "What kind of cake?"

"I don't know."

"What was your mother's favorite?"

Natasha's dark eyes brightened. "Chocolate. Definitely, chocolate."

"Is there a bakery in town?"

"It went out of business, and Miss Megan only bakes pies for Arlene."

The song on the radio ended, and another Keith Urban song began. Back-to-back Urban. As Beth would have said, the universe always sent messages. "Turns out one of my many odd jobs was as a bakery assistant. I can make it."

"Really?" the girl almost squealed.

"Absolutely. And maybe we could have it at the gravesite, and you can be in charge of serving it?"

Natasha looked puzzled. "What's wrong with Winter Cottage?"

Lucy arched a brow, considered sugarcoating the story, then decided that if she expected the truth, she'd better be willing to give it. "The road crews found a well on the property. And they think there are bones in the bottom that have been there a long time."

"No way!" Natasha's eyes widened as she drummed her fingers on the seat. "Who do you think it is?"

"I have no idea."

"Can I see it?"

"It's taped off right now. The sheriff is figuring it out."

"Cool. Can we still bake the cake?"

"Sure. But we'll need to stop at the store."

While Natasha prattled about her theories on dead bodies, Lucy drove to the market and parked. Dolly waited in the car while she and Natasha hurried inside and collected the ingredients as well as more school lunchbox fixings for Natasha.

At checkout, Natasha and Paula theorized more about the body as the news was already making the rounds in town. Lucy charged the supplies to her account and loaded up the groceries.

"Hey, if you drive another mile past Winter Cottage, we can see Hank's new winery. It's not done yet, but it's pretty cool."

Lucy didn't know a lot about Hank's operation here and realized she was curious. "He won't mind?"

"Naw. It's wintertime, so there's not much to do with the vineyards. Kind of the closest he comes to a slow time."

"Let's have a look." She drove past the turnoff to the cottage another mile and a half until she spotted the directional sign pointing to Beacon Vineyards. She took the left onto the dirt road.

"Hank wants a paved road, but he says it'll have to wait," Natasha said. "Money's tight."

As they made their way closer to the water, she saw a large metal-framed warehouse that honestly wasn't much to look at. She spotted Hank's truck and parked beside it. Out of the car, they were greeted by the sounds of hammers and Hank's deep voice.

Lucy and Natasha pushed through the door, and both watched as Hank, on tall scaffolding, peered into a large stainless-steel vat. Wrench in hand, he worked on a valve below him as another young man held a section of piping in place beside the vat.

"Hey, Hank!" Natasha said.

He looked around, his gaze a mixture of annoyance and worry until he saw Lucy standing beside Natasha. "Everything all right?"

"Natasha wanted to show me around," Lucy said. "If this isn't a good time, we can leave."

"I'll be right down." He spoke to the man on the other side of the tank, and when he seemed satisfied with his answer, climbed down the side of the scaffolding. "We're trying to get the new tanks installed," he said. "Like any task, the first time has its challenges."

"I hear you," Lucy said. "The next tank will go up in half the time."

"That is the hope," Hank said.

"Boy, you've gotten a lot done," Natasha said. "This room was empty the last time I was here."

"We're making progress," Hank said.

Lucy looked around the room, and though he was in the process of installing equipment, she could see that this was one heck of an undertaking. "This the first time you'll make your own wine?"

"Correct," he said. "We've always had a great reputation when it comes to selling our grapes but have never made our own. Hopefully, by this fall after the harvest, we'll be able to reserve some of the crop and make a run at our own label."

"You've gotten all this accomplished since you returned home in the last six months?" she asked.

"I've been thinking about it for a couple of years."

"Are those tanks stainless steel?" Lucy asked.

"They are. We'll age our chardonnay grapes in there for nine months. The beauty of stainless steel is that the taste will be pure. We have ancient shell in the sandy loam soil, and it imparts a great flavor in the grapes."

"I don't know much about soil," Lucy said.

"Basically, we have sand particles in our soil, which means it has to be watered and fertilized frequently. The shore is a beautiful place to live, but the land makes you work for everything."

No truer words spoken. "What's the grand plan?"

"After we get this equipment installed, the next phase is to build a tasting-and-event room. Events are not only a moneymaker but also help with publicity. Part of the fifteen-year plan."

"Fifteen years. I'm impressed."

"This is just the beginning."

She could barely hold down a job for more than a year, and he was writing out fifteen-year plans. "I envy you your dedication. It's good to be a part of something bigger."

"Hank," the man from above called. "I got that bolt loose."

"Great. I'll be right up." He jabbed his thumb over his shoulder. "I've got to get back. I'll see you two later."

Natasha clasped her hands together. "Don't work too hard!"

Lucy smiled at Hank, but as she turned she was amazed at what he'd accomplished and what he was building. As easy as her life was in Nashville, she had no roots or anything to call her own.

Ten minutes later, she pulled into the driveway and past the flapping caution tape ringing the well.

"Stop!" Natasha said. "I want to see it."

"We need to leave it to the sheriff. And there's no telling what other wells are out there."

"So cool."

She drove slowly over the graveled road and was glad to be able to park right by the kitchen under the side portico. More progress. She was moving in the right direction.

She unloaded the groceries as Dolly and Natasha ran around the yard. She then refilled the dog's water bowl and dug out a chew stick from the day's haul at the store. Dolly and Natasha burst through the side door. Dolly lapped up the water while Natasha dumped her backpack and shrugged off her coat.

"Are you hungry?" Lucy asked.

"Starving."

"Sandwich?"

"Two would be better."

"Didn't you make yourself something for lunch today?"

"I did, but I think I have a hollow leg. I'm always hungry." She washed her hands. "I can make the sandwiches if you want to start on the cake."

"Sure. That works."

Lucy washed her hands and moved into the pantry in search of pans. The small storage room was a time machine. Its three walls were lined with floor-to-ceiling shelves filled with pots, pans, glasses, serving platters, and crystal punch bowls. All the pieces showed the worn patina of items that had been well used over many years. This house had been built for entertaining.

As Natasha bit into her first sandwich, Lucy found a set of round cake pans, a ceramic mixing bowl, and a white platter. She washed off each piece and, turning a switch, watched as the gas heat clicked on. "Okay, we're cooking, girls."

It took her less than twenty minutes to mix the cake batter, butter and fill the pans, and place both in the oven. She set a timer on her phone. Forty minutes. She took ten minutes mixing up the chocolate icing with a large wooden spoon until the butter blended perfectly with the powdered sugar and cocoa.

"When were you a baker?" Natasha asked.

"I was about eighteen. And I wasn't exactly a baker. I worked in a bakery. I've worked a lot of jobs like that. Shoe salesman. Waitress. Bartender. Sketch artist. Nothing too memorable."

"Whose picture did you draw?"

"No one in particular. Tourists mostly. I'd set up my easel and pencils. It never took long before someone stopped and wanted their picture drawn."

"Could you draw me?"

"Sure. Start your homework, and I'll get my pad." She retrieved her sketchbook and pencils and found Natasha sitting at the kitchen island with her books open.

Lucy fished out her phone, turned on her downloaded Country's Best playlist, and started to draw the girl.

"My face is too plain," Natasha said without looking up.

"Why do you say that?"

"I don't look like anybody. I'm dark like my mother but not pretty like she was. And I don't look like Dad at all."

Lucy drew the outline of her face. "It's okay to have your own special look."

Natasha frowned, twisting her finger around a dark curl. "Everyone says you look just like your mom."

"I do."

Natasha looked up. "Were you sad when she died?"

Her chest tightened and her breath caught. "I was and I still am. She wasn't perfect, but she worked hard all her life to make a home for me."

"How old was your mom when she died?" Natasha asked.

"Forty-seven," Lucy said. "A short run."

"My mom was forty-one when she died," Natasha said softly. "A short run too."

Vulnerability and sadness drained the energy from Natasha. What could Lucy say to bring back her smile? She wished the universe would send her a clear, concise message right about now for the little girl.

On the sketchpad she shaped the girl's almond eyes and filled in the irises. Though Natasha's expression had just saddened, Lucy drew bright, expressive eyes and lips that curled into a smile.

"My dad came to the school today," Natasha said. "The principal told me. She also said she called Hank."

Lucy shaded the soft ringlets framing the girl's face. "Your father called me too."

Natasha nibbled her bottom lip. "What did he say?"

"He was a lot of bluster."

"He can be mean."

"I've handled enough guys like him. Don't worry."

"He knows I'm staying here."

"And so does Hank and the sheriff. And both aren't more than ten minutes away. And honestly, it would take a tank to bust through one of the doors in this house."

Natasha relaxed a little. "And he's too big to get through my window. Which I blocked with a big box, by the way."

Deflecting the subject, Lucy asked, "Do you have any pictures of your mother?"

Without a word, Natasha unzipped a side pocket of her backpack and pulled out one. "Mom and me, when I was a baby."

Lucy studied the image of a thin, pretty African American woman holding a two-year-old with a wide grin and a wild spray of hair. They were standing beside a popcorn stand, and in the background, red and yellow balloons rose up to a bright-blue sky. "Where was this taken?"

"In Norfolk. We went to the zoo. My dad was having a good day, and he came with us. He took the picture. Anytime I smell popcorn, I think of her."

Lucy took the sketch of Natasha out of her notebook and laid it on the counter. She began to draw the girl's mother, capturing the woman's bright smile and the look of utter joy she emanated in that moment.

Natasha rested her chin on her hand and watched as Lucy shaded around angled cheekbones and full eyebrows. "She usually didn't wear her hair loose like that."

"I like her this way," Lucy said. "She looks happy."

"She does." Natasha was beaming.

"That's how you should remember her," Lucy said.

"I try to, but sometimes I remember how sick she was at the end."

Lucy understood how hard it was to hold on to the best memories. The good memories of Beth had been crowded out with moments of Lucy trying to get her to the bathroom before she got sick, the head-aches and the medicines that made her mother weep, and finally the falls that left her mother's legs and arms bruised.

She wanted to remember the Beth in the videos. The woman who was excited and ready to tackle life. She handed the sketch to Natasha and waited.

"She's so pretty," Natasha said.

Lucy slowly put the two sketches side by side and still said nothing. The universe had sent its message.

Natasha was silent for a moment. "I do look like my mom. Can I frame them?"

"Sure. I'm sure someone sells picture frames in town."

"Can I put them in my room now?"

"Sure. Why don't you do that while I ice the cakes?" Lucy fished a roll of tape out of a drawer that appeared to be filled with all the things that had no other place to be.

"Okay." She took the tape and sketches and dashed to the door but stopped. "If anyone knows how that body got into the old well, Mrs. B did. She lived here, like forever."

"I think you're right."

"We need to keep watching the tapes. I bet she tells us."

"Agreed."

Lucy had just finished icing the cake when the front bell rang. Wiping her hands, she glanced through the windowpanes flanking the door. Hank stood on the front porch with a pizza box in his hand. She tugged her sweater down, stood straighter, and moistened her lips before she unlatched the locks.

CHAPTER FOURTEEN

Lucy

January 16, 2018

Since they'd seen him at the winery, Hank had changed into clean jeans and a V-neck sweater. His hair was damp from a shower. She caught the scent of sandalwood soap. He held up the pizza box. "I know how that kid can eat."

"She just ate two sandwiches, but I'm sure she'll eat more." She stepped aside. "Come on in."

"Something smells good."

She closed the door behind him and locked it. "Chocolate cake. Natasha said food should always be served at a funeral." She shrugged. "Worse case, she'll be having cake for breakfast day after tomorrow."

"Where is she?"

"Putting a few things away in her room."

"Which is hers?"

"The blue one across from mine."

He strode into the kitchen, and as he set the pizza box down, he spotted her sketchbook opened to a street scene she'd sketched in Nashville. "That's really good. You did that?"

"It's a hobby."

"A hobby? Mind if I look?"

Smiling, she closed the book. "It's just scribbles."

"More than that. You ever take lessons?"

"No. Just picked up tips here and there." She turned to the cabinet and pulled out plates. "What's the status of the bones in the well?"

"That's my other reason for coming. Rick and I are going to excavate the site in the morning, and then we're sending it off to the state lab."

She nodded. "Natasha and I were just going to watch more videotapes of Mrs. B."

"Tapes?"

"Turns out, Beth interviewed Mrs. B right before she left town for good. Started as a history project, and then Mrs. B hired Beth to tape her full story."

"I didn't realize that."

"I found the tapes in a box in a parlor closet. You're welcome to join us. If anybody would know who or what might be in the well, it would be her."

"Sure. I've got some time."

"Would you like a glass of wine? I picked up a couple of bottles in town."

"Sure."

"It's from the corner store, so I don't know what a wine grower would make of it." She grabbed a couple of glasses and a bottle from the fridge.

He found an opener in a drawer and poured two glasses. "They carry quite a few blends there that are really good, including this one."

"I've got to say, I'm very impressed with what you've done at the winery. Looks like you've got a great vision for this place."

"We'll see if I can pull it off."

"Am I standing in the way of your plan?" she said.

He studied her a long moment as if wrestling with what he'd say next. "Lucy, there's something I've been meaning to discuss with you about the land."

"Okay." She took a sip but didn't take her eyes off him.

"My father planted his grapes thirty years ago on the land adjacent to Winter Cottage. Samuel leased the land to my father for one dollar a year."

Lucy let the remark sit there. Hank still had some explaining to do.

"He really did us one hell of a favor. There were times I don't think we'd have made it if not for that agreement."

"So how do I figure into this?"

"The lease Dad and Sam signed expired upon his death."

"And you need a new agreement from me."

"I do."

"Why didn't you just tell me from the start? After what I saw today, I'll do whatever I can to help. I'll sign a new lease agreement."

"Really?"

"Just be up-front with me, Hank, and we'll be fine. Draw up the papers."

"I have them in my car."

"Get them now. I'm feeling generous."

He rose and left for his car as Natasha and Dolly rushed down the stairs.

"Is that pizza?" Natasha asked. "Oh, I love pepperoni." She picked a piece from the box and took a bite.

The door opened, and Hank strode into the kitchen. "Hey, kiddo." He laid the one-page contract on the table and handed Lucy a pen.

"This is just a lease agreement?" she asked.

"Correct."

"For how long?"

"Another decade. A dollar a year. I can leave it for you to read."

She scribbled her name on the line. "As long as you're straight with me, we're good. And for once I like being a part of something bigger than just slinging drinks."

Silent, he studied her, and for a moment she got lost in those eyes before she handed him the signed document.

"Lucy, draw Hank," Natasha said. "He's pretty good-looking for an old white guy."

Hank cleared his throat. "Not so old."

Natasha giggled. "Ancient."

"I'm game if Lucy is," Hank said.

Drawing could be an intimate exchange. When she drew someone on a Nashville street corner, she was giving them a piece of themselves— a glimpse into who they were at that moment. She'd just done that for Natasha. But to draw Hank, and to allow herself to study his features and his expressions, left her nervous and exposed.

With the two staring, for her to refuse would make something out of what really was nothing.

"Sure. Why not?" Lucy accepted.

She opened the pad and took a long sip of wine. On the Nashville strip she also drew caricatures, and in this moment she needed a laugh.

She drew quickly, sketching out his face and exaggerating his square jaw. She penciled in large, broad shoulders, and in one hand he was holding a bottle of wine, and in the other a strip of caution tape she'd seen him wrap around the well. The waves of the bay swirled in the background, and in the distance sat Winter Cottage. Glancing at Natasha, Lucy drew the girl's youthful face with full expressive eyes and a wide grin. She added curls, and in one hand was a math book and the other a slice of pizza.

Natasha looked at the picture and immediately giggled. "Luceee."

Hank didn't try to look, but he sensed Lucy was lampooning them. "Can't wait to see it."

She turned the sketch around for him to see. "What do you think?"

"I don't have a lantern jaw."

"And did you see me?" Natasha asked.

"I did. But I don't see Lucy. Where are you in the picture?"

"Draw yourself." Natasha pushed the paper back toward Lucy to finish. "You have to be in our picture. And so does Dolly."

"You heard the girl." There was a dare in Hank's tone.

She sketched herself with her crazy, long hair and a Nashville T-shirt, jeans, and cowboy boots. Dolly ended up with a wide grin and a chew stick under her paw. Natasha giggled.

Hank also laughed. It was deep, rich, and warm. "Well done."

"Can I put that up in my room too?" Natasha asked.

"It's Hank's picture," Lucy said.

"It's all yours, kid." He grinned.

Natasha scooped up the picture. "I'll be right back."

"I'll set up another video," Lucy said, grabbing her glass as she walked.

"Don't start without me," the girl shouted as she ran up the stairs with Dolly on her heels.

Hank followed Lucy into the parlor, his footsteps defined with confidence.

She picked the next video in the stack. "I've already watched two." She pulled sheets from more of the furniture and, with his help, set two more chairs by the old VCR and TV. Natasha whirled back into the room within moments and plopped in the chair by Hank.

Lucy hit "Play."

CHAPTER FIFTEEN

Beth

May 22, 1988

Beth sits next to Mrs. B, looks back at the camera, and smiles. "Sunday tea with Mrs. B," she says.

The older woman wears a blue suit trimmed with red brocade and tailored to fit her body perfectly. Her hair is twisted into a bun, and she's wearing panty hose and dark, sensible shoes. "Why do you always wear that broach?" Beth asks.

"It was made for me by a dear friend, and I'm very fond of it."

"What's the design?"

"It's a songbird."

"Who made it?"

She is silent for a moment, and then an old secret rises up, and she says, "Jimmy. He was quite talented."

"That's ivory, right? Scrimshaw?"

"Many a seaman found hobbies to pass the time. For him it was carving ivory."

"When did he give it to you?"

"A story for another day, child. Today I want to tell you about the wedding day."

"For Mrs. Lawrence and Mr. Buchanan."

"Yes."

"Well, I'll get out of the shot." Beth scrambles off camera. "Take it away, Mrs. B."

Claire

January 20, 1916

On the day of the wedding, Claire rose early, still too annoyed and angry with Jimmy and Victoria for their poor choices of the other night. Victoria was a fool. She always would be. But Jimmy—Claire expected he would have had some common sense.

She moved to her window and looked out over the courtyard. There would be no hunting on this wedding day. She was disappointed when she didn't see Jimmy gathering his group of wealthy hunters who so admired him. He was their pied piper, and they loved his tales of adventure.

Wrapping a shawl around her shoulders, she padded down the hallway to her workroom, where Mrs. Lawrence's wedding dress hung on the sewing mannequin. She turned on the overhead electric light, which cast a warm glow over the rich satin.

The finishing work had been done at Winter Cottage in the early-morning hours when the house was quiet. This was the time she did her best work. Now, as she touched each pearl bead, pleat, and strip of ribbon, she recalled each morning when she had risen to just catch a glimpse of Jimmy traipsing off with his merry gang.

Yesterday, when she'd heard the hound dogs barking, she'd risen and watched for him. But this time he had looked up toward her window and their gazes met. Claire didn't step back into the shadows or look away. It was Jimmy who yielded first.

Footsteps creaked in the hallway, and she turned to see Mrs. Lawrence standing in the doorway. Her long, dark hair, streaked with strands of gray, flowed around her shoulders in a dramatic flair befitting of her rumored theater past.

"It's a work of art," Mrs. Lawrence said.

"Thank you."

"I know you put a good bit of yourself into the dress," she said. "No one creates beauty like this without giving of themselves."

"I wanted it to be perfect."

"And it is." Both stood in silence as Mrs. Lawrence traced embroidered songbirds. "Victoria came in late the other night."

Claire didn't respond.

"I've known the girl since she was seven. She's impulsive and selfish. She's lucky you were there to see her upstairs and that her father was too inebriated with spirits to hear her tiptoeing into her room."

Claire kept her gaze on the songbird, wondering why Jimmy had allowed this to happen. Couldn't he have been the one man to resist Victoria?

Mrs. Lawrence smiled and pushed a stray red curl from Claire's face. "Men can be quite helpless around her. She knows it and uses it well." She fingered a delicate pearl sewn into the waistband. "I'd also not judge any good man for a foolish mistake."

"No, ma'am."

Mrs. Lawrence stepped back from the dress. "Today has finally arrived."

"Yes, and it will be beautiful."

"Mr. Buchanan would not have wanted it any other way." She squeezed Claire's hand with the warmth of a kindred spirit. "I've not eaten in weeks in preparation for this day. I do hope Mrs. Latimer has prepared ham with her biscuits this morning. Now eat up and let us get this day started."

———— ♧∽♧ ————

The day was perfect. The sun was warm, the sky was a crystal blue, and there was not one cloud in the sky. A flock of geese flew overhead, honking a most perfect salute to the couple who loved the outdoors.

Claire was with Mrs. Lawrence in the back of the small stone chapel in town, fluffing the ivory silk. The pearls caught the morning light and glimmered like the waters of the bay.

Mrs. Lawrence was radiant and glowing in a dress that hugged her curves in such a way that erased decades and transformed her into a blushing bride.

Claire wore a green velvet dress, originally made for a woman in Newport who had changed her mind at the last moment. The seam-stress in the shop had traded the dress for Claire's help in a month of Sunday-afternoon sewing sessions. She'd been saving the dress for this day, wanting to make an excellent impression.

In the rich folds of an elegant dress, she wasn't the lost little girl who'd been abandoned by this town. When she was dressed in her best, she was a worldly woman of substance and daring who could rise to any heights. She also hoped Jimmy Latimer would see her and dream of her for the next thousand nights.

Claire was the last to take her seat in the back row beside Mrs. Latimer, who wore her gray wool Sunday dress. Claire had cro-cheted a strand of lace and sewn it on her collar as a surprise. The older woman had fussed, said she didn't need anything so fine, but she stood just a bit straighter.

Victoria and Robert sat in the front row. Victoria was dressed in a rich ice-blue velvet dress that fitted her trim waist. Brocade on the hem and cuffs added sparkle and set off her blonde hair and pale porcelain skin to perfection. Robert's suit, like his father's, was made of black broadcloth, and the frock coat, trimmed with satin lapels, pinched in a little at the waist. A freshly starched collar sat high, and his trousers were slender and sharply pressed.

When the ceremony ended and Mr. Buchanan kissed his new bride, Claire ducked out to signal the five horse-drawn carriages that awaited the wedding party. Jimmy stood by the last carriage, arms folded, a cigarette in his mouth. When he saw her, he dropped the smoke in the dirt and ground it out.

Since the night Victoria had appeared at the kitchen door, disheveled and with no sensible explanation for her whereabouts, he'd kept himself busy either at the lighthouse or with the early-morning hunters.

Applause pulled Claire back, and as the new Mr. and Mrs. Buchanan emerged and took their posts by the bottom step, Claire arranged the new bride's tulle veil in a gentle waterfall behind her. The guests greeted husband and wife and then formed double lines. As the new couple moved through the cheering gauntlet, a flurry of rose petals fluttered around them.

Claire watched as Victoria walked past without so much as a nod and settled into the second carriage with her brother. Robert kept his gaze ahead, silent, almost brooding.

Claire approached the last carriage and paused by Jimmy. In a low voice, she said, "Victoria leaves a wake of sad, longing faces behind her. She's claimed more men's souls than I can count."

Jimmy looked at her, his expression more quizzical than dark. "She's not claimed me." He set the step stool down in front of the driver's seat. "I've got you in the front seat. There's no room in the back."

If he thought he was forgiven, he was wrong. "What about your mother?"

"She prefers the carriage's interior." He pulled off his gloves and offered his hand to Claire.

Claire refused his hand and climbed into the seat, taking care to arrange her skirts. Jimmy strode to the back and helped the others into their seats.

The carriage dipped as he climbed up on his side and took the reins. With a snap of his wrists, the horses began to move.

"You look nice," he said.

Heat rose in her cheeks, and she was annoyed with herself for being so affected by a few sweet words from him.

"Is that a blush, Miss Claire?" His was the devil's grin, and it had the power to make her knees weak.

"I'm pleased that you noticed how well I sew."

"I suppose the stitching is all fine, but not a man here today was thinking about needle and thread. They were noticing how the dress looks on you."

"I don't want your flattery, James Latimer."

The carriage wheels rolled through the sandy soil. "Then will you accept my apology?"

When she looked up, the too-confident grin was gone, and his blue eyes telegraphed longing. "I want us to be friends, Claire, now more than ever."

"Why now?"

"Because I've received orders for a new ship. I'm to be a captain this time. When I got the word, I thought of telling you first."

Knowing he was leaving softened all the anger she was desperately trying to cling to. "You've sailed before."

"The war in Europe is going poorly, and it's just a matter of time before America is drawn in."

"But you're safe. You're a merchant marine. You're not a combatant."

"The U-boats don't agree. They're sinking ships all along the English coast. Their plan is to starve Europe of naval supplies." He gripped the reins, and she sensed that nervous energy bubbled in him as it did in the younger male servants when the topic of the war came up at the dinner table.

"When do you leave?"

"A week." He glanced toward her, his eyes bright. "I don't want there to be anything bad between us."

"Why can't you just stay here?"

"And continue to lead the old men on their hunting expeditions?" he asked harshly. "My time here has always been considered temporary as I waited for my next ship."

"You could make a fine life here. You've done enough, and everyone here doesn't want to see any harm come to you."

His jaw set into a grim line. "I want more, just as you do."

Suddenly, she blamed Victoria for all this. She fancied he'd have stayed longer if not for that spoiled woman who had dallied, grown bored, and put him back on the shelf like last season's frock.

An azure sky drifted past them as they made their way down the dirt road toward Winter Cottage. She couldn't keep the bitterness from her low voice. "She's not worth this. She's not worth what that war will do to you."

He wrapped the reins around his hands. "This has nothing to do with her."

"Have you told your mother?"

"No. You're the first, and now that I'm looking at your sour face, I'm sorry I did."

Sadness tightened her chest, and she was forced to sit in silence for several minutes before she could bring herself to say, "I don't have a sour face."

"You look like you've bitten a lemon."

Claire studied his proud, angled face, and she wanted to cup it in her hands and kiss him. She wanted to order him to stay here, where it was safe and far away from the madness of Europe.

She didn't say any of that but huddled behind the silence that lingered between them.

They rode the rest of the way back to Winter Cottage and pulled up behind the other carriages. Mrs. Latimer and a kitchen girl got out of the carriage, but Claire couldn't bring herself to leave. Time with Jimmy had always been precious, and now it may be over.

She stared ahead, her hands gripping the purse she'd proudly chosen to match her dress. She twisted toward him, and he turned. Suddenly, she sensed an understanding between them that hadn't existed. She didn't care that he'd chosen Victoria over her before. All that she knew was that if she was going to kiss him, it had to be now. People would see, of course, but she would manage the whispers and gossips. *"Who dares, wins."*

His seat creaked as he turned to her. "Can you do me a favor?"

"Of course." She moistened her lips.

He watched the crowd of guests and servants vanish into the house. "Can you get a message to Miss Victoria?"

Her heart seized and she froze. "What?"

She didn't want to talk about his affection for another woman. She wanted him to see her and everything she'd done today expressly for him. She swallowed the lump in her throat. "What do you want me to say?"

"Tell her I'll marry her, if she'll have me."

"Shouldn't you ask her this question directly?"

"I've tried to get her alone the last couple of days, but she's avoided me."

"She won't marry you," Claire said.

"The offer needs to be made."

Victoria wouldn't accept his offer of marriage because she was destined to marry money, and candidly, Jimmy was beneath her. She wanted the big church wedding that would be the society event of the year. She'd never be satisfied with a small country affair, holding a handful of winter flowers days before her sea captain husband left for his next voyage.

"I'll talk to her tonight."

As much as she wanted to stomp off, she didn't. "Take care of yourself, James Latimer. Don't take any foolish chances."

———— ❧ ————

When Claire entered the room, Victoria sat at her dressing table, looking into the mirror as she brushed her hair with a silver brush that had been her mother's. Without the hints of rouge and lipstick, Victoria looked pale.

"I believe you have made your name today in the world of fashion. Everyone was talking about the dress you made for my stepmother," Victoria said.

Claire closed the door behind her. She had several cards from ladies wanting to discuss a position in their home.

Victoria twisted in her seat and faced her. "I'm glad for you. You work hard, and it's wonderful that you'll be acknowledged."

Claire approached. "I spoke to Jimmy today."

Victoria's brow knotted, but she didn't say a word.

"He'll marry you."

She started to brush her hair again in long, steady strokes. "He's being foolish, of course. You know that."

"Do I?"

A delicate brow arched. "Claire, tell me you're not buying into this Romeo-and-Juliet fantasy. I could never marry Jimmy. He's being honorable, but I must be practical for the both of us."

"What if there's a baby?" Claire whispered.

Pure laughter bubbled from her. "Don't be so dramatic. That would not happen to me."

"Because you wish it to be so doesn't mean that it will be."

Victoria turned back toward the mirror. "You're worrying over nothing."

"And if I'm right? He'll be off to sea and you'll be alone. The war will ensure there are no trips abroad."

She looked up beyond her reflection to Claire. "You're jealous because it's not you. You want his baby in your belly and his ring on your finger."

"I do. I see no shame in admitting it."

"And have you told him?"

Claire was suddenly angry, not at Victoria or Jimmy but at herself. She'd had moments she could have shared her feelings, but she'd been afraid to breach the silence and find rejection or, worse, his pity.

"If you want him, you better find the courage," Victoria said.

"He doesn't want me."

"Do you know that for certain?"

"No."

"Then I suggest you find him. As you said, he might not return."

Claire's anger nearly drove her mad over the next few days. She lost count of the number of times she walked toward the boathouse to see Jimmy and then lost her nerve.

Claire heard her father had returned from his short voyage along the coast and would be in town for the next two days. She could easily have avoided him, but as she walked up to the Jessups' for supper, carrying belated Christmas gifts for her brothers and the Jessups, she detoured. She wanted to see the cottage that she'd lived in for the first twelve years of her life. The home her whole family had shared before everything had unraveled.

She gripped her small satchel of wrapped gifts. Her fingers ached as she walked along the sandy road. When the time came to turn onto the path toward her father's cottage, she hesitated as her bravery waned. Drawing in a breath, she pressed on until she saw what remained of the Hedrick family home.

The white paint had faded, and the red tin roof had rusted in the salt air. The gardens her mother had planted and cared for had long since succumbed to weeds. The yard was filled with scrap wood, an overturned boat, buoys, crab pots, and all kinds of clutter men liked to save. There were no lights on in the house, and the scent of bread baking was now just a distant memory.

Claire knocked on the front door and waited. When she didn't hear a sound, she twisted the knob and opened the door. The house was dark and smelled of mold and musk. "Father?"

The silence enveloped her, making her feel less welcome. She stepped softly through the house, touching the wingback chair where her mother had sat and shown her the magic of needle and thread. She closed her eyes and could almost hear her laughter.

Clenching her hands, she crossed into the kitchen, expecting the warmth she'd remembered but finding a cold cast-iron stove, dust on the floor, and the wooden family dining table now covered in ropes and pulleys. The only hint of life was an unwashed cup and bowl in the sink.

Through the back window, she spotted her father standing on the dock that stretched fifty feet out into the bay.

He was wrapping a rope around his arm, just as he had done a million times when she was a child. His broad shoulders stooped slightly, and the hair that peeked out from the knit hat was no longer a blend of salt and pepper but stark white.

There was a part of her that felt pity for him. He'd been dealt a harsh blow when her mother died and he was faced with raising seven children with a merchant marine's job waiting. He'd had only difficult options before him.

But another part of her embraced the hard kernels of anger that had not softened over the years. He should have been more careful with her mother. He should have known childbirth was a dangerous undertaking for her when she'd almost died after her fourth birth. But he'd wanted a son. And when she finally gave him a son, he'd wanted another and then another. And she'd obliged until her body simply failed.

The wind blew off the sound, billowing his jacket. He would be gone again tomorrow. She drew in a breath. "Father."

Gnarled fingers stopped winding the rope. He didn't turn right away.

"Father," she repeated.

This time he did straighten his body and turn. His face was thinner and more weathered than she remembered. A scar on his chin peeked through the thick gray stubble.

Gray eyes narrowed.

Did he know which of his daughters had returned? He'd farmed out his boys to the Jessups but had banished all four of his daughters.

"It's Claire," she said.

"Aye, I know who you are."

"I wasn't sure you'd recognize me."

"You look as angry as you did the day you left." He dropped his head and, reaching for a rag in his pocket, wiped the dirt from his hands.

She had been angry. She was still. But she refused to allow that emotion to dictate what she said now. "I brought you a gift for the holidays. I know they've passed, but this might be our only chance." She stepped toward him and handed him a scarf she'd made and wrapped in blue tissue paper. "It's not much."

"I don't have anything for you."

"It doesn't matter."

He studied the wrapped package in her hand for so long she thought he didn't want it. Finally, he accepted it, and tore open the blue paper, exposing a green scarf knitted from thick wool.

"My stitching is better now," she said. "I made that for you shortly after I left. I thought we'd be home for Christmas and I could give it to you." Her voice dropped. "I suppose I'm as stubborn as you. I was determined to give it to you."

With a trembling hand, he traced some of the knots. "Why did you make this for me?"

"Mom always made you scarves." She'd worked hard on knitting and had always been proud of the work.

He fingered the green wool threads. "Come inside the house."

She followed him to the kitchen, this time not as jarred by the changes in her family home.

"It's not what it was," he said, reading her mind.

"How could it be?"

He grunted and then vanished into the living area. She didn't follow, not wanting to see any more evidence that the life she'd once loved was truly forever gone. Sadly, these images would be the ones that would linger.

He returned holding a small ivory box that fit into the palm of his hand. It was made of whalebone, and its lid was covered in delicate triangular etchings. A small gold lock fastened in the front.

"It belonged to your mother," he said. "Or it would have. She died before I could give it to her."

She stilled, not trusting herself to speak. For so long she'd felt abandoned, alone, and lost.

"When we sailed to New England, there were always whalers in the pubs. I crossed paths with one each year, and he was always on hard times. I'd buy him a few beers, and he'd give me a bit of his handiwork."

She accepted it from him and carefully opened it. Inside was a compass, only it was no simple tool. The tiniest of etchings created intricate patterns that not only marked north, east, south, and west but also displayed very precise degrees between each of the major points. In the center was the image of a snow goose.

"He made one for each of you girls. Each of the boys got knives. I gave the other children theirs, but you wouldn't have anything to do with me after your mother died. You slapped my hand away when I offered it as you were leaving."

She remembered feeling so lost and afraid. She'd wanted nothing from him in that moment. It had been easier to be angry than acknowledge the pain she'd felt over losing her mother and family. A year later when the agony of loss had faded to a dull ache, she could admit she missed him and this town. She'd asked him in her first letters why he'd never sent for her, but of course he'd never answered any of the letters. "Why didn't you ever send for me?"

He lowered his head and cleared his throat. "I went to sea right away. I've not been back much since."

"We needed you."

He shoved his hands in his pockets. "You were best to live somewhere else. There was no life for you here without your mother. I wasn't enough."

"You were."

"What kind of life would you have had, raising your six brothers and sisters and working yourself to the bone? You'd have been an old woman by the time you were eighteen. But now look at you. You look so fancy. The Buchanans have been good to you?"

"Yes, they have, Father."

"I knew they would be." He shook his head. "I almost didn't recognize you when I first turned."

She closed the box. "I'm going to the Jessups' for a late Christmas lunch. Come with me. We'll see the boys together."

He shook his head. "No, Claire. There's no place for me at that table."

"If there's a place for me, then there's one for you."

His face hardened. "No. But you go. Make sure the boys are minding Sally. Her baby is due any day."

179

Tears clogged her throat, and before she thought twice, she closed the distance between them and kissed him on the cheek. "Happy Christmas, Father."

He sniffed and coughed. "You best get going. Don't want to keep them waiting."

As she left, she sensed this would be the last time she'd see her father—standing on the front stoop of their old home, clutching the scarf.

It was another mile of walking to the Jessup family's farm. The winter winds quickly overtook what heat the sun provided. The cold sliced through the layers of her jacket, forcing her to burrow deeply as she made her way along the graveled road. Shoes designed more for style than function pinched her toes. Her cheeks were chapped from the wind, and she sniffled constantly to control a runny nose.

The Jessups lived in a small house on the ocean side of the shore. They weren't wealthy by the Buchanans' standards but had done well enough, making their money fishing and selling Chesapeake Bay duck to the restaurants in Norfolk.

She knocked on the front door and heard a peal of laughter and the clamoring of young feet. The last time she'd been home, the youngest of her brothers, Michael, had been four years old, Joseph five, and Stanley six. Claire should have come to see them right after her return but had been good at finding excuses not to see the children her father had struggled to keep close to him. She wasn't proud about this and pushed the thought out of her mind.

The door opened to Sally Jessup. Her belly had grown rounder since the dance, and her face radiated. "Claire, you have arrived! The boys are anxious to see you."

A loud thud echoed from somewhere in the house. A dog barked but sounded more excited than menacing.

"It sounds like they're full of energy." Smiling, she stepped inside, savoring the warmth and the scents of spices, yeast dough, and roasting meat.

"It's a regular day by most standards. Let me take your coat."

Claire shrugged off the coat and allowed Sally to take it. "Thank you for having me."

"Of course. We're family."

The house had low ceilings and whitewashed walls. The furniture wasn't ornate but practical, each piece having multiple functions. In the main room, she found her three brothers in a tangle on the floor in front of the hearth filled with a crackling fire.

In another corner was a handmade crib fitted with fresh linens. Claire's father had made that crib for her, and he'd carried it to the Jessups' house the day he'd brought his boys here. She'd been carrying Michael in her arms, and Joseph and Stanley had clung to her skirts. All three boys had been crying when she and her father had left. He'd taken her straightaway to the train station and told her he had made arrangements for her to live with the Buchanan family. He'd left her at the station and never once looked back.

"Boys, get up." Sally unfurled the knot of legs and arms and saw to it each boy was standing like a proper young man. "Claire, may I present my boys and your brothers." She laid her hand on the shortest boy first. Michael was gangly at fifteen. He had red hair like their mother and a splay of freckles that made him look more imp than human.

"Michael, you have grown."

He tugged at his shirt and pressed his head higher. "Thank you."

Sally then placed her hands on the shoulders of a dark-haired boy who had a long, lean face so much like their father's people. "This is Joseph."

"Hello, Joseph."

"And finally," Sally said, "the oldest of these ruffians is Stanley. Seventeen and now preparing for his first sea voyage."

"I'll be sailing with Jimmy," Stanley said with pride. "He's to be our captain."

"Yes, he told me," Claire said. She wanted to grab them all and sail back into the past. She wanted her mother to be alive and for her real family to be together again.

Sally squeezed her hand. "It's hard to let them grow up, but we must."

Claire stared at the faces of her brothers, each she'd helped deliver, and now found strangers looking back. Sally had done her best to write, but letters were a pale substitute for seeing first steps, baby teeth lost, or sailing lessons mastered.

"You'll all have to give me a minute, boys." Unwelcome emotion tightened her throat. "It's hard to reconcile the three young babies I remember with these strapping young men."

The boys regarded Claire with a mixture of curiosity and some trepidation. To the youngest two, she was not just a visitor but a potential threat to the only family they had known. "Where are our sisters?" Michael asked.

Like her, they'd been sent away. "Jemma, Sarah, and Diane are still working in different cities. I've seen them from time to time. They're doing well."

"When are they coming back?" Stanley asked.

At least the sisters had some memories and a photograph to memorialize their mother. The boys had only Claire and the stories she could tell. "I don't know," she said. "I hope soon. It would be nice if all the Hedrick children could be together again sometime."

Joseph frowned. "We are Jessups."

Claire could have argued bloodlines and finer legal details, but as she stared at Joseph's furrowed brow, so reminiscent of their mother's, she chose not to spoil this rare visit with an argument impossible to win. "I didn't mean to imply—"

"Of course you didn't," Sally said. "The boys know they were brought to me, but they're mine."

Their real mother had clutched her oldest two boys to her breast after they'd been born and wept tears of joy. Claire had bottle-fed Michael herself, rocking him to sleep each night while the other two slept on a bed beside her. "I know Christmas Day has passed, but I have brought you presents as well as gifts for Sally and Eric. Would you like to see them?"

"When Pa gets back from the dock. He's checking on his boat," Joseph said.

"We always wait for Pa to return," Michael said.

"Then we shall wait," Claire said. "Who would like to take these from me?"

None of the boys rushed forward. Finally, Joseph nudged Stanley, who stepped toward her.

As she handed Stanley the presents, she wanted him to remember her and to wrap his arms around her. She wanted him to see how much she loved him. She wasn't a stranger. She was his sister.

Stanley took the gifts and handed them to Joseph, who was still boy enough to give in to curiosity and search for the package with his name. Under the watchful eye of Sally, the gifts were set on the corner table.

The front door opened, carrying a bluster of wind and cold, and in stepped Eric Jessup. Claire smiled and took a step toward him, when suddenly Jimmy stepped over the threshold behind him. He pulled off his knit cap.

"Look who I found wandering around the docks," Eric said. "He said he expected to spend his last night in town packing, but I said that wouldn't happen."

Sally laughed, waddling toward Jimmy and giving him a big hug. "Welcome. I knew if I sent Eric out searching, it wouldn't be too hard to find you."

His arms came easily around her. "I don't want to impose."

"Ah! There's no such thing in the Jessup house. Everyone is welcome."

The boys didn't need prompting to greet Jimmy. They rushed up to him, battering into him like buoys in a storm. Laughter rumbled in his chest as he captured Michael and Joseph in headlocks. Both boys whooped and hollered, but Jimmy held firm until he heard from both, "Uncle!"

As he released the boys and straightened, his gaze settled on Claire. "Claire," Jimmy said. "I didn't know you would be here."

"Sally invited me. No better place to be on a chilly January day than with my brothers."

Michael tried to grab Jimmy's lapel in a surprise attack, but he easily held the boy at bay. "I came by Winter Cottage last night. Mother fed me, but I didn't see you."

"I retired early."

"Boys!" Eric said. "Come and help me get a few more logs for the fire." Instead of waiting for an answer, he grabbed Joseph and Michael by the collars. Stanley had sense enough to follow.

Sally followed her men toward the kitchen. "We'll be eating in fifteen minutes."

"Can I help you?" Claire asked.

"No, you may not. I expect you two to warm yourselves by the fire and enjoy the company of one another."

When Sally vanished around the corner, Claire heard herself blurting out, "I told her. I spoke to Victoria."

Jimmy squared his shoulders and lifted his chin, ready to accept his fate. "And?"

"She wishes you well, but she declines your offer."

Jimmy moved closer to the fire. The light from the flames added shadow and depth to the lean lines of his face, making him look more attractive than she'd ever seen him. "I thought as much."

"I'm sorry."

"Nothing to be sorry about. It's over and done." He held his long fingers out in front of the blaze, warming them. He was too proud to complain. "It's for the best."

"Are you disappointed?"

"No. Relieved."

Claire studied his angled features, watched as they slackened a notch, and recognized the truth behind the words. A smile flickered on her lips. She reached out and took his hand, wanting to wrap her arms around him.

"Supper!" Sally shouted from the other room.

She began to pull her hand free, but he held tight for a beat or two and then released it. They walked side by side into the dining room and took their places at the long, rectangular table.

Sally had prepared a feast that consisted of three roasted ducks, fried oysters, cornbread, stewed tomatoes, and mashed potatoes. On the sideboard, there were an apple and a pumpkin pie.

"You have outdone yourself, Sally," Claire said.

"Not the fancy fare of Winter Cottage," she said as Eric helped her into her seat at the end of the table.

"I believe you could challenge Mrs. Latimer, though I will deny it if you tell her so."

"I won't be the one to tell Ma she might have to crown a new contender," Jimmy said.

That jostled nervous smiles from the boys, who relaxed a bit. As the meal progressed, the boys warmed up to Claire, and their laughter returned. She enjoyed the duck and even found it in her to tease Jimmy about the first time he drove the motorcar. He accepted her ribbing with an easy nature, and by the end of the meal, she felt at home on the shore for the first time in a long time.

After both pies had been devoured, they moved back to the parlor, where the boys opened their gifts. She'd made shirts for each and was pleased she'd guessed their sizes correctly. There was a lace collar for

Sally and a scarf for Eric. She'd even fashioned a christening gown for the baby.

When it was time to leave, Jimmy and Claire refused Eric's offer of a carriage ride, and they set out on the road back toward Winter Cottage. The air was brisk, and a full moon was rising.

Now that they were alone, all the things she wanted to say were swallowed by fresh nerves and fears. Words failed her. As they walked in silence, she grew more frustrated for anything to say that might break the damnable silence.

"Where will your ship be sailing?" she finally asked.

"The Caribbean and then on to England. We'll be carrying oil."

"Isn't that dangerous?"

"Ah, it sounds worse than it is. Not so different than steaming up the coast to Boston."

"It's very different. There's a lot that can go afoul on the open water."

"And there's a lot that can go right." Moonlight caught the glint of his even white teeth as he grinned. "Are you worried about me, Claire?"

"Yes."

"I'm glad to hear it. I was afraid I'd ruined things between us."

"There's never been an understanding between us," she said. "But I was hurt you initially picked her over me."

"I didn't realize you were interested."

The words raced to the front of her brain, and before she could censor them, she said, "I've been interested in you since the day you fished me out of the water."

Silently, he studied her.

Without much thought, she reached out and took his hand in hers. All these weeks, these years of wondering what it would be like to kiss him had built up to this moment. She should have been nervous because that was what she did. But she didn't give a thought to right or wrong.

His fingers felt cold as she intertwined hers. He looked down, but he didn't pull away. Buoyed by the small victory, she turned and kissed him on the lips. He stood stiff, but when her lips lingered, he wrapped his other hand around her waist and pressed into her kiss.

He kept Claire's hand, and they walked back toward the boathouse. He was leaving tomorrow, and she wanted him more than ever before. She stopped as they approached, knowing Jimmy's room was on the second floor.

Again he studied her, a muscle pulsing in his jaw. "Are you sure? Neither one of us can blame this on gin."

"I'm sure."

He pulled her inside the door and up the narrow staircase that led to the second floor. Moonlight streamed into the narrow room onto his neatly made cot. To the right was his fully packed seaman's bag.

She tugged off her gloves and removed her hat, setting both on a writing table. She draped her coat over the desk chair and then unfastened the front buttons of her bodice. He stepped toward her but didn't touch. She could hear his breathing made ragged by desire. She brought his hand up to her breast. His hooded gaze dropped to the creamy mounds, and he kissed each one.

For the next couple of hours, she found the boldness that had eluded her for so long. She stripped before him. Kissed him. And when he moved inside her, she boldly called out his name with breathless wanting. She didn't think about tomorrow. Just this one perfect moment.

The town of Cape Hudson took care of its own. Whether it was a cleanup after a storm, a family on hard times, or a secret in need of keeping, the town closed ranks when the times required it.

That summer, the mood in town was shifting. Europe was at war, and though America had not entered the war, many of the town's young men in the merchant marines had followed Jimmy, ready to brave the Atlantic's increasingly dangerous waters.

The town would weather a hurricane in late September that would ravage the boats and homes on the bay and strip the fields bare. Days later, the town would also circle around an infant boy who came to be known as Samuel. This new baby would join the Jessups' Christmas table, and he would grow up to be a seaman like Eric, the man whom everyone in town considered his father.

Only two people truly knew Samuel's rightful heritage. One of those people was Claire, and she'd sworn never to tell.

CHAPTER SIXTEEN

Lucy

January 17, 2018

In the predawn hours, Lucy lay in her bed, eyes closed, and rolled onto her side in a tight ball under the covers. The air was cold and the bed warm, and she was certain she imagined the sound of Nashville's traffic on the street outside her apartment window, the strumming of a guitar, and the smell of eggs and bacon drifting in from a neighbor's apartment. She heard breathing and imagined Raven lying beside her. It was a peaceful, quiet moment that was so sweet and perfect she wanted to hang on to it.

The breathing grew louder into whimpers and snorts, and the thump, thump of a dog's tail forced her to crack open an eyelid. Reluctantly, she twisted her head to find Dolly staring at her.

"Dolly," she muttered.

The dog sat up, barked. Time to go out.

She picked her phone up off the nightstand and checked the time—5:50 a.m. "No. Not doing it. Too early." The dog nudged her. "I took you out just before bedtime."

Dolly licked her face, forcing her to relent. "Give me a second. I just want to lie here a minute longer."

Dolly woofed.

"Please." She'd been reduced to bargaining with a dog.

Dolly nudged her with her nose, forcing her to sit up and swing her legs over the side of the bed. With a longing glance back at her bed, Lucy disappeared into the bathroom. Minutes later when she emerged, she was dressed and had her hair pulled back into a ponytail.

"Come on, let's get you outside."

Out in the hallway, she glanced into the blue room and saw the girl curled on her side. In a matter of days, she'd gone from being strings-free to being responsible for a dog, a house, and now a kid. That Nashville apartment life she'd dreamed of was so far away it might as well have been on the moon.

She and Dolly were halfway down the steps when she heard Natasha cry out. "Lucy!"

Lucy paused on the step. "I'm here. Just letting Dolly out."

The girl rushed out of her bedroom wearing sweatpants and a Donald Duck T-shirt. Her hair was a wild spray of black curls framing a face tight with panic. "I thought you were leaving."

"Nope. Dolly just needs to pee, and I need coffee." The grandfather clock in the hallway chimed six times. "Get showered and dressed, and I'll make us some breakfast. I promised Hank I'd get you to school by seven thirty."

Natasha rubbed her eyes and yawned. "I want to see the bones."

Bones. Right. Tack that onto her list of newfound issues. And don't forget Natasha's crazed father, Brian. "School first. Besides, it'll take all day for them to make any headway."

"I don't like school."

Lucy started down the stairs. "Don't want to hear it, kid. Not before coffee."

She left the girl staring at her as she let Dolly out into the brisk, cold morning air. The sun wouldn't rise for nearly an hour, but the morning sky was bursting with countless stars. Light from Nashville always overshadowed the night, and she rarely got the full effect of the stars and moon. As Dolly sniffed and ran around, she couldn't help but be in awe of the beauty both around her and overhead.

The dog hustled back into the house, and she locked the door behind her. There'd been no calls from Brian Willard, but better safe than sorry.

Fifteen minutes later, Dolly had gobbled her food while Lucy sipped her first cup of coffee and greeted Natasha as she trudged into the room and sat on the barstool by the center island. Her hair was still a wild spray of curls in serious need of taming. "Coffee?"

"With a lot of milk and sugar."

"Coming up."

She poured a cup half-full of coffee, then topped it off with milk and a couple of teaspoons of sugar. She grabbed a paper napkin, set it in front of Natasha, and placed the cup on it. The kid still looked wild-eyed and worried.

"So do you come here often?" Lucy teased.

Natasha looked up over her coffee cup, rolling her eyes. "This isn't a bar." Sauciness chased some of her fear away. Better.

"So you don't want me to take your breakfast order?"

"People don't eat in bars."

"Sure they do. But I don't have nachos or burgers right now. How about eggs and toast?"

A smile teased the edge of her lips. "Okay."

"Okay, what?"

"Thank you."

She selected a country-western tune on her phone, and while it played, she rummaged for pans and all the fixings.

"Do you always listen to country-western music?" Natasha asked.

"Always."

"I'm not crazy about it."

"And I suppose you like all that techno stuff that isn't even real music."

"It's real."

A cast-iron skillet heated on the stove as she broke eggs into a bowl. "I like the kind of songs that require a person to play a musical instrument and sing with their own voice."

Natasha slurped her coffee. "Could I get a tattoo like you?" she asked.

The sudden pivot had Lucy retreating. The egg in her hand missed the side of the bowl, and when it cracked, half the shell landed in the mix. "No. You're twelve."

"I don't see why that matters. I'm pretty grown up for my age."

She picked eggshells out of the collection of yolks. "It matters."

"Can I get blue hair like yours?"

"Why do you want blue hair?"

"I hate my hair."

"I like your hair. Women pay top dollar for those curls."

"It's not straight and blonde like yours. It's all curly and kinky."

She pushed a wooden spoon through the cooking eggs and put a couple of slices of bread into a toaster. "After breakfast, I'll fix your hair."

"It's not going to look like yours."

"It's not supposed to. You have your own style, and you rock it." Lucy served up breakfast on plates, grabbed a couple of forks, and set it all on the island. Butter from the fridge and more coffee for both.

She bit into the eggs and was almost tempted to take a selfie to commemorate the fact she was up before sunrise and eating real food. "How did your mom use to do your hair?"

"I don't know." Her frown was sad, not angry. "I should know that."

"It's okay that you don't remember. I'm already having trouble remembering Beth's face and voice."

"You have the tapes."

"True. But that's not the Beth I knew."

The girl pushed her eggs around, and when she tore off a piece of toast, she fed it to Dolly.

Lucy took another swig of coffee and rose. "I'll be right back."

"Where are you going?"

"Trust me." She hurried upstairs and, from her bathroom, grabbed a wide-bristle brush, dry conditioner, and a bag filled with hair fasteners and clips.

When she returned, Natasha had taken a few more bites, and Dolly was conning the kid for another nibble. "Stop feeding the dog."

"But she's hungry."

"She's already been fed this morning. She's running a scam on you and playing you for a sucker." Lucy set her hair supplies on the island. "Finish and I'll begin."

Curiosity pushed aside some of the apathy. "Begin what?"

She shrugged. "Finish."

"Fine." The girl gobbled down several more bites, and when the plate was clear, Lucy picked it up and set it in the sink. "How do you know about my kind of hair?"

"I worked with a few African American gals. I used to listen to them talk about hair. I'm no expert, but I bet I can make something happen."

"Sometimes Mom braided my hair."

"I can't braid, but I have an idea." She moistened a paper towel, wrung out the excess water, and then smoothed the damp towel over the girl's hair, which she realized was more tangled and delicate than she first thought. Next she smoothed the leave-in conditioner on her hair and worked it through.

Natasha sighed and closed her eyes. What was it about getting your hair done that made life seem a little better? Slowly, she worked through the tangles, separating the curls and smoothing them out.

"I haven't had my hair done in a long time," she said. "Brenda didn't have time, and that's not the kind of thing you'd ask Hank."

"No, he doesn't strike me as a hair-and-beauty expert."

Natasha giggled. "Not even close."

"There must be a place around here that does hair."

"There's Christy's across Route 13."

"Okay. I'll see what they have. I could use a trim too." She smoothed more conditioner on the ends and then after drying her hands brushed the front of Natasha's hair flat. Next came the red headband to hold back her hair. The overall effect was pretty cute.

"Go have a look in the mirror upstairs, and don't forget to brush your teeth."

Brown eyes brightened with what felt like real emotion, not the pretend smiles the kid wore as a mask. "Okay!"

She jumped up, and Dolly, without a second glance, followed her up the stairs. Lucy cleaned the kitchen and made a couple of sandwiches for lunch. She tossed in a bag of chips and an apple. By the time Natasha came downstairs, backpack slung over her shoulder, she was smiling.

"You like?" Lucy asked.

"Not bad."

"High praise." She checked the time on her phone. "We have to go."

The drive to school took under fifteen minutes. She pulled up to the bus ramp. "Have a great day."

"New hair, a funeral, and a dead body. This is going to be the best day ever."

"We aim to please."

Natasha kissed Dolly and scrambled out her door. She was halfway out of the Jeep before Lucy realized she'd not taken her lunch. She rolled down the window, called out, and Natasha bounded back and grabbed the bag.

Lucy shifted her Jeep and drove back to Winter Cottage. When she arrived, the sheriff's cruiser was on-site alongside Hank's truck. They'd maneuvered a ladder down into the well, and Hank looked ready to climb down.

She parked behind Hank's truck and, hooking a leash on her collar, pulled Dolly out.

Hank watched the pair approach as he pulled on black latex gloves. "Natasha off to school?"

"The package has been delivered."

"No issues?"

"Smooth sailing." She smiled at Rick. "Morning, Sheriff. Can I get you two coffee?"

"Thanks," Rick said easily. He removed a tarp from the back of his truck and spread it to the right of the well. "Maybe after we see what we've got waiting for us down in the hole."

"Sure."

Rick slipped on a headlamp and clicked it on before climbing over the side of the well onto the ladder.

"Do you all know when the well was first sunk?" Lucy asked.

Hank shook his head. "I went over the papers on file at the clerk's office, and apparently six wells have been sunk on the property in the last hundred years. But it's more likely it predates 1918."

Rick started down the ladder, the light shining off the circular stone sides that extended down fifteen feet. He inched lower and lower until finally he ducked out of sight.

Hank grabbed a digital camera from the front of his vehicle and began taking pictures. Tensing, she inched closer and peered down. Rick's headlamp cast a narrow band of light on the stone walls, the shallow puddle of water in the bottom, and the collection of bones that lay against the north wall.

"Do the bones look human?" Hank asked.

"Hard to tell. And there's a lot of sediment." He fished a camera from his pocket and took pictures of the well and the bones before tucking it away. From another pocket, he removed a plastic evidence bag and began to pick up the bones. He was several inches into the muck when he removed what looked like a human skull.

"That answers one question," Hank said.

"Who do you think it could be?" Lucy asked.

"No idea."

As Rick continued to dig in the muck, Lucy took Dolly inside and put on a fresh pot of coffee. She found a thermos in the pantry, washed it out, and filled it with coffee. Grabbing a couple of mugs, she left Dolly behind with a chew stick and returned to the site as Rick handed the bag of bones to Hank.

"Not exactly CSI," Rick said. "But I think I collected most of them." He hoisted a muddy boot over the side of the well and then the other. He was covered in mud from his midcalf down.

Hank studied the skull. "There's one hell of a crack in the side of the skull. I don't know if it happened in the fall into the well or before."

Rick carried the bag to the tarp and carefully began to arrange the bones he'd collected.

Hank stripped off his latex gloves. "Thanks for the coffee."

Lucy poured him a cup. "Want to take a guess?"

"Nope. Whatever clothes the person was wearing are long gone, and if they were wearing anything metal like a ring or watch, it's either gone or sunk into the muck."

"Never a dull moment around here, is it?" she asked.

Hank sipped his coffee. "Usually, it's not this exciting. You must have brought it with you."

Rick rose and stripped off his gloves before accepting coffee from Lucy. "Not much I can do on my end. I'll bag all this up in evidence bags and drive it down to the state medical examiner's office in Norfolk. They might be able to figure out who our mystery person is."

"Do you have any idea how long the body's been down there?" Lucy asked.

"I'm no expert on bones, but they're pretty brittle," Rick said. "Rough guess, several decades."

"Wow." She looked back at the house. "Mrs. B would have been living here then."

"Well, if she knew, she took this secret to the grave with her," Hank said.

Hank and Rick had left by noon, giving Lucy the afternoon to shower and watch another tape of Mrs. B and Beth. She was growing accustomed to seeing her mother young and excited about life.

She pulled away, not learning much from the tape, and made her way upstairs to finish her hair and makeup. She chose a hunter-green sweater, jeans, and her cowboy boots.

When the front bell rang, it was 3:30 p.m. on the dot, and after a quick glance out the side window, she opened the door to Hank. He was dressed in a dark suit, a white shirt, and a blue tie. His hair looked damp from a shower, and she had to admit that for an uptight guy, he looked pretty sweet.

She allowed Dolly to rush past her, barking and wagging her tail. His gaze swept over her. His frown deepened. "Are you ready?"

"Beth would roll over in her grave if I showed up in a dress and heels."

"So am I overdressed?"

"Is that what you normally wear to a funeral?"

"It is."

"Then you're fine. Beth always insisted people be themselves." For most of the years she'd been with her mother, she'd worried. Would Beth pay the rent? Would she cook dinner? Would she show up at school late? But for all Beth's faults, there was a lot of good. And that's what she wanted to honor today. She deserved it.

197

"The cake is in the kitchen. Let me just run upstairs and get the urn?"

"Sure."

She hustled up the stairs, grabbed the urn off her dresser, and as she hurried down the stairs said, "If you can carry this, I'll get the cake."

He took the urn as she hurried into the kitchen, and she gathered the cake along with a plastic grocery bag she'd filled with paper towels and a handful of plastic spoons. There was also a serving knife made of a lovely silver. Beth would have laughed at the fancy knife, but down deep she'd still have liked the gesture of people gathering. Though Lucy could have invited the townspeople back to the house and made it an even fancier affair, Winter Cottage didn't feel like her home, and it had never been Beth's. Better to just keep the ceremony at the gravesite.

Dolly trotted out beside her toward Hank's car. He was just closing up the tailgate and had opened the door when the dog hopped in without hesitating.

Lucy settled on the front seat and balanced the cake on her lap as she fastened her seat belt. Hank slid behind the wheel, and they were moving.

"Don't be surprised if a few more trickle in. It's a small town, and everyone knows everyone."

She wasn't sure how she felt about dealing with a handful of strangers today. Beth had died less than a month ago, and she'd thought she'd made peace with her passing, but now as she sat there, emotions stirred and groaned.

Natasha was waiting for them in front of the school. She had her backpack slung over her shoulder. There was a mix of hope and trepidation in her smile as she searched the line of waiting cars.

"Be sure to compliment her hair," Lucy said.

Hank studied the girl. "She looks different."

"Don't say *different*. Say *nice*."

"Roger that."

When Natasha spotted Hank's truck, her smile broadened so wide, it fired up emotions in Lucy simmering beneath the surface.

The girl slid into the back seat and rubbed Dolly on the head. "Oh my God, I can't wait to eat the cake. Where are we going to eat it?"

"It's a pretty day, and I packed a blanket. Maybe a picnic near Beth's spot?"

"Seat belt," Hank said. "And I like the hair."

Natasha clicked her belt and absently touched a curl. "Thanks! I've never had a picnic at a graveyard before."

"It would have been right up my mother's alley," Lucy said. "She'd have loved it."

"My mom's service was held at the Baptist church. They were supposed to bury her right after the service, but Dad hadn't paid for anything, and the funeral director wanted his money." She looked out the window, absently rubbing Dolly's chest.

Lucy blinked. "What happened?"

"Funeral home gave us a discount because the embalmer liked my mom, and the church raised the rest. Maybe you could come with me sometime, and I could show you her place."

"I'd like that," Lucy said.

"What's the deal with the bones?" Natasha asked.

"They are human," Hank said.

Natasha's eyes widened. "No way."

"Way," Hank said. "Sheriff took them to Norfolk this afternoon. By the way, Rick says if he can get back in time, he'll stop by the service, but with traffic chances are slim."

"I appreciate the effort," Lucy said, touched.

"Do you really like my hair?" Natasha asked.

"I do," Hank replied.

"Really?"

"Absolutely."

She relaxed back in her seat. "I do too."

Hank drove through town and out to the beach road. Five miles later he turned onto a road flanked with dried cornstalks harvested months ago. Dirt kicked out around the tires, creating a brown plume that followed them toward an open field.

Parked on the field were at least two dozen cars and trucks. "Are we in the right spot?" Lucy asked.

"We are." He parked behind a white SUV marked SHERIFF and shut off the truck.

"All these people knew my mother?" Lucy asked.

"Folks have come to pay their respects. It's a close town."

"I should have baked a bigger cake," she said.

Hank took the cake from her and handed it to Natasha. He retrieved the urn with Beth's ashes. "Do you want to carry these?"

"I suppose." She accepted the urn, hesitating as she stared at the crowd of strangers waiting by the wrought-iron fence.

"Go on," Hank said softly.

She drew in a breath and walked across the grass field as Dolly ran ahead, greeting everyone. To her, they were all old friends.

An older man dressed in a suit similar to Hank's closed the gap between them and was the first to greet her. "Lucy, I'm Noah Garrison. Hank's father. My wife, Nancy, and I came to pay our respects. Sorry we weren't here to greet you, but we've been traveling. We knew your mother in high school."

Lucy remembered her mom talking about Noah on the tape. She'd vowed to get a date with him as soon as he broke up with his girlfriend, which didn't appear to have happened.

Nancy stepped forward, placing a gentle hand on Lucy's arm. "Your mama and I were cheerleaders together. My word, you look just like her."

"She never talked about this place," Lucy said.

Nancy squeezed Lucy's arm. "It's all right. None of that matters now. Come on inside the fence."

Several others greeted her, including Faye Reynolds, who stood by a folding table covered in white linen and filled with an array of covered-dish meals.

"Natasha," Mrs. Reynolds said. "Go on and put that cake on the dessert side of the table."

"Did you make all this?" Lucy asked.

"I made my sweet-potato casserole, but we all brought a dish," Mrs. Reynolds said. "The Beth I knew would have wanted her last gathering to be a celebration."

Why had Beth run from this town and these people who cared enough after a thirty-year absence to gather and celebrate her life? Lucy hesitated a moment before she trusted her voice not to break. "Thank you."

Lucy stepped inside the fence, noticing the collection of stones marking the lives of the Jessup family. These were her mother's people, her people. There were graves for Sally and Eric and the five boys: Stanley, Joseph, Michael, Aaron, and Samuel—who she knew now was her grandfather. Beside Samuel was the spot for his wife, Donna, and next to her was the grave for Beth. There were other graves, names she didn't recognize, but her attention was pulled toward the newest grave. The headstone read, SCOTT JESSUP, UNITED STATES MARINE CORPS, 1989–2017. On top of the stone were two overturned shot glasses.

"So do you want to say any words?" Hank asked.

Lucy tore her gaze away from the stone. "Beth wasn't big on ceremony, but I can say a word or two."

As everyone gathered around and grew silent, she gripped the urn as a flood of emotions washed over her. She choked back tears, but several still spilled down her cheeks as she knelt in front of the hole. She set the urn in the ground.

"You're home, Mama," she said. "Here's hoping you find the peace you never knew. Here's hoping your folks are waiting for you and whatever drove you away is long forgotten and you can forgive each other."

She gathered a clump of the damp, sandy soil and clutched it in her fingers. "Bye, Mama." She tossed the dirt onto the urn, rose, and stepped back.

Hank came up beside her. "There are a few folks here who would like to say a word about your mother. Do you mind?"

"No. I'd welcome it."

Noah Garrison was the first to speak. "It's been thirty years since I've seen Beth Jessup, but right now as I look at her daughter, I feel like the last three decades vanished in a blink. The last best memory I have of her is about a month before graduation. A few of us were leaving for the beach, but she was staying behind. Beth said she was working on a secret project and couldn't be pulled away. She gave me a big hug and asked me to bring back the biggest seashell I could find." He drew in a breath and released it slowly as he reached in his coat pocket and pulled out a conch shell. It was bleached white with MYRTLE BEACH painted on the side. "I couldn't believe she took off without a word. I couldn't find the actual shell I brought back, but I found this one at home." He walked up to the grave and laid it inside. "I always tell my kids to keep their word. I promised her a shell."

He stepped back next to his wife and threaded his fingers between hers. Next to speak was Mrs. Reynolds. She adjusted her glasses and cleared her throat. "Beth was one of my best students. I knew she had so much potential, and I wanted her to realize that potential. She was troubled, but I thought if I prodded her and raised her expectations, she would realize she could be so much more." Mrs. Reynolds held up a folded yellow piece of paper. "She left before I could issue the last report card. I told her she could get straight As if she applied herself." She shook her head. "All As and an incomplete. I think she purposefully didn't turn in that last project just to prove me wrong." She laid the card in the grave next to the shell.

The last to speak was Arlene. She'd changed out of her waitress uniform and let down her red hair. With a shrug of her shoulders, she said, "Beth would have had a fit if she saw all the grim faces. She'd have told you to lighten up." Arlene fished her phone out of her pocket. She pressed the screen and "Don't Worry, Be Happy" started to play.

Natasha came up beside Lucy and slipped her hand into hers.

This quirky kind of gathering suited Beth perfectly. When the song ended, Lucy wiped away tears as a laugh stuttered over her lips. She squeezed Natasha's hand.

Megan had arrived, and she stood outside the wrought-iron fence. She raised a hand when her gaze met Lucy's.

"This is supposed to be a celebration. So please start eating." A rumble of laughter came over the crowd.

The sound of screeching wheels rumbling up the road had everyone turning to see a beat-up red pickup. A disheveled man wearing faded, torn jeans and a scuffed leather jacket got out of the truck, swigged the last of his beer, and tossed the can in the front seat. He ran stout fingers through his shoulder-length hair and shouted, "Am I late?"

Natasha groaned and shrank closer to Lucy. "Oh God, it's Dad."

Hank and his father cut away from the crowd and moved toward Brian Willard, stopping him a few feet from the entrance to the cemetery.

Hank said something to Willard, but his voice was low and didn't carry far. Willard frowned, and when Noah reached for his arm, he tugged it away.

"What? I'm here to pay my respects. I knew Beth better than any of you dumbasses," Willard shouted.

He looked past Hank and Noah to Lucy, his eyes transfixed for a split second. "I swear it's just like looking at Beth. She was a sweet, fine-looking girl." He shrugged. "Of course, she could be a lying bitch who would cut your heart out as soon as look at you."

"That's enough," Hank said. "Time to leave."

Willard jerked away from Hank's grip. "I told Beth if she left me, her life wouldn't amount to shit." His gaze roamed over to Lucy. "Looks like I was right."

If she'd been behind her bar, she'd have been reaching for the Peacemaker right about now. "Get out of here."

"*Whoo-wee,*" Willard said, laughing. "And I can see you have your mother's fire in your eyes. When she looked at me like that, I knew I had a wildcat on my hands."

This time, when Hank grabbed Willard's arm, the man couldn't wrestle free. Hank shoved him forward with a hard thrust that sent Willard tripping several steps before he caught himself. He jerked his jacket back in place and stabbed his fingers through his hair. "If she's in town to find her daddy, she's going to have to look far and wide. That Beth never met a man she didn't like."

Noah shoved Willard toward his truck. Willard held up his hands. "Fine, I get when I'm not wanted." He leveled his gaze back on Natasha. "You can stand over there and pretend you're going to find better, but I'm your daddy, and no fancy hairdo is gonna change that. We're blood."

Willard's laughter rose up, sending a chill down Lucy's spine. As much as she wanted to discount him, he was the kind of man Beth had always gravitated toward. But it was the expression on Noah Garrison's face when he looked at her that stole her breath away. In one glance, he telegraphed a lifetime of pain and regret.

And she realized with a mixture of relief, happiness, and regret that he had inadvertently shared something with Beth. He dropped his gaze back toward his wife. They looked at each other. She smiled at him, but her expression and body language were cold. There was an old wound between them.

The concerned look the couple shared mirrored Lucy's.

She had to wonder if Noah Garrison was her father.

CHAPTER SEVENTEEN

Lucy

January 17, 2018

When Hank, Natasha, and Lucy parked in front of Winter Cottage, they all sat in silence for several beats until Dolly broke the ice and started barking at a squirrel.

Natasha opened the door and the dog rushed out. "Lucy, you going anywhere?" she asked.

"No. Staying right here."

"Your hair really looks great," Hank said.

Natasha nodded. "I know. But thanks." The girl took off after the dog, running toward the reeds ringing the edge of the bay's shore.

"So what is Brian Willard's story?" Lucy asked.

"What you saw today pretty much sums him up. Natasha's mother was the parent. And since she's been gone, he's gone downhill even more. Sadly, the selfish bastard is trying his best to drag Natasha with him."

"He knew my mother. So did your dad."

He watched as the dog ran in and out of the reeds. "So it seems."

Leave it to Beth to create drama from the grave. "Thank you for today, Hank."

"Sure."

"Why are you being so nice? You already have the lease signed by me."

"I did what's right." When he turned toward her, his eyes were direct and wary all at once. "And I'm still not convinced you're going to stay. This is not an easy place to live. Hell, the town is on the verge of dying, and I don't know if I can save it."

"Then why are you trying?"

"Family. Tradition. I grew up here and sank deep roots. You haven't, Lucy. Beth didn't."

She got out of the car and took her cake plate from the back before she called to Natasha and headed to the front door. In front of the door was a plastic grocery bag filled with old articles that looked like they'd been printed from microfilm. Mrs. Reynolds had delivered on her promise.

The girl and the dog bounded up to the front door as she heard the wheels of Hank's truck crunch over the gravel driveway.

She pushed open the door and turned on the light. The high ceiling and the tall expanse of windows added a chill to the house. The stark walls and the shadowed corners still offered little welcome. This house didn't care if she stayed.

"Is there any cake left?" Natasha asked.

"None," Lucy replied.

"Too bad. Super good. You did a fantastic job with it."

"Thanks."

"Maybe you could teach me how?"

"Sure. But don't you have homework?"

"Always, but it can wait."

Lucy hadn't eaten any of the covered dishes. She'd been too busy fighting nausea, sadness, and grief as she tried to absorb so many stories about Beth. The community had circled around her. Embraced her. But she'd also felt suffocated.

"Have you watched more videos of your mom?" Natasha asked.

"I watched an hour's worth earlier today."

"We could watch more now. Make popcorn or something."

In the kitchen, she turned on the hot water tap, which spit out cold water for a good thirty seconds before it slowly warmed. She washed her hands and dried them. She needed a break from Beth before she dived into the next video.

"Snack. Homework. Then popcorn and movie."

"Ah, come on," Natasha said. "That can wait."

"That's what I used to say to my mom."

"And what did she say?"

"She'd say, 'Okay, go watch TV.'"

Natasha put her hands on her hips. "And you turned out okay."

Lucy shook her head. "You don't want to end up like me, Natasha. Tending bar is okay, but it means long hours and hard work. It would be a waste of your sharp mind."

"You don't have to be a bartender anymore. You can stay here and fix up Winter Cottage."

"And then what?" The question was meant more for herself than the girl.

Natasha shrugged. "The house is always going to need someone."

"I don't know anything about taking care of a house."

"Hank does. He'd help."

"I know he would."

Lucy knew they weren't talking just about the house as she sliced a loaf of bread and spread butter on several pieces. She handed one to Natasha and bit into the other. She thought about Hank today, showing up at her front door dressed in a coat and tie. No man had ever put on a suit for her. She also knew he had something to do with the freshly cut grass at the cemetery.

"I mean, he could be your half brother," Natasha said. "That would be kinda cool to have a brother, wouldn't it?"

If the girl had dumped a bucket of ice water on her head, she couldn't have rattled her more. She was now very aware that Beth could have slept with Hank's father.

"Eat."

Natasha tore off a piece and handed it to Dolly. "Kinda weird, I guess."

"Yes, it is." From the plastic bag, Lucy pulled articles Mrs. Reynolds had given her about Winter Cottage. Most were published in the local paper, but a few had appeared in the *Virginian-Pilot* based in Norfolk.

The first article dated to 1916 and featured the wedding photo of George Buchanan and Elizabeth Lawrence.

The newly minted Mr. and Mrs. Buchanan stood in front of the cottage. Mrs. Buchanan's dress was a creamy satin with a beaded bodice and yards and yards of tulle that the wind gently teased. Mr. Buchanan wore his evening coat with tails and a top hat. Her smile was brilliant, and his chest puffed with pride.

Next to the couple were two smartly dressed young people. The girl was stunning, dressed in a velvety dress with a matching fur-trimmed hat that framed blonde curls and sharp cheekbones. She wasn't smiling, but her clear, light gaze telegraphed an impish charm that would have been hard to resist. The young man, tall and slender, looked very much like his father. This was Victoria and her brother, Robert.

Lucy studied Mrs. Buchanan's wedding dress more closely. She recalled the portrait that she'd found in the closet. It was the same dress, but not the same bride.

The next article featured a local man, James Latimer. His picture was printed above the fold, which was no wonder because he could only be described as breathtakingly handsome. Many would have picked up the paper just to admire him. His gaze bore a gravity that saved him from ever being described as pretty. If anything, it made him a man's man and all the more irresistible. She could see why the young

Claire and Victoria had been drawn to James Latimer. The headline read LOCAL MAN TO COMMAND MARIAH.

Lucy felt a sense of pride as she thought about Jimmy rising through the ranks.

Feeling hopeful, she flipped to the next article, dated August of that same year. This headline was far more ominous, THE MARIAH LOST AT SEA, and the article explained how the ship had been torpedoed near Nassau by a German U-boat. She'd never known Jimmy and the men who served under him, yet the weight of this loss bore down as she thought about the young girl who had lost so much.

"Damn it," she muttered.

"What?" Natasha asked.

She showed her the article. The girl read it and shrugged.

Lucy's nerves were scraped raw from her mother's passing along with the memorial service. She dug through the papers, searching for any article that would reveal the fate of the men on the *Mariah*. She found a small mention in the Norfolk paper about the *Mariah* that said twenty crewmembers, including Jimmy Latimer and Stanley Hedrick, had been among the survivors picked up by a fishing vessel.

The immediate sense of relief Lucy felt was quickly dashed by the next paragraph, which stated Isaac Hedrick had been lost at sea. The old sailor was survived by his seven children, Catherine "Claire," Jemma, Sarah, Diane, Stanley, Joseph, and Michael.

"Poor Claire lost her father, but at least her brother and Jimmy survived," Lucy said.

"Why are you crying?" Natasha asked.

"It's sad." Lucy wiped a tear away and flipped to the next article. It noted that Mr. Robert Buchanan had been commissioned into the army in late summer 1916. Mrs. B had said the first time she'd danced with Robert at the locals' party the winter before, he'd been in a fight, but there'd been no mention of military service.

The next article announced the fall 1916 wedding of Robert Buchanan to Miss Catherine Claire Hedrick. She wore an ivory wedding dress and stood alone on the front lawn of Winter Cottage with the bay behind her. Full white clouds lingered in the clear sky, and a gentle breeze caught the veil.

Claire, a servant in the Buchanan household, had married the heir to the family fortune. Surely the wedding had been something of a shock, if not a scandal. And what about Jimmy? Lucy studied the young Claire's face. She was smiling, but her eyes didn't sparkle, as you'd expect from a bride.

The couple planned to live at Winter Cottage, rather than in New York City.

The next piece was dated March 1917 and included a picture of Sally and Eric Jessup and their five boys. The older three boys were teenagers, whereas the younger two were babes in arms, one a small infant and the other just over one year old. Eric Jessup had won a commendation for rescuing sailors during a hurricane.

Lucy knew from the last tape that the three older boys were Claire Hedrick's brothers. The baby that Sally had been carrying during the wedding festivities in January 1916 would have been the older of the two children held by Sally in the picture. The youngest, her fifth son, was Lucy's grandfather, Samuel.

Lucy stared at her adoptive great-grandmother's smiling face as she stared at her husband. Sally was radiant, surrounded by the men in her life.

The last piece told the story of another man claimed by the sea in 1917, which Lucy now understood was the price of living in a community like this. The local sheriff said Mr. Robert Buchanan had taken a boat out in a horrific storm. His body had never been recovered, meaning the grave in the cemetery was empty.

Hank

Hank parked at the top of the circular driveway outside his family home. It was a brick two-story colonial with hunter-green shutters and a white front porch that wrapped around the house. He got out of the car and strode toward his parents' house. They'd not spoken much at the funeral, but he knew he and his father needed to talk about Beth.

On the porch, wind chimes danced in the breeze. He opened the front door and was greeted by the scents of his mother's spaghetti sauce brewing on the stove. She'd started the tradition of having spaghetti on Wednesdays when Hank and his sister were young. Mrs. Garrison insisted the family ate together that one day of the week.

"Mom!" he said.

"In the kitchen pantry."

He found her rearranging cans, something she did when she was upset or worried. "What's going on?"

"Why does anything have to be wrong for me to clean?" she asked.

"Mom. You clean when you're annoyed."

She brushed hair out of her eyes with the back of her hand. "The funeral service. Beth Jessup and I were the same age. All I can remember is a young girl who was nice to me when she found me in the ladies' room crying. I'd just found out I was pregnant with you, and I was ter-rified. She hugged me and told me I would be fine."

His mother and father had married right before graduation of their senior year in high school. At that time, she had been eight months pregnant. The family had circled the wagons around the young couple, who despite the odds had gotten college educations and raised Hank and his sister. "I didn't realize you knew her that well."

"We were all friends. It was such a small community. Everyone knew everyone."

The fact that his parents had married before graduation didn't get his father off the hook when it came to possibly having gotten Beth pregnant. If anything, it made the need for clarification all the more important.

His mother sniffed and wiped her eyes with her sleeve. "Beth's daughter looks so much like her. It's like looking into the past. What's she like?"

"She's a good person."

"Is she keeping the house?"

"I don't know. She's not used to this kind of responsibility, and now she has a big decision."

"I think it's sweet she's taken in the Willard girl. God knows that child needs a break."

"She sure does." Impatience nipped at him. "Where's Dad?"

"In the shed out back. He's fixing the lawnmower."

"Thanks."

"Everything all right?"

Hank kissed her on the cheek. "Never better."

He strode out the back door, trying to picture his father as a newly married husband with a baby on the way. The pressure must have been tough. His parents had been great, and he had no complaints, but they rarely talked about before he was born.

Hank found his father in the shed working on a red lawnmower. He'd pulled off a spark plug and was holding it up to an overhead light.

"Dad."

His father removed half glasses and smiled. "What brings you by?"

"I'm going to be blunt, Dad."

A grin deepened the lines around his father's mouth. "You have been since you were two, son. What's up?"

Hank closed the door to the shed. "Did you sleep with Beth Jessup? Are you Lucy's father?"

Noah Garrison stiffened and glanced toward the window, making sure his wife wasn't close. "No. I'm not Lucy's father."

"Then why are you looking around for Mom?"

"Because I came damn close to messing up everything I had with your mother. We'd put all that behind us until today when that damn Brian Willard showed up."

"What happened between you and Beth?"

"Your mother was about eight months pregnant. She was terrified about having a baby and certain all her plans for college were ruined. She was understandably emotional. And that's not to say that she doesn't adore you more than anything," he was quick to add. "The minute you were born, she was in love."

"I know all that. I'm concerned about the month before Beth left town. But you need to be honest with me, Dad. Are you Lucy's father?"

Annoyance flashed in his dark eyes. "Like I said, no."

"You're sure?"

"Yes, damn it, I am." His voice had risen a notch, and it took a moment for him to regain composure. "I came close, but I didn't sleep with Beth. And why do you care so much?"

"It's just important to me."

"Why? Do you like Lucy?"

"I've known her two days. And I'd bet my last dollar she'll be back in Nashville by the end of the month."

"Son, if she's anything like her mother, she won't stick around. I'm amazed Beth didn't take off sooner. She was always a restless soul, but after her mother died and her father went back to sea, she had nothing to anchor her and got into the habit of thinking that drifting through life was normal." He shrugged. "If Lucy leaves, that would be good for you. That means you get the cottage."

"Exactly. It would make all my plans fall right into place."

"What about the lease on the land?"

"Lucy signed the extension. We're good for another ten years."

"So why are you frowning?"

"I'm not."

"You come charging in here to find out if I had an affair over thirty years ago. Asking me if I'm Lucy's father. And yeah, kiddo, you're frowning more than usual."

Hank sat on a stool by the workbench and picked up a wrench. "I've got so much riding on this project, Dad. It's not just me. It's my guys. The town. The vineyard has helped, but developing the land beyond and scaling up production is going to make a huge impact on this area and their lives."

"I appreciate your loyalty to your men and the town. But you don't owe them a career and a place to live."

"Yeah. I do owe them all."

Noah was silent for a moment, and then, squaring his shoulders, he clamped his hand on his son's shoulder. "Like you said, Lucy is most likely going to be gone by the end of the month. This is a beautiful place, but the pace is slower, and it's not for everyone. She looks like a big-city girl. Not that I'm saying there's anything wrong with that. It's just she might not like it here."

"I know."

Noah shook his head. "There was a wildness in Beth that was intoxicating. She could light up a room. No high school gathering was really fun until she showed up. But she could be self-destructive. She had brains and could have done anything with her life."

"And she got pregnant in high school. Like you and Mom?"

"Yes, but we had your grandparents. Otherwise, we'd have been in a world of hurt. Beth didn't have parents to back her up. By the time her father returned from sea, she was gone."

Noah shook his head. "I've thought about Beth over the years and wondered why she vanished like she did. Both Mrs. B and Samuel knew about Lucy, and Mrs. B did send money, but she died when Lucy was just over one year old. And as wild as Beth could be, she had her pride. She wouldn't have asked Samuel for help."

"Lucy said she and her mother had their differences. I guess stubborn runs through that family," Hank said.

"Samuel could be bullheaded. But he was a good man. If not for him, your mother and I couldn't have planted the vineyard when you were little."

"Lucy said there are several tapes of Beth interviewing Mrs. Buchanan."

"She left right before graduation. If she had a project, I never heard about it."

"Do you think that project is the reason she left the property and house to Beth and Lucy?"

"I don't believe that's the reason. Mrs. B was very loyal to family. I can't imagine her breaking with tradition and giving it to someone outside her bloodline."

"What kind of connection did Mrs. B have with the Jessup family?"

"Well, the Jessups raised her three younger brothers, and I believe she was always grateful for that. But she did permit Samuel to live in the gatekeeper's cottage when he finally married in the late 1960s."

"But why not leave Winter Cottage to one of her blood relatives? Samuel was the Jessups' boy."

"I don't know," he said as he took the wrench from Hank. "When do you meet with the bank?"

"Two days."

"What are you going to tell them?"

"I'll tell them Lucy renewed the lease for the next ten years."

"Which is good, but a lease is not leverage."

Hank shook his head, never imagining that the dream that had been so black-and-white could now be in doubt. "I don't know."

CHAPTER EIGHTEEN

Beth

May 29, 1988

As the camera is rolling, Beth Jessup sits in Mrs. Buchanan's chair in Winter Cottage's main parlor. The bay is to her back. The sky is clear.

She wore her black sweater today and left her long blonde hair loose around her shoulders. She even put on makeup, adding blush to make her cheeks rosier and mascara to make her eyes pop.

Beth moistens her lips and tugs the cuff of her sweater down to hide the bruise, which looks worse than it is. *"Mrs. B is keeping me waiting. She does this sometimes. I can't get mad. She's almost a hundred years old, and some days she's slower than others. Totally cool."* She glances toward the door. *"I just wish today she'd hurry up. I've got a date."* Her smile is sly. Wicked. *"A secret date. And as usual, I'm playing with fire, but then, what's the fun of life if you always play it safe?"*

There is a noise in the background and then footsteps. Beth rises up out of the seat and says, *"Hey, Mrs. B. Looking mighty fetching today."*

"Thank you." Dark circles ring Mrs. B's eyes, and her skin looks paler than normal. She's in her wheelchair today, and a young African American girl no more than thirteen is pushing the chair. The girl is as

thin as a reed, and her dark hair is braided. She's wearing jeans and a pale-blue shirt.

Beth moves the regular chair Mrs. B uses so that the young girl can push the wheelchair into the spot. She sets the brake and then takes the time to arrange the blanket on Mrs. B's lap. Mrs. B has never been filmed in the wheelchair before. *"All set, Mrs. B?"*

"Yes, thank you, Grace. I'll ring when I need you."

The girl leaves and quietly slides the pocket doors to the parlor closed.

"Rough night?" Beth asks.

"I didn't sleep well. Too many dreams." She drags out the last word for effect.

Beth knows Mrs. B wants to be asked about the dreams. But she's enough of a diva to wait and be asked.

Beth is glad to oblige. She's grown fond of the old lady and likes to hear the stories about Claire and Jimmy. *"Okay, I'll bite. What did you dream about?"*

Mrs. B studies her manicured fingers. *"You're not really interested."*

"I am."

"You're not." She waves her hand dismissively.

Beth arches a brow. *"I didn't think you played games, Mrs. B. I thought you were a straight shooter."*

A bit of the moodiness chasing Mrs. B dissipates. *"I don't know what you're talking about."*

Beth shakes her head. *"Please."*

A spark of laughter flashes and, like a streak of lightning, is gone as quickly as it appears. *"You're saucy. You remind me of Victoria."*

"You've said that before. What happened to her?"

"She died an old woman several years ago. It doesn't matter."

"Okay, so this is the day of half answers? Are you going to tell me about Jimmy or not?"

"First, child, tell me about that bruise on your wrist."

Beth tugs the sleeve again. *"It's nothing."*

"So I'm not the only one who gives half answers."

She shrugs, acting like it's not a big deal, hoping it chases away the memory behind the bruise. *"This guy I'm seeing was playing around. He got too rough, and I bruise easily. He said he was sorry."*

"Does he hurt you?"

Beth flexes her fingers, wishing they didn't tremble when she was scared. *"No. Like I said, it was an accident."*

"I had accidents like that once. My husband was always around when they happened."

She plucked at an invisible string on her skirt. *"When my husband drank before we were married, he could be rather charming. But after I got pregnant and the stress mounted, he wasn't so sweet when he drank."*

"You haven't talked about your husband much."

"Then today, I shall."

Claire

September 1916

The breeze from the bay did little to soften early September's intense heat, which had blanketed the town for nearly two weeks. Claire had arrived in late April. The trip was not planned but necessary. Claire had returned to Winter Cottage to carry out her employer's wishes.

Today she had chosen a soft white muslin dress that hung loose and skimmed her ankles. Her red hair was tied up on top of her head with a white bow. She'd walked into town to visit the post office, hoping for a letter from Jimmy. He would send letters and trinkets to his mother when he reached ports, but it had been nearly six weeks since she'd heard from him. Claire always fetched the letters. The two would huddle together during the quiet moments of the summer days, and she would read to Mrs. Latimer.

His last letters were full of short sentences. *It rained today. Oranges in the port of Nassau. U-boat sightings two hundred miles north. Isaac and Stanley fare well. Tell Claire I miss her.*

Though the war had yet to pull America into the fight, she'd heard stories of more men joining the merchant marines. These men made supply runs that kept Britain stocked with fuel and food.

Jimmy's ship transported fuel, and already this year, the *Mariah* had made her third Atlantic crossing. If a ship could survive the two-week crossing to England, their cargos were sold quickly and the profits were bountiful for the company. But the threat of the U-boats, which had claimed dozens of ships, was increasing.

Claire sifted through the rest of the mail. A large envelope from Mrs. Buchanan was postmarked California and addressed to Claire. She opened it and found several letters from Victoria's cousin, Edward, which Mrs. Buchanan had quietly forwarded to Cape Hudson. Edward wrote Victoria almost weekly.

Returning home, Claire pushed through the front door of Winter Cottage. The windows were open, allowing a heavy breeze to cut through the humid air. The rattle of pots and pans drew her into the kitchen, where Mrs. Latimer stood over a cutting board centered in the island. She was kneading bread.

"Is there any news?" Mrs. Latimer asked, looking up. Sweat dampened her brow and her blouse. She didn't like working in the kitchen in the summers.

"Only letters for Victoria. How is she doing today?"

"Upstairs, resting. Not happy with the heat." Claire had also forgotten about the summer heat. She'd grown spoiled by summers in Newport, Rhode Island, with the Buchanan family.

"I'm sure the weather is far lovelier up north than it is here. Tonight's dinner is going to be simple. Bread and cold meats. I don't have the fortitude to cook a full meal."

"That's fine. No one has much appetite in this heat." She nodded toward the stairs leading to the second floor. "How is she *really*?"

"Miss Victoria is in a foul mood. Wishing she were home. Wishing she'd not been such a stupid girl."

"Perhaps the letters from Edward will cheer her up."

"That girl is a lucky one. If not for the threat of war, she'd be the center of gossip this summer. Everyone would be wondering why she missed the summer season." Mrs. Latimer tsk-tsked. "If they only knew she wasn't on a grand adventure with her stepmother but instead upstairs hiding her pregnant belly."

Two months after the night Victoria had slipped into Winter Cottage disheveled and careworn, Victoria had realized she was pregnant. She'd tried to keep it secret, but Claire was the first to notice. She'd been fitting the girl with her summer wardrobe when she'd noticed a slightly protruding belly. The average person would not have noticed such a slight change, but Claire, who was attuned to the bodies of the women she dressed, had. Mrs. Buchanan had been in the fitting room, and she'd seen Claire's awkward pause. Her gaze had trailed to her stepdaughter's belly, and she too had then been in the inner circle.

In Claire's world, a pregnancy would have cost her job. Her family would have shunned her, and she'd have been a pariah. But for Victoria, a girl destined by birth for a great marriage, this misstep required complete discretion. In a normal year, Victoria would have been sent to Europe for a grand six-month tour. But Europe was too dangerous with war.

Several hideaways had been discussed, but ultimately Winter Cottage had been chosen. The residents, mostly supported by the Buchanans, had understood what to do. As far as the New York socialites knew, Victoria was in California.

Mrs. Buchanan had asked Claire to accompany Victoria because she trusted her completely with the secret. And if anyone should ask, Claire could say she was making the girl's wedding trousseau.

No one in town had made a single comment when the two arrived in late April. Claire had been able to hide the girl's growing belly for a time, but finally it had become impossible. Her tiny frame had nowhere else to hide a baby. Now she was weeks away from birth, and Claire was as many days away from returning to her old life in New York. When Claire had first arrived, she'd been counting the days until she could return to New York or Newport, but as the summer had lumbered on, she'd started to fall in love with Winter Cottage and the Eastern Shore again. She would truly miss this place.

The rattle of an automobile pulled Claire toward the front of the cottage. It was a sleek blue roadster with nickel trim that glistened in the sunlight.

Out stepped Robert, dressed in an army officer's uniform that fit his lean, trim frame in a way that made him look quite attractive.

"What is he doing here?" Mrs. Latimer said. "He couldn't know about Victoria, could he?"

"I don't know."

"Go and talk to him and find out. If he goes upstairs, he'll discover Victoria's situation. And you know how those two bicker."

Robert shrugged off his uniform jacket, carelessly tossed it on the back seat of the car, and wiped his forehead with a handkerchief. He'd never visited Virginia in the summer and clearly didn't look to be enjoying himself.

"I suspect he already knows about his sister," Claire said. "He plays the party-boy part well, but he's cleverer than his father gives him credit for."

"Well, find out. I have dough on my hands, and you just about grew up with the man."

Claire summoned a smile and went out the front door. She came down the steps. "Mr. Robert. What brings you to Winter Cottage?"

He unfastened the collar's gold stud. "I had no idea it would be so damn hot and humid. How have you and Victoria tolerated it?"

"I'm sorry, not quite sure I follow?"

"Don't give me a quizzical look. I've not lost my mind. I've come to see my sister. I know my stepmother has been forwarding her mail here."

Claire stood very still, not sure how far to press the lie. "Who told you such a thing?"

"Elizabeth's maid is a charming young girl, and she let it slip Edward was writing Victoria. It took a little detective work to trace my sister to Winter Cottage, and I can tell by your face that I'm right. And in case you're worried, Father still has no idea about my sister's change in summer venue, though it would serve the pompous bastard right to know his angel had fallen."

A discreet woman knew when an employer was fishing for information and never rushed to confirm or deny. "And how are Mr. and Mrs. Buchanan?"

"I'll tell you over a whiskey."

"Does Mrs. Buchanan know you're here?"

"Pour me a whiskey, and I'll tell you anything."

He followed her into the house and down the long hallway to the parlor. She and Mrs. Latimer kept the windows closed during the day and the shades drawn to hold in the cool air, but by late afternoon, the heat ultimately thwarted their best efforts, and the house grew stuffy and hot.

In the parlor, she pushed back the thick green velvet curtain and tied it back. A twist of an iron handle released and opened the window, allowing in a warm, thick breeze. She continued to do this until all the windows were open.

From the liquor cabinet, she removed a bottle of whiskey and a crystal tumbler. She filled the glass and handed it to Robert.

He accepted, gulped it down, and handed her the empty. "Another, please, and you should have one too. God knows my sister has likely made you earn it."

She poured him a second glass and, despite her better judgment, poured one for herself. While he gulped, she sipped.

"So how is she?" he asked. "Or are we going to keep playing this game?"

"She's fine."

He studied the amber liquid in the design cut into the glass. "I assume she's pregnant. That's the primary reason young girls go on unconventional holidays."

All he had to do was climb the stairs to the second floor and get one look at his sister and the jig was up. "Her time is near, and she's not comfortable. The heat does not help."

He studied her over the rim of the crystal tumbler. "Do we know who the father is?"

"She won't say."

"I assume it's not Edward. If it were, Elizabeth would have arranged nuptials posthaste, and that poor sop would have gladly chased her down the aisle."

She sipped more, enduring the smooth burn that eased some of the tension from her body. "She's very tight lipped."

"A little late for that, don't you think?"

She swallowed a grin. His humor always had a way of cutting to the quick.

He held up his glass to her. "You're a good, loyal woman. I doubt anyone else could have gotten her out of the city and kept the secret so well. I assume Elizabeth is paying you and Mrs. Latimer well."

"She has always been generous with me."

"Is my sister at least contrite?"

She regarded the amber hues catching the light in her glass while praying for the right words. "She has become quieter the last few days. The baby is active and kicks often. It's all more real to her now."

His expression turned cold. "She's not getting attached to it, is she? Because we both know she can't keep it."

"She understands a plan is in place for the child."

"Who?"

"I think it's best I not say. The fewer who know, the better."

"Does Elizabeth know?"

"She asked me to make arrangements, and I have. The baby will be fine."

He tossed back the last of the whiskey. "Well, tell Mrs. Latimer I'm here for the duration. Victoria is a twit, but she's family, and family stays together. And it will be nice to have a secret from Father for a change."

"Of course."

"Is there a doctor in town?"

"The closest is in Norfolk. But there's a midwife. I visited her this morning."

"Excellent. Claire, how about you join me for dinner? You're a clever woman, and I could use good conversation and maybe a game of gin."

Robert, in his own way, was charming. Perhaps it was the uniform, but she found the idea of dinner exciting. "Of course. What time?"

"We'll say seven."

"It might be a cold supper. Mrs. Latimer didn't cook today."

"As long as there's whiskey, we will be fine."

A loud scream from the kitchen cut through the house. Claire rose quickly and hurried across the house and into the butler's pantry. She found Mrs. Latimer in a heap on the floor. She clutched a letter in her hand and was sobbing.

Claire dropped to the ground and took the woman's face in her hands. "What is it? Tell me."

Tears streamed down Mrs. Latimer's face. "One of the sailors brought me this."

Claire slowly pulled the letter from Mrs. Latimer's grip and carefully smoothed out the crinkles. The letter was from a shipmate of her father's, a Mr. Rory Tucker, who was now convalescing in a hospital in the Bahamas. The *Mariah* had sunk in the Caribbean. Many of the men had died outright, including Isaac Hedrick, but Jimmy had pulled Stanley Jessup through the water to safety.

Claire struggled to take in a breath as her head spun. The sea her father had loved so much had finally claimed him. "Jimmy and Stanley are alive," she said.

Mrs. Latimer shook her head. "Read on."

She scanned the letter, reading Mr. Tucker's next account, which he said was confidential and not to be shared in the papers. Though Stanley had been sent back to Cape Hudson, Jimmy had joined the crew of the *Reverie* as captain after influenza had swept through their ranks. Two days after he took command, the *Reverie* had been low in the water, heavy with fuel and munitions, when another U-boat's torpedo had struck the side. The ship had exploded instantly and sunk immediately. There were no reported survivors.

She was transported back to the day they'd laid her mother's coffin in the ground. She'd held a crying Michael close as her other siblings gathered around her. The bottom had fallen out of her life, and neither she nor her family was ever the same, but they'd all found a way to patch together the pieces.

Now those stitches ripped and the fabric shredded.

Footsteps sounded behind her, and she heard Robert ask what was happening. When she couldn't speak, he laid his hand on her shoulder and asked again. She'd never heard him speak so gently.

A breath shuddered through her. "Stanley is safe, but my father and Jimmy are gone," she said. "Their ships sank."

"Oh, Claire, I'm so sorry." Robert reached for Mrs. Latimer and, supporting her, wrapped her arm around his neck. Claire rose and took the old woman's other arm.

"My Jimmy. My Jimmy," Mrs. Latimer wept.

"I'm here, Mrs. Latimer. I'll take care of you," Robert said.

The woman gripped Claire's hand. "You won't leave me, will you? You'll stay with me?"

Claire kissed her on the side of her cheek and dried her tears. "I'm not going anywhere."

Over the next week, Claire spent time with Robert every day. He was patient with her melancholy and accompanied her on long walks along the beach. Mrs. Latimer had returned to Annapolis, Maryland, to be with her sister, leaving Victoria's care to Claire. Robert joined Claire and Victoria for dinner each evening, and he was the one person who could buoy her spirits.

The more time Claire spent with Robert, the more she saw him in a different light. He had a biting but funny sense of humor and reminisced about several hunting expeditions starring Jimmy, who had rescued several hunters either stuck in the reeds or nearly shot by an oblivious hunting companion. Claire relished these stories and grew closer to Robert.

On the sixth day, a summer storm blew up the coast. The rain churned up the bay and soaked the ground while the wind rattled the windows and bent the old oaks that had seen many storms before. The storm also brought cooler temperatures that seemed to ease the swelling in Victoria's ankles and hands.

Robert and Claire were walking along a shoreline littered with driftwood. The sky was a deep blue and the breeze soft and cool.

"I received a telegram from my father," Robert said. "I'll be leaving for France in a month. Father knows a general who needs an attaché, and time in the military would make a man of me, he says. Though we both know good and well that I won't see any fighting."

"So your father knows you're here?"

"Ah, he does. And he now knows about Victoria."

"How?"

"It doesn't matter how."

Jimmy was now beyond any earthly retribution. "What does he plan to do?"

"Nothing. He concurs with Elizabeth's plan. Victoria will return to New York this fall, and in the spring, she'll wed Edward."

"Does Victoria know this?" Claire asked.

"Not yet. Better to see the baby's delivery over and done with, and then you'll escort her home. She'll learn of her fate while I suffer my own."

"Are you afraid to go to Europe?"

"No. It's a reasonable enough job for a man of my station. Father thinks I'll be best suited for politics one day, and military service is always a plus," he quipped. "Father always gets his way." He picked up a stick and slung it into the bay. "Always."

"I certainly didn't when my father sent me away as a child. You are a grown man, Robert."

He stared out over the water, watching as the sun sparkled on the waves. "Father has leverage. He'll cut off all my funds, and he'll do the same to Victoria if she doesn't marry Edward." A crooked smile teased the edge of his lips. "My sister and I excel at many things, but being poor is not one of them."

In this moment, she felt sad for the whole Buchanan family. They'd all had such hope in January, and now they were all adrift. She threaded her fingers through his as they walked along the shore to the dock that stretched out into the bay.

Robert turned to her and carefully brushed a curl from her face. "You're a beautiful woman. The most sensible woman I have ever met. I have always thought that about you, Claire."

"I'm not beautiful," she said gently. "I make the best of what I have in beauty and life, nothing more."

"Don't sell yourself short, Claire. You're a beauty. There's Victoria's beauty, the classical look, but it is fragile and will wither with time. You have a striking, unforgettable look that will only grow lovelier."

Heat rushed to her cheeks, and as his hand lingered, she leaned her head slightly into his touch. "You're too kind."

A smile quirked the edge of his lips before his brows knotted. He angled his head, closed the distance between their lips, and gently kissed her.

She closed her eyes and thought about the first time Jimmy had touched her lips. He had tasted of honey. Smelled of sandalwood and salt air.

This kiss was simple enough, but it reminded her of loving Jimmy. And suddenly, she was so desperate to feel any connection that she couldn't resist whatever this was.

Claire inclined toward him, allowing her breasts to rub against his chest. He cupped her face in his long hands and kissed her again. However, this time the touch wasn't light or exploratory but betrayed a hunger she'd only glimpsed in him over the years. When he reached for her breast, whatever momentary spell she'd been under vanished, and Claire realized with painful clarity she was not in Jimmy's arms.

She pulled back and moistened her lips. "I cannot."

His dark eyes were sharp and pointed. "Why not?"

"I have a life of service with your family. And I won't be the silly girl conscripted to the shadows whom you trot out when you feel bored."

A muscle pulsed in his jaw. "This isn't about boredom."

"Isn't it?" She stepped back.

"What if I were to ask you to marry me?"

"I'd say you were a fool, and perhaps a cold compress on your head would cure that feeling. Your father would never allow it."

He laid his hands on her shoulders. "I mean it, Claire. Marry me."

"Why me? There's a line of women in Newport who will make you a far better match, Robert. A life in politics isn't feasible with a downstairs wife."

"You're smart, clever, and clearly very loyal. You would be the perfect wife for me. Marry me. Today."

Reason told her to take a step back even as her mind swirled with the possibilities. "You're not thinking this through."

"I'm being very reasonable. I've never been more reasonable. We will get married today."

"And then what?" She was forever looking beyond the next three stitches to the greater pattern.

He traced his hand over her shoulder. "My family will accept us in time, especially when the children come. The storm will pass, and my family will come around."

Warmth from his hands warmed her shoulders. "Robert, you're playing a dangerous game with me."

He kissed her on the nose. "I'm not. I'm very serious. Never more serious. And I want to do it before I leave for France." His hand slid to her belly. "If I should do something stupid and get myself killed, I'd want to know there might be a piece of me in you." He took both her hands in his. "Marry me, Claire."

And for the first time since she'd slept with Jimmy, she allowed herself to dream beyond the possibilities of just owning a small seamstress shop.

"You don't know what you're getting yourself into." Her tone softened as her mind wrapped around the possibility.

"And what else is new? A life with me will never be dull. Marry me."

"Yes."

He reared back and cocked his head. "You will marry me? Now? Today?"

"Yes."

Robert wrapped his arms around Claire's waist and, lifting her off her feet, twirled her around.

———— ⚬⚮⚬ ————

They were married in the chapel in Cape Hudson on a warm September day. Robert wore his traveling suit, and she wore Elizabeth's wedding dress, which she'd so carefully packed away after the January wedding earlier that year.

The satin and beaded waistband reminded her of the love she'd felt when she'd sewn the dress. Each stitch, each fold and handmade lace had been infused with her love. Now she prayed that love would find a new life with Robert.

They spent their wedding night in a small inn, savoring each other's bodies, eating roast duck and chocolates for dessert, and drinking wine and laughing. Their lovemaking wasn't infused with passion but felt like a renewal of life.

The following day, Claire and Robert arrived back at Winter Cottage to find Victoria in her bed, clutching her belly.

"Help me, Claire," Victoria said.

Claire held her. "I'm here. It will be fine."

She sent one of the boys for the midwife and remained at Victoria's side as the contractions came faster. It took less than three hours for the little slip of a girl to give birth to a healthy, squalling boy who was well over eight pounds.

Electric light flickered in the room as Claire washed off the baby, taking great care as she swaddled him just as she had with all her siblings. She searched for traces of Jimmy in the little face and imagined the babe's frown mirrored his father's.

As the midwife cleaned up, Claire carried the baby into Robert's room, where he waited by the window overlooking the bay.

"Is he healthy?" Robert asked.

"He's perfect." As the child greedily tried to suckle her finger, warmth and love nearly stole her breath away.

"You've arranged for his care?" His signet ring clinked against the glass in his hand.

She raised him up to the light. He was the last piece of Jimmy on this earth, and she wanted to keep him for herself. "Would you like to hold him?"

He shook his head. "I'm not very good with the little creatures."

"I all but raised my siblings. They aren't as delicate as you think."

"I'd rather not."

"He's your nephew."

"He's not mine. He's Victoria's mistake."

"Robert, he's no mistake. He's your flesh and blood. I would like us to raise him as our own."

He shook his head as his brow arched. "Do you really think my father would allow that? Our marriage will test his patience. Raising Victoria's bastard would send Father over the edge." He finished his glass. "The sooner we get rid of the child, the better."

She clutched the baby to her breast and felt him begin to root. "Do we need your father? We can do this on our own."

"I'll not risk my future to raise my sister's bastard. And I want you to swear you will never tell anyone about him. If word leaks out about this child, my father will punish us all, including the boy."

She was losing Jimmy all over again, and yet she couldn't find any words.

He gripped her wrist, his fingers biting. "Swear to the secret."

Tears burned her eyes. "For the child's sake, I swear."

He rose, that bright smile blooming again. He brushed a curl off her forehead. "Now, take the boy. I'm sure someone is waiting for him."

The *someone* was already preparing the cradle for the boy and washing clothes that would be his. Claire knew the boy would be loved, but as she turned to leave, she realized she would never love her husband.

She bundled the baby up and carried him to the small cottage at the end of the sandy road. The front of the property was filled with boats in need of mending, and the house was full of children and laughter.

Sally Jessup hadn't quite weaned her son, Aaron, who was almost seven months old. She'd reared the three older boys while her husband worked two jobs to feed the mouths he had. Sally opened the door, and with Eric standing beside her, she beamed when she saw the baby.

"It's a boy," Claire said.

Sally's smile widened. "Another boy. Well, I certainly know what to do with boys."

Claire knew Sally would love the boy just as her own flesh. But that didn't soften her resentment as she recalled the moment she'd laid Michael in this woman's arms. Drawing in a breath, she gently placed the baby in Sally's arms. "Yes, you're good with boys."

Sally peered in the blanket at the small pink face and touched his button nose with her fingertip. "I've heard rumors from the Buchanan house about this baby."

"I can't say, but you're a smart woman, Sally. You will know the right thing to say."

"Where's Miss Vic—the mother?"

"She'll leave the cottage soon. She won't return."

"And she has agreed to this?"

"She has."

"What about your husband?" Sally said.

"He wants the same." Claire dug into her satchel and pulled out an envelope filled with cash. "This will help with your expenses."

"You can keep your money," Eric said. "We'll take him regardless."

"I know," Claire said. "That's why I'm giving him to you."

With tears in her eyes, Claire bent over and kissed Jimmy's son and left, vowing that the boy and all his children would want for nothing.

CHAPTER NINETEEN

Lucy

January 17, 2018

Lucy stood in the center of the house, feeling a restless energy. No wonder, with the move, the cottage, the kid, the funeral. The list was growing. But knowing why she was unsettled didn't make it go away. She could pick up and leave, like Beth had done when she couldn't handle the energy building inside of her, or she could make the best of it like she always did.

"Natasha, how well do you know this cottage?" she asked.

Natasha looked up from her sandwich and shrugged. "Pretty well."

"What does that exactly mean?"

"I know it really well. When I was here alone, sometimes I'd look around. I didn't take anything. I was just curious."

"I believe you. Have you ever been in the attic?"

"Sure. It's got some neat stuff up there. Trunks, old furniture, a mirror. Kinda cool."

Lucy retrieved her flashlight and clicked it on and off several times. "Want to go exploring? I've only glanced up in the attic, and I need a break from videos."

Natasha gobbled the last of her sandwich and gulped her juice. "Yeah. Come on, Dolly."

The dog looked up at Natasha and wagged her tail.

"Lead the way," Lucy said.

Natasha dashed up the first, second, and third flights of stairs with the dog on her heels, barking and wagging her tail. Lucy followed, not quite sure what her expectations were for this adventure.

On the third floor she paused to look. There were ten rooms, but all were smaller. Each room was painted white, and the furniture, if there was any remaining in the room, consisted of a twin bed with dresser and mirror. Every other room had a dormer window allowing natural light.

"This is where the servants lived," Natasha said.

"Claire's room was on the third floor at the end of the hallway." Lucy paused at the door and opened it, stepping in. She moved to the dormer window and stared out over the property that stretched to the paths leading to the lighthouse and boathouse. How many mornings had Claire stood here and watched Jimmy?

"Are you coming?" Natasha said from the doorway. "The attic is right here."

"In a minute. I want to see what Claire saw over a hundred years ago."

She then joined Natasha in the hallway, where the girl opened the doorway to the attic and then clicked on a light and tossed an imp's grin back at Lucy. "Come, if you dare, my lady. This is where the ghosts of Winter Cottage dwell."

Lucy clicked on her flashlight and placed it under her chin, knowing the light caught her hair and shadowed her face. "I do dare. Do you, child?"

Natasha laughed. "I don't scare that easy."

"One of my many jobs was to give ghost tours in Nashville. I can tell a scary story."

Natasha shook her head. "Ghosts and goblins don't scare me. Besides, if there were ghosts, my mom would have come back and given me some sign. And she never did, so no such thing as ghosts."

"Fair point."

The stairs were made of rough pine wood, and the stairwell walls were covered in an unfinished bead board.

"How often have you been up here?" Lucy asked.

"Five or six times. I don't rush it because I know I'll miss something."

"And you've been to the basement?"

"I have. But it's not as fun. That's mostly crammed full of lawn equipment and outdoor furniture. Nothing as cool as the attic."

Lucy flipped a switch she'd not noticed before, and more lights flickered on.

"The house was the first to have electricity in the town," Natasha said. "And it got its running water from a bunch of wells and a couple of cisterns."

"How do you know all this?"

"I asked Mrs. Reynolds. I like to hang out in the library, and she likes to talk about the cottage. She's worried it's going to die." Natasha walked toward four large black wardrobe trunks. "I know she's glad you're here."

"I'm glad someone is happy."

"You might look a little flaky, but once the town gets to know you, they'll figure out you're just like them and here to save the house."

The girl's faith in Lucy was unsettling. "Natasha, I haven't made any promises. You understand that, right?"

Natasha shrugged. "Yeah, whatever. Ready to see the trunks?"

"Seriously, Natasha, I don't know what I'm going to do."

"I know. I get it."

The girl's attention seemed to have shifted to the first four-foot-tall trunk. It would have taken a grown man to move it while empty and perhaps two or three when it was filled with garments and shoes.

"Have you ever looked inside these?" Lucy asked.

"Never got around to it, but I've always wanted to."

Tucking her flashlight under her arm, she opened the trunk's lid. Inside were clothes carefully covered in muslin garment bags, hanging on hooks. She ran her hand along the bags' fabric, thinned by age, and thought about all the clothes Mrs. B had worn in her videotapes. She had been a woman who cared about appearance, and she would have cared for her clothes, saved them as cherished friends.

Releasing the fabric ties at the top of the bag, she unfastened each large button until the bag fell open to reveal a burgundy satin suit jacket, trimmed in fur around the collars and cuffs. The waist cut in sharply and was belted with an embroidered strip of satin. The skirt flared at the hips and fell to just above the ankles.

Lucy ran her hands down the sleeve to the cuff and turned over the edge to find dozens of perfectly neat hand stitches.

She rested her flashlight on the top of the bureau and removed the jacket from a hanger wrapped in satin. The coat smelled of mothballs, but the richness of the fabric was too much to resist. Carefully she slid her arms into the fabric sleeves. The fabric stretched smoothly over her back, allowing her to fasten the three buttons at the fitted waist.

"There's a mirror over here," Natasha said.

Lucy faced the oval mirror, which was streaked where the silver backing had faded. She didn't know much about fashion, but she knew this dress had been made before Jimmy had died.

In the jacket she found herself straightening her shoulders and feeling different. It was hard to wear such a lush jacket and not feel special.

"I'm trying to picture Claire arriving here and wearing this." She ran her hand over the cuffs trimmed with fur. "She spent days, maybe weeks choosing an outfit, whereas I showed up in torn jeans and a Nashville T-shirt. But then Claire had to prove her worth to the town that had sent her away."

"Pretty fancy," Natasha said.

"It is. You want to try it on?"

The girl's eyes were equally hesitant and excited. "You think Mrs. B would mind?"

"I don't think so. I think in a lot of ways, she was just like us." She slipped off the jacket and slid it on Natasha's thin frame. Standing behind her as they both looked in the mirror, Lucy brushed the shoulder and straightened the collar.

Natasha studied the covered waist buttons. "And she made this herself?"

"She was a seamstress."

Lucy helped Natasha out of the coat, rehung it on the padded hanger, and replaced the muslin cover. For the moment she'd worn the jacket, she'd felt different. She wasn't some commoner raised by a single mom who'd spent her life scraping by. She was special.

She flashed her light around the attic, letting it go where it may. Whatever she did with this cottage, she would have to do something with the clothes. Perhaps a museum or a collector. Hank had been clear he wanted the property and the water access. The cottage and these treasures didn't fit into his plan.

They kept rooting through the attic, digging through dusty boxes crammed full of black-and-white photos, old light fixtures, a chair with a torn cane seat, gilded picture frames, and a table that had a large gash sliced down its center. All the pieces had been sent to the attic, a kind of purgatory between the downstairs and the rubbish bin.

"Hey, look at this box," Natasha said.

The girl knelt in front of a steamer chest. Its edges were neither smooth or feminine, but instead rough and worn. Carved on the lid were the letters *JL*.

Lucy traced the letters. "James Latimer. Jimmy."

Natasha rattled a lock fastened to the center latch. "Locked."

"What would his locker be doing up here? His family should have ended up with this."

"Wasn't it just his mom and him?" Natasha asked.

"You're right. Maybe there wasn't anyone to take it." And Claire had loved him.

"You can tell Mrs. B hadn't forgotten him," Natasha said. "Her voice always softened when she talked about him."

The girl was right. Even after eighty years, the woman had not forgotten the man who had saved her from the turbulent bay waters. "Can you help me get it downstairs?"

"Yeah, sure." She pushed back a dark lock of curled hair. "This is way better than homework, or Nashville, I bet."

It was all interesting. But was it enough to stay and give up her life?

They each lifted an end and carried the heavy locker down the first set of stairs. After a moment to catch their breath and shut off the lights, they worked their way down to the first floor.

Dolly ran ahead into the kitchen and barked. Lucy followed. When they reached the first floor, they found Hank standing by the center island with two boxes of pizza and a six-pack of soda.

"I'm starving," Natasha said. "How do you always know when I'm hungry?"

"You're always hungry," he said. He flipped open a box, revealing a cheese-and-pepperoni pizza as he shifted his attention to Lucy. "You didn't eat today. Figured you'd be hungry. And pizza is the only real take-out option in the off-season."

A smile spread across her face. "Thank you."

"I'm starving!" Natasha picked up a gooey piece, letting the cheese wrap around her finger. She pinched off a chunk and handed it to a waiting Dolly before she bit into the slice. "We found a chest," she said.

Hank crossed to the sink and grabbed the roll of paper towels. He tore off a section and handed it to her. "Did you?"

"James Latimer's."

"Who's that?" Hank asked.

Natasha waggled her eyebrows. "The guy Mrs. B loved before Mr. B."

Hank grinned. "Really? Mrs. B had a secret life?"

"Secrets are like buried treasure here," Lucy heard herself say as she grabbed a slice.

"My family and I are an open book," Hank said.

"What's that mean?" Lucy asked.

"Dad and I had a frank discussion today," Hank said.

"So is he Lucy's daddy?" Natasha asked.

"He. Is. Not. Natasha." He grabbed a slice for himself and bit into it. He always spoke clearly. But now, if it were possible, the words had an extra-sharp edge.

"Is that what he told you?" Lucy asked. "Because sometimes people are not totally truthful, Hank."

"Not my father. He's ready to take a DNA test to put this thing to bed immediately."

"Really?" Lucy asked. "He'll have a DNA test?"

"Absolutely. Anytime. Anywhere. His words exactly."

Lucy had learned to spot BS in seconds while tending bar. It was a skill honed while serving thousands of drinks to a cast of characters and charlatans. "I might take him up on it."

"I hope you do."

The three ate, talking about the chest, the discoveries in the attic, and Natasha's excitement to share in school what she'd found today. There was a normalcy about it all that was a little unsettling.

Lucy faced two hard truths. This cottage, this life, was already tugging at her. It would expect a lot from her. And she was afraid she wouldn't measure up. The second truth was that nothing lasted forever.

Lucy glanced at the clock. "Natasha, it's almost eight. You need to get ready for bed."

"I never go to bed before eleven."

"Not here," Lucy said. "Lights out at nine."

"That's too early. I'm in fifth grade."

Lucy shrugged. "I feel your pain, kid. I do. But I won't be far behind you. It's been a long day."

"But what about the chest?" Natasha asked.

"I'll bring some of my tools tomorrow," Hank said. "We can open it after school."

"Promise?" Natasha arched a brow, daring Lucy to join the long line of people who'd broken promises to her.

Another promise. Lucy wiped the cheese from her hand and stuck out her little finger. "It's a deal."

Natasha wrapped her pinkie around Lucy's, holding it tight. "Swear?"

"Swear."

The subtle tension rippling through the kid's body eased a fraction. She released Lucy's hand and took another bite of pizza. "Can Dolly sleep with me?"

"Take her out for a quick walk first."

"Okay." She grabbed another slice.

Lucy handed Natasha the flashlight. "Stay close to the house. I don't need you to find a new well the hard way."

"Got it." Natasha winked at the dog, and the two dashed outside.

Hank wrapped the last uneaten slices in cling wrap and put them in the refrigerator. When he turned, he looked at her with such seriousness it unsettled her. "I meant what I said about the DNA test."

"I understand."

"If he said he didn't sleep with Beth, then he didn't."

She held up her hands. "Accepted."

He crossed the room until he was inches from her.

"Why do you care, Hank?"

His aftershave blended with his masculine scent and body heat. And the way he looked at her made her chest feel tight as her stomach fluttered.

He raised his hand to her face and cupped it. Rough calluses brushed her cheek. She didn't want to kiss him, because she knew she'd like it. And liking always led to disappointment.

Still, she leaned in toward him just a fraction. She couldn't seal the deal and press her lips to his. But she could offer a hint to see if he was paying attention.

He was.

Hank raised his other hand and very gently pressed his lips to hers. The almost chaste kiss vibrated with energy and was about the most erotic experience of her life. She moistened her lips and hovered within inches of him. Again, he pressed his lips to hers, but this time there was a heightened urgency that stirred a primal pull. She imagined taking him up to the pink bedroom and . . .

The front door banged open. "Success!" Natasha shouted. "Number one and two!"

Lucy stepped back from Hank and pressed her fingertips to her lips, drawing in a breath before she turned and crossed to Natasha. She blinked, tried to shake off the kiss, and scrounged a smile. "So you're headed up?"

"I am."

Beth had been more of a high-fiver than a hugger kind of mom. She'd treated Lucy like a friend more than a daughter, so whatever mothering had happened between them Lucy had to initiate.

Lucy wasn't Natasha's mother, sister, or cousin, but as she stood there feeling blown away by Hank's kiss and the emotions of the day, she couldn't let the moment pass. And a high five sure didn't cut it.

She took Natasha's chilled fingers in her hand and squeezed. "Thank you for today."

The girl's wide-eyed expression softened, and then she frowned. "Yeah, sure. No sweat."

"I couldn't have done it without you." A lifetime of hiding had her scrambling back toward the practical everyday things that didn't require thought. "I'll take you to school tomorrow. If you want cold pizza, I can pack it for your lunch."

"Cool." The girl turned, stopped, wrapped her thin arms around Lucy, and hugged her. For such a skinny kid, she hugged like she was drowning and holding on for her life.

Lucy slowly raised her arms and held the girl. "Maybe chips and a bottled water too."

"Perfect." Natasha broke away quickly and bounded up the stairs with the dog on her heels. The girl's laughter mingled with the dog's bark.

"I'll see you back here tomorrow afternoon," Hank said as he came up behind her.

"Really? Okay?" She swallowed, searched for a steady voice, and faced him. "I'm sorry, why're you coming back tomorrow?"

He crossed the entryway and paused at the front door. "To open the chest."

"Right, yes. Of course. Like opening Al Capone's vault."

When the door closed behind him, she expelled the breath she'd been holding. Somewhere in the walls a pipe clanged, and in another room, a window rattled.

"Mrs. B, your cottage is sucking me in, and you and I know there's always another shoe to drop. What aren't you telling me?"

CHAPTER TWENTY

Lucy

January 18, 2018

Lucy dropped Natasha off at school at eight. The library wouldn't open for another two hours, so she took Dolly to the shore at the edge of town and walked the beach for almost an hour before she loaded the dog back into the Jeep and took her back to the cottage. After changing quickly, she arrived at the library when it opened at ten.

Mrs. Reynolds was behind the front counter, frowning at a computer screen. When she felt the rush of cold air trailing behind Lucy, she looked up and smiled. "Lucy. How are you doing?"

"I'm well."

"What can I do for you?"

"I'd like to find out more about James Latimer. I think I found his sea chest in the attic of Winter Cottage."

"Really? Now that's fascinating. I've been pulling anything I could find about the area just before World War I. Retrieving those articles for you just got me to wondering.

"James was a jack of all trades, like many of the men in these parts. He was a gunner for the rich hunters."

"A gunner?"

"Basically a guide. He took wealthy hunters to the best spots for hunting duck. I read a diary account that said he knew the waterways on this island better than anyone in the county. And when he wasn't doing that, he manned the lighthouse as an assistant keeper. On top of that, at seventeen, he joined the merchant marines. Jimmy was home on leave, as he often was in the fall, and his first day back, he swam out to a capsized boat and saved a young girl from drowning."

"Mrs. B talks about him saving her."

"Really? The girl was never identified in the papers. Interesting. He continued to rise up through the ranks in the merchant marines, and shortly before the war broke out, he was a captain with his own ship."

"The *Mariah* and the *Reverie?*"

"That's right. But how did you know about the *Reverie?*"

"Mrs. B's tapes. She also talked about having dinner with him and the Jessups before he left on his last tour. She was worried sick about him."

"In this small town, I imagine everyone was saying a prayer for them. And folks were hearing stories about the German U-boats sinking any ships they could."

"It was awful to discover he died at sea."

Mrs. Reynolds adjusted her glasses. "He didn't die at sea. He survived that attack."

"Really? Are you sure?"

"There was an explosion aboard the *Reverie* when it was struck by a torpedo. The first reports indicated all men were lost at sea, but that wasn't true. Jimmy was badly burned while saving over a dozen men. When he was released from the hospital and arrived home in the summer of 1917, everyone rushed up to see him. The folks were appalled at his condition. Several accounts mentioned that the right side of his face was a solid, indistinguishable mass of scar tissue. Jimmy retreated to the boathouse and became a recluse."

Lucy thought about the young, beautiful man Claire had loved. He'd been a man who'd risked his life for the people of this town. "What happened to him?"

"Not long after he returned, he went out in a storm with Robert Buchanan, and neither came back."

"Why would he go out in a storm with Robert?"

"The sheriff asked Mrs. Buchanan several times, but she said she didn't know. And if she did, she took the truth to her grave."

"Were Robert and Jimmy friends?"

"My grandmother remembers Robert. He wasn't well liked in town. There were rumors that he gambled and drank. His father's fortune had made him less of a man."

"Did Mrs. B know her husband's true nature?"

Mrs. Reynolds shook her head. "There were theories, but no one really knew."

"What were the theories?"

"Robert and Mrs. B's marriage did not go over well with the senior Mr. Buchanan. He banished Robert to Winter Cottage with a very small allowance. Robert contracted influenza even before his troop ship set sail for Europe. In the end he never got beyond the New York City docks. He returned to Winter Cottage ready to divorce his wife, but she was very pregnant at that point. He had no choice but to wait, and the longer he waited, the more resentful he became. He drank a lot, and some of the servants saw bruises on Mrs. B's arms. James Latimer wouldn't have been the kind of man who would tolerate behavior like that."

Natasha

Natasha was proud of herself. She'd gone a whole morning without wanting to punch anyone, curse, or cry. She'd paid attention in English class and knew all the answers in math and in history, and she'd shared what she and Lucy had found in the attic. The teacher and kids were really interested. It was a cool story. And it was hers to tell.

So when she came out of the school ten minutes early, she didn't mind the cold, and she wasn't thinking about where she was going to sleep tonight, if she'd have food in her belly, or if her father was going to make trouble. She was thinking about the trunk that had belonged to James Latimer. He'd been a sailor. He'd traveled the world. A kind of hero. And maybe he'd brought back buried treasure.

The rumble of her father's truck engine was her first yank back to reality and a clear sign that the good times never lasted. At first she kept walking and didn't dare turn around. Sometimes he just hovered, usually in his truck because his knees were bothering him. Old football injury, he once said.

But as the engine grew louder, she tightened her hand on the strap of her backpack and turned to face him. It would only be worse if she ignored him when he caught up to her.

Her father parked and eased out of the cab, but he kept the engine running. A beer can tumbled out after him. He moved slower these days, but she wasn't fooled. All he had to do was land one punch to flatten her. "Natasha!"

She glanced around and was sorry now for being early. She stepped back, hating herself for not being brave enough to hold her ground. But both knew one of his backhanded slaps always softened up whatever toughness she'd mustered for the rest of the world.

"Come here," he said. He was smiling, but he always smiled when he wanted something.

Her chin trembled, but she still raised it in defiance. "I'm waiting for Lucy."

He looked around, didn't see anyone yet, and took a step toward her. He winced as his knee buckled a bit. "I need to talk to you. Now."

Maybe she could outrun him now, but there'd always be a later. "I don't want to talk now, Dad."

The smile melted faster than butter on a hot day. "Get in the truck. I'm picking you up and taking you home."

She looked around, seeing the first few students trickle out. The last bell would ring soon, and everyone would be out here. "I'm staying with Lucy right now. I'm not staying at home."

Like a snake, he struck, closing the distance in a blink, and grabbed her arm. They'd not called him "Lightning" in high school for nothing.

"Let go of me!" He reeked of beer, whiskey, and body odor all rolled up together.

He twisted her arm, and pain shot up through her body. "I don't appreciate your back talk. Your mama had a mouth on her, and I never did like it either."

Natasha cried out and dropped to a knee. "Daddy, just let me go."

"I'm not letting you go until I get you home and you tell me all you know about your new friend." He wrenched her arm, and she cried out. She could swear bone was breaking. Excruciating pain and nausea overwhelmed her.

And then when she thought she couldn't draw in another breath, she heard the honking of a horn, a dog snarling, and a woman screaming. It was fury unleashed and closing fast on her.

Her father tightened his grip. As she looked up, Lucy was teeing up her baseball bat, and Dolly was ready to take a bite.

Lucy's face was twisted with fury, and she looked a little possessed. "I'll crack your skull right where you stand if you don't step away from that kid."

"What do you care how I discipline *my* kid?"

"I've cracked more skulls with this bat than I can remember, and adding yours to the list won't mean much to me. In fact, I might land in jail. But I promise you that you'll be eating through a straw for a long time." Dolly growled and moved forward. "And my dog bites."

Her father's smirk faded, and his grip loosened. "To hell with you."

Natasha jerked away from him, holding her arm and not sure if she should stay or run. She looked toward the entrance of the school, and a teacher with a cell phone was already calling someone.

Her father lunged toward Lucy, but she was already in midswing. She caught him on the shoulder with the bat. He hollered and jumped back. "What the hell? You hit me?"

Dolly got between him and Natasha and started snapping.

Lucy cocked the bat for the next swing. "And I'm just getting warmed up. Maybe I can get in a few more swings before the sheriff arrives. He should be here any second."

A crowd of kids was gathering, and a teacher ran out of the building toward them. If her father thought he could sneak in here, grab her, and run, then he was wrong. And mention of the sheriff was enough to take some of the wind out of his sails. Natasha knew he hated backing down, but he hated jail more.

Holding his shoulder, he fumbled for the handle of his truck door and flung it open. He cursed a few times and then shouted, "This ain't over between us."

"Oh, you can count on that, Brian," Lucy said as she came up to the passenger side. "I promise you I'm not finished with you yet."

Her father shifted into first gear and lurched forward, punching the gas and speeding off.

Lucy and Dolly looked at each other and then at Natasha. Teachers gathered around her. Mr. Cook, the PE teacher, asked her if she wanted to coach girls' softball. Mrs. Daniels, the principal, said the sheriff was on his way.

But Lucy barely nodded to them all as she crossed the sidewalk to Natasha. "Are you okay, kid?"

"I'm fine, now." Dolly came up to her and licked her hand.

"What about your arm?" Lucy's breathing was still quick, and she still gripped the bat as if expecting more trouble.

Natasha rubbed the dog between the ears. "Daddy turned my arm pretty good. But I don't think it's broken."

"That's not up to you to decide. I'm taking you to the doctor." Lucy hugged her close. She melted into the embrace, and it felt almost like the times her mama used to hold her. Tears choked her throat, and as much as she wanted to be brave, she started to sob. And they weren't cute, pretty tears like Angie Hanover cried when the teacher asked where her homework was. They were big, slobbery tears.

But they didn't seem to bother Lucy, who held her closer and patted her back with a hand that trembled just a little.

The principal prattled on to Lucy about how they were sorry. Natasha had slipped out a little early. Normally there's a teacher on duty. Lucy nodded politely and said they'd talk about it later. Not to worry. She had it under control.

As they walked to the Jeep, Lucy fished out her cell phone. "Hank, this is Lucy." Natasha missed most of what Lucy said because she shot the words out so fast, she might as well have been firing a machine gun. "Right, got it."

Lucy opened the front door of her Jeep. Dolly jumped onto the seat and then into the back as Natasha settled inside. A kid from the school handed Natasha her backpack, which Lucy stowed. Lucy reached in her glove box, dug out some clean fast-food napkins, and handed them to her.

"What about the chest?" Natasha blew her nose. "I've been waiting all day to find out what was in it. I don't want to go to the doctor. I'm fine."

"Not about what you want right now, kid. Hank's meeting us at the clinic. He said the town doc can check your arm and x-ray it."

She thumped her head against the headrest in frustration. "Ahh. This sucks."

"It could have been a hell of a lot worse, kid."

Lucy

When Hank pushed through the door of the doctor's office, his expression bordered on murderous. His keys and phone were gripped in his fists, and he was wearing faded jeans, dusty work boots, and a jacket that read BEACON VINEYARDS. He strode toward the front reception window and leaned in until the nurse on the phone hung up. "Where's Natasha?"

"Doctor's with her now," the nurse said quickly.

Lucy rose along with Dolly. The adrenaline bump that had sent her charging out of the car had faded, and her body was spent. She smoothed shaking hands along her jeans. "Hank, she's in X-ray."

Hank looked at her with eyes clouded with rage and worry. "What happened? Why weren't you there?"

"I was a few minutes late getting to the school, and Natasha apparently slipped out of school early. I was in the library. Lost track of time and then had to run back to the cottage to get Dolly."

He held up his hand, a signal he didn't want to hear the rest. "What happened?"

She brushed a lock of hair from her eyes. "Her father showed up, and he tried to force her into his car."

Hands on hips, he leaned toward her. "But he didn't, correct?"

"No, I arrived in time. Her arm was badly twisted, and the doctor wants to make sure there isn't a spiral fracture. He should be out any moment." She desperately wanted him to hold her. During Beth's illness, she'd made several trips to the emergency room, and she'd grown to hate everything about it.

But Hank's rigid body offered no invitation or tenderness, and his entire demeanor made her feel worse.

"Jesus, Lucy, I trusted you," he said.

"And I was a minute late," she retorted. His words were like a spark to tinder. Everything that had frustrated her over the last five months combusted into flames. "I don't need you standing here and judging me."

"You were late," he repeated.

"One minute!" Dolly's ears perked, and she nudged closer to Lucy.

"Lower your voice," he said.

"Why?" she said loud enough for everyone to hear. "The whole damn town knows each other's business, and I'm sure they're all talking about what a screw-up Lucy Kincaid is now."

A muscle pulsed in his jaw. "No one is saying that. I'm not." He shoved out a breath. "They're saying you were a badass."

She shook her head. In truth, she'd been terrified. She'd had no idea what she was going to do or how she was going to stop a six-foot-two bully. She'd broken up her share of bar fights, but there had always been a bouncer who'd had her back. Willard would have killed her if he could.

When she didn't speak, he took her hand in his. "I'm sure he's nursing a few bruises. Where's Rick?"

"He's in there talking to Natasha now. Why didn't he arrive sooner? This is a small town."

"It's just him on the police force, and he covers a large area. He's got a part-time deputy, but it's mostly him."

Her temper was cooling and her nerves calming. She liked holding his hand.

"What were you doing at the library?" he asked.

"Reading up on Winter Cottage." The history had grabbed her by the collar and wouldn't let go. She'd actually been resentful when the alarm on her phone sounded and she had to get up and leave to get Natasha. But she could never tell this to Hank. He was a man who always did the right thing. He wouldn't have been late.

Rick came out from the examining room and crossed the lobby directly to Hank and Lucy. "You can relax," he said. "She's fine. No breaks. Maybe a sprain, so the doctor is wrapping it now."

"When can we see her?" Lucy asked.

"It'll be a few more minutes," he said. "And while we got the time, why don't you tell me what happened. Natasha gave me her version, but she's a little dopey on pain meds now. She keeps saying you can swing a bat like a pro."

"It's a bat I kept behind the bar in Nashville. I brought it with me from Nashville just in case I had trouble on the road. When I pulled up and saw Natasha struggling with her dad, I didn't think twice about grabbing the bat." Recounting the story triggered another surge of adrenaline. "Have you found Willard?"

Rick flipped a page in a small notebook. "We're still looking for him."

"When you do, he's going to tell you I hit him with the bat," Lucy said. "He's right, and it wasn't a glancing blow."

The sheriff's mouth quirked, but he didn't allow a smile. "You were defending Natasha, correct?"

"She was screaming," she said. "And I once learned in a self-defense class that if you're going to take a swing, you better make the first one count."

Hank muttered something under his breath. "He could have killed you."

"Like I said, I figured I'd only get one time at bat."

Rick's expression lost all traces of humor as he scribbled a few words in his notebook. "Hank's right, you don't know Brian. He would have snapped your neck."

"And we all know he's hurt Natasha before," Hank said.

"I hear you," Rick said, "but I have to make sure I understand what happened if this ever gets to court."

"Why would it go to court?" Hank said.

"Everything seems to make it to court these days," he said. "But Lucy doesn't have to worry. I've spoken to a few folks at school, and they said exactly the same thing. Brian rolled up, exchanged words with Natasha, and seconds later she was screaming and trying to get away."

The sounds of that child's screams would rattle in Lucy's head for a long time. "Can I see her now? I'd like to take her back to the cottage." She couldn't bring herself to say *home*. The word *home* carried with it a lifetime of obligations that still scared the hell out of her.

"Sure, the doc should be done now," Rick said.

"I'm going with you," Hank said. His jaw was pulsing again, and his tone verged on terse, but his fingers had relaxed from tight to loose fists.

"Sure," Lucy said.

"She's in cubicle six," Rick said. "One more question. Where's the Peacemaker?"

"She's in the car."

"She?" Rick said.

"Sure, why not?" With Dolly trailing behind her, Lucy pushed through the doors and strode straight to cubicle six. She swiped back the curtain and found Natasha sitting on her bed, grinning and hugging her arm, which now rested in a sling. The swoosh of the curtain made the kid flinch as her head swiveled around. When she saw Lucy, the stress wrinkling her brow eased a little.

"Luceee. Dolleee," Natasha said. "I've been asking for you."

The kid was loopy, which was for the best. Lucy came up by the bed and carefully took Natasha's good hand in hers. "I'm sorry I wasn't there when you got out of school."

"Late, *schmate*. Anything under an hour isn't late. Not late at all. I was early. I wanted to open the chest." She rolled her head toward Hank. "Look, the gang is all here."

"Hey, kiddo," Hank said.

"I should have been a little early. I'm sorry."

"Who'd ever have thought my dad would be on *time*," Natasha said. "He's never on time. *Ever.*" Her brows drew together as she eyed Lucy. "You sure did hit him hard. I've never seen him that mad before. I thought he was going to kill you."

Hank's frown returned, and the fingers of his right hand flexed, reminding her of a boxer before he gloved up. "Sheriff Rick is looking for your dad, Natasha."

"He's violated his parole," the girl said. "He won't want to go back to jail. He'll be hard to find."

"That's too bad," Lucy said. "Because Rick is going to find him and lock him up."

The girl didn't express relief as most might expect. Instead, her worry deepened with the lines in her forehead and around her mouth. Lucy understood. As much as the girl feared her father, he was her only family. And though he was the devil in many respects, he was the devil she knew. He was family. Blood. And it did count, no matter what anyone said.

"Ready to go back to the cottage?" Lucy said.

"You still want me?" Natasha shook her head. "With Dad running around, that's probably not too smart."

"The doors have good locks," Lucy said. "And the walls are a couple of feet thick."

"And until your father is caught," Hank said, "I can stay at the cottage."

"Would you?" Natasha sounded relieved. "I mean Lucy can wield a bat like nobody's business, but it might take more than a bat the next time Dad stops by."

"As long as it's okay with Lucy," he said.

Natasha, Hank, and Dolly looked at her. Natasha was hopeful. Hank's gaze challenged. Dolly's tail was wagging. She could take care of Natasha and Dolly without Hank. She knew how to be careful. But the reality was she had to sleep sometime, and this wasn't just about her. She had to think about the kid. And if she could just get over the idea that Hank would be sleeping down the hall, well, she would be just fine. "Sure."

"He can stay in the yellow room," Natasha said.

Right. The one that was connected to the pink room. "Sure."

"Can we open the trunk when we get home?" Natasha asked. "Everyone at school is curious to know what's in it. I want to tell them what we found tomorrow."

"Let's see how you're feeling. And you might not be going to school for a few days."

"Why not? I have a story *and* a sling. I want to go."

Hank grinned. "Never thought I'd hear you whining about not going to school."

She rubbed her hand over her injured arm. "Hank, you should have seen Lucy. She looked like Wonder Woman."

Hank allowed a slow, lazy grin as his gaze slid over her. "Really?"

"Not that dramatic," Lucy said.

"I wish I'd seen it," he said. "The sheriff said folks are all talking about it."

That warmth that seemed to spread through her body when he was around started heating up again. And seeing as they were going to be in adjoining rooms, she knew there would be trouble if she didn't check her feelings for Hank.

"Enough about my crime fighting. Let's get Natasha home," Lucy said.

"Yes, ma'am." And as he rose he whispered, "Can't wait to find out where you keep the Lasso of Truth."

CHAPTER
TWENTY-ONE

Beth

June 5, 1988

Beth is over a half hour late, and when she pushes through the sturdy door of the cottage, she can see Mrs. B is annoyed. The old woman has a thing for punctuality and says tardiness is right up there with stealing. *Time is our most precious thing*, or some BS like that.

Her stomach is queasy, and she has one hell of a headache, but she tries not to think about either. She wonders what is happening in Paris or Nashville now. She bets people in big cities live happy, exciting lives.

Beth opens the pocket doors leading into the parlor. "Hey, Mrs. B. I'd blame it on traffic, but we don't have any around here."

The older woman is dressed in a pale-green dress with three-quarter-length sleeves made of a knit fabric. There is a matching belt at her waist. As always, she's wearing her ivory pin. The old woman's hair is styled in a twist, which Beth practiced the other night but found that her long blonde hair refused to stay pinned.

Beth's hands tremble as she tucks her hair behind her ear and begins to rummage through her camera bag for the microphone. She's glad she has Mrs. B today. It's a bright spot in a world that is getting more and more confusing.

"What is wrong with you?" Mrs. B asked.

She doesn't look up, afraid her face shows her fear. "I'm late. Isn't that enough?"

"You look pale."

"I'm pretty white, even in the summer."

"You also look upset."

"Because I'm late. I know how you hate it."

The old woman scoffs. "You've never been upset by tardiness before. I doubt you've ever been worried about time. What is wrong with you?"

Some of her frustration bubbles to the surface. "It didn't go so well with Noah. I made a play for him, and he said no. Did you know he married his girlfriend? And guess what, she's pregnant." Beth shrugs. "I thought she was getting fat."

"I wasn't aware of the baby. His father and grandfather are honorable men, and he's a good boy. And I like his girlfriend." A delicate gray brow arched. "I told you he was committed to Nancy."

"It was stupid. I get that. I just wanted a little bit of nice in my life." Her grin is exaggerated. "What is Noah's kid to you? Some great-great something?"

"Great-nephew," the old woman said.

"More babies for Winter Cottage. You like babies, right?"

Beth wonders why the hell she's talking about babies as she sets up the camera on the tripod. There are times when she kinda wishes the old lady were her grandmother or distant relative. It would be a comfort to be able to share with her. But if she tells the old lady how she's screwing up her life, then she'll see disappointment and regret. Beth can't bear that.

"Where's your father?"

"He's still at sea. He'll be home in a couple of weeks."

"Is anyone staying with you at your house?"

"I've been staying alone since I was fifteen. I'm fine."

"What is that on your wrist?" Mrs. B asks. "Is that a bruise?"

Beth glances at the ring of purple around her wrist and carefully tugs down her sleeve. "Nothing. I'm fine. We better get started if we're going to tape today. Mrs. Reynolds is super excited. Says I'm exceeding her wildest expectations."

Mrs. B was having none of it. "No one should leave bruises on you, Elizabeth."

"It was an accident." And it kind of was. If Beth had known one joke would have pissed him off so much, she wouldn't have made it. "Don't look at me like that."

"Like what?"

"Disappointed."

"I understand more than you realize. You think I'm a silly old woman. But I have seen nearly a hundred years, and I know when an accident is not an accident."

Mrs. B looks ready to interject more wisdom Beth doesn't want to hear. How could this rich old woman really know? She lives in a big house and has all the money in the world. Bad stuff doesn't happen to people like that.

Beth hits "Record" and says, "Rolling."

Claire

October 1916

Robert went off to his war, and Claire was glad to see him go. As she'd kissed him goodbye, they'd both looked into each other's eyes, and she saw her own feelings mirrored back. Their impulsive marriage had been a terrible mistake. She knew he feared his father's reaction, whereas she couldn't forgive him for refusing to adopt Victoria's baby.

Shortly after his car drove away, she climbed the stairs to check on Victoria. They'd be leaving for New York in a week or so. However, the girl was still in bed, and her body burned with a raging fever.

Claire sat at Victoria's bedside for the rest of that day, applying cold compresses and feeding her peppermint tea to reduce the fever.

After Victoria's body broke into a sweat and her eyes cleared, she was still too weak to sit up, lying curled on her side and silent. Despite repeated telegrams from Mrs. Buchanan, Victoria was not fit to travel.

Finally, as Victoria's health improved enough to travel, Claire's faltered. She thought perhaps she had caught whatever illness her younger charge had contracted, but she soon realized she was pregnant.

The train ride north was a long, miserable journey. Her waistband now tightened against her expanding belly, and Victoria, who was not the least bit pleased about her marriage to Robert, remained mutinously silent through the trip. With each lurch and rock of the train, Claire's worry and nausea grew as she thought about facing the Buchanans.

When they stepped out of the carriage in New York's Upper West Side, the fall air was crisp and cool. The Buchanans' residence was heavily influenced by French architecture and contained works of art that dated back to France's King Louis XV. Inside, there were three elevators, eight fireplaces, a large banquet hall, and a swimming pool. The garden behind the house was as large as a city park and filled with topiaries, a fish pond, and several water fountains. Anyone who lived on the Eastern Shore would never understand Winter Cottage's humble moniker. But as she stood here now, she understood.

Claire had always entered the house through the back entrance, but now she had to resist the urge to do so. Pressing a handkerchief to her lips, she pulled back her shoulders and followed Victoria inside.

Victoria climbed the stairs, and as she reached for the front door, it swung open to Edward. Her cousin wasn't the most handsome man, and his body never did justice to his tailor's work, but the bright smile on his face showed how much he'd missed Victoria.

Victoria normally shooed him away when he beamed like a puppy dog, but this time she wrapped her arms around him. "I have missed you, Edward."

Edward embraced her, a mixture of love and relief softening his features. Then he lifted his head and addressed Claire with a mixture of pity and disappointment. "Claire."

"Mr. Edward."

"You're wanted in the study," he said.

"Of course."

He took Victoria by the hand and pulled her into the study, leaving Claire to follow. The study was a massive room with floor-to-ceiling bookshelves filled with leather-bound tomes. A portrait of Mr. Buchanan's father hung above a gray marble fireplace, and a hand-made red-and-navy Turkish rug warmed the floor. Mr. Buchanan stood by his wife, who sat in a burgundy tufted chair.

"Daddy," Victoria said, crossing the room.

Her father embraced his daughter, and he kissed her gently on the forehead. "I understand you haven't been well."

"It's the reason Claire and I couldn't travel home until now."

"We were worried about you."

"I'm no worse for the wear," she said.

The father held his daughter back, inspecting her thin frame, and then smiled. "I think you and Edward should have something to eat. You're too thin. I know Cook has made all your favorites."

"Yes, Daddy," she said.

Victoria tucked her arm into Edward's, and the two left Claire alone with people who had been a part of her life for nearly sixteen years. However, this new relationship they shared made them virtual strangers.

Mr. Buchanan walked to a large mahogany desk and sat behind it while his wife rose and closed the door to the study. "It looks like you've taken good care of Victoria. I'm grateful, and it's the reason you're here now."

He was treating her like a servant, ignoring the wedding vows and the growing baby in her belly. "She's young and strong and I think has recovered fully."

"Good."

"You received Robert's telegram about our wedding."

He studied papers in front of him. "I did. It's why I've had annulment papers drawn up."

"Annulment?" she asked.

"You didn't think I'd stand for Robert's latest rebellion, did you? You're another one of his messes that I have to clean up." He tipped the nib of his pen in an inkwell. "You'll be compensated."

"We were lawfully wed," she said. "And before you proceed, you should know that I'm pregnant with your *next* grandchild."

The word *next* cut between them. Perhaps if Mr. Buchanan had been kinder, or if Victoria had uttered one word of thanks, she'd have thought twice. Or if she'd been feeling better, or if Robert had been at her side, or if Jimmy were alive. *Or, or, or.* But none of those options were available to her, and she could not afford to be docile. If she didn't play her best card now, she'd never get another chance.

Mrs. Buchanan came to stand beside her, inspecting her breasts and her belly. She shook her head, looking up at her husband.

"How do I know it's Robert's baby?" the old man countered.

"It's Robert's baby, and I'm sure there are several people in the village who would testify that I was almost never seen in town through the summer and was always accompanied by Mrs. Latimer."

"I could bring witnesses to say otherwise."

"Yes, you could. And I could bring witnesses who can speak about the baby Victoria delivered five weeks ago. I'm sure Edward would not have to dig too deeply to find the boy." She was playing with fire, but she sensed her father-in-law's fear of a scandal outweighed any action against the child.

Mr. Buchanan tossed down the pen, splattering black ink on the paper. "What do you want?"

This world, *their world*, would never be hers, nor did she want it to be. She wanted what was hers. "To return to Winter Cottage. I want the house deeded in my name, and I want a trust set up to take care of me and my child."

"Don't forget your husband. He's a part of your new package."

"Of course."

He opened a box, counted out cash, and set it on the edge of his desk. "Go on then, take your money and get out of here. I'll have papers sent to your hotel room by tomorrow."

She swayed on her feet, half hoping she didn't disgrace herself and throw up on his carpet. The door opened with a small click, and she turned to see Mrs. Buchanan standing by the door. Her gaze was soft, but her chin was tipped up in resoluteness.

She left through the front door, praying she and Robert could make a good life.

———— ✌ ————

Robert's military service could only be described as a disappointment. He'd contracted influenza before he'd set sail and spent the last half year recovering in a friend's home in Baltimore.

When Robert stepped off the train carrying his bag, it was nearly April, and the weather had turned bitterly cold. His tie was loosened, and his cap set back on his head. For most men, she wouldn't have thought twice about the casual stance, but that wasn't Robert. He had always been so careful about his appearance.

Her belly was heavy when she hurried up to him and wrapped her arms around him. Slowly his hands came up, and she felt him embrace her. "You smell good," he said, burying his face in the crook of her arm. "All I've smelled for the last six months is sickness."

She kissed him on the cheek, wishing she were excited to see him. The last few days, there'd only been dread and worry. "I'm glad you're home."

As a husband and wife, they were strangers, but months alone had sown the seeds of hope that once the baby was born and her body returned to normal, she'd feel the desire she knew a woman could have for a man.

"Home. I suppose this is home for me now." He looked around the town's small train station and then at her with such dissatisfaction she felt like she'd been struck.

She smiled, putting mental distance between herself and his disappointment. "I know it's been hard for you, being so ill, but the salt air cures most ills."

They walked to the waiting carriage, and he helped her climb aboard and then sat next to her. A boy who worked at the cottage had come with her, and he drove them home. They sat in silence, each lost in their own worries.

When they reached Winter Cottage, Robert helped her down, and she waddled into the house. Mrs. Latimer, thinner and grayer now, greeted them. "Welcome home, Mr. Buchanan."

"Thank you," he said. "If you two don't mind, I'd like to rest. Claire, would you bring me up a decanter of bourbon?"

"Are you sure you should be drinking?" she asked. "You've been sick."

"I'm surer now than ever." He shrugged off his jacket, handed it to her, and climbed the stairs.

Mrs. Latimer accepted the coat as she shook her head. "Be careful," she said. "He's looking for someone to blame for his turn of fortune."

She heard the door close upstairs. "He asked me to marry him. I'm carrying his child."

"And you're the reason he's banished from New York."

She smoothed her hands over her belly. "I was trying to protect his child."

"Yes, you were." Mrs. Latimer smoothed her hand over the coat, absently checking the pockets as she always did when one of the men returned home. In the right breast pocket she found a small, empty flask. "Be careful."

"Make him a sandwich. I'll take it up."

Mrs. Latimer carried the coat with her into the kitchen, leaving Claire to fill a decanter with what little bourbon remained in the house. Without the influx of winter hunters or the Buchanans, luxury items that had been restocked almost daily were ignored. Mr. Buchanan had deeded her the house, but the money set aside for its maintenance had been put in a trust that maintained the house but paid its occupant a small stipend that covered only the most basic needs.

When the sandwich was ready, she carried the tray up to the second floor and knocked briefly before entering the blue room.

Robert stood by the window, staring at the lighthouse and the bay. His hands were in his pockets, and he'd removed his vest, tie, and shirt. He'd grown so thin, she could see the faint outline of his ribs through his knit undershirt.

"Why didn't you accept my father's offer?" he asked.

She set the tray down on a small round table. "We're lawfully married and expecting a child."

"Yes. We. Are."

"Are you sorry I didn't take the money and sign the papers?"

Facing her, he crossed the room and laid his hands on her shoulders, rubbing her smooth skin. His hands had grown rougher since their wedding night. And his touch was bolder, not seducing but demanding.

Husbands were supposed to want their wives. Her father had loved her mother. She'd sacrificed her life to give him the sons he wanted. But as Robert pushed the cotton away from her shoulder and kissed the naked flesh, she didn't feel love but hate.

The drip of his moist kiss on her skin sent ripples of angst, not desire, through her. Hands came up and squeezed her breasts hard, twisting her nipple until she pulled away in pain.

"Robert, perhaps this is not the best time," she said.

He wrapped his hand around her wrist, tightening until those calloused fingers manacled around her skin. "How can you reject a husband you accepted over a fortune?"

She pushed his hand away. "What has changed so much? I thought I was protecting our marriage—which you wanted."

"You're my wife. I'm your husband. This is what you're supposed to do for me, correct?"

"You weren't like this before."

He unfastened the buttons at the top of his pants. Their lovemaking in the days after their wedding had been discreet and modest. She'd yet to see him fully naked and wasn't keen to do so now.

He placed his hand to her belly and quickly turned her around, pushing her toward the wall. Her cheek hit the cool plaster and scraped against it.

Pain throbbed in her head. "Robert, no! Our reunion should be tender."

Rough hands jerked up her gown and exposed her knitted underwear. She felt him fumble against her bare skin, and when she wouldn't open her legs for him, he jabbed his knee between her thighs, prying her legs open. She wasn't ready for him, so his first attempt at entry failed. When she tried to move away from the wall, he laid his forearm against the back of her neck, pinning her. With his other hand, he repositioned, and this time he was ready for the resistance with force. He pushed inside her, tearing as he went.

She cried out, and tears filled her eyes. "Robert, why are you doing this?"

"Do you know why I married you?" he said with his second thrust. She closed her eyes, trying to drive the tension from her body.

"Because I was angry at my father. He'd forced me into the military. Said it would make a proper man out of me." He shoved into her again. "Said when I got back, I'd be grateful to marry the right kind of woman and follow his lead into business." He gripped her hips, his fingernails biting into her skin. "I found the least proper woman for him, determined to teach him a lesson."

Tears welled in her eyes as he pounded into her until guttural sounds escaped his lips.

He collapsed against her, pressing his chest against her back. Tears ran down her face as his heaving breath filled her ears. "He was so angry when I told him about you and then Victoria. I thought he would have a stroke. He begged me to let you go. I told him to pay you off, and when I returned home, we would start fresh. But you wouldn't take the money. So now we're here, trapped in this prison together."

He stepped back, fastened his pants, and crossed the room to the decanter. He poured himself a drink. When she turned, she didn't recognize the harsh features that took delight in her red-rimmed eyes and bruised shoulders.

For the next six weeks, she was never alone with him. He stayed in his room and drank. She slept with her door locked, a kitchen knife under her pillow.

Claire was nearly nine months pregnant when word came to the cottage that another man had returned home. It was Jimmy Latimer.

Jimmy had survived the ship that had burst into flames and sunk. He'd been in the Caribbean, healing from his wounds. But she would soon discover that he too wasn't the same man she'd once known.

CHAPTER
TWENTY-TWO

Lucy

January 18, 2018

Lucy helped Natasha up to her room and settled her under the covers.

"You were pretty great today," Natasha said groggily.

"I wish I'd been early."

Natasha's eyes drifted closed and then opened again. "Promise you won't open the chest without me."

"I won't."

The girl grabbed Lucy's hand, squeezing with a surprising grip. "Promise?"

"I won't."

Lucy tucked the blanket up under the girl's chin. She wanted to do more than just promise about the chest. She wanted to promise about the future and tell her everything would be all right. But she couldn't do that.

The smell of coffee greeted her when she entered the kitchen. Hank was standing by the counter, looking over some papers. He was frowning.

"Everything all right?" She crossed to the fridge and retrieved the milk.

"Bank stuff. I have a meeting in the morning."

"Tell me about your plans before I came into the picture."

"I wanted to develop a beach community. What little land is left in the Virginia Beach area is too expensive and overdeveloped. Jobs also would have come. It was ideal for a mixed-use development. There's also deep-water access. Should the vineyard scale up, thanks to your renewed lease, a winery man can be added, and he will enhance the area even more."

"I haven't even seen the vineyard except what I glimpsed driving onto the property."

"Not much to see this time of year. But I'll take you anytime." He shook his head. "Not everyone in town welcomes change, but it's now a matter of grow or perish. Families have been in this area since colonial times, but there are so few young families left. They need jobs to stay. The development could change all that."

"You're taking a big risk."

"I am." The coffeepot gurgled out the last of the brew, and he poured two cups.

She added milk to hers and remembered to put a bit more generous amount in his. "Why do you want to do this?"

"I've got to make this work. I have a thousand moving parts, and there's not much margin for error."

She sipped her coffee. He made his coffee as strong as she made hers. "You strike me as the kind of guy who doesn't lose often."

"Here's hoping."

"You don't have to stay here tonight. I really can take care of myself and Natasha."

He set his cup down carefully. "I said I would, and I will."

Truth be told, she didn't want him to leave, and that in and of itself was a warning sign. "You just said yourself you have a meeting tomorrow."

"I'll get up early. I've done it enough times before. Do you want me to open the chest for you?" The question put further discussion to rest.

"Natasha asked me to wait. She wants to see it opened. She's on enough pain meds, so she'll sleep through the night and into the morning."

"Good."

"What are you going to do about Brian?"

"He might be doing more than a little jail time, and he knows it. That makes him dangerous."

Lucy gave Hank a tentative smile.

"You've been here only a few days, and already you're making friends." An attempt at a smile suggested he was trying to lighten the situation.

A bigger smile tugged at her lips. "I thought this place was going to be a sweet little town. Instead, a crazy guy is stalking me, there are bones in my well, and the house is haunted. And there is the matter that no one can tell me who my father is."

His eyes glinted with humor. "Small-town living."

"You've got to admit, it's an odd place. I see the charm—the quiet has been a nice change, and it is a beautiful place."

"How's it going with the tapes?"

"I'm down to my last tape, so if Mrs. B has any secrets to share, she'd better do it soon, or I'll be back to testing the DNA of every man in town."

Hank rolled up his sleeves, revealing an antique gold wristwatch. "What was your mother like?"

"Beth was a good soul, and she loved me. She could never understand why she should clean a house or cook a meal when neither lasted. In her mind, her songs were her real legacy."

"How did she do?"

"A few small successes when I was younger, but she never made it to the Country Music Association Awards. I'm not going to pretend it was all wonderful. We went our separate ways for several years. I had been accepted to art school six years ago, but there was no money. I was trying to save, but she told me I was wasting my time on school. We fought, and I took a big break from her. We were still estranged when she became sick, but she called, and I came. By the end, we got past all that and had grown close again. My mom even said she wasn't mad at the cancer that was killing her because without it, she may never have gotten me back."

"I'm sorry."

"I really admire what you've done here for your family and the people in this town. I'm glad I could help in a small way."

"It was a big way."

"I wish I could do more."

A calm intensity smoldered in his eyes as he took her cup and set it beside his on the counter. He cupped her face in his hands and kissed her. She leaned into the kiss.

"You're sure about your father?" she said, pulling back.

"So damn sure," he said, his lips brushing hers.

A night with Hank could easily rank among her top-ten lifetime mistakes. But that was the thing about wanting and all the lust, desire, and craving that went along with it. It always shouted out warnings.

So when he took her by the hand and quietly headed toward the stairs, she followed. There were plenty of steps and moments for reason and common sense to find their voices. Yet there was nothing but the sound of stairs creaking.

He took her to the pink room. Moonlight streamed in through the window, illuminating the rumpled sheets on the bed she'd not made this morning.

He kissed her again, letting his fingertips trail over her collarbone and to the top button just above her breasts. He drew small circles on her skin and then unfastened the button. He hesitated, watching her face closely. "You sure about this?"

A chuckle rumbled in her chest. "If I waited for *sure*, I'd be waiting a long time."

He undid the next button, revealing the lace topping her bra. His palm smoothed over her breast, cupping it.

She reached for the hem of her blouse and pulled it over her head. "Seriously, yes."

He helped her tug the top free. Moonlight glistened on her skin, and he kissed the mounds of her breasts. A lump formed in her throat, and she struggled to catch her breath.

She stepped back and removed her bra. He was a step behind her but began removing his own clothes. Naked, she lay back on the bed. He slowly slid his body over hers.

She ran her hands over his thighs. His muscles were taut, and she could feel the urgency in his body that now mirrored her own.

When he kissed her, the world beyond the walls faded away. It was just the two of them.

Her own desires were building, and a part of her wanted to race to the climax.

But he was a slow and patient lover, taking his time and teasing her body, bringing it to almost the brink and then back again. When she thought she couldn't stand it anymore, she turned her sights on his body. She lost track of how long they played this erotic back and forth dance until finally neither of them could take it another step, and together they tumbled into the abyss.

January 19, 2018

When Lucy woke up, the morning sun was streaming through her windows, and she could hear footsteps padding in the hallway. She sat up, glanced toward the other side of the bed, and found only the impression of where Hank's body had been last night. He'd risen early, so quiet she'd not heard him leave for his meeting.

She glanced under the sheet, realized she was still naked, and quickly tossed the sheets back and scrambled to find her jeans and T-shirt. When Natasha appeared in her door, she was zipping up her jeans.

"Did Hank spend the night?" Natasha asked.

She cleared her throat, dug a band out of her pocket, and combed her hair into a ponytail as she hustled toward the door. "He did."

"His bed is made."

"You know Hank." She secured her hair. "He's a neat freak."

"Yeah. That's very Hank. Hey, can we eat? I'm starving."

"Sure. How's the arm?"

She wiggled her fingers. "Good. Did you open the chest?"

"Waiting for you."

"Where's Hank?"

"Norfolk. Meeting with investors."

Natasha rubbed her arm, wincing a little when her fingers touched her wrist. "Any word from my dad?"

Last night was the first night Lucy had slept really well in a long time. "Not that I'm aware of."

Natasha's brow wrinkled. "Don't be fooled. He's out there, and he's going to cause trouble."

She took the girl's hand in her own. "Hank and I will handle him."

Her head cocked. "You say that like you're a team."

The girl's leap wasn't as unsettling as it should have been. "That's hard to say."

"When will Hank be back?"

"Tonight."

"Cool."

"Need help getting dressed?" Lucy asked.

"No, Lucy, you can't see me without my shirt on. What if you see my bra?"

"News flash, I've seen bras before." The girl's frown reminded Lucy she'd gone through her own modest stage at about this age. "What if I promise not to look? I'll look away during the entire process."

She looked toward the door to double-check it was closed. "You swear?"

"Swear. You know, I've got the same equipment as you."

"Yours are much bigger than mine. There are other girls in school with big ones. Mine are puny."

"So were mine at your age."

"Really?"

"Really. I promise they'll grow to the perfect size, whatever that is."

With her gaze toward the ceiling, Lucy held the T-shirt up so that Natasha could slide her injured arm in first. The girl groaned and winced, but she worked the arm into the sleeve and then the other.

Natasha tugged her shirt hem down. "You didn't look?"

Lucy crossed her heart. "Didn't see a thing. You ready for breakfast?"

"I'm starving."

"Good, we'll eat, and I'll get you off to school." She reached for the brush, headband, and conditioner, and without a word, Natasha turned and let Lucy do her hair like this was a routine they'd always shared.

After breakfast, Lucy and Dolly dropped Natasha off at school. She waited outside as Natasha walked up to the front, proudly showing her sling to a couple of the girls. A teacher joined them, waved to Lucy, and they disappeared into the school.

She stopped at the grocer and stocked up on more bread and milk, then made her way back to the cottage. She let herself in the side door by the kitchen and loaded the milk into the refrigerator.

The sky was clear and the sun warm, and she didn't want to waste the time inside. She'd been to the lighthouse, but she'd yet to explore the boathouse where Jimmy had lived. She took a flashlight and the keys that Hank had given her, guessing one of them must unlock the boathouse.

From what she'd learned on the tapes, the boathouse was a quarter mile down the road, sandwiched between the lighthouse and the cottage. The boathouse wasn't visible from the road, but from what Claire had said, it was buffered by a stand of trees. She set out toward the trees with Dolly, enjoying the warmth of the sun on her face.

She spotted the two paths that cut through the trees. The one on the left went to the lighthouse, so it made sense the other led to the boathouse. Dolly noted Lucy's direction and raced ahead, barking as a couple of water birds flew out of the trees.

It appeared the path had been trimmed in the last couple of years, but the overgrowth of vegetation was currently winning. She carefully pushed back a branch with thorns and rounded a corner. A few more steps and there was the boathouse.

The structure was bigger than she'd imagined. It was more the size of a long, tall two-story home. Gray, perhaps painted white in the last year, the salt air was taking its toll. Several windows had been shuttered as well as its central door. Around the side, large sliding double doors closed off the water access.

Back around the front, she tugged on the large rusted padlock before fumbling with her keys and trying each. The first and second didn't fit, but the third slid into the lock. It took a little wiggling, but the tumblers turned, and the lock clicked open.

She threaded the lock's U-shaped shackle from the latch on the door. Dolly came running up, and Lucy attached the dog's leash to her collar and clicked on her flashlight. "Come on, Dolly, let's see what we can find."

A hard push opened the door while her flashlight skimmed over the ripples on the water in the center of the boathouse. There was no boat hanging from the pulley thick with cobwebs, but across the room, an old life preserver hung from a hook.

To her left was a steep set of stairs. She tested the first step with a hard thump to see if the wood would hold. It did, and she and Dolly slowly took each step up the darkened stairs until they reached the second floor where sunlight streamed in through salt-streaked windows. Several wooden boxes and crates were stacked next to a wrought-iron patio table and chairs. There was no sign of Jimmy's bed or the table where he'd done his work.

She moved toward the window that overlooked the lighthouse and beyond the cottage. How many times had Jimmy stood here before sunrise, dressing for the morning hunt? He'd have been thinking about the weather, the duck blinds, and the older wealthy men so ready to follow him.

As she turned from the window, the light cast a shadow over a loose board on the floor by the door. Curious, she crossed to the spot, knelt, and pulled up the plank. She shone her light into the space between the rafters and searched, finding only spiderwebs, dust, and crumpled newspapers.

She pushed up her sleeve and, drawing in a breath, stuck her hand into the space, gingerly skimming her fingertips over the rough wood until they reached the paper. She removed the wad, shaking the webs off it and her fingers.

She unwrapped the paper and found a gold pocket watch engraved with a delicate scroll. She opened it and read the name: *Robert Buchanan*. "Why is Robert's watch here?"

She ran her fingers over the delicate timepiece, and an odd sense of worry crept through her. Jimmy had never struck her as the kind of man who would steal, so what was he doing with the watch?

She shifted her attention to the newspaper, Norfolk's *Virginian-Pilot*, dated 1917. There was an advertisement on the page for furniture and another for a miracle healing cream. Below the ads were brief articles about stolen chickens, a broken window, a borrowed horse, and a local man who'd gone missing.

As she stared at the watch and the yellowed paper, she thought about the bones that had been found in the well. Her skin prickled, and she had the sense someone was standing behind her.

Dolly began to whimper.

"I hear you." Lucy rewrapped the watch and tucked it in her pocket. "Let's get out of here."

They eased down the stairs, locked up the door, and retraced their steps back to the cottage to find Megan's red truck parked out front and her standing on the front porch. Tucked under her arm was a large roll of paper, which looked like architectural plans.

"Hello," she said.

"Hi," Lucy said, smiling.

"I'm sorry I didn't stay long at your mother's funeral," she said. "That cemetery is emotional for me." Dolly ran up to her, and she automatically scratched her head.

"Please don't apologize."

"I was hoping you'd say that. I want to show you something."

"Sure." Lucy unlocked the door and grabbed a towel she now kept nearby to dry Dolly off before she set her loose. "It's probably been a while since the old floors have had a dog and kid running around. I can almost hear them groaning in protest."

Megan laughed as she shrugged off her coat and hung it on a peg. "The house has been waiting a long time for someone to breathe life into it."

"And I'm that person?"

Megan arched a brow. "I think we're that person."

"There seems to be a lot of hopes riding on me right now." She crossed to the coffeemaker and set it up to brew. "I've never had to worry about screwing up because there wasn't anything to lose, really. Now, a mistake could not only cost me but also a lot of other people."

Megan's brow knotted. "Then you're probably not going to like what I have to ask."

Smiling, Lucy shook her head. "Might as well spit it out. A few more bricks on the load won't make a big difference. Still have some apple pie."

"Perfect."

She grabbed plates and mugs from the cabinet as well as a couple of forks and a roll of paper towels.

Megan served up pie as Lucy poured the coffee. When they were settled at the table, Megan waited until Lucy had taken her first bite before saying, "I've toyed with the idea of a bakery, but I'm worried about raising a baby alone while balancing a sixteen-hour workday."

"Reasonable. It was always difficult for my mom."

Megan tucked a strand of hair behind her ear. "A few years ago, I came to Samuel and interviewed him about the house. He was very pleasant and told me all he could. After I gave him my final dissertation, I asked him if he'd be interested in renovating. Samuel declined, but I'm the eternal optimist, so I drew up plans, cost analysis, the whole deal. They're a few years old, but still very relevant." She unrolled the plans, smoothed her palms carefully, almost lovingly, over them.

"You showed these to Hank?"

"Our discussion about the house was more theoretical. Lots of *ifs*." She laid her palm on the plans and leaned forward. "I want this job so much," she said. "If I had a project like this house, it could be the cornerstone of my portfolio."

Her mother's dog, a 99 percent orphan, construction crews, a town crazy guy, and now a pregnant woman needed her. Lucy and Beth had lived in a place with no heat the winter she turned three. To keep them warm, her mother had piled so many blankets on them that she could barely move or breathe. But when she'd poked her head out, the cold had driven her back. "Can I think about it?"

Megan's eyes widened with so much hope. "Yes, of course."

"I'm not saying yes."

She held up her hands. "But you haven't said no, and I'll take it."

Lucy took a few more bites while searching for any kind of conversation that didn't have to do with the cottage. "So you moved from Richmond? I hear it's lovely."

"It's a great city. I love visiting. My late fiancé's family is from there, and when I'm in town, it's always nice to see them."

"They must be excited about the baby."

"We all are." She shoved out a breath. "They want me to move in with them. They want to take care of me and the baby."

"That's a generous offer."

"It is." She stabbed an apple with her fork.

"But . . ."

"They're very strong willed. And if I accept, things will be done their way. This is my baby, and I'm raising him on my terms."

"That's fair."

"My fiancé is buried at the Jessup cemetery. He was a marine pilot and killed overseas."

He'd been Scott Jessup. "I'm sorry."

She was silent, and then, "Can I ask you what it was like growing up with a single mom?"

"It's all I know. And it wasn't that bad. Not always easy. It would have helped to have a dad."

"You missed having a father?"

"Sure. Not having a dad made me different. Father-daughter dances are not quite the same when your mother comes with you."

"Have you found out more about your dad here?"

"My mom liked to date around. It could be any number of candidates, though Noah Garrison is certain he's 'not the father.'"

Megan held up her hands. "If you stick around, someone is bound to spill the beans."

"Maybe. Might be a case of 'be careful what you wish for.'"

Lucy was ten minutes early for the pickup line at school. The Peacemaker and Dolly were at the ready. Natasha was full of energy, and in the fifteen-minute drive back to the cottage, she chattered about the sling, Jimmy's unopened chest, which had all the kids guessing its contents, and cupcakes one of the kids' mom had made for her son's birthday.

Lucy parked near the kitchen entrance, and Natasha and Dolly bounded up the steps. She let the two in and set her purse and keys by the door. She made Natasha a sandwich and fixed herself a fresh pot of coffee.

"The kid's cupcakes were chocolate," Natasha said, settling on the island stool. "They were good, but not as good as your chocolate cake."

"Did your mom ever make cupcakes for you?"

"She wasn't much of a baker. All her stuff came out of box mixes, but they were pretty good."

"When's your birthday?"

"June first." Absently, she fingered the plans Megan had left behind. "What are these?"

They were another commitment. "Just papers," she said, putting them away. "Natasha, tell me about your mom. All I've done is talk about Beth, but I don't know much about your mom."

"No one ever talks about her anymore," she said softly.

"I am, now."

The girl's face softened. "She was nice. She had a gentle voice, and she liked to eat chocolate cake."

"You look like her."

"Do I? Her skin was a little darker and she was tall. She ran track in high school, though whenever we raced, I always beat her." She picked up a chip and frowned. "She was letting me win. I know that."

"She enjoyed watching you win," Lucy said.

"I guess."

She sipped her coffee. "What was her name?"

"Grace."

"Are your grandparents still around?"

"Trying to get rid of me?" Natasha asked.

"No, like I said, I don't know any of the history around here."

She tore the crust from her sandwich. "They died when I was two. It was some kind of fire. Mom said she never got over losing them. All she had left was Dad and me."

"I'm sorry."

"It was all okay when she was alive. She could keep Dad calm, and when he took off for a few days, it was okay because she was still there."

"She died of cancer." Lucy could say the words without her voice breaking, but speaking them hurt, maybe always would.

"Yeah. Two years ago." Natasha set down the sandwich and wiped her hands on the napkin. "I miss her every day."

"I'm sorry." She sipped the coffee. "What about your dad?"

"Why do you want to know about him?"

"I'm not trying to stir up trouble. I'm just trying to understand your father."

"My mom said it wasn't his fault he was so mean. His daddy was mean to him, and she said that's all he knew."

Beth had dated her share of guys who weren't the nicest of men. Though her mother had done her best to shield Lucy from whatever happened behind closed doors, she'd known when her mother was upset or trying to hide a bruise with makeup. But not all the guys Beth dated had been bad. There had been Tim, who drove a dump truck, and Joey, who'd played the guitar in the studio for anyone needing to record a song, and Alex, who'd already had four wives but wanted Beth to be number five.

It hadn't been totally terrible. And yeah, they'd had their ups and downs, but Beth had always tried to look out for Lucy when she was little. Maybe that was why she'd left Cape Hudson. Maybe she'd been afraid.

Of a guy like Brian. He had gone to school with Beth. He had played football like one of the boys she'd mentioned on the tape. And he could easily have left bruises on Beth.

Brian Willard.

Her father.

Jesus.

That possibility was reason enough to leave town, because if she did stay, he'd always be around, stirring up trouble. But leaving also meant abandoning Natasha to that creep, and she couldn't do that either.

If she tested her DNA with Natasha's, she'd know immediately if Brian was her father and Natasha her half sister. She'd be a real, live, living relative who could assume full custody of Natasha.

Damn. She had no idea how to raise a kid. Her only role model had done the best she could, but that wasn't the kind of life she wanted for Natasha.

What had started as a simple trek east to bring Beth home had taken so many twists and turns she wondered now if she would ever find her way back to Nashville.

"You look worried," Natasha said.

"Just thinking."

"You don't have to worry about my dad. He's going to be lying low for a while. He knows he screwed up, and he doesn't want to go to prison. Heck, he might have even left the area."

"You think he really left?"

"No. He's interested in this house."

"What about the house?"

"He's always wanted to get in the house. He said there was no reason for it to be empty while folks like him were living in a double-wide. He tried to break in a few times, but Mr. Jessup kept it locked up tight."

"But you got in."

"Only when Dad was away, and I never told him I could get through that basement window."

"Why didn't you tell him?"

"Because if he got into Winter Cottage, he wouldn't just live here. He'd strip it bare and sell it for parts. His daddy used to work here, and he didn't like Mrs. B."

"Your grandfather worked here?"

"Yeah. It was a long time ago. He did lawn maintenance for Mrs. B back in the sixties or something. Dad always called Mrs. B 'the Queen.' He said she was a townie just like the rest, but she thought she was better than everyone because of Winter Cottage."

"I didn't get that impression at all. She seemed real pleasant to Beth. She never put on airs."

Natasha bit into her sandwich. "I agree. She looked pretty cool."

The rumble of a truck and a vehicle door slamming out front pricked Dolly's ears, and she went running toward the front door wagging her tail. Lucy rose, and as she rounded the corner, she saw through the glass panels Hank standing on the front porch. A blush rose up to her cheeks, and leaving this life suddenly felt a little foolish.

Lucy unlocked the door and smiled. He was wearing his dark suit and had loosened his tie. "How did your meeting go today?"

"It went." He leaned in and kissed her lightly on the lips. "Rick tells me there's no sign of Brian."

"He's not been around here."

"Learn anything new from the videos?"

"No." The word tumbled out because she knew she was still hedging her bets. If Hank suspected she was Natasha's half sister, he'd insist she stay. It would mean giving up Nashville, her friends, and her old life. And as much as she liked Hank and Natasha, the idea of commitment terrified her. Jobs, school, or men had never lasted more than a few months, and she'd rarely mourned the loss longer than it took to down a few shots of whiskey. But if she failed these two, it would take more than whiskey to wash the guilt away.

"Did you open the chest?" Hank studied her closely, as if sensing something was off but he couldn't put his finger on it.

She managed a smile. "We've been waiting for you."

"Make me a sandwich, and I'll get my tools from the truck," Hank said.

"It's a deal." She was grateful for a mundane task to buy her time.

"Hey, is that Hank?" Natasha rounded the corner. "Where's he going?"

"To get his tools from the truck. After he eats, we're opening the trunk."

"Awesome!"

"Let's make him a sandwich."

They were in the kitchen, and she was slicing a ham sandwich on a diagonal when Hank reappeared with a leather tool belt in his hand. He shrugged off his jacket and laid it carefully over a chair.

Natasha got him a soda from the refrigerator. "We've been waiting for you."

"I heard. Thank you."

"Sure. Always. You're the Man, Hank."

He laughed as he unbuttoned his cuffs and rolled up his sleeves. Lucy raised her cup of coffee to her lips, mesmerized by his hands.

"So what was your meeting about?" Lucy asked.

"The development. These were potential investors."

"You told them I was here, right?"

"I did." He bit into the sandwich, taking extra care to chew on the meat and bread, apparently searching for the right words.

"And what did they say?"

He popped the top on his soda. "It's a wrinkle they were not expecting."

"I can imagine." She wondered if it was possible to truly feel at home in Winter Cottage. "So how did you leave it?"

"I thought maybe we could talk about that later. When we're alone."

"You don't want me to hear," Natasha said.

"That's right, kiddo. This is between Lucy and me."

"I'm almost grown up," Natasha said.

"Not as much as you think," he countered.

Lucy's sense of goodwill and excitement ebbed as the two chatted. She imagined promises Hank might have made on her behalf. Did he assure them she was leaving? Did he guarantee he had her backing? Did last night have an ulterior motive?

Lucy wanted to believe that Hank was an honest-to-a-fault, straight-shooting kind of guy. But she'd slung drinks in a town where deals and promises were broken as easily as they were made. Her chest tightened, and she could feel a dull throb pounding in the side of her head.

Hank rose and carried his plate to the sink. "Ready to open the chest?"

No. She wasn't ready. She wanted to drag his butt outside and have this out with him right now. What the hell had happened at the Norfolk meeting?

But Natasha's excited expression temporarily silenced her questions. "Let's do this."

Hank studied her as if he knew he'd somehow tripped a bad vibe. He allowed Natasha to take his hand and drag him and his tool belt into the parlor, where the chest had sat for the last two days. Dolly followed, leaving Lucy alone with her doubts.

Lucy set down her cup, taking extra time to rinse it along with Hank's, and then she placed both in the drainer.

"Luceee, come on!" Natasha shouted.

She dried off her hands and found the two staring at the roughly hewn box.

"I don't want to damage it," Hank said. "And seeing as we don't have a key, I'm going to take the back hinges off."

"Okay," she said.

He pulled out a drill and, after taking a moment to choose the right bit, plugged it in. He pressed the trigger, and the whir-whir of the bit echoed in the hall.

He knelt by the box as Natasha sat cross-legged on the floor, totally engrossed in what he was doing. That little girl wanted to belong so badly, and Lucy knew, no matter what happened with her and Hank over Winter Cottage, she'd have the DNA test done. And if it wasn't a match . . . well, maybe she'd find a way to get custody.

After about ten minutes of drilling and prying, Hank took off the last hinge holding the lid and box together. He unplugged the drill and set it aside.

He rubbed his hands together and deadpanned, "So you really want to open it?"

The girl groaned. "Yesss!"

"Lucy, are you ready?" he asked.

No, she was not ready for the avalanche of change that was rolling in her direction. "Open it."

CHAPTER
TWENTY-THREE

Beth

June 12, 1988

Beth has thrown up three times this morning. She wants to go to the Quick Mart and buy a pregnancy test, but if she does that kind of thing in this town, then everyone, including *him*, would know about the baby. In Norfolk, she can go to a clinic and get a real test. But that would require borrowing a car from her neighbor. He asks why, of course, and she then lies and says Mrs. B has moved their weekly meeting to Thursday and needs fabric samples. He gives her the keys, warning her to be back on the road by two to miss the afternoon traffic that really starts around three when the naval base workday ends.

What comes next is "the Visit," the plus sign, and the nurse's conversation about "options." On the bright side, she misses the traffic.

Mrs. B is moving slowly as she pushes her walker across the parquet floor of the great room, and she looks pale. Her young caregiver, Grace, is right behind her. The girl is quiet and looks a little too young in the nurse's uniform.

Mrs. B is wearing a pale-pink suit, which Beth recognizes now as Yves Saint Laurent. It's hard to spend any time around Mrs. B and not learn her labels. She accessorizes with classic pearls, the ivory broach, and very sensible but expensive chunky-heeled beige shoes.

Beth stands and helps Grace settle the old woman into her chair. They've met seven times now and have fallen into a kind of routine. Camera on tripod. Microphone set. Mrs. B adjusting her skirt and checking already perfect lipstick in a small handheld mirror.

After Grace closes the door behind her and they're alone, she says, "You never said who the father of Victoria's baby was."

"No, I did not," Mrs. B says. "I promised that I never would, and I have not."

"Why did you promise?" Most of the people in Beth's life have been fast and loose with promises, using them as placeholders to keep a temporary peace. Beth realizes she's not good with them either, but she swears she'll do right by her baby. Somehow.

"My husband, Robert, would have found a way to punish the child. And if I learned anything growing up in the Buchanan house, it was how to keep secrets."

"Can you tell me now? It's been over seventy years."

She is silent for a long moment. "Time does not change the fact that I gave my word."

"Did it ever make you feel bad to keep a secret?"

The woman studies her for a long moment. Does she notice her pale skin and fuller breasts? So far, the signs aren't too hard to hide, but that will change soon.

Mrs. B touches the broach on her collar and gently fingers it. "If a secret is meant to protect a child, then it's a necessary evil."

———— ⚬≈⚬ ————

Claire

May 16, 1917

Robert had left for Norfolk several days ago and said the trip was business, but Claire didn't really care. As long as he was gone, she would be fine. Since the night of his homecoming, he'd stayed in his room, alone. She'd telegrammed his father, informing him his son had arrived, and told him Robert was not doing well. The elder Mr. Buchanan had not responded.

The trap she'd so effortlessly stepped into bound her, and she saw little hope for herself. The darkness seemed to be closing in around her, and then like all storms, the clouds parted when she and Mrs. Latimer received word from town.

"Jimmy Latimer is alive!" the boy from the butcher exclaimed.

"What?" The baby kicked hard in Claire's belly.

"He's alive. The message came over the telegraph."

Mrs. Latimer crumpled in a chair and raised her apron to her watery eyes. "Are you sure, boy? Are you really sure?"

"Yes, ma'am. The men at the telegraph office checked it twice to confirm."

"When will he arrive?" Claire asked.

"Today on the afternoon train. He said he just wants his ma to meet him."

Mrs. Latimer wept. "Of course I'll go see him."

Claire rubbed her hand over her full belly. It had been over a year since she'd seen Jimmy. He would think her a faithless soul for not waiting, and he'd be right. She'd selfishly given in to sadness and now was paying the price.

"Is he hurt?" Mrs. Latimer asked.

"Telegram didn't say," the boy replied. "Just said he was coming."

When the boy left them, they sat in the kitchen, still as stone. "It can't be right," Mrs. Latimer gasped. "It can't."

Claire laid her hand on the woman's shoulder. "It's a miracle."

"And I'll never ask for another again." She raised a trembling hand to her hair. "I have to get ready. I have to ride into town."

"I'll have one of the boys go with you."

"Can I put Jimmy in the boathouse apartment?"

"Of course." Robert might argue later, but she'd worry about that then.

And so the two spent the next couple of hours preparing. While Mrs. Latimer tidied herself up, Claire cleaned the room over in the boathouse, sweeping out the dust and putting clean sheets on the bed.

At three o'clock, she waved as Mrs. Latimer climbed in the car, her cheeks flushed with happiness. Claire watched as the car rumbled away. There was nothing left for her to do but wait.

Two hours later, Mrs. Latimer returned to the cottage. Her face was ashen, and her hands trembled.

"Did you get Jimmy?" Claire asked.

Mrs. Latimer began to cry. "Yes."

"What is it?" Claire held her while she wept.

"How could the world be so cruel to a fine man like Jimmy?"

"What are you talking about?" Claire poured Mrs. Latimer a brandy and sat with her while she drank it.

"He's not the man that left."

"What's happened?"

"I can't speak of it." Worry gripped her voice. Claire settled the mother into her room on the third floor and set out to see Jimmy.

The wind was blustery and cold. She burrowed in the folds of her coat as she hurried down the road, telling herself that whatever it was couldn't be that bad, while she also steeled herself for what was to come.

As Claire walked, the baby lay heavy in her belly. With each anxious step that led down the sandy path, she prayed it wasn't as bad as

Mrs. Latimer had described. A mother, after all, would be grieved by any injury to her child.

The tall grass brushed the hem of her skirt as she made her way to the boathouse. Her hand paused on the door latch as she struggled to calm her nerves. She smoothed back a curl, praying he didn't think less of her for not waiting for him.

Inside, the sound of a tool hitting metal clanged and echoed in the rafters above. She pictured Jimmy's broad, muscled shoulders wielding the hammer, and even given her advanced state of pregnancy, her womb tightened with desire.

She moistened her lips.

There was so much to tell him.

She knocked on the door, but when the clang of the hammer continued, she was too impatient to knock again. She pressed on the door handle, and when the latch released, she stepped into the boat shed.

The first floor of the boat shed was lit through the open doors where water from the inlet and bay lapped against the wooden sides. A skiff hung from a set of pulleys and ropes. Half its hull had been scraped of barnacles. Life preservers, hooks with long handles, and rope hung from hooks.

The hammer's blows were so hard, the floorboards rattled violently and kicked up dust.

She pulled the folds of her coat around her belly, suddenly embarrassed by her new pear shape. Even after her marriage, she'd dreamed of Jimmy's return, and each time she'd pictured herself with him, she was slim waisted and wearing her favorite burgundy dress.

She climbed the dark stairs, her hand skimming the roughly hewn wall. With each step she grew more nervous. Of course Jimmy had survived the downing of the ship. He was a strong swimmer, and if there were ever a man to persevere, it was him. He had a good and true heart, and God surely saved him for a good reason. She could handle this.

When Claire reached the second floor, she peered around the corner and saw him. Jimmy was standing with his back to her. He wore gunmetal-gray trousers, a black belt that cinched tightly at his waist, and the scuffed boots he had always worn. He'd stripped off his coat and wore only a collarless cotton shirt that showed off broad shoulders her hands had caressed as he'd made love to her. His thick blond hair had grown out and now dipped below his shoulders.

He raised his right muscled arm and drove it down onto an oar hook that she could see now was bent.

Clang. Clang. Clang.

She fancied those arms wrapping around her. God, if only word of his survival had returned to her sooner. She'd have waited and taken him.

The raised hammer stilled as he sensed her presence. He slowly lowered the hammer, and the muscles in his back bunched with tension.

"What do you want?" Jimmy said without turning.

His voice was rough, harsh, and for a moment she wasn't sure if this was Jimmy.

"Jimmy," she said. "It's Claire."

He gripped the handle of the hammer tighter. "Go away, Claire."

The rejection was so out of place she assumed she'd heard wrong. "Jimmy, it's *me*, Claire."

"I heard you the first time." He didn't turn, and a fresh tautness rippled through his shoulders as he straightened.

Boards under her feet creaked as she stepped closer. This close, she could smell his scent mingling with the salt air. To the right was a small cot, which he'd made years ago. It was the cot where'd they'd made love and huddled together until just before dawn. Beside it was an old, worn trunk with a stack of books upon it as well as a leather-bound journal.

"Go away, Claire."

Her hand slid to her belly. "You've heard about my marriage."

"Aye."

"I thought you were dead."

He stared ahead, silent, not turning toward her. His long, thick hair curled, hiding his face from her. "It's for the best."

She wanted to tell him it wasn't even close to the best. It was a tragic mistake, and she feared her growing hate for her husband would poison the child inside her. As if the baby read her thoughts, it just then kicked hard in her belly. But shame more than loyalty kept her silent. She didn't want him to know how much she despised and feared her husband.

"Won't you even look at me?" she asked.

"No."

Tears welled in her eyes. "Am I such a horrible person, Jimmy, that you can't even look at me?"

"Go away, Claire."

All that they'd shared. She'd given him her innocence. She'd protected secrets for him. Even when Robert pressed, even when he hit her, she'd not betrayed Jimmy.

Frustration crowded its way past the sadness and guilt. She crossed the room toward him and laid her hand on his shoulder. He flinched and stepped away.

"I won't let you just toss me aside as if I were nothing. We loved each other!"

He carefully laid his hammer on the table by his side and, fingers curling into fists, turned slowly to face her.

Anticipation grew to the point of bursting. How many nights had she dreamed of his stern, handsome face?

But all those dreams exploded in a rush of fear and disgust as he now faced her. The entire right side of his face was an angry pink scar. Half his nose and his right eye were missing.

She stepped back, unable to swallow the startled scream. She could feel his pain. This was a man she'd dreamed of touching again. Shivers of revulsion and terror cut through her. She was ashamed by her reaction, but fear gripped her completely.

As Claire backed up, she tripped. Reflex had him reaching for her, but she drew in her arms as she righted herself. The walls of the room shrank. The air grew heavy and putrid.

Clutching her belly with one hand, her other hand barely skimmed the wall as she took the stairs two at a time. She rushed out into the sunshine and sucked in fresh air as she tried to shove the image of Jimmy's devastation and destruction from her mind. Her Jimmy. What she'd seen in the boathouse was more demon than human.

CHAPTER TWENTY-FOUR

Lucy

January 19, 2018

Natasha could barely stand still as Hank carefully raised the lid from the chest and set it aside. Lucy's own excitement built as she edged closer and peered inside. On top was a neatly folded blue wool blanket that smelled musty. Moths had chewed away at the outer edges, leaving them frayed.

Lucy knelt in front of the chest. The wool fabric was scratchy to the touch, and she carefully set it aside. Underneath was an odd collection of items. There was a compass, a straight razor, a shaving cream bowl, an ivory comb, and a collection of chess pieces carved from whale ivory. There were books, including *A Boy's Will* by Robert Frost and *Tom Swift and His Air Glider* by Victor Appleton.

Lucy picked up one of the chess pieces, marveling at the minute detailing of scrolls and patterns. "There's a hairbrush and comb set in my room with markings like this."

"It's called scrimshaw," Hank said. "Sailors carved whale ivory in their spare time and sold it when they were in port. It looks like Jimmy had a talent for this."

Natasha held up a white horse. "This is a rook."

"Do you play chess?" Lucy asked.

"Not a lot, but I like it."

"I play too. Used to be my thing when I tended bar. Beat me in a game of chess, and your next drink was free."

"How many free rounds did you give away?" Hank asked.

"Not many," she said.

"I believe you have many hidden talents," he said.

The silkiness under the words glided over her skin, making her feel restless. "Natasha, I'll play you sometime."

"Cool."

Next from the chest was a macramé bracelet made of a thin rope braided in an intricate pattern. "That's a seaman's bracelet. It can be unwound if the sailor needs a rope," Hank said.

"What kind of downtime would this guy have?" Lucy asked.

"As a captain, not much. He was accountable for the ship, the cargo, and the men, in that order," he said.

Under three neatly folded shirts, she found a small picture frame featuring a woman surrounded by her five boys. The oldest three boys, who appeared to be in their late teens, were tall and gangly with splashes of freckles across their faces. A young boy with black hair and dark eyes leaned against his mother, who cradled a toddler with a thick shock of blond hair. The woman was smiling. Her sturdy face could never be considered classically beautiful, but there was a kindness and vibrancy in her eyes that was compelling.

Lucy turned the picture over and saw *Sally Jessup and her boys, 1920*. "The three older boys are the Hedrick children. The boy with the dark hair is Aaron, and the littlest one must be my grandfather, Samuel." She handed Hank the picture.

"The timing would be about right. He was almost hundred and one years old when he died this past September. He was a seaman, a captain in the merchant marines," Hank said. "Couldn't settle down until well into his fifties, when he finally married and had your mom. Even then, he kept mostly to the sea and was gone most of the time."

"Beth said she was on her own a lot as a child. I guess that's why she was never bothered about being by herself. In her mind, she could take care of herself." Lucy cocked her head. "Samuel looks like the picture I saw of Jimmy Latimer in the local paper," she said. There'd been so many years of not knowing where she'd come from. How many family-tree assignments in school had she fabricated to spare herself the embarrassment?

"So this James dude might be your great-grandfather?" Natasha asked.

"Maybe."

"Do you think Mrs. B was Samuel's real mother?" Natasha asked.

"She couldn't have been," Lucy said. "Mrs. B was married just days before he was born, and I've seen the photographs taken on her wedding day. The dress hugs her slim waist." She couldn't take her eyes off the little boy's striking eyes. "Samuel was born here the fall of 1916. The same time Mrs. B was at Winter Cottage with Victoria."

"Victoria was Samuel's mother?" Hank asked.

It all made sense. "And James was his father. The baby's birth would have been the kind of secret a rich family would want to hide," Lucy said.

"Victoria went on to marry my great-grandfather, Edward Garrison, a wealthy New York financier. She also never returned to the cottage," Hank said.

Natasha took the picture of Samuel, studying his face and then Lucy's. "So this means Lucy's related to James Latimer?"

"I suppose I am." And then to Hank, "Were there any whispers of a child's birth in your family?"

"There was never a word about Victoria giving birth out of wedlock, but then, that's the kind of thing families didn't talk about," Hank said.

Dolly rose, stretched, and walked toward the door. She glanced over her shoulder with a wistful "who notices me?" glance.

Natasha rose. "I got this."

"Are you sure?" Lucy asked. "Your arm."

Natasha wiggled her fingers. "I'm getting better. And Dolly is a pretty good listener."

"If she takes off after a rabbit, call one of us," Hank said. "And stay close to the house. Really close."

"Will do." The girl scrambled to her feet and vanished out the door with the dog.

"So if I'm descended from Jimmy and Victoria, and you're descended from Victoria and Edward, what does that make us? Very distant cousins?" She rose and stared out the window. "Any other excitement for today?"

"There is Brian. He's lying low, but he can't forever."

"And then what?"

"His parole will be revoked, and likely he'll do prison time. He was drunk on public-school property, and the judge was very clear that if Brian got into any more trouble, even jaywalking, he was going back inside."

Through the window, Lucy could see Natasha pick up a stick and toss it for Dolly to chase. The dog ran up to the stick, sniffed it, and kept running. Natasha chased after her.

"Dolly doesn't fetch," Lucy said, more to herself.

"Natasha will teach her," he said.

Lucy changed the direction of the conversation and asked, "How did your meeting go today in Norfolk?"

"We need to talk about that."

"Why?"

His face was angled, and the dimming light cast shadows. "They'll give me the loan provided you sign as well."

"Me?"

"You own the house and the land. I'm merely a tenant. Both are worth a lot. They want the collateral."

"So you want me to risk the only home I have ever owned."

"It's a big ask. I know that. I've put everything on the line to bring this town back."

She didn't think he'd meant to corner her, but she felt as if her back was to the wall. "And you expect me to do the same?" Her chest felt tight. "Why would you do that?"

"I didn't think it would be that big of a stretch. Lucy, I'm asking you to risk a place you're not even sure you want."

She was growing to love Winter Cottage, and the thought of putting down roots scared her. "You should have talked to me before you met with the bank."

Annoyance flashed in his gaze. "I'm talking to you now."

"You've implied promises on my behalf you had no right to. We've made no promises."

He closed his eyes a moment. "I thought we were further along in trusting one another."

It had been amazing. And that was what scared her. "It's interesting you mentioned that. Remember when I said working in a bar attuned my skills to spotting BS? I think you know who my birth father is."

He was silent for a moment.

She bored into him. "You do know." She shook her head. "It's Brian, isn't it?"

He held her gaze. "I never knew for sure, but I think he might be Brian."

Sadness mingled with frustration, hurt, and anger. "How long have you known?"

"When I spoke to your mother in September. She mentioned Brian's name, but she sounded so confused by the pain medicine. There were moments when she seemed to think she was back in high school."

Something deep in her ached. "Why didn't you tell me?"

"I really didn't know anything for sure. And honestly, I was worried what he'd do to you when he figured out the truth."

Seeing his logic didn't soften the rush of sadness. "It would have been the perfect way to scare me off."

"That would have been a cheap shot. Mrs. B left you Winter Cottage, and you deserved to decide how to handle it without Brian breathing down your neck." He reached for her, but she pulled away.

"You should have talked to me about Brian before you dragged me into your loan."

"You said you wished you could have done more to help. I took you at your word."

"It's not fair." Outside Dolly barked and chased Natasha in circles.

"If you're looking for fair, then you're out of luck, Lucy. Megan buried a fiancé when she was barely two months pregnant. I was a pallbearer at his funeral. Rick's picking up the pieces of his own life, and Claire spent a lifetime living with unfair. Life isn't fair."

He grabbed his jacket and stormed out the front door.

She stood in the house alone, listening to the wheels of his truck drive away. She raised a trembling hand to her head, irritated with him but more with herself. The phone rang, and she crossed to answer it. "Hello?"

"Lucy, this is the sheriff. I have news about Brian Willard. He just turned himself in. He's in a cell now."

"Thanks for letting me know, Sheriff."

"He wants to talk to you."

With an effort, she shifted her thoughts from Hank to Brian. "When?"

"Give him a couple of days to sober up. Can you come in on Monday morning?"

As much as she didn't want to deal with Brian, she had no choice. "I'll be there."

CHAPTER TWENTY-FIVE

Beth

June 19, 1988

Beth threw up this morning. That was bad enough, but the guy she's dating asked her to steal something from Mrs. B. He went to Maryland, bet big at the tables, and lost ten grand. There are men who are demanding money from him, and he needs her to steal from Mrs. B. When she refused, he shoved her into the shed behind his parents' trailer and set fire to the door. She kicked out a board in the back and crawled out, coughing and struggling to breathe. He was waiting for her. Smiling, he insisted she wouldn't escape the next time.

Now as her fingers curl around the antique box and tuck it in her pocket, she knows she could get several hundred dollars for it in Norfolk.

As she sets up the camera equipment for the last interview, Mrs. B sits calmly in her chair as she's done every other time. However, when the old woman looks at Beth now, she senses the old woman is on to her.

"You're pregnant," Mrs. B deadpans.

Beth thinks about the box in her pocket and is almost relieved the old woman doesn't know about that. "Do you have X-ray vision or something?"

"Once a woman has had a child, she can see the signs in another woman." When Beth readies to toss out a lie, Mrs. B holds up her lined, bent hand. "Who is the father?"

The lies fall away, and she is left with nothing but fear and worry. "Does it matter? I'm not even sure I'm going to keep it."

Mrs. B fusses with the folds of her dress before folding her hands in her lap. "Why wouldn't you keep it?"

"Then he'd have a hold over me. He's talking about getting married and being a family. He has no idea what he's talking about. If we lasted a year together, it would be a miracle."

With steel in her voice, Mrs. B asks, "Who is he?"

"Brian Willard."

"His father worked for me many years ago. The father was lazy and a drunk."

"He's in trouble with guys he owes money to." She thinks about the ivory box.

"That's why you stole the box?"

"What?"

"I've been in this room for so many years, I know when a tassel on those drapes is out of place. I see that one of my boxes is missing."

Desperation kept her from confessing. "I've got to get out of town, Mrs. B. I need to be as far from him as I can because the men chasing him are really bad. One of them threatened me. Said he'd kill me if I didn't call when I saw him."

"And you're going to get rid of the baby?"

Tears flow unchecked down her cheeks. "It's not like I want to. This kid is doomed if we stay in town."

"I'll give you money to leave."

"What?"

"I'll give you the money to move to Nashville and chase your dreams. Raise your baby. I'll make sure Brian or these men do not know how to find you."

"You'd do that? Why?"

"A woman should be allowed to raise her child in peace. I'm very good at keeping secrets."

Beth reached into her pocket, removed the box, and set it on the table.

"Fitting you'd choose the compass. It was always one of my favorites. Keep it. Bring it back to me when you're ready to return. Or tell your child to bring it back when she returns."

"My child won't come back."

Claire

May 17, 1917

Claire's labor pains began in the predawn hours the day after she saw Jimmy. Mrs. Latimer summoned a local midwife who'd delivered most of the babies on the shore, including hers. Robert was still in Norfolk, and a boy was dispatched to town to send a telegram.

The labor pains crushed through her, tearing and washing her body in agony. Mrs. Latimer held on to her hand as a housemaid fetched blankets. She knew she deserved the agony as the next contraction arrived. She had been cruel to the one man who had saved her life and loved her. He had needed her kindness, and she'd abandoned him.

"I shouldn't have rejected him, Mrs. Latimer. I shouldn't have been afraid."

The older woman pressed a compress to her forehead. "He sent a fright through me that stole my breath."

"But you didn't run."

"He knows you care for him."

"I should have found a way past the carnage and accepted him. And God is punishing me."

As labor drew on, she grew weaker, and her mind began to play tricks. God would punish her with a creature. What better revenge than to gift her with a child who frightened people away?

After twenty hours of labor, the midwife was still not to be found, she could barely breathe, and her body was so fatigued, she didn't have the strength to sit up. The women around her began to whisper with worry. Claire was losing this fight. She and the baby were going to die.

In the distance, Mrs. Latimer ordered all the women out of the room. As a shadow appeared at the door, none argued as footsteps hurried away.

"All right, Claire," Mrs. Latimer said. "It's time we birth this baby. We're going to do it together. Let's get you up."

"I can't."

Strong arms banded around her shoulders, pulled her forward, and Mrs. Latimer yanked off Claire's gown. As she was lifted from the bed and suspended, she cried and tried to get free. But whoever held her upright had a strong grip. Through haze and pain, she looked at the pair of hands, expecting to see Robert. But she knew those hands. They'd touched her with love and affection. They were Jimmy's.

Mrs. Latimer reached up into her. Claire thought she had suffered up to this point, but in that moment she thought her body would split in two.

"Push," Jimmy ordered.

"I can't," she whispered.

"Do it!" he said.

She hitched in a breath and then braced for the next contraction. When it came, she pushed, screaming and digging her fingernails into his arms.

Then came the rush of flesh from her flesh and the wash of blood, cord, and afterbirth. For several seconds, she hung suspended by Jimmy's strong arms as Mrs. Latimer swiped her finger in the baby's mouth, held the child upside down, and patted its back. Her vision went in and out of focus. The room filled with a troubling silence. God had willed her a deformed child, or he'd taken the baby.

And then, mercy. Claire heard the child's strong cry and Mrs. Latimer's exclamation that it was a strong, healthy boy. Later, when she awoke, the baby was sleeping in the cradle by the bed. Mrs. Latimer cooed over him, beaming with joy.

"Is he really all right?" she whispered.

Mrs. Latimer straightened, coming to Claire's side. "He's fit and fine," she said. "You did a good job for your first time."

"I couldn't have done it without you. And Jimmy."

Mrs. Latimer shook her head, brushing a curl from Claire's head. "It was just me, girl. Jimmy was not here."

"But I heard him."

"No," she said, tugging the blanket up. "You're mistaken. And you must never say another word about it. Do you understand?"

She closed her eyes. "Yes."

Robert returned home two days later, and he was thrilled with the birth of his son. He made promises of a fresh start and no more drinking. But bad habits aren't so easily banished. They bide their time and wait for frustration, doubt, and then temptation to do their bidding.

The baby was five weeks old when Robert decided he needed another trip to New York. He was going to personally deliver the news to his father. He was certain the boy, Robert Jr., would heal the wounds between his father and him.

Claire was glad to see him go. She could barely stand to look at him now, and when he leaned over the baby's cradle, it was all she could do not to scream and order him away.

When Robert had been gone two days, Claire worked up the courage to go see Jimmy. As Mrs. Latimer watched the baby, Claire wrapped a thick scarf around her head and headed out to the boathouse. She'd not seen Jimmy since the baby's birth, and she needed him to know how very sorry she was. She desperately wanted his forgiveness.

She found him on the second floor of the boathouse. His back was to her, and his head was bent as he worked on one of his carvings.

"Jimmy," she said.

His shoulders stiffened, but he didn't turn.

"I'm so sorry. I shouldn't have turned away."

"Forgiven, Claire. Now go away."

"Jimmy, I'll never turn away from you again."

He raised his head and stared out the window toward the bay. Slowly, he shook his head.

She crossed the room toward him and touched his shoulder. He flinched. But he didn't tell her to leave. She smoothed her hand up the side of his face that wasn't damaged. Jimmy was in this broken shell. He was trapped. Caged like she was in her marriage.

She settled her hand on his shoulder and raised the other to the damaged side. She started at his temple, feeling a thick scar that felt alien. He sat stock-still, gripping his fingers into fists.

She came around to face him, but he ducked his face. "No, Claire."

She raised his face toward her and looked at his wounds. The damage the war had caused. Tears filled her eyes as she thought about the proud young man who'd been so full of life and so ready to take on the world. She knelt forward and kissed his lips.

He stared at her, his eyes unblinking. "Claire."

"Why is it that life always got between us, Jimmy?"

"It doesn't matter."

She kissed him again, this time cupping his face. "It does."

She leaned back, reached for the button on her bodice, and carefully unfastened it. Her breasts were full of milk and spilled over her undergarment. She took his hand in hers and pressed it to her breasts. For several long seconds he stood there, his face downcast.

She leaned forward, wanting his touch. Unable to stand still any longer, he kissed the tender white skin, moaning with a mixture of pleasure, loss, and longing. She'd yearned for this. Lifting her skirts, she straddled him, pressing against his hardness.

With his gaze on her, he unfastened his breeches and freed himself. She lifted slightly and then lowered herself onto him.

He dug his fingers into her back as she steadied her hands on his shoulders and took all of him. In this moment, neither one thought about the outside world. It was just the two of them. She savored the whirlwind of sensations that drove them toward the edge.

When they tumbled over, she hugged him, dipping her head into the crook of his neck. "I love you, Jimmy," she whispered.

He raised his fingers to her face and gently traced them across her lips.

"I'll be back tomorrow night," she said.

"Don't."

"I won't leave you."

"Don't promise. Get home now before the storm. Live your life." She kissed him full on the lips. "I love you."

———— ❦ ————

Hours later, as Claire hurried down the sandy path toward Winter Cottage, the sky cracked with lightning. The air was thick with humidity, and fat raindrops began to fall. Jimmy had warned her of the weather and the coming storm, but she hadn't wanted to believe him.

Her breasts were full and beginning to ache as she thought about the baby waiting for her. As much as she now hated her husband, she could never say the same about her son. He was perfect. And whatever she had to do to keep him safe, she would move heaven and earth to do so.

When she stepped in the back door, she saw the tall dark boots and black coat hanging on the peg.

"Mrs. Latimer?" she said.

There was no answer except for her son's cries. She hurried up the back staircase to him. When she entered her room, a fire crackled in the hearth, and Robert was standing over the cradle.

"I sent her away." He touched the baby's foot. "They're such fragile little things," he said, straightening.

"Robert. I didn't expect you back until next week."

As he turned, a smirk jerked the corner of his lip. "Clearly."

He clutched the neck of a nearly empty liquor bottle in his hand. "I suppose it makes sense that you would fraternize with the help. Like begets like."

She stood very still, realizing the house was eerily quiet except for the cries of her son. Robert had sent away all the servants. "Did you visit your father in New York?"

"I did." He swigged another gulp of whiskey.

In faint electric light, she saw a bruise on his cheek. He'd been struck, and she wondered if his father had caused the injury. "You're hurt."

He crossed the space between them in two strides and drew back his hand, slapping her hard across the mouth. She tasted blood as pain shot through her body. "And now so are you. Consider that a delivery from my father."

For a moment, she couldn't catch her breath. The wide planks of the floor moved in and out of focus. "What happened in New York?"

Robert took a long pull on the bottle and leaned over the crib. "He's not my child, is he?"

She blinked in horror. She saw the darkness in his gaze and the pure violence that swirled behind it. "He *is* your son."

"Liar."

He struck her again, and she fell hard to the floor. He kicked her, his booted foot catching her stomach.

"You both have become a ball and chain around my ankle. Because of you two, I'm trapped in this godforsaken dump. There's nowhere else for me to go."

She fought through pain and a wave of nausea as he returned to the crib. She knew then that he didn't see an innocent child. He saw an embarrassment to his good name standing in the path that led back to his father's good graces. And with sickening clarity, she realized he was going to kill the child and her. He was going to erase his mistakes, free himself from exile, and return to his old glory in New York just as Victoria had done.

She couldn't let him hurt the baby. She wouldn't. As she pushed up to her feet, she stumbled to the side table.

"The bay can hide so many secrets," he said. "So many people have been lost. And with this storm, there's no telling who it will claim."

Robert was clever, and he no doubt had already concocted a story. Thunder clapped outside, and the winds howled. He'd been waiting for the storm, and she wondered if he'd even left for New York or had simply been hiding on the shore.

She could picture what was to come. He'd say mother and child had been lost at sea. She'd made a mistake and misread the weather. She'd done it before. God only knew why she'd taken the boy. She'd gone mad over the news of Jimmy.

As the baby cried louder, she could hear all the scenarios play out in his softly spoken voice.

Standing straighter, she wrapped her hands around the candlestick on the table. It was made of silver, and its octagonal base was heavy. She'd have one good swing, and it had to hit its mark. There would be no forgiveness if she failed.

As he reached for the child, she swung with all the force in her body. Metal crunched bone, and the shock of the impact rattled up her arm. He stumbled away from the cradle and righted himself on the mantel. He touched the back of his head, and when he saw the blood, the dumb look of shock on his face almost made her smile.

"You'll rot in prison for this," he said. He closed his eyes as if the room were spinning and dropped to his knees. "You'll never see your bastard son again."

And this time when she swung, a dozen images flashed in her mind, and the bloodied edge hit him square in the temple. His eyes rolled back in his head, and he fell flat to the floor. Her ears began to ring, and a cold spread through her limbs. For a moment, there was just Robert and her and the loudest ringing in her ears.

Claire then heard her son's cries grow closer, bringing her back to the present.

She dropped the candlestick and wiped the blood from her hands onto her skirt. She scooped up the boy and quickly shushed him as she pressed his mouth to her breast. Her head throbbed, and her stomach ached with the consequences that promised a fate almost as ugly as Robert's. It was all she could do to make her wobbly legs carry her to the rocker and sit.

She lifted her gaze above her son's sweet face to stare at the blood that pooled around her husband's dead body.

She didn't know how much time passed, but when the baby quieted, she rose, moved to the window, and stared at the choppy rough waters of the bay. They could swallow a man's body up. They could also spit him back out. Downstairs she heard Mrs. Latimer call up to her. Clutching the baby, she made her way down the center staircase.

Mrs. Latimer held up a lantern as the storm had knocked out the electricity. The soft glow of light illuminated the older woman's face crumpled with worry. Her fear grew as she saw the blood on Claire's skirt. "What has he done to you?"

"It doesn't matter."

"It does. It does."

"I need help." Claire's voice sounded far away and so utterly calm.

"Where's Mr. Robert?"

"Upstairs."

Mrs. Latimer grabbed Claire's skirt. "You're covered in blood. What has he done?"

"It's not all mine."

The older woman's eyes widened and then narrowed with steadfastness. "What did you do to him?"

"He's dead. I killed him."

Grim determination sharpened Mrs. Latimer's pale-blue eyes. "Is there anyone else in the house?"

"No. He sent them all away. He meant to kill the baby and me."

"Stay right here. Don't move."

Lucy

January 22, 2018

Lucy had barely slept. Every time she'd almost drifted off to sleep, worries about Hank, the land, and her father jostled her awake. After staring at the ceiling until 4:00 a.m., she finally couldn't stay in the bed any longer. She got up, dressed, and with Dolly on her heels, went to the kitchen and brewed herself a cup of coffee.

When she finished her second cup and was still no closer to understanding why she was so angry with Hank or maybe herself, she pulled out pots and pans and baked three dozen chocolate cupcakes, and when they'd cooled, she iced them. She didn't know how many kids were in Natasha's class, but any leftovers would make it to the teacher's lounge.

By the time Natasha woke for school, the cupcakes were boxed and ready to go. She was thrilled about the cupcakes but reminded Lucy it wasn't her birthday. She then quickly added it didn't technically have to be anyone's birthday for cupcakes.

Lucy and Dolly took Natasha to school and waited out front as she proudly carried her bounty into the school.

"Dolly, now it's time for Dad. Dad. I can't believe Brian is Dad."

She drove to the jail and, with Dolly in tow for moral support, pushed through the front door of the sheriff's office. Rick looked up from a stack of papers and rose to greet her. "Lucy, you doing all right?"

"I'm fine, Rick. Can I see Brian?"

"Yeah, sure. He's up. I just served him breakfast."

He crossed to a large door behind him. "He's in the last cell on the right. You can talk to him through the bars, but I've got to be present."

"Sure. I get that."

He unlocked the door, and she smoothed her hands over her jeans, wondering why the hell she was so damn nervous. She moved in front of the cell to find Brian sitting on a cot, his head in his hands. "Brian?"

He looked up, meeting her gaze. His eyes were bloodshot, but there was a clarity she'd not seen before. He actually appeared sober.

"I didn't think you'd come." He rose gingerly, wincing as he put weight on his right leg and limped toward the bars.

Rick stepped back, with Dolly beside him. He was trying to give them some privacy but remained within earshot.

"Part of the reason I came to Cape Hudson was to find out who my father was. And it appears that I have."

"One hell of a disappointment, I bet."

"I've heard so many versions from Beth of who you might have been that I wasn't sure what to think."

"I didn't used to be this guy. I was someone with real promise."

"Why are you telling me this?"

"I'm not really sure. I guess I'd like to think knowing my name is not enough."

To say she felt sorry for him was an overstatement, but good or bad, she wanted to understand him. "What happened between you and Beth? Why did you hurt her?"

He closed his eyes and shook his head. "It always got out of hand with us. If I was gasoline, she was the match."

"In the tapes she made with Mrs. B, there were bruises on her wrists."

"Like I said, we both weren't good together." He shook his head. "Did your mother ever talk about me when you were a kid?"

"Not once. All her stories about who my father was were fantasies made up for her benefit as much as mine."

He shifted his weight, grimacing.

"I heard you were in a car accident and messed up your knee."

He scratched the thick gray stubble on his chin. "It wasn't a car accident. That's what I told people. Beth's the reason I lost it all."

She rose to her mother's defense. "How is my mother to blame?"

"I used to sneak over to the casinos in Maryland occasionally to have fun, blow off steam, but mostly to bet. The people I hung around with knew I was good for the money because I was a big-shot athlete from the area who had a full scholarship to play college football." He shook his head. "You really want to hear about your old man? It doesn't get better."

There was no bravado, and she suspected it was hard for him to peel back the anger and remember what he could have been. "I do."

"I was ten grand down and in deep trouble. The casino boss said I could settle my debt by shaving points on my games once I made varsity. They said they'd even throw in an allowance each month. I was naive and desperate, so I just went along with it."

"Keep going."

"Beth got really pissed. She was mad that I didn't take her on the trip and called me a selfish dumbass. I got really pissed and told her I wasn't sending a dime of my money to her or her brat kid." He shook his head, like the retelling sounded worse out loud. "Like I said, it always got out of hand with Beth and me. I was cruel to her."

"You knew she was pregnant?"

"I did. Hell, I even offered to marry her, but she said no. Said she wasn't waiting around in this little town while I went off to college and became a football star." He threaded his fingers through his hair. "Loving Beth felt like a damned addiction. I couldn't take care of her the way she wanted, but I couldn't let go."

Of all the scenarios she'd imagined about a reunion with her father, she'd never pictured this. "What does this have to do with your knee?"

"She called the casino and told them I was going to screw them and not shave points. A few days later, a guy showed up and told me he'd give me thirty days to get the money. I got some of it, but not all. I made the mistake of threatening them with going to the cops. That afternoon, when I was crossing the street, a car came out of nowhere and clipped me." He shook his head. "It all went to shit after that. Broken leg. The scholarship. School. The leg never healed right, and the pain was constant. I started to feel sorry for myself and started drinking more. I've been hitting the booze hard ever since."

"Maybe Beth didn't feel like she had a choice."

He slowly shook his head. "She had a choice."

"I don't know what to say. I'm supposed to just believe you?"

"I'm not asking for anything. I'm not looking for your forgiveness. I just wanted you to hear my side."

"Okay." She didn't know if he was telling her the truth or not, but for the first time, she glimpsed some humanity in the man.

"I'm going to do some time. I broke my parole when I got drunk in public and came onto the school grounds. I'm likely looking at a couple of years." He reached for the bars, tightening his fingers. "Take care of Natasha for me. I'll sign whatever papers I need to sign. But she's better off with you. You're not like Beth or me. You're better than us both."

"I'll look out for Natasha."

He tried to thank her, but his voice caught.

"Take care of yourself, Brian."

He released the bars and stepped back. "Always."

Lucy and Dolly left the jail and drove to the beach. She let the dog run as she walked along the sand, not sure what to make of what she'd just learned from Brian. She wasn't sure if she even liked the guy, but she gave him credit for turning himself in and giving up Natasha.

He'd stopped running.

And maybe, it really was her chance to do the same.

She and Dolly got back to the Jeep, and she drove to Hank's office. Seeing a light on inside, she parked and the two pushed through his front door.

"Hank," she said.

Footsteps sounded on the second floor and then the stairs. He looked as if he'd just stepped out of the shower. His hair was damp and his shirt clean, but there were dark circles under his eyes. "I was just coming to see you."

"You must have heard Brian turned himself in?"

"I did. Rick called me last night."

"I went to see Brian."

He moved closer but didn't try to embrace her. "How did it go?"

"He told me his side of his relationship with Beth."

"Do you believe him?"

"Oddly, yes. He also asked me to take Natasha."

"What did you say?"

"I said yes."

"That's really great. Thank you."

"Don't thank me yet. You've seen the parenting stock I came from. It could be the worst thing for that kid. But hey, it takes a village to raise a kid anyway."

"You're not alone. You'll have our help."

She nodded, still trying to process it all.

"I'm sorry about the loan. I'm meeting with the bank this morning and telling them I overcommitted you."

"Yeah, I was thinking about that myself. Seeing as I'm staying, and I have a kid to raise, this town is going to have to stay alive. I'll sign after I've read the papers."

He took a half step toward her. "Are you sure? There's no turning back once it's done. We'll both have our necks on the line for a long time."

She reached out and took his hand, rubbing her fingers against the rough calluses. "Risk doesn't scare me. What scares me are secrets. Beth kept them all her life. You've kept a few. I'd rather have bad news straight up."

"Message received loud and clear." He tugged her gently, and she stepped the rest of the way toward him.

She traced her finger over his freshly shaved jaw and then kissed him on the lips.

"Welcome to Cape Hudson, Lucy."

CHAPTER
TWENTY-SIX

Mrs. Catherine Buchanan

June 26, 1988

Mrs. B sits alone in the parlor, staring at the camera. She's been waiting for Beth for almost an hour. The girl is always a little late, but this is ridiculous. The girl is fire, bright and entertaining in one moment and reckless in the next. She is her own worst enemy. Just like her father, and like her grandmother, Victoria, before that. She has none of Jimmy's temperance. Mrs. B thinks back to the moment she held Victoria and Jimmy's son in her arms on that long-ago night. The winds churned up something terrible, and the rains were strong. It was as if the skies opened up and wept for the child unwanted by his mother and unknown to his father.

When the clock strikes four, she realizes Beth has accepted her offer. She has run away with her unborn baby inside her. She's taken the money Mrs. B left out on the table by the front door. The money won't last her forever, but it will give Beth a start. Maybe she'll call once she's settled and the child is born.

"Ah, Jimmy," she said. "You've a strong-willed granddaughter, and I have no doubt her child will be as strong. I only hope one of them has your level sense."

She feels the wind blow across the back of her neck, and she knows Jimmy is close. He is always close. This has been their home for nearly seventy years.

She tips the edge of her glasses forward and studies the camera. The button on the right is the one that Beth always pushed before she told her it was recording. Beth never thought Mrs. B was paying attention, but she always has.

She presses the button, moves as quickly as she can, which isn't that fast, and sits in the chair. She fusses over her collar, touches her hair, and moistens her lips. A woman is never too old to be vain.

She begins to speak.

Claire

June 22, 1917

Of course, Claire knew she would go to jail. A poor woman who killed her husband from a well-connected family was always punished. Marriage was for better or worse, and it was her lot now to bear the worse.

She sat holding her son close as he rooted for her nipple, crying as if he needed comfort more than sustenance. He latched on to her breast and drank greedily, kneading her breast with his small fists. Soon he stopped whimpering and relaxed against her.

Robert's body had grown still as a stone, and a chill had crept into the room. She was terrified he'd rise up from the dead and tell the world what she'd done to him. And if the world knew what she'd done, her father-in-law would take her son and send her to prison.

Footsteps sounded behind her, and she tensed, expecting Mrs. Latimer to have fetched the sheriff. Stiff, she gripped her baby tight. She knew she could take the baby to the Jessups. She'd rejected the thought of her in-laws raising her son, and if Mrs. Latimer asked the town to hide the boy, they would. The Jessups were good people, and there was always room for another baby in that house.

Still, the idea of losing her son made breathing difficult.

Accepting what must be, Claire drew in a breath and rose. Jimmy stood in the doorway beside his mother, and she looked past him, but there was no one but the two of them.

He didn't try to hide his face, and she didn't look away. He was her beautiful Jimmy, no matter what.

He frowned when his gaze settled on the rising bruise on her cheek. Rage tightening his face, he walked to Robert and pressed his fingertips to his neck. "He's dead."

"Are you sure?" Claire asked.

"Yes. Very much. Give the baby to my mother, Claire."

"Why?" she asked. Was Jimmy to be the one who would deliver her to the police?

"I'll need help with the body," Jimmy said. "My right arm is not as strong as it was. My mother will tend to the boy and keep him safe."

Mrs. Latimer came back in then and crossed to Claire, who still couldn't bring herself to let go of her child. "He'll be safe with me. Go with Jimmy. He'll help us fix this proper."

She looked past Mrs. Latimer to her son. "You'll help me?"

Jimmy nodded. "Yes. But we must hurry."

Claire laid the baby in Mrs. Latimer's arms and kissed her boy on the head. "Thank you, Mrs. Latimer. Take him to the Jessup house if I don't come back."

"You'll be back."

"Why are you helping me? You know the consequences if we're caught."

Mrs. Latimer took Claire's hand in hers. "I'm the one who owes you thanks. You saw Jimmy when no one else could. And I'll always be grateful." A tear fell down her cheek. "Now you two get to work, and I'll clean the room. The other servants will be back in the morning."

"Why didn't you leave with them when Robert sent them away?"

"When I saw Mr. Robert, I knew in my bones there'd be trouble. I pretended to leave, but I came back and waited in the kitchen."

Claire squeezed the old woman's shoulder and stepped past her. She pushed up her sleeves and moved to the body of her dead husband.

As Jimmy elevated the shoulders, she grabbed the feet, and together they lifted. Robert had lost weight since his banishment to the shore, but even now his slender frame was awkward and unwieldy.

"What do we do with him?" Claire asked.

"Down the back staircase. I'll bring a cart around."

"The storm."

"It'll protect us."

Nodding, she gritted her teeth, and together they half carried, half dragged the body down the back stairs. Her muscles screamed, and her lungs burned from the exertion, but she kept putting one foot in front of the other. They crossed the kitchen, and when they reached the back door, her body was spent. She could barely catch her breath.

Jimmy turned to leave, and she grabbed his hand, pulling him toward her and kissing him. "I love you," she said.

He touched her face with his hand. "I love you, Claire. I should have seen it years ago. I should have wed that sixteen-year-old girl who thought she could sail the bay."

When he opened the door, the wind and rain pelted them, soaking her dress and plastering it to her skin. She looked down at her shoes, which had been covered in blood, and watched as the rain washed it away. They dragged the body across the back lawn toward the small sandy beach.

"I'll be right back," he shouted, his voice nearly lost in the wind. "Stay right here."

"Yes, Jimmy."

Jimmy jogged out into the rain and down the sandy path toward the boathouse. He didn't return for what felt like an eternity as she jumped at every crack of lightning.

Finally, she heard the rumble of a boat engine as it came out of the boathouse and around the canal toward the shore.

He jumped out, his booted feet hitting the water, and he strode toward her. Again, they heaved the deadweight and placed it into the boat. She hurriedly climbed aboard.

"No, Claire," Jimmy said. "I'll take it from here."

She grabbed his hand. "I want to help you. I don't want you to do this alone."

"No. Stay. This is my job."

"Where are you taking him?"

"Let me worry about that. Go inside to your son. And look after my mother. You're all she has now."

Lightning cracked, briefly illuminating the whitecaps. "You'll be back."

He hesitated. "Aye, I'll be back."

She kissed him, her hand cupping the broken side of his face. "I need you to come back."

He nodded. "And I need you to be safe."

Together, they pushed the boat back in the water, and he settled into his seat. A pull of the cord started the small engine, and he slowly pulled out into the bay.

Claire stood on the shore until the boat vanished into the darkness.

Mrs. Buchanan

June 22, 1988

Mrs. B looks directly into the camera. Gently, she touches the broach on her jacket. *"And of course, everyone knows Jimmy did not return. He took his boat into the heart of the storm. He and Robert were lost as his mother and I washed all traces of blood from the house.*

"And my secrets sank to the bottom of the bay forever."

CHAPTER TWENTY-SEVEN

Lucy

January 30, 2018

Lucy had DNA tests done and confirmed what she'd suspected. She and Natasha were half sisters. Brian Willard was her father. Custody of Natasha was settled relatively easily. Brian signed over custody as he'd promised, and she'd left the courtroom with some empathy for the man.

She wasn't sure why her mother had finally told her about Cape Hudson or why she wanted her ashes brought back. Maybe Beth thought enough time had passed and she needed to do right by Lucy even though she'd not been able to face the truth while she was alive. Lucy wanted to believe this and would until she knew differently.

Lucy and Dolly pushed through the front door of Arlene's and settled at the counter. She didn't need to pick up a menu.

Arlene grinned as she poured Lucy's coffee. "You look ready for bear."

She poured sugar in the coffee. "Morning drama. Just dropped Natasha off at school."

"What was it this morning?" Arlene asked.

"Like every morning. Her hair. She doesn't like the way the woman did it at the salon. The honeymoon is over," she moaned.

Arlene laughed. "Welcome to parenthood."

Lucy sipped her coffee. "We visited her mom's grave yesterday and rewatched some of Mrs. B's tapes. That always churns excitement." When Lucy pointed out the young caregiver in the tapes was Grace, Natasha cried as she watched it. However, the girl kept rewinding the tape again and again, until Lucy had the tape transferred to a digital format for fear it would break and they'd both lose what they had left of their mothers.

Lucy shook her head, still worried she was somehow going to botch parenthood. "Natasha is so positive and upbeat with the rest of the world, but she can be a moody teenager prone to slamming doors when she doesn't want to do her homework."

Arlene began to wipe the counter with a rag. "I never understood why that girl was always smiling and so eager to help. She was desperate for love, and now she has it. She trusts you. You're the safe place to vent her frustrations. Believe me. It's healthy."

"I hope so."

"You're doing fine with her. We're all proud of you. You've stepped into a crazy life, and you're managing so well."

"Thanks."

"So what will you have?"

"Pancakes to go. I've got to start packing the furniture. Megan wants to start the restoration soon."

Arlene shook her head every time Megan's name came up. "Bless her heart. How's she doing? Not pushing herself?"

"She's due in four months and has the energy of six people." Lucy also understood that kind of energy was often fueled by desperation. Megan hadn't spoken about anything beyond the house, but Lucy hoped one day she'd open up about what was driving her.

"Well, you make her slow down. That girl is living on nervous energy."

"Understood."

Minutes later, she took her carryout box and drove back to the cottage, pausing at the front entrance to take in the beauty of this majestic place. She then turned and looked toward the yellow caution tape still wrapped around the capped well. She thought about the bones that were still being examined in the state medical examiner's office. She'd told Rick about Robert Buchanan's watch that she'd found at the boathouse, thinking perhaps the body in the well was Robert's and that he'd not been lost at sea but buried. A seaman like Jimmy would have known dumping the body in the bay risked it washing up with the tide if he didn't take it out far into the bay and weigh it down.

DNA testing had been done on one of the body's back molars. It had been sent to the state lab and had been compared to Megan's dad, James, as he was Robert's grandson. The test had come back as negative. Rick had then gone back into the well, excavated deeper into the muck, and this time had found an old poker chip. Lucy thought back to the tapes and remembered Robert had had a fight with a man from the Franklin family. Mrs. Reynolds had searched the newspaper archives and discovered Kevin Franklin had gone missing in January of 1916. The Franklin clan had a reputation for gambling and later moonshining during the 1920s. Franklin's descendants had been traced, and this time the DNA test had been positive. Perhaps Robert had killed the man and stashed his body in the old well.

The familiar rumble of Hank's truck pulled Lucy into the present. She smiled and turned from the house where Megan and her crews would soon arrive and begin removing the old furniture that would be restored off-site and returned after the cottage renovation was complete.

Hank grinned as he crossed the front lawn in long, even strides. He was dressed in faded jeans, work boots, and a long-sleeve sweater. He and his father were scheduled to work in the vineyards this morning.

Spring would be here in a couple of months, and they needed to be ready.

Dolly barked and ran toward him. He rubbed the dog between the ears, and then he stepped up on the front porch and wrapped his arms around Lucy. He smelled of clean soap.

He sniffed her hair. "You smell like pie."

"It's my new scent. Megan bakes when she's nervous."

"How's she doing?"

"She's dedicated to this job. I've offered her one of the rooms upstairs while she gets to work on the guest house where Samuel lived."

"Is she going to take you up on your offer?"

"I think so."

He traced her collarbone with his finger. "You make pie sexy."

She laughed. "You aren't listening to me, are you?"

He kissed her. "I caught every word." And between more kisses, he said, "Megan. House. Pie. Renovation."

"Rick has a tendency to show up when she's here. He's always got a question or tidbit about the bones in the well. What's the deal with them?"

"Can't say." Hank just grinned and ran his hand down to her waist. "What are you doing for the next hour?"

A delicious wave of excitement raced through her. "Packing up furniture."

"Ah, sounds like hard work."

"Hey, eyes up here. I'm assuming you received your financial backing?"

"I did." His voice was now barely a whisper, and he seemed to be tamping down excitement as he placed his hands on her shoulders. "We'll be moving forward with clearing the additional parcels of land in the spring."

"That's very exciting. You've got to be proud."

"Between you and me, it's scary as hell. I'm betting the farm—*your farm*—to make this happen."

"Go big or go home."

He hugged her close. "You make me think it really will happen."

"It will."

"Natasha is at school, correct?"

"Until three thirty."

"And Megan?"

"In town running errands." She was starting to care less and less about packing those boxes. "I thought you had vineyard work this morning?"

"I do. Soon."

"Well, I was planning to wrap the smaller pieces for the movers who are coming in two hours."

"And if I helped you later today, would that free up some time?"

"Maybe." She smoothed her hand over his chest. The longer she was in this house and this town, the more settled she felt. Even though her life was busier than ever, the bone-weariness that had dogged her for a long time had lifted. "How shall I fill the time?"

He ran his hand up her sweater, and a thrill of excitement shot through her body. "I have an idea."

She laughed. "I think I'm going to like this."

READING GROUP QUESTIONS FOR

MARY ELLEN TAYLOR'S

WINTER COTTAGE

1. Both Claire and Beth were forced to leave their homes at a young age. How would their lives have been different if they'd stayed in Cape Hudson?

2. Claire believed that fashion had the power to transform anyone's life, but did it get her the life she truly wanted?

3. Did Hank take it too far when he committed Lucy's name to the new financial deal he'd negotiated with the bank?

4. Do you have a favorite passage or moment in *Winter Cottage*?

5. The winter season is an important part of *Winter Cottage*'s setting. How do you think the season relates to the characters?

6. If a movie were made of this book, who would you pick to play Claire, Lucy, Hank, and Natasha?

7. If you had to write an ending for Claire and Jimmy, what would it be?

8. Lucy strikes a truce with her father. Is this something that can last, or is this tentative peace doomed to fail?

9. How does this novel leave you feeling? Did you feel a sense of hope for Claire? What about Hank and Lucy?

10. How do you think the pending renovations for Winter Cottage will go? Do you think it holds more secrets?

Winter Cottage Apple Pie

For the Filling

- 1 tablespoon of cornstarch
- ½ cup of white sugar
- ½ cup of brown sugar
- 7–8 Granny Smith apples

Peel and thinly slice the apples. In a bowl, toss the apples with the sugars and the cornstarch. Set aside.

For the Crust

- 1 cup of butter, chilled and cubed
- ½ teaspoon of salt
- 3 cups of all-purpose flour
- 4–5 tablespoons of ice water

Place the cubed butter, salt, and all-purpose flour in a food processor. Pulse until the mixture resembles a fine meal. Still pulsing, add water one tablespoon at a time until the dough forms a ball. Refrigerate for at least one hour.

To Assemble the Pie

After one hour, roll out half the dough into a circle and place in a greased pie pan. By now the apple filling will have given off some of its juice. Strain the apple filling and arrange it on the bottom crust. Roll out the other half of the dough and drape over the filling. Pinch the top and bottom sections of crust together. Slice two slim vent holes in the top. Bake in a 425-degree oven for 15 minutes. Reduce the heat to 350 degrees and bake an additional 35–45 minutes.

Lucy's Chocolate Cake

For the Cake

- 2 cups of sugar
- 1¾ cups of all-purpose flour
- ¾ cup Dutch process cocoa
- 1½ teaspoons of baking powder
- 1½ teaspoons of baking soda
- 1 teaspoon of salt
- 2 eggs
- 1 cup of milk or buttermilk
- 1 tablespoon of espresso powder
- ½ cup of vegetable oil
- 2 teaspoons of vanilla
- 1 cup of hot water

Preheat oven to 350 degrees. Mix together the sugar, flour, cocoa, baking powder, baking soda, and salt. Blend together the eggs, milk, espresso powder, oil, and vanilla. Add the wet ingredients to the dry. Stir in the cup of hot water. Bake for 30–35 minutes until an inserted knife comes out clean.

Chocolate Icing

- ½ cup of butter, softened
- ⅔ cup of cocoa
- 3 cups of powdered sugar
- ⅓ cup of cold coffee
- 1 teaspoon of vanilla

Cream the butter until it is silky, then add the cocoa, powdered sugar, coffee, and vanilla. Whip until smooth. Ice the cake when it is completely cool.

ABOUT THE AUTHOR

Photo © 2017 Studio FBJ

A southerner by birth, Mary Ellen Taylor's contemporary stories intertwine her love of women's fiction and the history of her home state of Virginia. When she's not chasing her three dachshunds, she writes romantic suspense under the name Mary Burton.